THE NEW BREED

Book I
in the Magnificent

AMERICAN PATRIOT SERIES

The thundering seventeenth-century saga of Sir Richard Dunstable's evolution from English baronet to fiercely loyal American colonial . . . a heroic adventure of Indian attacks and loyal Indian companions, of opulent luxury and cruel poverty, of pleasure and sickness, love and pain.

Here is the enthralling story of one man, two women, and the building of a new nation. It is the epic of America.

THE NEW BREED
From the creators of
WAGONS WEST
and
THE KENT FAMILY CHRONICLES

THE AMERICAN PATRIOT SERIES

BOOK I

The NEW BREED

Douglass Elliot

BALLANTINE BOOKS • NEW YORK

Produced by BOOK CREATIONS, INC.
Executive Producer: Lyle Kenyon Engel

Library of Congress Catalog Card Number: 81-65420

ISBN 0-345-29483-1

Manufactured in the United States of America

This edition published simultaneously in trade and mass market.

First Edition: July 1981

Prologue

By 1649, the North American colonies were undergoing a rapid transformation. The new breed of hardy pioneers, settlers whose vision extended far into the future, was rapidly planting roots in the fertile soil of the New World. Farms were productive, towns were burgeoning, and the face of the land was being transformed.

As befitted the oldest colony, Virginia was the most advanced. Thanks to John Rolfe, tobacco had become the staple and vast fields were devoted to its planting. Now almost forty years old, the original Virginia colony had weathered well; its people knew the climate, the Indians, and the hazards of life, and their culture was spreading to many newer communities. The Virginians were closely tied to their homeland across the Atlantic, reflected in their manners, customs, and even household furnishings.

In contrast, the settlers of Massachusetts Bay and Plymouth colonies led a more rustic existence, largely due to the more difficult climate and their Puritanical beliefs. Boston had few structures that could be termed impressive, and for the most part it was a marshy, hilly town with no trees and muddy roads.

New Haven, although also founded by Puritans, enjoyed a greater prosperity, perhaps because its settlers were less rigorous in following their religious beliefs. Spacious homes surrounded the Green and commercial

1

trade became a stronger investment with each passing year.

Another town whose commerce was based on the waterfront was New Amsterdam, administrated by the Dutch. It was a rousing, rowdy atmosphere with people from many nations coming to trade, staying to live. The director-general, Peter Stuyvesant, was striving to provide order to the town by imposing stringent laws concerning the sale of drinks, and the conduct of citizens and visitors alike. Stuyvesant met with little cooperation among his merchants, who sent a letter of remonstrance to Holland complaining of government's interference with their money-making ability.

Perhaps the most intriguing of settlements was that of Providence Plantations, Rhode Island. Here religious freedom was a fact, not a dream. The residents enjoyed self-rule without their delegates having to swear an oath of allegiance to the British monarch. Roger Williams, founder of the colony, vehemently objected to such oaths.

Men and women breathed the air of freedom in North America, and that in turn gave rise to the new breed which was unique in human annals. For the first time anywhere an individual was judged by accomplishments, not family wealth or personal standing. A new breed truly was arising in this new land.

I

Precisely as England's many soothsayers and fortune-tellers had predicted, the sun did not appear over the British Isles on Tuesday, January 30, 1649. It remained hidden beneath banks of dark gray clouds, and an icy wind that blew in off the North Sea added to the discomfort of a confused and frightened people.

Late in the day, the inclement weather notwithstanding, Londoners by the thousands gathered in the open area outside the great Banqueting Hall at Whitehall Palace, where a black-wreathed platform topped by an executioner's block had been built. The victorious Puritan troops in their drab uniforms, the victors over the Cavaliers, or Royalist forces, in the civil war that had almost destroyed the nation, kept the throngs at a distance. Parliament was supreme, and as the members of the House of Commons filed out of the building and took their places in a special grandstand built for their convenience, a hush settled over the crowd. In the lead was Oliver Cromwell, soon to become Lord Protector of the Realm, his face solemn, his step decorous.

Royalist sympathizers averted their faces, and some murmured the epithet, "Roundheads." But they were careful not to speak aloud. Anyone who opposed Cromwell and his Puritans was in grave danger.

Fifty-nine somber men followed the members of the Commons and took their own seats on the opposite side of the executioner's block. Later to become infamous as the Damned Souls, they constituted the special high court of justice that had placed His Majesty on trial and found him guilty of "treason against Parliament and the nation." Now he would pay the penalty for his alleged crimes.

The black-clad, hooded executioner came through a side door, shouldering his heavy, razor-sharp ax, and many in the crowd shuddered. A number of the Puritans in the grandstand had the sensitivity to appear disconcerted.

The main doors opened wide, and Charles I, head of the house of Stuart, King of Great Britain and Ireland by the grace of God, stood for a moment and looked out at his subjects for the last time. His face was pale, but his emotions were controlled, and he was obviously prepared to meet his Maker. His long Stuart chin jutted forward, his thin nose quivered slightly, and there was cold contempt in his eyes as he glanced first at his judges, then at the Parliamentarians who were responsible for this violent miscarriage of justice.

Waving away two Puritan officers who would have assisted him, he mounted the scaffold alone, and the throngs pressed forward for a glimpse of his fine linen, his cloth-of-gold coat, silk breeches, gold-buckled shoes, and the exquisite fringe of lace at his wrists and neck.

Charles looked for an instant at Oliver Cromwell, then faced the crowd. "I do not recognize the right of the Commons," he said in his Scots' accent, "to stand in judgment of their sovereign liege lord." Turning quickly, he bowed to the hooded executioner, then removed a gold coin from his purse and handed it to the man. No matter what his supposed faults, Charles I never lacked the social amenities. The executioner produced a thong to bind the condemned man's wrists and

4

a blindfold to spare him needless agony in his final moments on earth.

"I need no restraints," Charles said. "I have lived a king, and now I die a king." With no one assisting him, he slowly dropped to his knees and placed his head on the block.

No one in the great crowd moved or spoke, but there were many who wept in silence, and even the most implacable of Charles Stuart's foes were compelled to admire his courage.

"I commend my soul to Almighty God," he said. "Executioner, do your masters' duty."

The great ax gleamed as it was raised high over the executioner's shoulder, and then it descended swiftly, making a quiet, almost gentle sound as it severed the head of Charles I, King of Great Britain and Ireland, from his body.

The messenger's footsteps echoed down the long, marbled corridor, interrupted several times by the palace guards. Each time, the messenger was waved by as the sentries became aware of the nature of his mission. At the last chamber, he was asked to be seated in a massive, red velvet chair by the entrance to the office. His instructions were to present the communiqué only to Cardinal Mazarin, and to wait for a reply.

"The messenger has arrived from England, Your Eminence."

"Send him in when I ring. You are excused, Deveaux."

Cardinal Mazarin was unique in Europe, perhaps in the whole world. Like his great flamboyant predecessor, Cardinal Richelieu, he was the first minister of the government as well as a prince of the Church. Promoted to the rank of cardinal for skillfully settling a political dispute, Mazarin had, in fact, never been consecrated priest. Unlike Richelieu, who dressed in gaudy civilian clothes and enjoyed showing off his power, Mazarin lived up to his nickname of the "Gray Spider." He was always dressed in the most modest of clericals, and only the red of his shirt and of his biretta distinguished him from an ordinary priest. He had refined, delicate features that caused him to resemble an intellectual, which he was. What the casual observer did not and could not know, however, was that he was also endowed with an inordinate, soaring ambition for France. He wanted his land to become first in power on all the earth, and he was willing to do anything to further that end.

The assistant turned on his heels and left quickly, closing the gilt double doors quietly. The cardinal turned to his two colleagues. "Be wary of your expressions. This fellow may be trained to read involuntary reactions. This message, on this particular day, can mean only one thing. Cromwell has done it. The King of England is dead."

The cardinal lifted a crystal bell from his desk, summoning the messenger. Reading the parchment, he excused the fellow.

Horace Laing and Jean-Pierre Colbert struggled to control their excitement. This was the moment for which Mazarin's agents had carefully planned. Their machinations could at last be implemented. The cardinal nodded to them: supremacy in Europe and the New World would soon be theirs.

"Your Eminence, do you wish for me to return to Virginia to await the arrival of Lady Dawn?"

"Yes, Monsieur Laing. We will continue as planned regarding the lady. Please, be careful with her face. We want her persuaded, but gently, gently. And control that mad-dog butler of yours. Our last recruit took weeks to heal. Lady Dawn is too precious for such antics. And before you leave, I want you to carry further instructions to Laroche in New Amsterdam."

Lady Dawn was indeed worth special handling. As a member of the highest English aristocracy, she was trusted completely by every man in the king's party. She could come and go at will, she could learn any secret of the machinations being conducted against the Lord Protector, Cromwell, and she was assured of a hearty welcome by almost everyone, even at the court-in-exile. Few other people had such qualifications.

The cardinal paused and jotted some notes to himself, then turned to his other compatriot. "Colbert, please continue with your excellent work. Lady Dawn should be nearing Dover now. Make certain she is not detained in her voyage to the New World by any ignorant Puritan constables. She is too dear to us to be thrown into the Tower to rot. This is your responsibility: make certain she reaches Laing in Virginia. Follow her to America, and use an alias when you book your own passage." The cardinal removed a suede sack of gold coins from his desk and placed it in front of Colbert, who picked it up, tossed it gently to ascertain its weight, and stashed it in his pocket.

"When do you want my next report, Your Eminence?"

"Soon, Colbert, soon. Your ship will be intercepted by one of our officers. You may give him a message for me. He will be in our camp. Do you have any questions?"

The men shook their heads.

"You are excused, then. I will be busy now with the young and impressionable Charles the Second." A slight smile played upon the lips of this man of God.

Sir Richard Dunstable had felt restless all day, and now, as he looked out at the trees on his heavily wooded estate in Lincolnshire, far from London, he decided he needed physical exercise. It was too late in the day to hunt in the royal game preserve, which was his privilege as the King's Forester, an almost meaningless title he had inherited along with his baronetcy from his late father. And he had read until the words melted together on the page, as he had done when he won honors at Oxford University.

But the lack of fresh air stifled him, so he went into his armory and took from their cases his favorite weapons, a riflelike musket and a double-barreled pistol, both made according to his own precise specifications by a London gunsmith. As an afterthought, he buckled on a belt that contained a half-dozen perfectly balanced throwing knives.

Several servants had been given the day and night off, so Richard was attended by a minimal staff in the manor house, but he enjoyed the relative solitude, just as he felt completely at home in the forest of oak, pine, maple, ash, and elm that comprised the royal game preserve. He sat and loaded his weapons, then seemed to uncoil as he stood and headed for the side yard. His gait was that of a natural athlete who had no spare flesh on his rugged six-foot frame, and as he headed toward the fringe of the woods, he inhaled the scent of the pines, faint but still discernible in this season when the snow lay on the ground.

Ladies who saw him often thought that he was wasted in the backwoods of rural England. His hair, naturally crisp and dark brown, was worn fairly short and was gathered in a tie at the nape of his neck. His hazel eyes were alert, reflecting an unusual quickness and intelligence. He was fortunate in that he was endowed with a physical strength and stamina. In the earlier stages of England's civil war when he fought with the king's men against the Parliamentarians, he had been known for his ability to spend twenty-four to forty-eight hours in the saddle without rest, and his feats of strength and of prodigy were legendary.

He had always found accomplishments easy to attain. He had taken honors at Oxford at the age of twenty in a study of England's relationship with France over the centuries; anything connected with the power balance between the two nations fascinated him.

Currently he was annoyed with himself because he had given up the fight against the Puritans too soon. In one battle, near Worcester, he and a group of five scouts had held off an entire battalion of enemy infantry for more than twelve hours, a feat that Cromwell's generals refused to believe. But then, recognizing the hopelessness of the Royalist cause, and aware, too, that there would soon be a price on his head unless he desisted, he had come home, determined to sit out the rest of the war. Sitting of any kind when action promised was very difficult indeed for Richard.

Richard halted, took quick aim at a small pine branch thirty paces away, and fired both barrels of his pistol in quick succession, smiling quietly when the acrid smoke cleared sufficiently for him to see that the branch had vanished. He searched for a more difficult target for his rifle shot, ultimately selecting a dead maple leaf that clung tenaciously to a branch on a tree behind the top of the pine. He took careful aim, braced for the recoil, then squeezed the trigger. The single shot echoed through the game preserve, and the leaf was gone. Moving closer to the woods, he threw each of his knives in quick succession at the trunk of a young gray birch, but he felt no satisfaction when he saw all six imbedded in the wood of his target.

Obviously his skills as a marksman gave him no pleasure today, the day the Puritans had sworn they would execute King Charles. A staunch Cavalier who had been a lifelong supporter of the Stuarts, Richard found it difficult to believe that even as arrogant a general as Cromwell would carry out the terrible threat. Certainly, had he known the king would be

9

tried like a common criminal, he would have joined the Royalist Army prior to its last, unsuccessful campaign. He was still sorry he had been dissuaded from that course by the Earl of Newcastle, one of his father's closest friends, who had told him repeatedly in recent years that the Royalist cause was hopeless and that Charles was sure to lose his head because of his unwillingness to compromise with his enemies. Perhaps it would have been better to die honorably in battle than to survive a murdered monarch.

Putting his gloomy thoughts out of his mind, Richard retrieved his knives, returned to the house for his sword, then went out to the stable and saddled his stallion, which he had named Prince Henry, after one of King Charles's sons.

Prince Henry was unique, and he certainly was Richard's most valuable possession. A great stallion, a sleek, jet black, standing eighteen hands tall, with a distinct temper and temperament of his own, he had been trained as a charger by one of the best equestrians in the royal stables. Richard was inclined to believe that the mount was as intelligent as a man, and treated him accordingly.

As dusk settled over Lincolnshire, Richard rode the two miles to the substantial wooden house of a local squire, William Hatcher. Ordinarily, the road was heavily traveled, but few people were abroad today, and Richard, pulling his cloak around him as protection from the raw wind, saw no one as he rode up one hill and down the next. When the Hatcher house appeared ahead, set back from the road, lights were glowing in several rooms, and Richard grinned when he detected a slight ruffling of the curtains in the parlor. His beloved Dorothea knew he would be on time and was waiting for him.

Richard dismounted, looping his reins over the hitching post. The front door opened as he strode toward the house, the aura of the oil lamp that Dorothea Hatcher held in one hand, lighting her hazel eyes and making her brown hair seem to glow. Even in the modest gown that befitted the daughter of the proprietor of a small estate, she looked lovely, and Richard reached for her as he came into the house.

Dorothea was attractive, her regular features and her youth standing her in good stead. A more experienced eye than Richard's would have been aware of the fact that she was beginning to show signs of putting on weight, signs that would be fully revealed in several years.

All Richard knew, to be sure, was that she was tall, supple, and comely. He lacked both the experience with women and the foresight to be able to see her in long-range terms, much less to realize there were limitations to her beauty. He would have been amazed had someone told him that in a few years Dorothea would become an ordinary-looking woman.

Dorothea evaded his embrace, closed the door, and motioned him into the parlor. As she unfailingly greeted him with a kiss that was his privilege to take as her future husband, Richard was somewhat bewildered by her reserve. "We need to talk quickly," she murmured.

Dorothea placed the lamp on a table and continued to stand as she turned to him. "Papa doesn't want me to marry you," she said, speaking softly but distinctly. "He's afraid that the king's supporters will be executed, or at the very least imprisoned, and he's certain the Roundheads will confiscate your property."

"But that's nonsense," he protested. "I'm protected by English law! We aren't living in the Middle Ages!"

"I'm just telling you what Papa says." Dorothea was deeply troubled.

"If you love me as much as I love you—"

"Papa says survival and the acquisition of worldly

goods are more important than love." She paused, then added uncertainly, "Just this afternoon he told me he's selected a more suitable husband for me: a Roundhead county commissioner who stands high in Cromwell's regard. . . ." Her voice trailed away.

"Good evening, Sir Richard." William Hatcher's bulk filled the entrance hall archway.

Richard turned slowly, struggling for composure, and the thought crossed his mind that the sudden change in Hatcher's appearance was remarkable. Instead of the swallow-tailed, embroidered coat and pale satin breeches he usually wore, he was dressed in unrelieved black that caused him to resemble an undertaker—or a Roundhead. "Your servant, Master Hatcher."

"Dorothea, be good enough to retire to your room," Hatcher ordered in a deep baritone. "I want a word in private with Sir Richard."

The girl stood uncertainly for a long moment, her eyes filling with tears as she glanced first at her father, then at Richard. Suddenly, she gathered her full skirt and fled.

Richard was not one to dissemble or evade issues, and he immediately took the initiative. "I gather from Dorothea that you no longer regard me as a suitable husband for her."

The heavyset man reddened. "We live in unsettled times, Sir Richard," he replied, apology and defiance mingling in his manner. "In the world that we knew, no bachelor was more eligible than you, a baronet with a fixed income and a fine estate, along with an extra income of three hundred sovereigns in gold each year as the hereditary King's Forester. Ah, you were a man to be envied! Unfortunately, you've been branded with the Stuart mark, and no father who takes his responsibilities seriously could permit his only daughter to marry someone whose future is uncertain."

"No one can look into the future, Master Hatcher," Richard protested. "You lose sight of an all-important fact, sir. Dorothea and I love each other!"

"As a realistic man of the world, I cannot allow myself to be swayed by the feelings of the young. My regret is genuine, Sir Richard, but Dorothea's betrothal to you is ended."

The girl was not yet twenty-one years old, and Richard knew she would not be married without her father's permission, but he would not give up without a fight. "I'd like to speak with Dorothea, if you please. We have an understanding—"

"Understanding be damned." Hatcher was unyielding. "My daughter is permitted neither to receive you nor to speak with you again." Trying to maintain his dignity, Hatcher led Richard toward the door.

Richard's temper flared, but he managed to hold it in check. If he were dealing with anyone but Dorothea's father, he would have challenged the scoundrel to a duel. But that would not help in the present situation. He was tempted to ask Dorothea to elope with him, but she was so gentle and meek that he knew, without asking, that she could not summon the courage to defy her father. Furthermore, by running away with Dorothea, he would create problems for himself with the Puritans who now held all posts of authority in Lincolnshire, men who already hated him. His only recourse was to find some way to speak privately with Dorothea in the days ahead and ask her to wait for him until the present political frenzy that gripped England died away.

"Your betrothal ring will be returned to you," Hatcher said as he opened the door.

"I prefer that Dorothea keep it," Richard replied stiffly.

As the girl's father well knew, the ring, which had belonged to Richard's late mother, was made of gold and set with diamonds and rubies, so it was valuable, particularly in these uncertain times when money had become scarce. Avarice gleamed in Hatcher's eyes, and he said quickly, "As you wish."

The door closed behind Richard. He stamped down the steps, mounted his horse, and venting his frustrated rage, he raced home at a gallop.

The front gate, set in two posts of stone that had been worn smooth by the elements over the centuries during which time the Dunstables had owned the estate, stood open. Ahead was the great manor house of solid stone, a dwelling that his ancestors had enlarged and modernized for more than four hundred years, and as Richard looked at it, he smiled grimly. How could the future of the man who owned such a place be uncertain?

He saw a strange gelding tied to the hitching post beyond the side, or family, entrance, so it appeared that Richard had a visitor. Hurrying into the house, he saw a man warming himself at the hearth in the two-story great hall.

William Cavendish, Earl of Newcastle, turned slowly to greet the son of his oldest and closest friend. Inexplicably, the silver-haired nobleman was subduedly dressed in dark riding clothes, with drab boots and tarnished spurs. He looked very tired, but the smile that accented his wrinkles also lighted his face. "I let myself in, Richie," he said. "Luckily, you keep this door unlocked, although that's foolish of you when Roundhead troops are arresting those faithful to the Crown. Lock them out—and you have the talent to shoot down a goodly number of them before they seize you."

"Surely the state of affairs in England won't degenerate that much!" The younger man clung stubbornly to his beliefs that the rights of individuals were inviolable and that every subject of the Crown enjoyed absolute protection under the law.

The earl found it difficult to believe that anyone could be so naive in an era when a bloodthirsty purge was sweeping the country. "King Charles, may God have mercy on his soul," he said, "was beheaded today at Whitehall."

Richard was stunned. He knew, of course, that the monarch had been tried and found guilty by a Puritan-appointed "special high court of justice," but he had refused to believe that the Parliamentarians who had seized power would resort to murder.

"I am on my way to France," Newcastle said briskly. "My arrangements were made well in advance, and a ship is waiting to take me to join Queen Henrietta Maria and her children, particularly young Charles, in exile. I'm traveling with an escort of twenty men who have concealed themselves behind your outbuildings. There's a price on my head now, but I've outwitted Cromwell for years, and I shall have the best of the bargain again."

His mind still reeling, Richard could not allow himself to forget his duties as a host. "Many of my servants won't return until tomorrow, which may be just as well, since I'm uncertain of their sympathies. But let me offer you a supper of cold beef and bread before you go," he said huskily.

"I can't spare the time," Newcastle said, then added pointedly, "and neither can you."

The younger man stared at him.

"The Cavalier planners have been preparing against this day of infamy for three years and more. We've had no illusions about the pious hymn singers who want to drink our blood. And there has been a good reason you haven't been allowed to take part in our more recent military campaigns. We could have used your

15

skills, but we couldn't risk losing you in battle. You've been saved to perform a special task."

"But—"

"Hear me out," the earl said. "You're an accomplished swordsman, and you know firearms better than most. No one is your equal at bringing down a stag or other game. You've stayed away from London because you've preferred the solitude of the royal game preserves, although why you should is something I can't for the life of me understand. Not that your lack of participation in the civil war will save you from the vengeance of the Puritans, you understand. You've made no secret of your Royalist feelings, and you hold the warrant of King's Forester. Our agents in the Puritan camp say you're scheduled to be arrested and thrown into prison tomorrow. If they take you, you'll spend the rest of your days rotting in a cell."

"I'll rid the world of a good many of the scum first," Richard vowed grimly.

Newcastle shook his head. "No, you'll do no such thing, because you won't be here. You're leaving tonight, too."

"With you, Uncle William?"

The earl smiled faintly. "You'll travel in another direction. You'll go to Bristol, where a ship whose master swears allegiance to young Charles the Second awaits you. He'll take you to the New World colonies."

"You're sending me to North America?" Richard could not hide his dismay.

"Yes, lad. The colonies are growing rapidly and are already of enormous importance to us. No matter how long it may take, we intend to place young Charles on the throne that rightfully belongs to him, and we'll need the support of the colonials."

Not yet resigned to his exile in a distant, barbaric land, Richard's heart was heavy as he listened.

"Your duties will not be onerous," Newcastle told

him. "You'll assess the sympathies of the colonials, and when possible, you'll work for the formation of a king's party. What's more, you won't be working alone. Our principal agent there is a man called Laroche. He'll be in touch with you, and you'll take your orders from him."

"How will I know where to find him? The colonies occupy a vast territory that stretches from Massachusetts Bay to Virginia."

The earl smiled and shrugged. "To be candid, I don't know. But Laroche has his own means of acquiring information, and he has told the Cavalier high command that he'll locate you. I'd guess that not many men of your stature go to America."

Richard couldn't blame anyone for not wanting to travel to that remote wilderness. "How long must I remain there?"

Newcastle shrugged. "How long will it take the people to see through the hymn singers and clamor for the restoration of young Charles to the throne?" He reached into an inner pocket for a sheet of folded parchment. "Here, lad, is a list of places where you'll stay on your journey to the White Hart Inn at Bristol. Some are private homes, and others are public inns. You'll be welcome at all of them. But avoid the main roads as you would the plague, and don't go near any large towns. The Roundheads are congregated in the cities, while most rural dwellers remain loyal to us."

Richard nodded as he studied the list of stopovers where he would be assured a safe, warm welcome.

"I hate to burden you with something additional," the earl said, "but it can't be helped. Are you acquainted with Lady Dawn Shepherd, the little-known daughter of the late Earl of Sturbridge? She's an exceptionally outspoken young woman, more's the pity for her. Her father tried to keep her concealed, for her

17

own safety, due to his political situation and her note-worthy beauty. Her friends know her as Mimi."

"I've never had the privilege of meeting her, Uncle William."

Newcastle sighed. "Mimi Shepherd has already arrived at the White Hart in Bristol and is in hiding there. The Puritans are determined to find her and make an example of her, so she desperately needs help. We hope you'll do what you can to assist her."

"In what way?"

"I suggest you work that out with her. She's certain to have ideas of her own which may or may not be valid. We must leave her future to your judgment."

Richard already had enough problems and resented the burden of looking after an earl's spoiled daughter. "How will I know her?"

For the first time Newcastle laughed. "She has red hair, and her appearance is striking, lad, to say the least. You won't need to be a Roundhead informer to recognize her."

"For your sake, I'll do my best."

The earl corrected him gently. "Not for my sake, but for that of the cause that both of us now represent. Write to me of your progress when you're able to do so. The master of the brig *Anne*, who'll carry you to the New World, will tell you which ships' masters can be trusted with correspondence. The letters will be brought to England, then smuggled across the Channel to me. I'll stay for a time with Queen Henrietta Maria at the Louvre and then I'll join my own family in Paris, but I don't yet know where I'll settle. We who are exiles will need to depend on the whims of the French."

A wave of compassion for the older man engulfed Richard. It would not be easy for one of the most prominent noblemen in the realm to live abroad with his wife, their children, and their grandchildren for an indefinite period, perhaps for the rest of their lives.

"I must be on my way." The earl took a purse from his belt. "I wish I could give you more than this, Richie."

"Keep it," Richard told him. "I have ample funds."

"Only the Lord knows when more gold will be available, so take this, along with your own money and valuables. When the Roundheads have discovered you've flown, there is little doubt they'll confiscate your entire estate. All of us are leaving behind precious belongings for the vultures, but it can't be helped," he added bleakly.

Richard accepted the purse, trying to assure himself that he would be expected to earn the money, that he wasn't taking charity. Newcastle went to a sideboard, poured two small glasses of brandy, then indulged in a curious gesture, extending his own glass over a carafe of water, then raising it in a toast. "Remember this sign," he said. "We drink to the king-across-the-water."

The younger man imitated the gesture, then gulped the potent brandy. "I shall not forget," he promised.

They clasped hands, and Newcastle murmured, "We shall meet again in better times." He slipped out through the side door. Moments later Richard heard the pounding of hooves as the fugitive and his escort started northward toward Scotland.

Soon he himself would be a fugitive, and he had no time to lose. Packing only his tooth-brushing twig, razor, and comb, along with a single change of clothes, he took his rifle, double-barreled pistol, plus a supply of ammunition and powder for both weapons, as well as his belt laden with throwing knives. Hastily packing a saddlebag with money and jewelry, he went to the library where he selected leather-bound volumes of the works of Sir Francis Bacon, several plays by Ben Jonson, and a book of sonnets by William Shakespeare. It

19

was a wrench to leave behind the many hundreds of books he had read and loved, but that could not be helped.

Pausing again, he studied paintings of his father, grandfather, and the earlier ancestors who looked down at him from the walls of the library. Even if he removed some from their frames, they would be too bulky for him to carry and would serve no useful purpose. Standing erect, he raised a gauntlet-gloved hand to his broad-brimmed, plumed hat in salute, then hurried to the kitchen outbuilding, where he made up a package of cold meat and bread to take with him on the road. Finally, he filled a feedbag for his stallion. He and Prince Henry had a long journey ahead.

Locking the door of the manor house behind him, he took care to shut the front gate, too, but the knowledge that the Roundheads would be forced to break in when they took possession of his home gave him little satisfaction. Resisting the impulse to look back for a last time, he mounted and started off down to the road toward the southeast.

No lights were burning in the Hatcher house when he passed it, and he bade a silent farewell to Dorothea. It was too much to hope she would have the strength to resist her father's efforts to give her in marriage to some prominent Puritan. At least Uncle William had verified why their betrothal had been terminated so abruptly; obviously Master Hatcher had been told in confidence that arrest, imprisonment, and confiscation of property awaited Sir Richard Dunstable. He would cherish Dorothea for the rest of his days, of that he was certain.

At the last moment Richard's resolve broke and he knew he could not tolerate the thought of going off without Dorothea. He dismounted, picked up some pebbles from the walk, then stood and, taking a deep

20

breath, threw them up against the leaded pane of her darkened window.

There was a long pause, and when no one replied he was on the verge of repeating his effort. Then, suddenly, the window opened. He caught a glimpse of his beloved Dorothea, her hair hanging loose as she peered out into the night.

"It's Richard," he murmured.

Dorothea was about to shrink back into the room.

"Wait!" he said. "Dorothea, I have no time to explain, but I'm going away—against my own will. I can't leave without you. Please, I beg you, come with me and we'll be married somewhere on our journey."

There was a long silence from above. "Dorothea!" His voice was more urgent. "I don't dare tell you more now, but—"

"It makes no matter," she said faintly, though there was a new resolve in her voice. "I can't go with you, Richard. I can't defy my father, or disobey him. If you go, you must go alone."

He was stunned. He had expected little more, but her refusal was so final that he abandoned all hope. He would have to make his future alone. He had no alternative.

Turning onto a little-used road, Richard made his way through the hills, his great stallion rarely varying the pace. A light, dry snow began to fall, whipped almost horizontal by stiff gusts that blew off the Irish Sea. The particles stung Richard's face, but he shielded his nose and mouth with his cloak, pulled his hat lower on his head, and rode on.

Not until an hour after daybreak did he come to a large, comfortable house, the first on the list that the Earl of Newcastle had given him. As nearly as he could judge, it was the country home of a squire, and a portly, middle-aged man in bathrobe and slippers answered his knock on the front door.

Richard removed his hat. "I am——"

"No names, please," his host replied, cutting him off. "Your horse will be attended, and you shall have breakfast, a warm bed, and another, more substantial meal before you leave. Sleep until you're awakened. We'll take full responsibility for determining when few Puritans will be abroad and it will be safe for you to go."

Richard slept for the better part of the day, and after eating a hearty supper—served by his host, although he could hear women's voices in the house— he tried in vain to pay for his lodging and meals.

"The risks you take are greater than my poor contributions to our mutual cause," the man told him. "All of us must learn to work together and make sacrifices in the long years that lie ahead."

The treatment was typical of the welcome that Richard received everywhere on his journey, and even the proprietors of public inns refused to accept payment from him. Certainly it was heartening to learn that, so soon after the execution of King Charles, a strong network of steadfast Royalists was already in operation. Riding steadily toward the southwest from his own home, not far from the North Sea to the west, Richard passed through Northampton, then avoided the picturesque villages of the Cotswold hills in Gloucester. He had friends in Oxford who would have welcomed him, but he resisted the desire to stop off for a brief visit. Recognizing the need for strict self-discipline, he followed the Earl of Newcastle's instructions to the letter.

Richard didn't realize it, but in a sense he was fortunate. He was already endowed with the spirit of independence that enabled him to make his own decisions, take his own actions, and accept responsibility for them. Orphaned a decade earlier while in his mid-teens, Richard and his appointed guardian quickly reached a mutual agreement that the lad could make his own decisions. Now, with an assignment in the New World waiting for him, he didn't know that he had already developed the qualities that made for success in the North American colonies.

Finally, late one afternoon, he reached the rough, brawling seaport of Bristol. After stopping to inquire about the location of the White Hart Inn, he made his way toward it through a maze of narrow, cobbled streets. Here he saw Puritans everywhere, distinctive in their suits, cloaks, and hats of black, brown, or gray, their women modestly attired in dark dresses and capes, many of them clutching prayer books as they walked to and from the interminable religious services, hymn-singing, and endless sermons for which their sect was noted. The majority, Richard realized, were honest, plain people, sincere in their beliefs, and it would be wrong to blame them for such outrageous excesses as the killing of King Charles perpetrated by their fanatical leaders.

The White Hart was a substantial three-story building of stone and wood. A stable boy came to take Prince Henry to the rear, and when Richard entered through the front door carrying his saddlebag, he stopped short. The proprietor, who came forward to greet him, was wearing the drab attire of a Roundhead. Richard was so startled that his face mirrored his dismay.

The man, short and swarthy, revealed the absence of several front teeth when he grinned. "I can't say as I blame you for being upset when you see Minter Lucey dressed for a masquerade. But when you're in old Rome, Sir Richard, you wear a toga so you look like the other Romans, if you get my meaning."

"You know me?" Richard was still uncomfortable, ready for violence should it be necessary.

Conscious of his wariness, Minter Lucey tapped a

23

keg of ale in a cubicle off the entrance hall, placed a small container of water on a nearby table, then went through the ritual of passing his mug over the water before returning it to his mouth and gulping the contents. "A friend of yours and mine it's best not to name, if you get my meaning," he said, wiping his lips on his sleeve, "described you to perfection. I wasn't expecting you for at least another day. You did well to get here so fast."

Relaxing with a smile, Richard released his grip on the hilt of his sword.

"I happen to know that Brennan doesn't expect you until late tomorrow at the soonest, Sir Richard."

"Who?"

"Captain James Brennan, master of the brig *Anne*." Lucey filled the mug, then thrust it at the guest. "Bristol hospitality, Sir Richard. The day the Roundheads ban drink—and there's talk of it in their church councils—I'll have to give up my disguise. Come along, and I'll show you to your quarters."

Richard sipped his drink as he followed the proprietor up the stairs to a small, second-floor suite that overlooked a lane outside the inn. The parlor and bedchamber were tiny and cramped, furnished with simple essentials that looked comfortable. The suite was badly in need of paint, and on one wall of the sitting room was a blank rectangle of a lighter color where a picture had been displayed.

Minter Lucey saw the visitor's inquiring glance. "A long time ago," he said, "our mutual friend gave me a copy of a painting of King Charles, bless him, painted by some artist. Name of Van Dyke. I felt in my bones what was coming when the Roundheads made poor Charlie their prisoner, and ever since then the picture has been hidden in my cellar." His sigh was lugubrious. "These are hard times, Sir Richard, and the worst is yet to come."

Richard was forced to agree.

"I gave you these quarters because you have the best view of the lane from here. Even though I've become as pious a Puritan as you'll find in Bristol town, all inns are under suspicion, so at odd times the comings and goings of my patrons are watched. You'll find this a most useful observation post. Besides," he added with a chuckle, "I'd be afraid to dislodge the occupant of the grand suite upstairs. As my pa always said, 'A sharp tongue is more to be feared than a rapier,' if you get what I mean."

"Indeed," Richard replied politely.

"Now that you're here safe and sound, I'll go off to my own house down the road. The staff will serve your supper in the dining room in an hour. If you're wise, you won't go out of the inn. There will be prayer meetings of thanks for the deliverance from the yoke of King Charlie all over town tonight, and no one is more suspicious of strangers than the faithful."

"I'll follow your advice, Master Lucey."

"For my own sake, as well as yours, I thank you kindly. It's a dangerous, two-faced game I play here, and I want no hymn-chanting constables snooping around my inn." Minter Lucey appeared on the verge of imparting a confidence, but changed his mind abruptly. "We'll talk again early in the morning, before you go off to meet Captain Brennan." He sidled through the door, closing it behind him.

Within moments, a servant in black livery appeared with a bucket of hot water and a basin. After washing away the grime of the road, Richard gratefully changed into his one clean outfit, deciding that if time permitted before he sailed, he would buy some needed additions to his wardrobe.

Strapping on his knife-belt and concealing his pistol beneath his coat, he went down to the ground floor, found the dining room, and seated himself facing the door at a small table. The other two tables were unoccupied.

The same servant appeared with a tureen of a thick mutton and barley soup, and after he placed it on the table, Richard ladled a generous portion into his bowl. Not only was he ravenous, but the small coal fire at the far end of the room was almost dead, and the soup warmed him. As he ate, someone else came into the room, and he couldn't help staring at the most flamboyant beauty he had ever seen.

The woman, who appeared to be in her early twenties, had glowing red hair that cascaded to her waist. Her gown was so daring and her use of cosmetics so lavish that only a courtesan or a great noblewoman—or someone who was both—would have had the courage to display herself in public in a manner certain to attract attention. She was tall, slender, and willowy, her low-cut emerald-green velvet dress revealing the cleavage between her high, full breasts, then nipping in her tiny waist and clinging to her long, firm thighs. Bright rouge accented her provocative lips, and she appeared to have rouged her high cheekbones, too; as if that weren't enough, a velvet beauty patch of emerald green was the focal point on one cheek. But her limpid eyes, which were enormous and matched her gown, were her most arresting feature. They were rimmed in black kohl with a black salve making her long lashes seem even longer, and on her lids was a substance of a delicate green.

She moved past him, hips swaying as she walked to the farthest table, and Richard instantly guessed she was Lady Dawn Shepherd, the late Earl of Sturbridge's daughter. The coal fire was reflected in her long gold earrings, a chain of gold dipped low in her cleavage, and her fingers were covered with rings. If she were truly the fugitive he believed her to be, she was mad for daring to make herself so conspicuous.

Paying no attention to the other guest, acting as if she were the only patron in the dining room, she waved away the soup that the servant brought her. The man reappeared with a roast of rare beef, and she took a slice of the meat, refused the roasted potatoes, and allowed herself to be served a portion of brussels sprouts.

Richard took every dish offered to him. Surely the young woman was aware of his steady, unwavering gaze, but she looked both past and through him, not once acknowledging his presence.

When the waiter brought glasses of wine, a thought occurred to Richard, and he asked for a carafe of water, too. After it had been served, he observed the ritual of drinking a silent toast to the young king-across-the-water. The woman hesitated for an instant, then went through the same motions. It was her prerogative to speak first, but she remained silent, so he concentrated on his meal, unable to fathom her strange attitude.

When the servant reappeared to clear away their dishes, she raised her voice for the first time, speaking in the clipped soprano of the upper class. "The savory was inedible last night, so I shall have none this evening," she said.

The man bowed and went off to the kitchen for a single portion of oysters and bacon, grilled on toast, which he placed before Richard, then retired.

The woman rose and paused for a moment at Richard's table. "When you're done," she murmured in an almost inaudible tone, "come to my quarters on the third floor." Not waiting for a reply, she swept out of the room.

The savory was delicious, Richard thought, and made a point of asking the servant to give his compliments to the cook.

"I'm the cook, your worship," the man said, bowing.

27

"There's none but me on duty here after dark. Now that we'll have peace, it may be that travelers will start a-coming to Bristol again."

Richard did not pause at his own suite, but went directly to the top floor, stamping his boots on the stairs to announce his approach. When he reached the landing, he saw a door had been opened, so he walked into a sitting room at least three times the size of his own. A jewel-hilted dagger in one hand, the woman appeared from behind the door then quickly closed and bolted it.

"There's no need to carve me, milady," he said as he bowed to her. "Sir Richard Dunstable at your service."

"I am not your lady," she replied coldly, raising her skirt and calmly placing the weapon in a sheath strapped on her calf. "Until further notice, I am to be addressed only as Mimi Shepherd, Sir Richard!"

"As you wish." He watched her as she poured wine from a pewter decanter into two glasses and handed him one. He was amused by her secretive air, just as he was irritated by her arrogance.

She waved him to a high-backed chair with a faded, tapestry-covered seat. "I have spent a full week in this primitive place," she said, taking a chair opposite his. "The only news I've heard in all that time until this morning was that poor, dear Charles is no longer in our midst. I haven't dared to go out-of-doors for fear the rabble will haul me off to one of their frightful gaols. Today, I was informed of your arrival, and you've come just in time to preserve my sanity."

He was less than certain that she was all that sane, but kept his opinion to himself.

"How soon can you make arrangements for my quarters on the ship, Sir Richard?" she demanded.

He knew nothing of her plans and made that fact clear to her.

28

"I sail to the New World on the brig *Anne,* as do you," she told him impatiently. "The very few I can trust tell me I'm not safe in England any longer, and because Queen Henrietta Maria dislikes me, I'm not welcome in France."

Richard jumped to the conclusion that the queen probably had no use for her because Mimi had enjoyed a dalliance with King Charles, who had frequently been guilty of indiscretions.

"I haven't chosen the colonies willingly," Mimi Shepherd said. "I regret to say there is nowhere else I can go."

"I hope to visit the ship's master tomorrow morning, and I'll do what I can for you, Mistress Shepherd. Are you expected on board?"

Her shrug was haughty. "I was told only that you would attend to the details. I prefer a spacious cabin on the port side, which will face toward the south crossing the Atlantic and should be warmer at this ghastly season of the year."

Her imperious manner nettled Richard. "I have no idea what accommodations might be available," he said. "I'll pass along your request to the master, but I hope you won't be disappointed if he's unable to provide what you want."

Her green eyes turned as cold as the ice on the eaves beyond the frosted window. "If you're concerned about my ability to pay for what I want, I assure you that I have more than enough money for my needs."

Her haughtiness was similar to that of so many other members of the upper nobility, and he realized that, in spite of her beauty, she would be anything but an ideal traveling companion. "I'll do what I'm able, Lady Dawn, but I make no promises."

"I've already told you, sir, that I prefer to be known as Mimi Shepherd."

His own nerves were raw after his long, hazardous

29

journey. "May I ask why, if you seek anonymity, you dress in a manner that will draw attention to yourself? Any man who even glances in your direction is certain to look a second time!"

She raised a thin eyebrow. "Now you sound like a Puritan, Sir Richard. I dress to please myself, as I've always done. I've remained in hiding here only because I promised poor Charlie that I'd go off to the colonies if anything unpleasant happened to him. If I had my way, I'd flaunt myself before Cromwell and all his mealymouthed followers—for the pure joy of watching the hypocrites gape at me!"

She seemed to be confirming his guess that she had been one of King Charles's mistresses. "It appears," he said, coolly polite, "that you fail to recognize the seriousness of your situation—or of mine. I've been charged with your safety. The Roundhead constabulary are searching all of England for you, and although they don't yet know I've come so far from my own home, I'm certain they're maintaining a sharp lookout for Cavaliers in every major seaport. So please stay indoors until I learn the exact hazards we face."

"I haven't shown myself beyond the front door of this horrid little place since I arrived, so your advice is unnecessary. But I reserve the right to change my mind."

Richard stood and bowed. "If you do, Lady Dawn, I shall feel I've been relieved of my obligation to assist you." He unbolted the door and went off to his own quarters. Uncle William had saddled him with a burdensome responsibility.

Sleeping soundly, as he always did, Richard awakened early the following morning. A different manservant brought him hot water for his ablutions and a mug of tea, and he went downstairs for a hearty breakfast of cold ham, cheese, smoked fish, and mild ale.

As he was finishing his meal, Minter Lucey appeared.

"I thought you might want advice on how to make your way around Bristol," he said.

"There are parts of town it's wise to avoid, I take it."

"Ah, you get my meaning. Puritan spies lurk in unlikely places."

"I'd be obliged for the most direct route to the waterfront."

Lucey gave him careful directions, then added quietly, "You'd be wise not to wear that hat, which advertises you as one of the king's party. Use this instead." He handed the visitor a drab black hat with a domed crown and rounded brim.

The offer was sensible, and Richard accepted it. His rifle would make him conspicuous, but he could hide his pistol and knife-belt under his cloak; only his sword would show, but the Puritan gentry carried sidearms, too.

"Members of the new constabulary carry long staffs and patrol in pairs, so you'll always recognize them. But beware of single loiterers who seem to have no occupation save that of leaning against buildings. Avoid looking directly at any you might encounter, if you get my meaning, and show no hesitation in unfamiliar surroundings. They'll be almost certain to question you if they discover that you're a stranger in Bristol."

Richard thanked the innkeeper, then set out for the waterfront. Following Lucey's instructions, he walked only a short distance down a street that ran parallel to the Avon River before he came to the stream's junction with the smaller Frome River. Together they formed a sheltered harbor at the head of the Severn estuary, and past rows of warehouses he could see the masts of ships tied up at wharves or lying at anchor.

Not slowing his pace, he went briskly past a score of vessels before he came to a weather-beaten brig with the name *Anne* painted in faded gold letters on her hull. She was no more than seventy feet long and, he guessed, did not weigh more than twenty-five hundred tons. Unfamiliar with the sea, Richard felt a knot forming in the pit of his stomach when he contemplated the dangers of making a mid-winter Atlantic crossing in such a frail craft.

He was alert to far more immediate dangers: at the foot of the wharf, a man in black, the brim of his hat pulled low, was leaning against a post. Any man who had nothing better to do in this raw, blustery weather undoubtedly was a Roundhead agent. Grateful to Lucey, Richard averted his gaze as he walked boldly past the spy and onto the wharf. The *Anne* was held in place by lines fore and aft, and he halted amidships, a short distance from a partly opened hatch.

"Ahoy, on board," he called.

After a long wait, a middle-aged seaman looked out through the hatch opening.

"I seek a word with your master." Richard knew the Puritan spy was listening.

The sailor's face did not change expression. "Who wants to see him?"

"Isaac Marker." Richard thought the Biblical first name was inspired and might lessen the agent's suspicions.

The seaman vanished, to return a few moments later. Climbing onto the deck, he placed a plank extending from the deck to the wharf.

Richard went on board, followed the sailor down a narrow ladder, and was conducted aft. The bearded master, James Brennan, wore a look of puzzlement on his lined, weather-beaten face as he stood at the entrance to his cabin, a charcoal brazier glowing behind him. "Master Marker?" he asked uncertainly.

Richard nodded, followed him into the cabin, and closed the door before he said, "I invented a name for

32

the sake of our friend at the foot of the pier. I'm expected, I believe. My real name is Dunstable."

Brennan grinned, his handshake a viselike grip. "You made it here safely, Sir Richard!" He went to a small keg, poured two mugs of foaming porter, handed one to his visitor, and went through the ritual of extending his own over an imaginary water receptacle. Richard did the same, and then they drank in solemn silence.

"I take it you had no troubles on the road, Sir Richard?"

"I avoided main roads whenever possible. One learns quickly how to become a fugitive."

Brennan nodded. "And no one followed you here?"

"Not to my knowledge, Captain."

"Good. There's an agent stationed day and night at the base of the wharf, but they think I'm one of them, and I've already been granted sailing clearance."

"When do we sail?"

"In a few days. You'll be notified about twelve hours in advance. I'll send word to you at Brother Lucey's place. But you can send your sea chests to me at any time, and I'll stash them in your cabin. Would you like to see it?" Not waiting for a reply, he led his passenger down a cramped companionway.

Richard peered into a tiny cabin with upper and lower bunks, a slab of wood that could be lowered from a bulkhead to become a table, and two stools that were fastened to the deck. A single, square window, tightly closed, admitted daylight, and an oil lamp stood on a shelf.

"It's not the most luxurious of quarters," the master said as they returned to his own cabin. "But you'll have privacy, which is more than can be said for those who'll share the general cabin."

"I was asked," Richard said, "to arrange accommodations for a certain lady."

33

Captain Brennan scowled. "If you refer to the daughter of an earl who died several years ago, there's no place for her on my ship," he said emphatically. "Word leaked out that she would sail with me, and I've been questioned by the new Puritan governor of Bristol himself. Naturally, I swore that I knew nothing about any such lady. They're taking no chances, which is the reason their agents are keeping watch on the *Anne*. They'll not only arrest her and haul her off to prison the moment they set eyes on her, but I'll be thrown into a cell, too, and my ship will be confiscated. There's no man more devoted to the Crown than I am, Sir Richard, but I'll be of no use to the cause if I'm behind bars and lose the *Anne!*"

"I see." Richard saw a great deal, and his mind worked furiously. The Earl of Newcastle had asked him to help Lady Dawn Shepherd, and he could not abandon her, particularly now that he knew the Roundheads were closing in on her. Obviously their plans had to be revised drastically, and the haughty noblewoman's demand for a cabin on the port side now seemed absurd. This new development forced him to take matters into his own hands, and he reacted accordingly. "The lady hasn't come to Bristol yet?"

"No, and I hope she doesn't! I don't know how the Puritans found out she was hoping to sail with me, but that's out of the question now!"

"I quite understand your position, Captain," Richard said. "I noted there are two beds in my cabin, and I wonder if I assume correctly that the second has not been sold."

The master shook his head. "There's no end of people begging for passage, but you're entitled to your privacy."

"Then I'd like to book passage for my serving lad and will pay you a double fare, of course. He's the

34

son of the butler who served my father before me, and I've promised to help the boy launch a new life in the colonies."

Brennan shrugged. "It's of no matter to me, Sir Richard. You'll be stumbling all over each other in that little cabin, but I don't mind, if you don't."

Richard immediately reached for his purse.

"Pay when we sail, not before."

"I insist on giving you an advance now." Anxious to close the agreement, Richard handed the master two gold coins. "I also wonder if you'll have room for my horse. I'll provide his feed and will take care of him."

"There's no space below, but you can quarter him near the fowl pens on the aft deck. Make certain he's supplied with enough blankets. You may pace him only when no one else is on deck. The Atlantic winds are chilly at this time of year, and I won't be held responsible if he becomes ill." Brennan then added, "I'll have to charge you full fare for your mount, if that's agreeable."

"I accept the arrangement, Captain." Richard gave him another coin.

The master slipped the gold piece into his pocket. "Along with your chests, send along any special foods you may want for a voyage of six weeks. Avoid perishables, and tell the shop clerks you intend the purchases for use on board ship, so they'll pack your goods accordingly." He paused and chuckled. "Mark you, don't bring too many delicacies, Sir Richard. You'll have to store the supplies in your cabin, and what with sharing the room with a boy, you'll scarce have enough space to turn around."

After a final exchange of amenities, Richard went ashore, taking care to pay no attention to the Round-head agent who continued to loiter at the base of the wharf. Losing no time, he hurried back to the White Hart.

Neither Lucey nor the manservant appeared in the parlor, so he went straight to Lady Dawn's suite on the top floor. He had to identify himself carefully, and not until she recognized his voice did she admit him. She had slept late, and although she had already applied cosmetics to her face, she was clad in a billowing, low-cut silk peignoir.

This touch of intimacy made Richard uneasy, but he knew they would be thrown even closer together if his daring scheme materialized. Mincing no words, he outlined the situation at the harbor and his own plan. The woman brooded in silence for a moment. "You're quite sure the Roundheads are keeping watch for me?"

"There seems little question about it. Someone apparently talked out of turn."

"I daresay that some members of my household staff in London are Roundheads." She sighed lightly. "Well, it can't be helped."

Richard had to admire her for showing no sign of panic.

Her elfin grin was unexpected. "Do you suppose you and I could tolerate living in such close quarters?"

"We'll have no choice if you're going to sail on the *Anne*. It's plain you must leave England. And if you can't go to France, you'd need a refuge somewhere else on the Continent."

"The German states are barbaric, the Dutch are dull, and the Spanish have no use for the English. That leaves only America, I'm afraid." She looked at him, her huge green eyes wide. "Do you actually think I can be disguised as a young boy?"

"We'll have to try," he replied. "I need more clothes myself, so I'll get you some appropriate articles, along with anything special you may want in the way of

36

food. As you've gathered, our space will be severely limited."

"I prefer to take as much of my wardrobe as I can salvage." She gestured toward several large leather boxes in one corner of her sitting room.

Richard made some rapid calculations. "One chest will take care of my needs," he said. "So I estimate we can squeeze in about half of those cases of yours."

"That's all?" She was dismayed, but was resolute. "I prefer saving my head. You realize, I'm sure, that I've placed my future in your hands."

"I've accepted the obligation, and I'll do my best, but I hope you'll remember that this type of problem is as new and strange to me as it is to you."

"Somehow we'll manage together, Richard." She smiled and extended her hand.

His hostility toward her melted away. "I wish us good fortune, Mimi," he replied. "We'll need all the luck in the world."

II

RICHARD bought enough new clothes for himself to fit into one sea chest, then went shopping for boys' clothes. Mimi Shepherd had told him her measurements, and he purchased shirts, a hat, smock, and breeches. His worst problem was finding boots and shoes for her; footwear worn by aristocrats was custom made by expensive cobblers, but there was insufficient time, so he had to do what he could in the Bristol shops that catered to common people.

His purchases would be delivered later in the day, so, satisfied with his morning's work, he headed back to the White Hart. Somberly clad Puritans were everywhere, but they went about their own business quietly, and none seemed to be aware of the inconspicuously dressed stranger in their midst. No Puritan agents lurked in the street near the entrance to the White Hart, either, so Richard was able to breathe more easily.

Minter Lucey met him in the front hallway. "Our other guest is being served a meal upstairs," he said, "because we have a visitor, someone who has come here at my invitation to meet you." He led the way into the parlor, where a young man in his early twenties, with pale hair and an athletic build, sat dejectedly in a corner, an untouched mug of ale on a table beside him.

"Sir Richard," Lucey said, "allow me to present Master Dempster Chaney."

Young Chaney tried to smile as they shook hands, but could not quite succeed. Lucey brought Richard a mug of ale, then discreetly withdrew.

Dempster Chaney was unprepossessing at first glance, but first glances were inclined to be deceptive. He appeared slight but was heavier and more solidly built than he looked and was endowed with wiry muscles as a result of years of hard work on his father's large agricultural estate. His pale hair and eyes gave him a rather nondescript appearance, but as Richard soon learned, a twinkle that appeared often in his eyes indicated there were hidden depths to him. He was dressed like most members of the upper middle class in stout, well-made boots and breeches, a leather jerkin, and an outer cape. Although the middle class was not inclined to carry weapons, a sword hung at

38

Dempster's side with such familiarity that it was obvious he knew how to use it.

"Have I gathered correctly that you wished to meet me?" Richard asked.

The younger man looked despondent. "Lucey insisted, but I know of nothing that you or anyone else can do for me."

He told his story succinctly. His father had been killed while fighting on the Cavalier side in the civil war. Then, Dempster had been ordered to withdraw from his studies at Edinburgh. Now the victorious Puritans had confiscated his estate and other property, leaving him penniless. And just yesterday the father of his betrothed had terminated the engagement.

Richard was struck by the similarity to his own case. Thinking of Dorothea, he felt sympathy for Chaney's plight.

"Robbin is a girl of great spirit," Dempster said, "and would defy her father. She'd run away with me without hesitation, but I'm virtually bankrupt now. I know of no way to earn a living other than in farming because I was not permitted to complete my medical training. I have no future here: Robbin's father would have no trouble following us, and the Roundheads would send me to prison for corrupting a girl who won't reach her twenty-first birthday for several months."

"You're more fortunate than you realize," Richard said. "Most young women are obedient to their fathers' wishes." He refrained from adding that Dorothea's subservience to her father's will had blighted his own life.

"Robbin would take any risk, Sir Richard, but I can't ask her to run away with me when I have no place to go."

39

Richard pondered for a time. "Have you thought of emigrating to the colonies in North America?"

"Frequently," Dempster said. "Most people there earn their livings on farms, or so I've read, and I'm prepared to work hard. But passage to the New World costs five sovereigns per passenger, and I don't have ten sovereigns to my name. Nor do I know of a ship that will sail to America in the immediate future. Not that it would be of any help if I did."

Rarely one to make impulsive gestures, Richard nevertheless felt envious of this young man whose sweetheart was self-willed. How different his own life would be if Dorothea had defied her father! "Get your girl," he said brusquely. "Go with her to Captain Brennan of the brig *Anne*. I prefer that you not mention my name, but you have my permission if need be. The only accommodations available are in a general cabin with other passengers—"

"We'll gladly suffer any inconvenience," Dempster interrupted. Slowly the gleam in his eyes faded. "But my basic problem is unsolved. I'd sell my sword, my last remaining possession of value, if I could get ten sovereigns for it."

Richard took two gold coins from his purse and silently handed them to the younger man. A broad smile wreathed Dempster's face as he took the money, then began to unbuckle his sword-belt.

"My own sword serves me well," Richard told him. "You may need your weapon before this adventure ends. Keep it."

"But—but how can I repay you?"

"Give your girl an extra kiss for one who doesn't share your good fortune."

Dempster started to speak, then thought better of it. Something in Sir Richard's troubled countenance told him it would not be wise to ask too many questions about his benefactor's life. "I hope I'll have the chance to show my gratitude to you," he said. "Will we meet again?"

Richard had no intention of admitting, even to a staunch fellow Cavalier, that he, too, intended to sail on the *Anne*. His safety and that of Mimi Shepherd depended on secrecy. "One often sees friends in this world when least expected," he replied vaguely.

Eager to be on his way, Dempster Chaney thanked him again, then took his leave.

Richard ate cold beef and bread alone in the dining room. His purchases arrived while he was eating, and after his meal he sorted them in his own suite, then went up to the third floor, a bundle under his arm.

"Your own seamstress and bootmaker could do far better for you," he said as the woman made the door secure. "These are the best I could find on short notice."

Mimi looked at the clothes Richard had spread out on a bench and laughed.

"There's no time like the present to find out if our ruse will be effective," Richard told her. "You might start by removing your cosmetics."

"I hadn't thought of that, but it's obvious I must." She went to her bedchamber, returning with her face scrubbed clean. He was startled to see that the absence of rouge, kohl, and other substances in no way detracted from her radiant beauty. For his taste, she looked even lovelier.

"What comes next?" she demanded, making a game of disguising herself.

"Do you have a razor or shears?"

She shook her head. "I have no need for either."

Richard went to his own suite, returning with his razor. He examined her critically, then said, "I dislike having to ask you to sacrifice so many inches of your hair, but I fear there's no choice."

41

"It will grow again, so that's the least of our problems. Are you a competent barber?"

"I've never in my life done anything like this. Hold still, and I'll try to cut it in a straight line." Grasping a handful of the long, red hair that tumbled down her back, he slashed it off at shoulder length.

Mimi sighed gently, but made no comment.

Richard concentrated on the alien task, and when he was done, he was relieved to see that he had cut her hair more or less evenly. Piles of the long strands were now disposed of in a basket.

She hurried into the bedchamber and stared at her reflection in the long pier glass hanging between the windows. "I no longer know myself."

"I must admit there's a change." He refrained from mentioning that she still looked exceptionally attractive.

"So much for minor matters," Mimi said as she turned to face him. "I'm in awe of your efficiency, but what do we do about two major problems?" She cupped her firm, full breasts in her hands.

He tried in vain to hide his discomfort. "This is the best I can manage," he said, and showed her a long strip of unbleached linen several inches wide. "Bind yourself in this to reduce the—uh—protuberances as much as possible."

"You'll have to do it for me. I couldn't make it tight enough." Showing no self-consciousness, she began to unbutton her dress. "You might want to fetch me the boys' smallclothes you bought, too."

Richard hastily went off to the sitting room for the underbreeches he had purchased for her, and when he returned to the bedchamber he saw that she was stark naked, except for a flimsy silk chemise and pantalettes that gave her no apparent concern. She showed no embarrassment, but Richard was very conscious of her appearance and his reaction caused her to giggle.

Her slender, feminine body so aroused him that even though he stood at arm's length, color flamed in his face as he handed her the underbreeches.

Mimi was amused as she donned them. "Oh, dear. They're far stiffer than my silks, but I'll try not to scratch or squirm. Now, stand behind me and wrap this strip around my breasts."

He marveled at her tranquility. Dorothea would have been overcome by embarrassment, but Mimi Shepherd seemed unconcerned. He wound the cloth twice around her breasts and tugged gently.

"Much, much tighter," she commanded. "Never fear, I'll tell you quickly enough if you're hurting me."

He pulled harder at the ends of the cloth.

"Enough," she said at last. "Tie off the ends, and cut away what isn't needed."

He did as she had ordered, then finally looked at her. She was examining her reflection critically in the pier glass. "Not long ago young Richard Lovelace promised he'd write an ode that would immortalize my bosom. I'm glad he can't see me now." Her breasts had been reduced to a fraction of their normal size, but no one would have mistaken her for a man.

She climbed into a pair of breeches, stuffing the boys' shirt of coarse wool into it, and then pulled a thick smock over her head. "Not bad," she said after analyzing her reflection again. "What do you think?"

"You should pass muster," Richard told her, and returned to the sitting room for one more item, a cap with a peaked visor. "Pull your hair behind your ears when you wear this," he told her.

The cap did a great deal to assist with her transformation, but Mimi was not yet satisfied. "Something is still wrong," she said.

Richard laughed for the first time. "I don't believe those diamond earrings are quite suitable," he said.

43

"You'll need to take off your rings, cut your finger-nails, and remove that lacquer from them, too."

"When you next see me in this disguise it will be perfect," she said. "How long will I be obliged to wear it on board the ship?"

"That will depend on circumstances," Richard replied.

"We shall have to change the circumstances," Mimi said, wriggling and scratching first her thighs, then her back. "You can't imagine how grateful I am to be a woman. I'd go mad if I had to spend the rest of my days in clothes that itch as if I were being pursued by all of the Puritans' devils."

"It's bad enough," he said, "that the Puritans themselves are hunting for you."

Dempster Chaney waited impatiently until late afternoon, then walked up the path beside the Avon River to a neighborhood of substantial houses and large gardens. These were the homes of Bristol's successful merchants, physicians, and lawyers, all of whom had been unwavering in their loyalty to the Crown prior to the steady series of defeats suffered by the Cavaliers in their war with the Puritans. Now the atmosphere had suddenly changed. No families hosted dinner parties, musical instruments were banished to attics, and a new Nonconformist church was built, which everyone attended in appropriately dark attire.

Dusk was falling as the young man cut through a number of gardens, then paused in what Robbin's father had been fond of calling his grove of statues. Here life-sized reproductions of ancient Greek statues were scattered, and only recently Dempster had remarked to Robbin that soon her father would be obliged to smash the nude figures or clothe them in attire of which the Puritans would approve. This evening they were still in place, however, offering an area of concealment that was useful.

A lamp was lighted in Robbin's second-floor bedroom, and Dempster's heart pounded. He picked up a handful of small pebbles, crept closer to the house, and tossed the stones up against the panes of a leaded glass window.

Elsewhere in the house, a dog barked furiously, then was silenced.

Robbin's father rarely left the place, and if her older brothers had come home from their shop, she would find it difficult to sneak out. Dempster waited as patiently as he could, his temples throbbing, and just as he stooped to pick up more pebbles, the window opened. Robbin appeared, squinting her eyes as she peered out into the darkness.

Dempster caught a glimpse of her blonde hair, paler than his own, and beckoned silently. At last she saw him and understood. The window remained open as she withdrew. He continued to stand, shifting his weight from one foot to the other, until he realized that anyone who glanced out into the garden could see him. Still staring at the open window, he reluctantly withdrew to the grove of statues.

A short time later, a bundle was thrown out of the window, landing with a soft thud on the snow-spotted ground. Dempster resisted the urge to sprint forward and pick it up. Obviously Robbin had been waiting for him and had made her preparations in advance.

A rope made of torn and tied linen sheets was lowered, and a moment later Robbin herself appeared. She climbed to the sill, hampered by her long dress and voluminous cloak, then slowly lowered herself hand under hand down the outside of the ivy-covered wall. The task was almost too great for her, and when she paused for a moment, balanced precariously by resting her foot on the top frame of a window, she appeared to be in danger of falling. Dempster had to curb his instinctive desire to cross the open yard and reach up for her. Overcoming her panic, the girl tightened her grip, then descended more slowly. Dempster's arms ached as he watched her. Ultimately her feet touched the ground, and she snatched her nearby bundle. Knowing where her beloved would be waiting for her, she gathered her skirts and ran as fast as she could to the grove of statues. They embraced, kissing fiercely.

"I won't be missed for about an hour, until I'm called to the dinner table," Robbin whispered. "Then all pandemonium will break loose, and Papa will scour the town for me. Andrew and Theodore are both home tonight—worse luck—so they'll help him."

Robbin was tiny, but her size was belied by her efficiency. She had a nose that was abbreviated and best described as pert, and her figure could have been called pert too, but she moved briskly, with a self-assuredness that more than compensated for the youthful or girlish look that she conveyed. Her hair was as pale a blond as Dempster's and her eyes, which were enormous, were an even more brilliant shade of blue. She was one of those people who seemed to be forever in motion. Even when she was not moving, her features remained animated, and she seemed to exude tremendous energy at all times.

Dempster took the bundle, held Robbin's elbow to guide her as they started across the gardens that would take them to the path beside the Avon, and nodded. Only now did he realize she looked like a Puritan maiden in her black dress with white collar and cuffs, dark bonnet, and ankle-length black cape. "We should have enough time if our luck holds."

"Where are we going?" She took long strides to keep up with him, trusting him completely.

"Wait until we're in the clear," he said.

She was content to accompany him anywhere. "I knew you'd find a way to come for me," she murmured.

Not until they reached the path and it turned into a street nearer the center of Bristol did Dempster explain their situation in full detail.

"Sir Richard must be a wonderful man."

"He appears to be, but we'll discuss him later. We're going straight to the brig, and if I can obtain passage we'll stay on board. I'll find some excuse for the captain so it won't be necessary for us to go ashore again. If our luck is good, your father won't think of having the ships in the harbor searched. He'll probably assume we've gone to London for the help of friends there."

"I think you're right. At least I hope so." Her breath was short, but she managed to ask, "When will we marry, dearest?"

"As soon as possible. But first we need to free ourselves. When did you start dressing like a Roundhead?"

"Today, when I'd hoped you'd come for me. I thought we'd be far less conspicuous if I looked this way."

Dempster nodded in approval. As always, Robbin was a step ahead of him in her thinking.

They were approaching the waterfront now, and having learned the location of the *Anne* before going for the girl, he led her toward it, his grip on her arm tightening when he saw the Roundhead agent on duty at the base of the wharf.

"Who is that man?" Robbin murmured.

He shrugged. "He appears to be watching for someone."

"It won't be you or me," she replied. "So let's walk more slowly and give him enough time to look at us."

Dempster obediently slowed his pace. The Puritan

47

studied them, directing most of his attention to the young woman. He seemed satisfied and averted his gaze.

A seaman, who was coiling a line on the deck, put down the plank that enabled them to board the ship, and they were taken to Captain Brennan's cabin. Dempster introduced himself, then added calmly, "This is my wife, Captain."

Robbin felt as if a bolt of lightning had struck her, but her gentle smile did not waver, even though she realized that she and Dempster would be forced to live a lie until they reached the colonies and could find a clergyman to marry them. But the technical sacrifice of her honor for a time was a small price to pay.

"We're told you sail soon for the colonies, Captain."

"Aye," Brennan replied. "My first port of call will be Boston."

"That's our destination," Dempster said glibly. "Can you find room for us?"

"There are two places left in the general cabin, but you'll share it with three others."

It was not easy for Dempster to say, "We don't mind."

Robbin nodded cheerfully too, although her heart sank. The lack of privacy on board the brig might make it necessary to wait until they reached the New World before she and Dempster slept together.

"I charge five sovereigns a head," Captain Brennan said sternly. "Payable in advance."

Dempster handed him the gold coins. The brig's master held them to the light and bit them before he was satisfied. "You have passage," he said. "Come back at this same time tomorrow for the sailing."

"We wonder," Dempster said, his voice even in

spite of his fears, "if we might stay on board until we sail."

Robbin astonished her betrothed by speaking in the thick accent of Northumberland. "We'll save a tidy sum," she said, "and I be weary after spending so many days on the road."

"Stay, if you like," the master told them. "But my cook won't come aboard until dawn, so you'll get no meal before breakfast tomorrow."

"Oh, we've had our supper," Robbin lied. "So we're much obliged to ye."

She was even more extraordinary than Dempster had known.

The master conducted them to the large cabin. "If you decide to stretch your legs ashore," he said, "just remember the sailing hour." Nodding to them, he left the cabin.

"So far so good," Dempster said when they were alone. "Where did you learn that north country accent?"

"There are many things about me that you don't yet know," Robbin replied demurely. "I thought a woman's touch was needed so we could stay on board. That's why I intervened. It's important that we not leave this ship. We've found favor with the gods and goddesses of the Greeks, Romans, and Norsemen who protect lovers, and we're not going to offend them by taking needless chances. We'll be that much hungrier for breakfast after we've fasted tonight."

She was right, as usual. "We'll have a long evening ahead of us, but at least we'll be safe."

The young couple assumed that the other passengers who would occupy the cabin with them would not arrive until the following day, so they could start their honeymoon without delay, even though their wedding necessarily had to be postponed. "The time

49

will pass quickly," Robbin said with a broad smile. "We'll find ways to keep busy."

Richard was eating breakfast when a member of the *Anne*'s crew brought word to the White Hart that the brig would sail on the early-evening tide. Minter Lucey took the word to Lady Dawn, but she remained secluded in her suite. Later in the morning she sent for the manservant, saying her traveling cases were ready.

When Richard saw her three leather boxes, he shook his head. It would be difficult to find a place in the cabin for his one small sea chest, but it was apparent that the daughter of a prominent earl did not think in terms of others' convenience. The day passed slowly, and at noon Richard ate heartily, enjoying his last meal on land for many weeks to come.

Midafternoon he went to the stable himself for Prince Henry and walked the horse beside the cart in which Lady Dawn's many belongings, his few possessions, and the fodder and blankets for his mount were piled. Captain Brennan materialized to supervise the stowing of the various possessions on board, and Prince Henry was penned in an open stall built for him on the aft deck.

Minter Lucey was waiting at the inn when the young baronet returned, and Richard frowned as he said, "The Roundheads have doubled their watch. There were two agents standing duty at the wharf just now."

"Another is just down the street a short distance, where he can keep an eye on the front door," Lucey said. "I wonder if they've caught wind of something."

"We'll find out soon enough," Richard replied.

The innkeeper nodded dolefully. "Yes, it's too late now to change your plans, if you get my meaning."

"There's no other way to leave," Richard replied, conscious of the mission the Earl of Newcastle had asked him to perform regarding the Royalists in the American colonies.

"You don't think the lady will be recognized?" Lucey asked.

A voice came to them from the staircase. "I don't recognize myself, Master Lucey," Mimi called, approaching them in boys' attire.

The innkeeper, who had known nothing of the scheme, could only gape at her. Richard examined her carefully and could find no fault with her appearance. Her nails, which had been cut short, were free of lacquer, she wore no jewelry of any kind, and her bulky smock, along with the band of linen she had managed to affix by herself, made her prominent breasts inconspicuous.

"I gather you approve," she said to Richard, turning slowly for his benefit.

He told her about the increase in the Puritans' watch. "I have no idea whether they've learned specifics or are just being more careful because they know the *Anne* is sailing this evening. But we can't afford any slips."

Mimi thought for a moment, then went to the hearth and, after drawing a finger across it, added a smudge to the bridge of her nose and one cheek. "I believe I could pass as a boy in the slums of London now," she said.

She might be selfish and indifferent to the rights of others, but Richard had to admire her courage. Oliver Cromwell had been gallant in his treatment of Queen Henrietta Maria, permitting her to go freely to France with her children, in keeping with his frequently quoted statement that Puritans do not wage war against women. But others who had been close to King Charles would be made to suffer for their sins. The daughter of the

51

Earl of Sturbridge, who appeared to have been one of the monarch's mistresses, would spend many years in prison and be subjected to endless humiliations should she be captured.

Lucey was still apprehensive. "What you've done is very clever," he said, "but it may not be enough. I'm sure there's time for me to locate eight or ten Royalists who know how to handle swords. I believe you should have an escort."

Mimi deferred to her protector.

"That wouldn't do," Richard said. "We'd be calling attention to our flight, and a battle would surely develop on the wharf. Even if we succeeded in sailing, it would take time for the brig to make her way out of the Severn estuary and Bristol Channel into the open sea. A swift rider could carry word to the coast, and a warship would overtake us easily. Remember that the Roundheads control the New Model Navy now. Not only would we be captured, but the master of the brig—who is useful to our cause in many ways— would be exposed also. We'll keep to our plan and hope for the best."

Lucey had been overruled and could only bow in resignation. "Let me offer you a drink before you go," he said. "A part of poor King Charles's wine cellar was brought here, and I've been told to use it as my own."

"So you should, Master Lucey," Mimi said as she watched him pour brandy into three glasses. "Richard and I are escaping to a new land, primitive though it may be, but you're staying on here to face countless dangers every day of your life."

The innkeeper smiled and shook his head as he placed a small bowl of water on a table. "If I do say so, your ladyship, I have a rich, strong voice, and as long as I sing the Puritans' hymns loudly enough in their church on Sundays and at their prayer meetings,

I'll be safe, if you get my meaning. Most of them squeak like mice when they sing."

He, too, had real courage, Richard thought.

Mimi raised her glass and savored the brandy's bouquet. She was reminded of the brandy-flavored plum pudding that was a staple feature at all family meals at her father's estate in the winter. No dinner would have been complete without it, and she almost succumbed to a nostalgia for a past that could never be retrieved. "What a lovely, familiar aroma," she said, and for a moment threatened to become tearful. But she recovered quickly and went through the ritual of toasting the young king-across-the-water. "To Charles the Second," she said softly. "To you, Master Lucey, and to our success in reaching our destination."

They drank in solemn silence. The brandy, richer and more mellow than any Richard had ever tasted, warmed his throat as it slid down. "We'll be on our way," he said, glancing out of the nearest window at the gathering dusk. After shaking Lucey's hand, he threw his cloak over his shoulders, clapped the detested Puritan hat onto his head, and picked up his rifle. "Boy," he ordered, "carry this for me."

It took a moment for Mimi to realize he was speaking to her. "Is it loaded?" she asked in alarm.

He shook his head. "My other weapons will speak for us if they're needed. Walk a half-step behind me, no more and no less, and keep up the pace. We're not going for a stroll."

"Yes, master," she replied, her tone mocking. "Be good enough to remember that nature made your legs longer than mine, and these shoes are an abomination."

"Come along," he said, and stepped boldly onto the street. He saw the Puritan agent standing in a doorway and pretended to ignore him. The Puritan stared hard at the man and the boy, then lost interest in them.

"We've passed the first test," Richard said as they rounded the corner. "Am I walking too fast?"

"I'm doing my best," Mimi replied grimly. "So far, I'm keeping up with you."

They did not speak again until they drew close to the waterfront. "Steady now," Richard said. "The real test is directly ahead." His companion made no reply.

He emerged from the street closest to the *Anne* and, looking across the street, saw the two Puritan agents. Crew members were busy on the deck of the ship, their bustle indicating they were preparing to sail. The agents looked searchingly at Richard, whom they knew now by sight, and then they devoted their full attention to the boy who was struggling in an attempt not to fall behind.

The half-light of nightfall was deceptive, but an additional diversion was needed, and Richard felt inspired. Without warning he increased his pace. Then, as he approached the two Puritans, he halted abruptly.

"Boy," he roared, "I've warned you for the last time not to lag behind. You have feet and legs! Use them!"

Giving Mimi no chance to reply, he reached out and cuffed her hard with an open hand across the side of the head. She staggered but managed to regain her balance, then half-walked, half-ran as Richard headed for the plank that extended from the wharf to the deck. The agents lost all interest in the pair. They had been warned that Lady Dawn Shepherd might appear in disguise, but it was inconceivable to them that the most celebrated beauty at the court of the late Charles I would be subjected to a severe cuffing.

Ignoring the plank, Richard leaped across the open space onto the deck. Mimi hesitated, the sight of the black water far below making her apprehensive.

Richard had intended to let her fend for herself, but every moment's delay was dangerous. "Boy, for tuppence I'd leave you behind," he shouted as he reached for her arm, then hauled her onto the deck so savagely that he sent her sprawling. One of the Roundhead agents snickered.

Allowing Mimi to pull herself to her feet, Richard called, "Good evening, Captain. I trust I haven't kept you waiting."

"You're just in time," the master replied from his quarterdeck. "In another ten minutes you'd have found me gone."

"We'll go below now," Richard told Mimi, and preceding her to the open hatch, he quickly climbed down to the inner passageway.

She followed more slowly, her step tentative on the ladder. He waited, then silently led her to their tiny cubicle, walking ahead of her into the cabin. She closed the door behind her, then said in a cold rage, "You could have warned me that you intended to beat me and knock me down."

"My apologies, but I didn't think of that treatment until the time came. You must admit it was effective. I saw the agents' faces, and they knew you couldn't be the only surviving member of Sturbridge's immediate family."

"My ears are still ringing. Do you frequently beat women?" she demanded sarcastically.

"This was the first time—and, I hope, the last. Besides, I cuffed my stupid servant, not you. Let me make amends. The lower bunk is yours."

She sank onto one of her leather clothes boxes and looked around slowly. "You and I will share this—this wardrobe closet—for the next six to eight weeks?"

He shrugged. "I tried to tell you. Queen Henrietta Maria's accommodations when she sailed to France were little better than this."

55

"I was intending to avenge myself," she said with a faint smile, "but I'm afraid I'll have to give up my plans. When two people are crammed together like this, they are obliged to make concessions so they don't kill each other."

Richard grinned, then sobered as they heard shouts and pounding footsteps on the deck above. Drawing his double-barreled pistol, he moved quickly to the locked door.

"What's wrong?" Mimi asked, her voice lowered.

"It may be nothing, it may be significant. I'm ignorant of what is and isn't normal on board a ship. But we've come this far unscathed, and I'm taking no chances." He stood still, close to the door, his pistol cocked.

Mimi did not speak until they heard the ship's timbers creak faintly. Then she jumped to her feet and peered out of the square window. "We're moving! We're leaving the wharf!" She sounded ecstatic.

Richard left his post long enough to join her at the window and saw for himself that the brig was underway, moving at a snail's pace as she threaded a path through the crowded harbor. A feeling of great relief swept over him, but he remained cautious. "This is the start," he acknowledged, "but we're not out of trouble yet."

She looked at him with mischief in her green eyes. "I do declare, sir, you're as determined as Puritan clergymen to stifle joy!" Giving in to a sudden impulse, she threw her arms around his neck and kissed him soundly.

The startled Richard could not help responding, and for some moments he returned the kiss, holding the woman in a firm embrace. Then he disengaged himself and took a single backward step, which was as far as he could go without falling over one of her leather boxes. "Allow me to say something," he said, curbing his desire. "I do not address this remark to my companion, Mimi, or to Lady Dawn Shepherd. I speak as a man whose baronetcy places him at the bottom of the order of nobility and whose blood therefore is far more red than blue. I speak to a very attractive woman with whom circumstances—not of her making or my own—force me to share these cramped quarters. I am not a seducer. I do not engage in idle love-making. But my ability to control my natural urges is limited. If such a gesture should be repeated, I shall not be held responsible for the consequences."

"I'll remember your warning, sir," she said with mock gravity, but her ebullience was not to be denied. The danger of capture and imprisonment was fading, and her spirits continued to soar, so she laughed quietly and at length. "Do I have your permission to change into my own clothes and resume my true identity?"

"You may not!" he replied emphatically. "Until we're clear of British territorial waters we could be halted and searched at any time by a New Model Navy warship. You can be sure that detailed descriptions of you—and possibly of me—have been distributed to the captains of the navy. So far we've managed to elude our pursuers, but it would be unfortunate if you were hauled back to England in chains."

"I'd regard it as somewhat worse than misfortune," she murmured, his cold logic quickly restoring her sense of balance. "As much as I hate this uncomfortable disguise, I'll continue to follow your directions."

Her penitence softened him. "It will do no harm," he said, "if we go up to the deck to watch our departure. Just remember, speak to no one, because your voice will give you away."

They went down the companionway to the ladder, which Mimi climbed with some difficulty, and then she meekly followed him to the starboard rail. The *Anne* was still crawling, with only her jib raised, but soon she left the harbor behind, and Captain Brennan called a series of commands, relayed by a mate to the crew. The large sails overhead were unfurled, opening with a cracking sound and filling rapidly in the chilly breeze, and the brig seemed to leap forward through the choppy waters of the Severn estuary.

For some moments the couple looked back at the lights of Bristol, which gradually grew smaller in the distance. A sense of sadness, so deep that it caused him physical distress, crept over Richard. He was leaving the native land he loved, going into exile in a distant country, having committed no crime other than that of being totally loyal to a king whose ancestors had been well served by many generations of Dunstables. The House of Commons supposedly represented the people of the realm, but the present members were bigoted zealots who had killed the monarch, caused thousands to shed blood, and divided the nation.

Richard would do what was required of him in the colonies to rid Britain of the Puritan scourge, but a lump formed in his throat when he realized he might be forced to wait many years before he would be welcome here. Depending on the strength of the Puritan conquest, he might die on alien soil.

Mimi grieved for her England, too. She stood rigidly still, her fists tightly clenched at her sides, and silent tears rolled slowly down her cheeks. Richard could say nothing to comfort her, but he placed a hand on her shoulder for a moment, and he could feel her relax slightly. Neither realized it, but their mutual grief brought them closer together.

Others obviously felt as they did. Some distance down the deck, a short, squat woman in her forties, poorly dressed, was weeping copiously. A youth in his late teens, dark and also short, made clumsy, ineffectual attempts to comfort her.

Then a couple who had been standing at the port rail hastily crossed the deck, and a beaming Dempster Chaney extended his hand. "I didn't know you'd be making this voyage, too, Sir Rich—"

"No titles, if you please, Master Chaney," Richard said, interrupting him. The young man understood and presented a beaming Robbin to his benefactor.

Richard, who made no attempt to introduce the boy at his side, was pleased that he had helped the pair. Robbin was very pretty and young, reminding him of Dorothea, and he felt a fresh stab at what his fealty to the Crown had cost him.

Dempster and the girl related their story briefly, saying they had come on board the previous day and had not gone ashore again. Obviously, their efforts had succeeded, for they had not been found by her father.

"We have only one problem now," Robbin said, "and I'm afraid it can't be solved until we reach the colonies. We had no opportunity to be married before we sailed."

Mimi tugged at Richard's sleeve and whispered to him, "That's no problem. The captain can marry them."

Richard repeated her statement. The young couple, knowing nothing of the customs of the sea, were both astonished and overjoyed. "We'll go to him at once!" Robbin cried.

"He's busy, and he needs to keep watch for warships that could halt us and return all of us to Bristol," Richard said. "I urge you to wait until we put the British Isles behind us."

Further conversation on the subject was delayed by the approach of the short woman, who was still red-eyed. The youth who had stood beside her trailed

59

her. "Mollie Williams is me name, and this here is me son, Bart," she announced. "I've been quiet long enough, and now I'll speak out as loud as I please. God preserve the soul of King Charlie, and may He soon put young Charlie on the throne!"

"Amen," Mimi muttered inaudibly. The others nodded in solemn agreement. All, it was plain, were Cavalier sympathizers.

Mollie Williams lost no time in telling her story to the sympathetic audience. She had served for many years on the staff of Whitehall Palace as a cook, she declared, adding proudly, "Many's the roast I grilled for King Charlie, and many's the sole I poached and boned for him."

"You were discharged?" Richard asked.

She shook her head. "I walked out afore I had trouble. The poor need to be meek, like the Lord said, so I kept me mouth closed tight and stayed at me stove all the while that Charlie was off fighting the Roundheads. But Bart here, he thinks he's as good as a duke or a marquess. He lost his twin brother, me dear son, John, in the fighting. Since that day, he's shot off his fat mouth, telling all who'd listen to him that the Roundheads are scum!"

"So they are," her son pronounced defiantly.

"There's none will deny it, lad," Mollie told him as she shook her head sadly. "But the likes of us can't afford to speak free. When a Puritan investigator came to the Whitehall kitchen and asked me so many questions I scarce knew me own name, it was time for us to be on our way. Every last farthing I'd saved took us to Bristol and bought passage."

"It was worth it, Ma," Bart said, reviving an old quarrel. "Now we're free!"

"The likes of us will never be free," she declared. "But here we be, in this tub that tips and swoops and

60

bounces, so there's naught we can do to turn back the clock."

A gong sounded below.

"I think the passengers are being called to supper," Mimi whispered to Richard.

He repeated her observation, and they obediently trooped down the hatch and made their way forward to the small wardroom, barely large enough for a round table and straight-backed chairs, where the *Anne*'s two mates had already seated themselves. Again, when names were exchanged, Richard carefully refrained from introducing the boy who moved to the place beside him.

The cook appeared with a pot of a steaming thick soup, which he placed without ceremony in front of the first mate. Then the officer began to ladle the soup into bowls. "Ladies and gentlemen," he said, "enjoy the fresh foods while you're able. Soon enough we'll live on beans, bacon, hardtack, salt fish, and bully beef. You'll lose weight before the voyage ends."

"Those of us who like sea fare may gain weight." The speaker was a late arrival who came into the wardroom, bending so he wouldn't hit his head on the bulkhead above the entrance. He was tall and thin, with a balding head and small, piercing eyes; his deep blue velvet coat, cream-colored waistcoat, satin breeches, and ruffled shirt instantly marked him as a Cavalier. His smile, as he took the one vacant chair without apology, resembled a grimace, and looking slowly around the table, he introduced himself only as Robertson.

Richard wondered if the man had dared to walk past the Roundhead agents on the wharf in attire that clearly identified him as a Royalist. If he had, either he was very bold or he lacked common sense.

Mollie Williams chatted at length, Richard made an occasional comment, and Robbin and Dempster joined in the talk, too. But Robertson made it impossible for others to know him. He lapsed into complete silence, saying nothing about himself and making no comment on any other subject. But he was not indifferent to the fellow passengers with whom he would live in close quarters for the next month and a half. On the contrary, he stared intently at each of them in turn.

The man's steady gaze irritated Richard, and he felt uneasy when Robertson concentrated at length on the boy who sat obediently, saying nothing. Mimi seemed to fascinate him, and he scrutinized her repeatedly. She handled the situation with aplomb, eating steadily, never glancing in the man's direction, and pretending to be unaware of his interest.

The main dish was mutton, served with boiled potatoes and greens, and all of the passengers except Robertson took the advice of the first mate and left the hardtack untouched. "You'll have your fill of it soon enough," he told them.

The dessert was pudding so sweet that Richard took only one taste, as did Mimi.

"If you ain't eating your pudding I'll relieve you of it," Bart said. "I were taught never to waste food, weren't I, Ma?" He half-stood and reached for the two plates.

"You was taught manners, too," Mollie said. Her son ignored the remark and quickly gulped the puddings.

After the meal ended, Dempster and Robbin went out to the open deck again, for a time preferring the cold to sharing their cabin with Mollie, her son, and the dour Robertson. Richard and the boy went directly to their own cabin.

Mimi removed her cap and shook out her hair as she sat on a leather box. "If that man had stared at me for one moment longer," she said, "I think I would have screamed. Do you suppose he was trying to memorize my features and every angle in my face?"

"I have no idea," Richard replied. "But I don't like him. Say nothing of any significance in front of him, and we'll keep him under observation, at least until we learn more about him."

"What harm can he do?" She peeled off her smock and began to unbutton her coarse shirt.

Richard turned away from her, deliberately averting his gaze, but he couldn't avoid seeing the frilly silk nightgown she took from a clothing box. Keeping his hands off her when she was easily within reach was going to be an even more difficult problem than he had anticipated.

"What a blessed relief to be rid of that breastband," Mimi said behind his back with a sigh. "You were very clever to think of it, but I can't help wishing you were less ingenious."

He fled to the companionway, waiting there until he felt reasonably certain she had changed into her nightclothes and completed her ablutions. Then, when he returned to the cabin, he deliberately extinguished the oil lamp before undressing and climbing into the upper bunk, which was barely long enough for him. "Good night," he called.

There was silence for a moment, and then Mimi said, "I'd like to ask you something, but you needn't answer my question if it makes you uncomfortable. Are you afraid of me?"

Richard chuckled. "Not of you, but of myself. Only a few days ago I was engaged to marry the prettiest girl in Lincolnshire. Now, through a turn of events, I'm sharing these close quarters with the loveliest woman in all of England. I find the situation disconcerting."

"You think I'd give in to you if you tried to make love to me?"

As always, Mimi knew what she was doing in the realm of sex. She had not been the mistress of the late King Charles, nor had she engaged in any other affairs that had been attributed to her, but that didn't mean she was sexually inexperienced; quite the contrary. Like so many members of her class, she had taken lovers as she chose them, and she had made her selections with great care, enjoying the favors of perhaps a half-dozen distinguished men over the years. Considering the fact that she was in her mid-twenties and that her being of one of Britain's first families offered unlimited opportunities, she could not be considered sexually promiscuous by the standards of the time.

"I hadn't thought of how you'd respond." He was being honest with himself as well as with her.

"Take my word for it, Richard, I'd allow you no liberties, even though the strains in the cabin might become intolerable."

"I'm glad to hear it."

"I'm no angel," Mimi said, "but I'm not promiscuous, either, at least according to my standards. I won't pretend I must be romantically committed before I'll make love to a man. I'm not all that certain I've even been in love. But I must know him well, have confidence in him, and feel close to him."

Richard's relief was mingled with a sense of regret. "You'll be safe with me because we're strangers."

She chuckled. "Do you think Newcastle would believe that?"

"No," he replied slowly, "but Uncle William is a worldly man."

"Poor Charlie would have taken my word. He accepted anything I told him."

Richard did not know what to reply. For a moment Mimi was silent, and then she said, "You think I was Charlie's mistress." She was stating a fact, not asking

64

a question. "I could read it in your face the first time I mentioned him."

"Your relationship with King Charles is none of my business."

"Nor anyone else's, although half the court was convinced I slept with him." There was a curious, melancholy note in her voice. "Well, I didn't. My father's summer estate was just down the road from Charlie's hunting lodge in Scotland, and I knew him almost as well as I knew my own parents. When I was a little girl, I discovered he had been attentive to my mother before he married that horrid Henrietta Maria. When I was six or seven, I think it was, I had a romantic daydream—a fantasy—that Charlie was actually my father. Poor Mama never looked at any man except my father. Then, when Papa died, Charlie took me under his protection. I was just growing up, men were paying attention to me for the first time, and it was a great help to pretend that Charlie was my lover. I was spared the persistent attention of rakes and fortune hunters. Charlie played the game so enthusiastically, as he did everything, that even the foolish Henrietta Marie snubbed me."

"You needn't have told me any of this," he said, "but thank you."

Her sigh floated up to him. "Ah, well, none of it matters anymore. The Sturbridge estates have been confiscated, and no doubt our possessions will be given to some of Cromwell's cronies. The only funds left to me are in my purse, and when they're gone, I'll be forced to depend on the charity of old family friends. So I needn't worry about fortune hunters. The others I can handle."

"You sound quite sure of yourself."

"You must have seen the dagger I keep strapped to my leg. It has a sobering influence on unwanted advances." She laughed, then said, "Sleep well, Richie."

He was startled by her use of the diminutive version of his name, which was what his parents had called him and was known only by a handful of close family friends. Apparently Uncle William had told Mimi more about him than he had realized.

The cabin was chilly, but it was warm beneath the blankets, and, ordinarily, Richard would have dropped off to sleep almost at once. Instead, he remained wide awake. He could not rid himself of the tensions he had endured since he had been forced to leave Lincolnshire so hastily, and the proximity of the ravishing beauty in the bunk below his further disturbed him. As the brig plowed through the rough waters of the Bristol Channel, rolling and pitching endlessly, she was carrying him farther from Dorothea.

The time had come, he reflected, to try to put dear Dorothea out of his mind for all time. Soon she would be wed to some Puritan functionary whom her father regarded as a suitable mate for her, but even that was irrelevant. She had been forcibly removed from his orbit, and never would she be his. All the same, he told himself, he would continue to love her in spite of his efforts to the contrary.

When he awakened at dawn, Richard felt confused. He realized he had been dreaming, but he couldn't quite decipher whether Dorothea or Mimi had been present in the dream. When he climbed down from his bunk, he saw that Mimi was huddled beneath her blankets, and he could make out only the crown of her red hair. He washed and shaved in very cold water, not learning until later that reasonable quantities of hot water could be obtained from the galley.

Then, he went up to the aft deck to attend to his horse's needs. Prince Henry was frisky, ready for a gallop across rolling fields, and Richard stroked his muzzle softly. "You'll have to be patient, my friend," he said. "I'm allowed to walk you when no one else is

66

on deck, but we won't be able to romp until we reach Boston."

The expression in the mount's alert brown eyes seemed to indicate that he understood what his master was saying to him. In any event, he seemed comforted.

The *Anne* was moving slowly now under reduced sail, and a thick gray-white fog that hid her upper sails from view enveloped the entire ship. It was impossible to see more than a few yards in any direction. Richard walked his stallion for the better part of an hour, pacing up and down the deck. Except for the mate who had the watch and the quartermaster at the wheel, the vessel seemed deserted.

The sounding of the breakfast gong brought the passengers to life. Captain Brennan elected to join them at the table, and Mollie Williams endeared herself to the entire company by offering to help in the galley whenever she might be wanted there. The master promptly accepted, and after she had gone off to consult with the cook, she announced that she would prepare one of her special stews for noon dinner.

The last to appear was Mimi, wearing her boy's attire, and there were no signs of the strain in her face; her eyes were so clear that she could have been a lad in his early teens. The dour Robertson, who answered in monosyllables when remarks were addressed to him, again studied her.

"We're moving through the Bristol Channel," Captain Brennan told the passengers. "A little later this morning, when the fog clears—as it will—you'll see Wales on the horizon to starboard if you look sharp. We're sailing close to Devon and Cornwall on the port side, so land will be much easier to see there."

The entire group laughed when Robbin asked, "If ye please, Captain, which side be port and which be starboard? I'm terribly confused."

Even Robertson smiled.

"Nothing to be ashamed of, missus. Port is left, and starboard is right. You may wish to remember it easily by recalling that port and left have four letters each," answered the ship's master.

At the end of the meal, as the others began to file out, Dempster said, "Captain Brennan, can you spare my wife and me a minute of your time?"

"Several minutes, if you wish," he replied genially, and looked at his fat pocket watch. "I'm not due to relieve the mate on duty for another half-hour."

Suddenly, the scarlet-faced Dempster became tongue-tied. Robbin had to speak for them. "It's this way, Captain," she said, deciding to terminate her north country accent along with their ruse. "Master Chaney—well, he isn't actually my husband yet. We were eloping when we came to the *Anne*—"

"—and because we stayed on board," Dempster cut in, finding his voice, "we had no opportunity to go before a minister. We're told you have the authority to marry us. Will you?"

Brennan looked at the earnest young couple who were holding their collective breath as they awaited his reply. "Why were you eloping?" As a father with a daughter of his own, for whom he had named his brig, he believed he had the right to inquire.

"Robbin's father forbade us to see each other again," Dempster said, "because I made no secret of my Cavalier sentiments. He became a turncoat, and for his own protection he would have given her to some filthy Roundhead."

"I'd have preferred to die," Robbin said fiercely.

The ship's master made up his mind quickly. "Very well, as a devoted subject of Charles the First, I know your feelings. Come to my cabin, where I keep my *Book of Common Prayer*—well hidden, of course, so the Puritan customs inspectors won't find it and de-

stroy it. I'll have you wed in no time, and this afternoon I'll write out a certificate for you to prove you've
legally become man and wife."

When they reached his cabin he raced through the
ceremony, halting abruptly only when they discovered
that Dempster had no ring to put on his wife's left
hand. Robbin solved the problem by taking a plain
ring from her right hand.

After they had been pronounced man and wife, the
captain said it was time for him to go to the quarterdeck.

"Just one more favor," Robbin said. "Everyone
thinks we've been married earlier, and it would be
embarrassing if they learned the truth about us."

"Only Sir Rich—ah, Master Dunstable knows our
real situation, and I'll explain to him in private,"
Dempster added.

"I don't talk out of turn," the captain said, and left
them.

They wandered hand in hand to the prow, where
they found Richard standing with his young servant,
both of them straining for a glimpse of land as the fog
began to lift.

"We're married now," a happy Dempster said.

"The captain just this minute performed the ceremony in his cabin," Robbin added.

Mimi could keep silent no longer. "How wonderful!" she exclaimed, and impulsively kissed the bride,
then the groom.

Her clear soprano could have been that of no one
but a young woman, and the honeymoon couple stared
at the boy incredulously.

Richard tried to repair the damage as best he could.
"There may be more than one secret on this ship that
needs keeping," he warned somberly. "Off yonder you
see the coast of Devon, crawling with Puritans. Off to

the right that smudge is Wales, where there are still more Puritans. We'll be obliged if you'll keep your discovery to yourselves until we're certain that all danger is ended."

III

THE *Anne* sailed out of the Bristol Channel, leaving Land's End behind and moving into the open Atlantic Ocean beyond the Isles of Scilly. The passengers rejoiced, believing it now unlikely that the brig would be intercepted by a New Model Navy warship. But Richard questioned the master closely on the matter.

"It all depends," Captain Brennan said. "If I happened to be carrying someone the Roundheads really wanted—which I hope I'm not—and they knew he was on board, we wouldn't be safe until we sailed at least another hundred miles from Britain. Then our chances would improve because no ship is easy to find in a sea as vast as the Atlantic."

Richard immediately urged Mimi not to abandon her disguise as yet, and she agreed cheerfully, in spite of the acute discomfort caused by the tightly fitting breastband and her need to keep silent in the presence of others. "I trust your judgment," she said. "If I didn't, I wouldn't have come this far."

Gradually they were getting to know each other better, and in the cramped cabin they established routines that permitted each of them some privacy. To

Richard's surprise, Mimi insisted on making up the sheets and blankets on both of their bunks every morning.

"There's no need for you to do a servant's work for me," he told her. "I'm capable of making my own bed."

"You don't understand," she replied proudly. "Never in all my life have I done anything practical like making a bed. I'm hoping that before this voyage ends, I can persuade Mollie to teach me to cook."

He grinned broadly. "Forgive me for smiling," he said, "but I can't picture you settling down into domestic life as a housewife in a colonial town like Boston."

"I have no intention of going to Boston," Mimi replied.

He was surprised. "Oh?"

"You know so much about me already that you may as well hear the rest," she said. "Newcastle and several others told me to go to a town in the Virginia colony called Middle Plantation. Near it is a large plantation owned by a wealthy, devoted Cavalier whose name is Horace Laing."

"I've never heard of Master Laing, but there's no reason he should have been mentioned to me."

"All I know is that he has helped any number of the king's party begin new lives. I can't possibly go back to England until young Charlie gains the throne —if he ever does—so it may be a long while before I go home. Years ago, Captain John Smith, one of the first New World settlers of Virginia, was my parents' guest. They repeated his tales of Virginia to me since I was a child, so perhaps I'll settle there."

"But what will you do?" Richard wanted to know.

"If land is still cheap, I hope my funds will be sufficient to buy a small plantation that Master Laing will help me find. Then I'll hire a staff to operate it for me."

"That makes sense," he said. "Certainly help won't be expensive. Why, on this ship alone, Dempster and Robbin don't have a penny, and Millie Williams admits that she and her son are paupers."

Their talk was interrupted by the shout of the lookout. "Sail ho!"

Richard always carried his knife-belt, but now he also strapped on his sword before they hurried to the open deck.

The other passengers were clustering there, too. "There she is, off the port bow," Dempster Chaney said, and pointed.

Mimi instinctively moved closer to Richard. A thorough New Model Navy search was certain to reveal her identity.

The ship was still little bigger than a white dot on the horizon, but she grew larger moment by moment. Captain Brennan, standing on his quarterdeck, caught Richard's eye and shrugged. He could not outrun a warship, and a battle would be suicidal, so he would be compelled to submit to any indignity imposed on him. As a seasoned commercial mariner, he expected the worst while hoping for the best.

The intruder drew still closer, and it became evident that she was a warship, a frigate of twenty-four guns.

"Sir," one of the mates said, "shall I direct the men to assume their posts?"

"It's not necessary just yet," Captain Brennan replied, and raised his voice. "Bos'n, you may raise our ensign."

"Raise the ensign," the boatswain called.

Within moments, the Union Jack was fluttering at the brig's masthead. The frigate hoisted her colors too, and the passengers were relieved when they saw the gold-and-white lilies of France. Robbin was the first to identify it. "The *fleur-de-lis!*"

Richard smiled at Mimi. "We have nothing to fear now."

She was wildly excited and drew him apart from the others. "You're quite certain she's French? That this isn't a New Model Navy trick of some sort?"

"We can only hope it's not. If it's French, we have nothing to fear."

She nodded, then turned and went below.

Somewhat mystified by her unexplained leave-taking, Richard returned to the deck rail and watched the warship as she bore down on the little brig. He knew that the First Minister of France, Cardinal Mazarin, the guardian of the Boy-King Louis XIV, was a staunch supporter of the House of Stuart. Queen Henrietta Maria was the sister of the late Louis XIII, and Mazarin had given refuge not only to her and her children, but to many nobles who had followed the British royal family into exile. There was no possibility that any of the passengers would be taken prisoner and turned over to the Puritans. Even Mimi, should her identity become known, would be safe; French officers, always aware of the latest gossip, would be delighted to tell Queen Henrietta Maria that the young woman she disliked was en route to the New World.

Ultimately, the frigate sent up a signal that read: *Heave to.* Captain Brennan had no choice and complied with the order. A longboat, manned by eight oarsmen, was lowered from the upper deck of the warship into the water, and a junior officer in a blue-and-white uniform climbed down a ladder to it, followed by a dozen soldiers armed with muskets and bayonets.

"Why in the devil should the French send a party to board me?" Captain Brennan demanded, thinking aloud.

No one could answer his question.

As the longboat started across the open water, Mimi emerged from the hatch. The boy had been transformed into the dazzling Lady Dawn Shepherd, daughter and heiress of the Earl of Sturbridge. Her low-cut gown of pale green velvet hugged her incomparable figure, sandals with towering heels added to her height, and on her head was perched a feathered Cavalier hat, jauntily cocked to one side. Diamonds glittered at her throat, ears, fingers, and wrists. She wore cosmetics suitable for an appearance at a Stuart court.

The brig's officers, crew, and passengers gaped, and Captain Brennan broke the silence. "I'll be damned," he said.

Mollie Williams dropped to the deck in a deep curtsy. "I was sure I knowed you," she cried. "Lady Dawn Shepherd it is, God save us all."

Only the man known as Robertson seemed not particularly surprised, and a tight smile compressed his lips as he stared.

Richard grinned broadly as he bowed and offered Mimi his arm. "You do know how to put on a first-rate show," he said in a low tone.

"I decided to greet our visitors as myself. This dress is rather fetching, don't you think? It's one of my favorites." Seeming impervious to the cold, she was enjoying herself, relishing the sensation she was creating.

The French officer came on deck, his men close behind him, and stopped short when he caught sight of the radiant beauty. Then he remembered his duty and marched stiff-legged to the quarterdeck. His troops, obviously accustomed to such maneuvers, promptly formed a half-circle around the raised quarterdeck platform.

The officer saluted smartly. "Enseigne Le Brun of His Christian Majesty's Navy," he said. "I regret the inconvenience I caused by halting you on the high seas, Captain, but this cannot be helped."

"Why can't it?" Captain Brennan was not intimidated.

"Our countries are close to war, Captain, because your usurper government chose to remove the head of the unfortunate King Charles. Cardinal Mazarin himself has issued a directive to all ships of His Christian Majesty's fleet, ordering them to halt all British merchant ships and to remove any Puritans of consequence. If you understand French, I shall gladly read the order to you."

"I don't know a word of your language, and I assure you there are no Puritans in this company. On the contrary, I'm carrying some Cavalier refugees to the New World."

"I do not doubt your word, sir," the Frenchman replied in his strongly accented English. "But you will not object if I interrogate them myself. Your cabin will be fine for the purpose."

"I prefer you use the saloon." Brennan was retaining what he could of his dignity. "The bos'n will show you the way."

The officer returned to the main deck and doffed his helmet to the little group of passengers. "I offer you my apologies in advance," he said politely, "but together we will make our little chats as brief and as painless as possible. I shall interview you one at a time. Is it possible that any of you speak French?"

Mimi took a single step forward, her manner beguiling. *"Mais oui, Monsieur l'Enseigne."*

The officer's eyes widened. *"Après vous, mademoiselle,"* he replied. She nodded, then preceded him to the hatch, quickly disappearing.

Mimi was unique, Richard thought, grinning and shaking his head. Within moments, the officer would forget his reason for questioning her.

The others quickly surrounded him. "We knew your boy-servant was a woman," Robbin said excitedly. "But is she really Lady Dawn Shepherd?"

"Indeed."

"Is it true that she and King Charles—"

"Mistress Chaney," Richard said, "there are matters I shall not discuss with anyone."

Dempster scowled at his wife. "You knew there was and still is a price on her head? The Roundheads are anxious to capture her."

"So I gleaned," Richard replied dryly.

Captain Brennan beckoned him. "I regret, Sir Richard, that you didn't take me into your confidence. As captain of this ship, I have a right to know the true identities of my passengers. I further regret that it's too late to change the cabin arrangements."

Richard had to bite back a smile.

There was nothing more the ship's master could say, but at least he had the satisfaction of knowing that the most prominent Cavalier he had ever carried on the *Anne* was being safely transported through England's waters.

Mimi remained in the saloon for more than a quarter of an hour, and when she returned to the deck, her smile indicated that all was well.

Richard was summoned by the French officer and had no difficulty in establishing his credentials. The post he had been forced to abandon as the King's Forester clearly defined his loyalties, and his examination was cursory. He carefully made no mention of the assignment that awaited him in the New World, and after a brief conversation, he was excused.

Dempster and Robbin were of little interest to Enseigne Le Brun, and soon were dismissed, as were Mollie Williams and her belligerent son. Somewhat to Richard's surprise, however, Robertson spent an inordinately long time below with the French officer.

"I wonder what they're talking about," he said to Mimi.

"I can't imagine," she replied. "Did you notice that Robertson didn't seem in the least surprised when I appeared as myself? He acted as if he had known or guessed my real identity from the onset."

When the enigmatic Robertson finally returned to the deck, his face was expressionless. He was accompanied by Enseigne Le Brun, who made it his business to question the ship's officers briefly. These interviews took place on the quarterdeck because it would have been an unpardonable insult to ask Captain Brennan and his mates to go below for the purpose. Even though the search was illegal, the French officer was observing the proprieties.

At last, Le Brun and his troops departed, the officer bowing low over Mimi's hand and flirting gallantly with her before he climbed down the waiting ladder. But the *Anne* was not yet free to resume her voyage and had to wait until Le Brun gave his report to the *capitaine* of the frigate. Then signal flags were raised on the warship: *You may proceed.*

"The French may be the allies and supporters of the Cavaliers in our time of need," the fuming Captain Brennan said after giving the order to weigh the anchor and hoist the sails, "but I can't abide their arrogance. I'd be tempted to make common cause with the Roundheads if we go to war with them."

Bart Williams felt the same way. "When that fop was a-talking to me," he said, a knife sliding down into his hand from beneath his sleeve, "it was all I could do to keep from carving him."

Mollie shook her head. "The sailors would have hanged you from their warship's yardarm. Will you never learn to curb your bad temper?"

"I didn't do it, Ma," he said, then added under his breath, "more's the pity."

77

The passengers dispersed, and Mimi asked Richard to wait for her on deck. Going below, she made a bundle of the boys' clothes she had worn. Then, returning to the deck, she ceremoniously threw them overboard. "May I never be forced to disguise myself again."

Richard was about to reply when he saw Robertson watching them from the opposite side of the deck. Mimi saw him, too. "He makes my flesh crawl," she said. The angry Richard started to cross the deck, intent on forcing a confrontation, but Robertson bolted, hurrying to the hatch, and disappearing from sight.

"He can't go very far," Richard said, returning to Mimi's side. "Sooner or later we're going to find out why he's so interested in every move you make."

When the *enseigne* returned to the French frigate, he moved directly to the *capitaine*'s quarters, as he had been instructed. From a pocket inside his uniform, he removed a parchment envelope and placed it on the desk before his superior officer. Then he stepped back and stood silently at attention.

"Thank you. You are excused. Please inform the crew to prepare to sail for France. I assume this communiqué is from Monsieur Colbert?"

"Oui, Monsieur le Capitaine."

"You have done well." The *capitaine* waved away his junior officer, then opened the envelope from Colbert. Mazarin's agent's message was brief:

Dawn Shepherd is on board, without incident. She is sharing a cabin with Sir Richard Dunstable, who is acting as her watchful escort. It will be necessary for me to eliminate him at my earliest convenience. I will keep you informed of our progress upon reaching Boston, then will follow the lady to Virginia.

C.

The *capitaine* smiled as he leaned back in his chair. The cardinal would be pleased with the message, and having been the catalyst, perhaps there would be a reward in it for him. He refolded the report and locked it in a small chest, still reflecting on fantasies of himself wearing, perhaps, the rank of *amiral*.

A new atmosphere prevailed that evening at the supper table in the saloon. Mollie was obsequious, Dempster and Robbin were deferential, young Bart seemed awed, and even Captain Brennan treated Mimi with great respect. Only the enigmatic Robertson remained silent, as always.

Mimi, who was in high spirits, knew she could not tolerate their formality for the duration of the long voyage. "I'm the same person I've always been," she said, "and the only difference is that now I can speak without fear of giving myself away. This adventure wasn't of our making, but we're comrades, and we're going to a land where, I'm told, the highborn enjoy no special privileges. So, for all our sakes, let's try to remember this is a ship, not the audience chamber at Whitehall!"

The ice was broken, but the others still found it difficult to relax. Mimi realized she had to go still further. "Robbin," she said, "I envy your long hair. It will take years for mine to grow that long again. Since I miss having my own to arrange, perhaps we could spend some time tomorrow fashioning yours in a new style." The younger girl was delighted and flattered.

"Mollie," Mimi continued, "the next time you make your wonderful stew, please take me into the galley and show me how you do it. I've never boiled a kettle of water, but there's no telling how much I'll be forced to fend for myself in America, and it's time I learned how to be more self-sufficient."

Richard nodded in silent approval. Even Mimi herself failed to realize how profoundly her tribulations were changing her nature. She always would be an aristocrat, as would he, but her escape and life on board the cramped ship were making her far less arrogant and selfish. Her friends in London, whoever they might be, would be surprised to see her chatting amiably with a middle-class girl and a cook, smiling genially at a sea captain who in status was far beneath her, and making small talk with Dempster, who only months earlier would have been overwhelmed to have been given a post on her household staff.

Richard knew that he himself had changed. It was impossible to maintain the barriers demanded by protocol and custom when he and Mimi lived in such confined quarters. Worst of all, she was so lovely, so naturally seductive that he knew he wanted her, but was troubled because he realized at the same time that by no stretch of the imagination was he in love with her. Dorothea remained his ideal, and although she was unattainable, Mimi was too sure of herself for him to lose his heart to her. Something in his own nature demanded a soft, yielding woman. It did not occur to him that he was not the product of a typical Cavalier family. Indeed, he would have been stunned had he known that his moral standards were remarkably similar to those of the Puritans he despised.

After supper Mimi remained behind in the saloon to teach an eager Robbin and Dempster how to play cards. Richard stopped in the cabin for his cloak, then went up to the deck to walk Prince Henry, who had been more restless than usual that day. Thick clouds concealed the stars and moon, and the sea was rough, with water breaking over the bow as the brig dipped into a trough, then climbed to the crest of the next wave. The mate who had the watch and the sailor at the wheel on the quarterdeck were fully occupied with their duties. The *Anne* was tossing and pitching violently and erratically, which created problems with walking the horse. The steed was unsteady on his feet, which made it necessary for Richard to hold the reins taut and move slowly. The spray soaked the deck, making the task even more hazardous, so after a few minutes he returned Prince Henry to the stall, groomed and fed him, then covered him with blankets. The horse was withstanding the rigors of the voyage well.

Emerging from the stall, Richard stood for a time at the fantail. The night was so dark that he could see the ship's wake for no more than a few yards, and the waves that loomed above the brig were black and menacing. But the cold sea air was invigorating, so Richard lingered, unwilling to return to the stuffy wardroom. Only the instincts developed and sharpened during the years he had spent in the forest of the royal hunting preserve saved his life. He heard nothing, but sensed the presence of someone behind him, and turned just as Robertson, a sword in hand, lunged at him. Richard barely managed to sidestep in time, and the blade missed his body by inches. Robertson grimaced, poised for another thrust. The moonlight broke through a rift in the clouds, enabling Richard to distinguish his opponent's blazing eyes.

Richard's first thought was that it was almost impossible to defend himself. His own sword and pistol were stored below in the cabin because there had appeared to be no need to carry them to the deck. His only weapons were the throwing knives in the belt that he habitually wore.

The wind howled through the lines above from prow to stern, making it unlikely that the pair on the quarterdeck would hear him if he shouted, and the horse's stall blocked their view of what was happening. Robertson, whatever the reason for his seemingly

81

inexplicable attack, had chosen the right time and place for it.

"Have you lost your reason?" Richard demanded.

"You've been in the way long enough," the man said. "Now that Lady Dawn has come into the open, it's time to be permanently rid of you."

The statement made no sense to Richard, but there was no opportunity to analyze it. Robertson lunged again, balancing as best he could on the heaving deck. The erratic movement of the ship saved Richard this time. The sword aimed for his heart just missed him, and Robertson's momentum carried him to the rail beyond Richard, forcing him to grip it in his free hand so he wouldn't be thrown overboard. This momentary respite gave Richard the chance to collect himself. He drew one of his knives, aware that he could not afford to miss.

Robertson laughed harshly at the sight of the knife. "Would you duel with toys, Sir Richard?" Lifting his blade to the guard position, its tip at eye level, he advanced slowly, carefully, his elbow bent, making certain that his next thrust would be effective.

Richard did not move. Continued evasion would result in his death, and he realized he had to find his target with a single knife, throwing it before the man could strike for a third time.

Their eyes met, and each could read death in the other's grim gaze. This was a duel, however unfair, in which no quarter would be given. Robertson poised for his thrust. Exerting no visible effort, Richard utilized his many years of training as he released his knife. The blade flew through the air before Robertson could lunge, penetrating the man's left eye and embedding itself in his brain. He toppled backward onto the deck, dying without making a sound. At the same instant, his sword flew from his hand, clattered

82

onto the deck as the ship lurched, then vanished overboard.

Richard stood for a long moment, his entire body bathed in cold sweat. His skill had prevented his own murder, but the realization dawned on him that he was confronted by a grave problem: if he went to the officer of the watch and Captain Brennan came on deck, it would appear that he had cold-bloodedly killed Robertson. It would be difficult for anyone to believe he was telling the truth when his attacker's weapon had vanished into the sea.

Leaping forward, Richard dropped to one knee and with great effort managed to draw his knife from the dead man's head. Wiping the blade on Robertson's breeches, he saw that little blood had been shed, which was all to the good. The sea spray was becoming heavier, and the salt water was washing away the blood.

Desperately wanting to learn the reason for the attack, Richard made a swift, thorough search of the man's pockets. His fingers closed over a small, leather-bound notebook, but the night was too dark for him to read the contents here. Besides, he could not take the time now. The man's other pockets were empty.

It was necessary to dispose of Robertson's body. Still on one knee, Richard pushed it close to the edge of the deck, and the movement of the ship did the rest. A savage lurch sent the body overboard, and it slid into the black sea below, disappearing from sight.

Standing again, Richard made an effort to compose himself. Only a few minutes had passed since he had emerged from his horse's stall, and he knew of no reason to believe that the men on the quarterdeck would point a finger of suspicion at him when Robertson failed to appear. He started forward along the wet deck, walking slowly, and paused to call a greeting to the mate.

"You'd best go below, Master Dunstable," the officer called.

"I was attending to my horse."

"Fair enough, but don't tempt the sea. The deck isn't safe for an evening stroll."

Richard nodded in pleasant agreement and went below. Mimi hadn't yet returned to the cabin, so he sought her in the saloon.

She looked up from her card game, saw his troubled eyes and pale face, and immediately excused herself.

"We'll play again tomorrow," she told Robbin and Dempster, then silently went with Richard to the cabin. Something in his manner prompted her to ask no questions. He bolted the door behind them, then told her what had happened in the duel and its aftermath, omitting no detail. She, too, was puzzled by Robertson's single, enigmatic remark.

Color drained from her face, but she remained seemingly calm. "You were right to act as you did," she said. "Captain Brennan may be a loyal Cavalier, but he would have been obliged to place you under arrest and hand you over to the authorities in Boston for a trial that would have been very difficult to win. Are you sure the sea washed away the blood?"

"It was gone by the time I left the deck. Now, let's see what this notebook tells us."

They sat side by side on the lower bunk and opened the little leather-bound volume.

"It's written in French," Richard said in surprise.

"So it is. And it seems to be a dated diary, started a year ago in London."

"I'm afraid my French isn't very good, and Robertson's handwriting is only partially legible to me."

"I'll translate—" Mimi broke off and gasped. "It's all about me! He kept a journal, and I am the subject." She was silent for a time as she scanned the pages. "Robertson had me under observation for a full year.

84

Charlie was off fighting the Roundheads, and, as you know, he surrendered to the Scots, who handed him over to Cromwell. There was almost no activity at Whitehall. I was living quietly in my family's town house, and he has recorded every move I made: the names of my guests, the people at whose homes I dined, my companions on horseback rides and at the theater. This is incredible."

Not wanting to interrupt her reading, Richard remained silent.

Mimi was flushed now. "His facts are remarkably accurate, but he also speculates outrageously. He suspects that Newcastle, the Lord Chamberlain, and the Earl of Lindsey were my lovers! Really! All of them friends of my father who were keeping watch over me!"

He smiled quietly.

Again she gasped. "Robertson followed me to Bristol and knew I was at the White Hart. He records your arrival, and he realized what was afoot when you went down to the docks to see Captain Brennan. He admired my disguise, but it didn't fool him for a minute. By that time he had already arranged his own passage on the *Anne*."

Robertson had been no fool, Richard thought.

"You seem to have infuriated him. Listen to this: 'Dunstable has become her protector and must be removed. His presence can prove very harmful.' What do you suppose that means?"

He thought hard, then shrugged. "I'm afraid we'll never know. Was he vindictive toward any other man?"

"Only the Earl of Lindsey, whom he seems to have forgotten after his first visit to my house."

"How odd. Perhaps Robertson was in love with you and resented the proximity of anyone who appeared to be close to you."

"That's possible," Mimi said, "but his tone doesn't indicate it. The flavor of these notes is—strictly objective. Only the comment about you is in the least emotional, and even then his dislike seems more professional than personal. How I wish I'd known that every move I made was being watched for months and months!" She shuddered, then instinctively rested against his shoulder. Richard put an arm around her for comfort.

"I've had no private life for a full year. How awful!"

"Well, no harm has been done."

"You could have been killed tonight!"

"I must admit I find it odd that Robertson would go to extremes to get rid of me. I can only think he wanted no one nearby who would be able to help you."

"But why, Richie?"

"I'm not sure. I find many entries in this journal strange," he said. "Robertson knew we met and saw through your disguise, but he made no attempt to prevent us from boarding the *Anne*. A single, quiet word to the Roundhead agents at the pier would have resulted in our immediate arrest."

"The worst part is remembering that his eyes seemed to cut through me." Mimi was working herself into a highly emotional state.

Richard continued to deal with realities. "What I find even more puzzling is that he elected to write this diary in French, since I assumed he was an Englishman. I can't imagine the Puritans hiring a French agent to keep watch on any Cavalier's movements."

"Nor can I. I like to think of myself as resourceful, but this is too much." Again she shivered.

His grasp tightened. "Robertson, whoever he may have been, never will be able to harm you in any way."

Mimi looked up at him, her green eyes troubled.

"I'm still frightened. I suppose it's knowing that everything I did, every move I made for a whole year was being recorded, and presumably reported to someone who was Robertson's superior."

"You're safe now," he said, "especially with Robertson himself gone."

"But why did the Roundheads choose me as the subject for such a careful watch? Why me?"

"How actively were you involved in Cavalier politics, Mimi?"

"I wasn't. In this past year when the Royalist cause was declining so severely and London became a dangerous place for Cavaliers to gather, many meetings took place at my town house. I believed, as did Charlie's principal supporters, that it was a safe place. I didn't dream the Puritans knew when people like the Earl of Lindsey sneaked into London for a day or two."

"If they had known, they could have arrested every last man who was trying to restore King Charles to his rightful place on the throne. They could have advanced their eventual victory, and Cromwell, with all his faults, is wise enough to have known it."

"Yet no active steps were taken."

"I keep coming back to the fact that this journal was written in French," Richard said. "Now I can't help wondering whether Robertson may have been an agent in the employ of France—or on the personal payroll of Queen Henrietta Maria."

"The stupid woman disliked me intensely—for reasons you know. But I didn't set eyes on Charlie during this past year, and she knew there was no way we could have come together. Even if I had been his mistress at one time, she would have accomplished nothing by having my movements watched. Besides, as she must have guessed, he really did sleep with two ladies at the court, and both of them visited him in Scotland.

Henrietta Maria has never been one to squander money."

"That leaves the French government," he said.

She shook her head wearily. "Mazarin knows who is and who was powerful in England. Surely a man that shrewd had no false illusions about me."

"We're reduced to one last possibility," Richard said. "For the sake of argument, let's assume that Cardinal Mazarin learned that secret meetings of the Cavalier high command were being held at your house. By keeping you under surveillance, he could have easily learned the identities of every active Royalist leader."

Mimi brooded in silence for some moments, then said, "Logical enough. That sort of operation would be typical of Mazarin. But why would his agent continue to follow me after I became a helpless refugee, and then try to kill you when you became my sole source of protection?"

"I have no idea." He placed both hands on her shoulders. "All I know is that we've experienced a nightmare. Fortunately, we knew nothing about any of it until tonight, and now it's ended. We'll keep the notebook, and tomorrow I'll ask you to read it to me, word by word, to see if we find any additional clues. But no matter what we learn, if anything, the problem has been solved. I'm still alive, and you're free to live as you please."

She absorbed what he said, closed her eyes for an instant, and then returned his unblinking gaze. Neither of them knew why it was happening, but he embraced her, she slid her arms around his neck, and as they embraced, they kissed fervently. Their ardor increased, Mimi's lips parted, and soon only their mutual desire mattered. They disrobed in almost unseemly haste, then began to make love in earnest. Mimi, suffering no inhibitions, was as forthright as a lover as she was in every other aspect of her life. Richard no longer cared that he did not love her. He wanted her desperately and reveled in the knowledge that she was willing.

The tiny cabin became still smaller, and the lower bunk was their whole world. Their caresses became urgent, and when they ultimately mated, their explosive frenzy culminated in a burst of ecstasy.

Not until they grew calmer did they become aware of the chill in the cabin, and Richard drew the bedclothes around them.

"I knew it would be like this," Mimi murmured as they became locked in a fresh embrace.

"You knew it would happen?"

"Well," she said with a smile, "I play a fair game of whist because I know the odds. And I couldn't imagine that a healthy man and a healthy woman, both compatible in many ways, could stay apart when they're spending the entire voyage in a space this cramped."

"I fought it," he admitted.

"Why?"

He hesitated.

"Why, Richie?" Mimi insisted.

"Since you force me to be less than a gentleman, I'll tell you. You're not only beautiful beyond compare, but you're lovely in many ways. You're honest and good. In spite of an inborn arrogance, you mean harm to no one. Yet, with all of these qualities, I don't think I love you. However," he added hastily, "I'm not certain I really know the meaning of love."

Her laugh was full-throated. "Be comforted, my dear. I'm not in love with you, either." She snuggled closer, her body pressing against his. "But I do enjoy our relationship more than any other."

They made love again in a more leisurely manner,

exploring and arousing, postponing their climax until they could wait no longer.

The wind shrieked, and the little brig rocked and pitched in violent spasms, her timbers groaning in protest. But all was serene in the cramped cabin.

"Do you want me to go to the upper bunk?" Richard asked at last.

"Don't you dare!" Mimi said. "After this, I intend to make only one bed in the mornings."

"So be it," he replied with a grin.

"You know," she said drowsily as she nestled in his arms, "we'll have no trouble passing the time for the rest of this long voyage."

Young Charles II stared at the canopy of his lavish bed. He was unable to sleep again tonight, and his bedclothes were wrapped uncomfortably around his legs, resulting from his futile efforts to find a suitable position for slumber.

There were so many weighty concerns rolling around in his mind, all seeming to defy attempts for resolution. His life was out of control. He grieved for his father, he felt himself to be politically adrift and financially dependent, and his mother was thriving in her homeland of France and seemed none too anxious to return to England with her son on the throne.

Giving up all hopes of sleep, young Charles sat up in bed, pulled aside the bed curtains, and lit the candle on the night table. He considered ringing for his manservant, but decided against it. There was no need for two people to go without sleep.

He was surprised to hear a light tapping at the door of his bedchamber. Had his servant heard him thrashing around the bed?

"Yes, you may enter," young Charles called.

The door opened slowly. Standing in the doorway was a young and radiant woman, holding a candle that softly illuminated her face. Charles sat transfixed, looking at her. Neither one moved nor spoke for several moments.

"May I come in, Your Majesty? I am Anne-Louise. I have been sent to you by the Prime Minister of France." The woman moved toward Charles's bed and sat at its foot. He looked at her closely, mesmerized by her beauty.

She was satisfied to let him gaze upon her, giving him time to acclimate himself. "You see, Your Majesty, there are many levels, many aspects to our hospitality. It has been noted by your hosts that you look tired. The cardinal suggested I help you to pass the long hours of the night."

The cardinal had suggested more than that. He had closely supervised her selection from among a number of women for this specific duty. She had her long, blonde hair loosely arranged atop her head so it would fall past her shoulders by removing a single hairpin. Her first meeting with young Charles was orchestrated so his first glimpse of Anne-Louise would be softened by candlelight.

"Your Majesty, may I pour you something to drink?"

"Yes, I would like that."

Anne-Louise stood and moved slowly toward the decanter and crystal snifters. She poured a drink for the young man and brought it and her candle to his bed. Handing him the brandy, she placed her candle carefully beside his own, then sat next to him on the bed. She must proceed slowly so Charles would consider the conquest his.

"You wish nothing to drink?"

"No, thank you, Your Majesty. I have come here for your own pleasure, and to serve your needs." Anne-Louise had been warned not to join Charles in his drinking.

Anne-Louise sat quietly by Charles, aware of his decreasing suspicion and tension. He sipped the brandy in silence, without taking his eyes from her face. When he had finished, she took the snifter from his hands and placed it on the table. She blew out one of the candles, came back to Charles, and removed the pin from her hair.

When Robertson failed to appear at the breakfast table, the first mate observed that in all probability he was suffering from seasickness.

"I feel none too hearty meself," Mollie Williams declared.

"We were a little queasy during the night," Robbin said, "but we appear to have found our sea legs."

"How long do you suppose this storm will last?" Richard asked coolly.

The mate shrugged. "We should see our way through the worst of it in a few more hours. But this is just a taste of what's to come. This is the season for gales in the Atlantic, and the next one could well stay with us for a week."

Mimi's hand found Richard's beneath the table. If the other passengers knew from the way they looked at each other and touched that they had become lovers, no one was disturbed. Robbin had slept with Dempster before they were married, Mollie had long enjoyed a scullery-eye view of the upper class, and the temperamental Bart was of an age when only his own feelings mattered.

Ever since Mimi had revealed her real identity, all had assumed that she and Richard were lovers, and neither the passengers nor the officers thought less of them for it. The crew envied Richard but respected Mimi, while Robbin and Mollie condemned neither. It was taken for granted that bluebloods made their own rules and were responsible only to themselves, and that even the nobles who had joined the Puritan cause would not alter their personal habits.

Late in the morning, Captain Brennan became mildly concerned and sent a crew member to the general cabin. The seaman reported that Robertson's bunk, concealed behind boxes of cargo for which there had been no room in the hold, had not been used the previous night. The entire ship was searched, but no sign of the missing man was found.

Captain Brennan made a laconic notation in his log: "Passenger Robertson lost overboard last night during gale." That was the end of the matter. Robertson had been so aloof that no one missed him.

His disappearance had not only changed the lives of Mimi and Richard, it made a difference to the Chaneys, too. They rearranged the location of their own bunks. Captain Brennan, aware of their situation, had several crew members move the cargo boxes, which were filled with the iron skillets and kettles eagerly sought after by those in the New World. After the crates were lashed to the nearest bulkhead for security, Robbin and Dempster finally had a private corner. They kept their voices down at night because otherwise Mollie and Bart might have been disturbed from their rest, but the young couple soon learned there was little need for conversation.

Mimi and Richard spent the better part of two days reviewing every word in Robertson's diary, but could find no clues that explained his behavior or indicated the identity of his employers.

"If you don't mind," Richard said, "I'll send the notebook to Newcastle, in France, via Captain Brennan at the end of the voyage. It may be of more significance to him than it is to either of us."

"Please do," Mimi told him. "There's nothing in those pages that I care to hide from the people who are struggling to put young Charlie on the throne." A sudden thought struck her. "How does it happen that you're going to America rather than to France? I know Lindsey has a great need for officers who are skilled swordsmen and who know how to use fire-arms."

Not even to her could Richard reveal his mission. "I'm being sent to the colonies," he said, his voice unintentionally curt.

Mimi knew enough about Cavalier politics not to press him. "I just wish they had given me something useful to do," she said, and dropped the subject, refraining from bringing it up again.

Dempster volunteered for the formidable task of teaching Mollie and her son to read and write, and devoted the better part of each morning to instruction. Mollie was a surprisingly apt and devoted student.

"Just imagine me being able to read a book!" she exclaimed enthusiastically. "Just like the Duke of Buckingham!"

Bart, on the other hand, showed no interest in learning. "I've never knowed nobody who could write a word or even read his name," he said. "Why should I bother? It ain't going to help me earn a living."

Every afternoon Mimi played cards with the Chaneys, who were becoming increasingly proficient, but Richard did not join them. Games bored him, and he confessed that his father had not been able to kindle his enthusiasm for chess, either. He preferred to spend his afternoons reading various volumes borrowed from Captain Brennan's small library.

Mimi became increasingly fond of the Chaneys, and one evening she seemed disturbed, but said nothing until she and Richard retired to their cabin. "I'm only slightly older than Robbin and Dempster," she said, "but I can't help thinking of them as naive. I don't think you'll believe what I've just learned today.

They're traveling to the New World without a penny between them."

"I know," he said, and told her he had provided the funds that had enabled Dempster to buy their passage.

"They'll need money after we land," she said. "They don't seem in the least concerned, but they'll need funds for food and lodging until they find work. I'm going to find some way, without embarrassing them, to make them a gift of cash before we reach Boston."

"I've fully intended from the start to help them," Richard said, "so I wish you'd leave it to me. Dempster is a proud and sensitive lad, and it would mortify him if anyone offered him charity. He'll take money from me more readily because I'll offer it to him as a loan."

"I see." It was obvious she was disappointed, if not annoyed, at not having her own way.

"If you wish," he suggested, "you might make a gift to Mollie. I believe her purse is more or less empty, too, and it would help her if someone gave her a start."

"I'll do it." Her quick smile forgave him. "What about Bart?"

"Helping his mother will be enough."

"You don't like the boy?"

"I neither like nor dislike him," Richard said. "This afternoon I grew tired of reading, and when the garbage was being thrown overboard I went up to the deck with my pistol to keep my eye and hand sharp. Bart coveted my pistol and actually wanted to know what price I'd ask for it. He's a volatile lad, with no notion of good sense. I'm afraid he'd spend a gift on a weapon that could create problems for himself and his mother."

"You're the only man I've ever known who has valid

reasons for everything that should or shouldn't be done. Do you have any other suggestions, Richie?"

"Indeed I do, my lady. Stop talking so much and get undressed—or I'll be forced to remove your clothes myself."

"What a lovely idea," she said.

The final weeks of the voyage seemed endless. The brig was buffeted almost incessantly by strong winds, the seas ran high, and the sun rarely appeared in the dreary, leaden sky. Crew members worked day and night in the open, their clothes rarely dry, their meals abominable, and yet their attitude was unfailingly cheerful. They did what was required of them, and if they complained, it was not in the presence of the passengers.

"As one who grew up near Bristol," Dempster said, "I've always taken seamen for granted, more or less. I wish I had the stamina of the civilians who sail on merchantmen and those in the old Royal Navy, too."

"Oh, you do, darling," Robbin assured him.

"I don't mind spending fourteen or more hours a day in the fields," he said, shaking his head, "but I've had enough of the sea to last me for the rest of my life."

"I so hope we will make good lives for ourselves in the colonies," his bride said.

"I intend to succeed," he told her, "if for no other reason than because I'll never have to sail back to England. Once we make a home, we'll stay there—even when young Charles gains the throne!"

Perhaps the worst of the voyage was the monotony of the diet. The hardtack was soggy, the bully beef had lost its taste, and the boiled beans needed seasoning to make them palatable. The mere thought of salt fish caused passengers and crew alike to shudder. Even the inventive Mollie Williams, who continued to as-

96

sist the cook in the galley every day, could no longer invent ways to make the meals more appetizing. "There's just so much a body can do to bully beef and salt fish," she said. "If we had more spices and herbs it would help a mite, but we don't." So the same dishes were served at virtually every meal, and passengers and crew members lost their appetites. The seamen, having known what to expect, continued to eat in order to keep up their strength, and the civilians, for want of anything better to eat, followed their example.

As the *Anne* drew nearer to Massachusetts Bay, the need to make specific plans for the future became more urgent. Dempster and Robbin tentatively decided to stay in the colony, go west to the frontier country, and establish a homestead of their own if they could find sufficiently attractive land for farming. Captain Brennan told them that free acreage was available, but made it plain they would encounter difficulties.

"The American wilderness isn't like English farm country," he said. "You'll have to build your house, uproot trees, and clear the land. That could take months of hard work. By the time you're ready to start planting, it might be too late to reap a harvest in the coming season."

Dempster refused to feel discouraged. "If I must," he said, "I'll find work with someone else this year, which will give us time to find the right property for ourselves. All I know for sure is that I can grow crops in just about any kind of soil."

Mollie Williams was overwhelmed by the gift of cash made to her by Mimi. "This will give me a chance to look around and find what's best for me. I want to settle in some place where Bart will be able to make a good life for himself, too. If we like Boston, maybe we'll stay there. If not, we had a scullery maid at Whitehall who went to Providence Plantations, so maybe I'll look her up."

The plans made by Richard and Mimi were more complicated. He intended to remain in the capital of Massachusetts Bay long enough to make his own soundings regarding the feelings of the people about the relative merits of the Cavaliers and Puritans. Mimi, however, would stay only for four days and then sail to New Amsterdam before going on the last leg of her voyage, which would end at her destination, Middle Plantation.

"We'll have a few days together in Boston, at least," Richard said.

She nodded. "But we'll need to be careful. If we share the same quarters, there's certain to be talk that will find its way back to London."

He had no intention of allowing her to become involved in a scandal. "There's only one inn of substance in Boston, Captain Brennan tells me. The Sign of the Bear, it's called. I'm hoping they'll give us accommodations near each other."

"I'd like that," she replied with a smile.

"I've been doing a great deal of thinking about you and me, Mimi," he said. "Are you quite sure you want to go on to the plantation of this Horace Laing in Virginia?"

"I believe so. From what I've gathered, the winters in New England are even worse than in Scotland."

"I don't know where I'll make my permanent headquarters," he told her. "It depends on the way my—uh—mission works out. But you may want to reconsider your own arrangements."

She didn't understand what he was trying to tell her, and raised an eyebrow. He had thought of many ways to say what he had in mind, but had discarded all of them. "If you wish," he said bluntly, "we could be married."

She was so startled that she had no immediate reply.

"I realize," Richard said uncomfortably, "that it would be a step down, a long step down, for the daughter of a belted earl, who already has a title in her own right, to become the wife of a mere baronet, but I nevertheless extend to you my offer."

Mimi began to chuckle, then halted herself sharply. "I beg your pardon, Richie," she said. "I didn't mean to laugh, and I'm not making sport of you. The truth of the matter is that I'm overwhelmed."

He bowed, still waiting for her reply.

"Do I gather correctly that you've recovered from your love for the girl you left behind in Lincolnshire?" There was no flippancy in her manner.

"I'm no longer certain of what I feel for her." He had done his best to put Dorothea out of his mind and had not been completely successful. "What I do know is that you and I have been living together all this time, and we're compatible."

Mimi wondered if he had been overcome by shyness, which wasn't like him. "Are you trying to say you've fallen in love with me?" she asked, prompting him.

Richard frowned and shrugged. "I'm confused by our intimacy," he said. "Ask me that same question with a sword pointed at my heart, and I'd be forced to say that I don't know. I honestly don't think I am in love with you, but I can't swear to it."

"If this is any comfort to you," she said with a broad smile, "I don't believe I love you, either."

"That relieves my conscience somewhat."

She looked hard at him. "Yet you'd do this for me?"

"Of course, if it's what you'd want."

An expression of wonder crept into her eyes. "I don't think there are many gentlemen of your caliber in our world these days. Buckingham gives a girl an expensive bauble and goes on to the next, and there are dozens like him."

"I had only a nodding acquaintance with Buckingham. I know nothing about his private life."

"What I know is only hearsay, I'm pleased to report." Her smile faded. "First, I thank you with all my heart for your proposal, but my own conscience forces me to reject it."

"The offer remains open if you change your mind."

"That's unlikely," Mimi said, and slid her arms around his neck. "I suggest we enjoy to the hilt the time we have left together—and let the future take care of itself."

IV

Boston, the capital of Massachusetts Bay Colony, was a strange town, unlike any place that either Richard or Mimi had ever seen. It had a population of almost three thousand inhabitants and was growing rapidly, but it bore little resemblance to any community in England. Perhaps the proximity of the endless North American wilderness, a vast sea of trees that extended for many hundreds—perhaps thousands—of miles to the north, south, and west, was responsible for its unique qualities.

Already a major seaport and the largest town of Britain's colonies on the continent, it nevertheless was only recently becoming influenced by cosmopolitan sophistication. Few taverns that catered to seamen were to be seen in the port area, and as Richard would learn when he made inquiries to satisfy both Mimi's curiosity and his own, there were no bordellos within the town limits, although night walkers were apprehended without warrant and presented to the courts for punishment.

The main portion of the town, which extended from the harbor past Beacon Hill, was still growing rapidly, with only a few buildings of stone or brick. Most, including a majority of the churches, shops, and dwellings, were made of wood, preferably oak. That made sense, since trees were the New World's least expensive commodity, but what was surprising was the relative absence of large homes. Even those who already had become well-to-do lived modestly in simple houses of one or two stories, many of them little more pretentious than log cabins.

Although founded nineteen years earlier, Boston had few public gathering places of consequence other than the churches. The court was housed in the First Church, and the governor's mansion, a two-story house of white painted clapboard, stood between the Common and Fort Field. There were no meeting houses, no theaters, and no other places of entertainment. Only three streets had been cobbled, although a few more would be paved when the warmer weather came, and most roads were rutted, with ice and snow caking the frozen mud. Several roads were pebble-paved down their center strip, making use of the round stones from the area's shorelines.

Many residents were attired in drab clothes, as Mimi noted immediately. Men and women alike dressed in blacks, dark browns, and grays, and the children were smaller versions of their elders. Only a very few wore clothes imported from England. Most wore suits, dresses, and cloaks of a locally made material known as linsey-woolsey, a mixture of wool and linen or cotton that was durable but shapeless.

The only note of color was provided by the copper-skinned American Indians, who roamed through the streets in large numbers, the men painting their faces with streaks of color that identified their various tribes. The Wampanoags, in particular, under the leadership of Massasoit, had long enjoyed friendly relations with the colonists of the Bay Colony. Indian men and women alike wore clothes of supple animal skins, and the costumes of the women were decorated with dyed porcupine quills and beads of many hues.

A huge area that extended from Beacon Hill toward the waterfront was known as the Common. From spring through late fall this was a carefully tended pasture, dotted with relatively few trees, as was the case in all of Boston, where milk-producing cows were permitted to graze. All citizens had the right to entrust their cows to William Hudson, the herder for the town, who would drive the animals to the Common each morning and return them at the sunset. Many families owned at least one milk-producing cow.

The Sign of the Bear looked as primitive as the rest of Boston, but the interior, although simply furnished, proved to be surprisingly comfortable. Richard and Mimi were given adjoining second-floor rooms without asking for such quarters; later, they would discover that they had been assigned the only private rooms in the place. All other quarters were dormitories, each of which housed as many as a half-dozen visitors.

While Mimi luxuriated in a hot bath, the water having been poured into a tub four feet long, Richard exercised his horse. Prince Henry celebrated his release from the shipboard pen by cantering spiritedly through the muddy roads, and Richard soon found himself in the open countryside. This was an area in which farms predominated, most of them small, interspersed with patches of deep woods. The man and his mount felt at home in the forests, and Richard reflected that, while Boston seemed alien, this taste of the American wilderness buoyed his spirits.

He returned to the Sign of the Bear after a brisk, two-hour ride that did wonders both for the stallion and for the rider. Then, after bathing quickly, he joined Mimi in her room. Already dressed for the evening in a form-fitting gown of emerald silk, she sat at a small table, applying cosmetics with the aid of two smoking pine knots and an oil lamp. "I'll be ready as soon as I can manage," she said. "The lights here are dreadful, and apparently smokeless French tapers are too expensive for the colonials."

Richard sat in a straight-backed chair while he waited for her. "The weather is so raw and cold," he said, "that I suggest we eat right here in the inn this evening. I did a bit of scouting and saw a few taverns in the neighborhood, but none of them looked very appetizing."

When the woman completed her toilet, they descended to the ground floor, and there the proprietor approached them hurriedly, a look of alarm on his face. "Lady Dawn!" he said, obviously concerned. "Surely you don't intend to appear in public looking as you do!"

Richard bristled, but controlled himself sufficiently to speak quietly. "Do you find something objectionable in Lady Dawn's appearance?"

"Not I, Sir Richard," the man protested. "I worked in a London public house for years before I came to Massachusetts Bay and built this place. But this is Boston. When a woman makes an exhibition of herself with her arms bare and her chest—uh—exposed, she's placed under arrest and is forced to spend two days sitting in the stocks. No exceptions are made, and I'd hate to see Lady Dawn in trouble."

Mimi made no attempt to conceal her amusement.

103

"Perhaps," Richard said, "we could be served our dinner in Lady Dawn's room."

"I'm afraid that can't be done, either, Sir Richard. I could spend a month in prison for fostering personal relations between unmarried persons of opposite sexes."

Richard and Mimi exchanged incredulous glances. The innkeeper drew himself up to his full height. "Lady Dawn, Sir Richard," he said, "this is Boston!"

"I would venture a guess that the Puritans control this community," Mimi said.

"Your ladyship, Boston was founded by Puritans. I'm sure that no city in England is as firmly in the Puritan camp. Those who are of other persuasions," the man added, "soon move. Some have founded new towns elsewhere in Massachusetts Bay, and a good many are now making their homes in Providence Plantations and other portions of Rhode Island. The Boston Town Council, made up exclusively of churchgoers, tolerates no dissent and no disobedience of its laws."

"You've convinced me I'd be wise to conform," Mimi said.

The innkeeper walked beside her to the staircase. "I'm grateful for your understanding, your ladyship. If you appeared in my dining room as you're now dressed, I could be arrested."

"I have a strange notion," Richard said as he and Mimi ascended the stairs to the second floor, "that I won't be tarrying overlong in this town myself. I just want to assure myself that our host isn't exaggerating."

Mimi found a jacket with a high ruffled collar and long sleeves among her belongings, and she donned it over her dress. Then, laughing at the local customs, they went down to the dining room. There they ate before a roaring log fire, and new surprises awaited them. The oxtail soup was delicious, the venison steak, which had been marinated in wine and herbs, was extraordinary, and the apple pie, enclosed in a crust rather than served in a deep dish as it was in England, was unlike anything they had ever eaten. The portions were so large, Richard could eat only part of what was placed in front of him. With their meal, they were served drinks of hard cider that had been produced locally.

The other guests were even more fascinating than the unusually good food. Two young, bearded French fur traders in buckskins appeared to have returned recently to the comparatively civilized atmosphere of the town from a hunting and trapping expedition in the northwest. Loud and uncouth, they drank enormous quantities of liquor, and they used language that would have made a London slum inhabitant blush. Three other men, who seemed to be local merchants, were clearly offended by the traders, first viewing them with disdain, then turning their backs to the rustics.

"It is a wonder to me that such conduct hasn't resulted in their arrest," Mimi said after she and Richard returned surreptitiously to her chamber.

"Well," he replied, "the Puritan standards of this colony, at least, aren't those we knew at home. I'd guess that allowances must be made here for the concentration of the Puritan population."

"I predict that as the wilderness settlements grow and become stronger, the clergymen here will lose their control over the people. Until then, I'm glad I won't be living here. Why, the way all those men were staring at me, I'd swear they've never seen a woman wearing rouge or rimming her eyes with kohl. I'll need to use cosmetics lightly while I'm here, or I might be sent to gaol for wearing too much."

He grinned as he watched her disrobe, then followed her example. "I guess I'd be horsewhipped if they caught me going to bed with you."

105

"I shudder to think of what they'd do to me. I just hope the other colonies are less prim, or I'll have to buy an entire new wardrobe."

Richard made certain the bolt that kept the door locked was firmly in place before he and Mimi went to bed.

Taking no chances in the morning, Richard made his own bed look as if he had slept in it. After changing his clothes and shaving, he went for a ride on his horse before joining a demure Mimi for breakfast. Her face was bare of cosmetics and her attire was modest, but the other patrons, all of them male, nevertheless gaped at her. She had an inner quality, Richard reflected, that drew men to her.

After breakfast he went on a long, solitary walk to acquaint himself with the town, and many of his earlier guesses were confirmed. In spite of the overlay of Puritanism that was evident everywhere, the shopkeepers and others with whom he conversed were earthy people. A few disliked the overzealousness that had been imposed on them, but were afraid to speak their minds as they pleased. Some cautiously admitted, in response to Richard's casual, leading remarks, that although they were Puritan sympathizers, they condemned the brutal execution of Charles I, of which they had learned from the officers and crew of a ship that had reached port only a few days earlier.

"The Puritan leaders here are serious, right enough," a cobbler said, "but the day we kill somebody here for his beliefs, I will pack up my family and move to another area. I go to our church, sing our hymns, and listen to sermons that last all through the Sabbath. But if our Puritan leaders go too far, my conscience will suffer for it. I came here to be free, I did, and no one is going to push me into corners!"

Reviewing his estimates of Boston's loyalties, Richard visited as many local establishments as he could until it was almost time to return to the Sign of the Bear to meet Mimi for the noon dinner. A watery light from the sun was shining in a pale sky, the wind had died away, and he took his time, strolling down a cobbled street.

"Richard!"

He was startled to hear someone call his name.

"Richard!" The deep voice came from an unpainted single-story wooden building.

He hurried toward the window reinforced with metal bars about six inches apart, stretching from top to bottom.

A haggard Dempster Chaney stared out at him. "Thank God you happened to walk past this awful place. Robbin and I have been thrown into the Boston gaol, and they're holding us in separate cells!"

"What in the devil did you do to be arrested?"

"The devil's own work, or so they told us. We were wandering around, seeing the sights of the town —such as they are—when we were arrested for committing a sin."

"You and Robbin?" Richard was stunned. "What sin could you have possibly committed?"

"We were holding hands," Dempster said bitterly, "and when we stopped at the edge of the Common, we kissed. A constable took us straight to the church, and when the justice learned we had only ten sovereigns, the money you gave us before we landed, he took it from us. He also sentenced us to thirty days' imprisonment because the fine for this offense was more than we had. I haven't seen Robbin since yesterday, and I'm going out of my mind with worry."

"Don't despair," Richard said. "I'll do what I can for you."

He raced back to the inn, and when he told Mimi what had happened, they promptly postponed dinner.

Instead, they asked for directions, then walked quickly to the Strangers' Court, which was two town squares away.

Justice Platt had just concluded his morning session in court and was about to return to his house for a two-hour dinner recess. But his bailiff, impressed by the refined appearance of Sir Richard and Lady Dawn, went directly to the magistrate to convey the visitors' names. The magistrate immediately consented to see them.

Clad conservatively, like almost all Puritans, he nevertheless bowed from the waist when the couple came into his tiny office, where several books of law sat on a wall shelf. "What progress Boston is making when people of your stature visit our fine city. Welcome, milady. Welcome, Sir Richard."

Richard decided to soften the harsh approach he had intended to take. "We're overwhelmed by Boston, Your Honor," he said. "But we are saddened, too. We have just learned that two shipmates of whom we're very fond have run afoul of the law and have been imprisoned."

"I think it unlikely that friends of yours could have committed a serious crime," Justice Platt replied gallantly. "Their names?"

"Master and Mistress Dempster Chaney."

The judge opened a ledger and moved a forefinger down a closely written page.

Richard's quick, warning glance told Mimi to control her temper.

"Here we are," Justice Platt said, and frowned. "Dear me. It grieves me to tell you that your friends committed no ordinary crime. They have sinned."

"What was the nature of their sin?" Mimi asked sweetly.

"They dared to embrace and kiss in a public place!"

It was Richard who had to make the effort to speak

108

calmly. "You realize, Your Honor, that they are legally man and wife."

"No matter, Sir Richard. In fact, all the more reason for them to behave in a seemly manner in public. When married couples feel the need to embrace—which is discouraged but not forbidden—they are expected to do it in strict privacy. The Chaneys might well have contributed to the corruption of the single men and maidens of Boston."

Mimi knew how to handle this bigoted representative of the Massachusetts Bay law. "They are so young themselves, Your Honor, that they were no doubt carried away by passions they couldn't curb. As you say, their conduct was unseemly, at best. But forgiveness is a virtue that all of us strive to acquire, so I do hope you can show forgiveness to these poor sinners."

"The law requires justice, not forgiveness, milady," Justice Platt said severely.

"What are the specific penalties of the law for this couple's grave offense?" Richard asked, his serene façade beginning to slip.

The judge crossed the room and picked up a law book. "This volume just arrived from London, where it was published by some of our dear colleagues. I find it both useful and enlightening. I don't suppose you're familiar with it?"

"As a country dweller," Richard murmured, "I've had little to do with the law."

Mimi carefully refrained from adding that, until recently, a member of her household staff took care of legal matters on her behalf.

Justice Platt took his time thumbing through the book, at last finding the citation he was seeking. "Here we are. The suggested fine is twenty-five sovereigns. Since few sinners can afford to pay that sum, they cool their ardor behind prison bars. The practice hasn't yet

109

been established in London or other cities in England, although soon the unholy there will learn their lessons, too. Here we find it much easier to keep them under control."

Richard was struggling with his anger now, so Mimi took the initiative. "We understand the Chaneys have already paid a fine of ten sovereigns. May we be permitted to supply the funds necessary to terminate their incarceration?"

"That's generous of you, milady."

She opened her purse and quickly had the gold coins in hand.

"I must make my acceptance of the fine conditional. I shall order this errant couple released into your custody and Sir Richard's, but there is no proper place here for people of that sort. They must leave Boston no later than sundown tonight!"

"It's you who show true generosity, Your Honor!" Mimi placed the gold coins on his desk.

Richard marveled at her seeming sincerity and told himself that her high position in the peerage had robbed the theater of a superb actress.

Justice Platt scribbled a few lines on a sheet of parchment with a quill pen, signed his name with a flourish, sprinkled the ink with talc and, after dripping tallow from a burning candle onto the page, affixed his seal. "I hope it will be my pleasure to see both of you again," he said. "Mistress Platt will regard it as a privilege if you will pay our humble home a visit."

"I'm afraid the visit will need to wait for a short time," Mimi said, picking up the sheet of parchment and waving it in the air to dry. "I sail very soon for Virginia."

"I'm leaving Boston in the immediate future myself," Richard said, then forced himself to add,
"but I shall call on you without delay when I next come to town."

"I look forward to that day, Sir Richard." The judge bowed them out.

When they reached the street, Mimi breathed in the cold air deeply. "I thought I'd suffocate in there."

"I was afraid I'd create a real problem by slicing off his buttons with my sword. If the penalty a married couple must pay for the sin of embracing in a public place is twenty-five sovereigns, the Puritans are mad indeed! Once they try to enforce laws like that in England, there aren't enough ships in all of the country's ports to accommodate the emigrants who'll be clamoring to come to the New World."

"But not to Boston," Mimi said as they started toward the prison.

"No, not to Boston while the Roundheads rule here, that's sure. I don't dare stay more than a short time myself, or I'm certain to be in trouble. But the situation here isn't totally as it appears on the surface. I started to test the temper of the people this morning, and I was pleasantly surprised." He had no intention of going into detail until they were alone.

The gaoler who sat behind a desk in the bare prison office was eating a slab of meat between two chunks of bread when the pair arrived. He did not rise, and they saw no need to identify themselves as, continuing to eat, he very slowly read Justice Platt's order. It occurred to Richard that the man had difficulty in making out the meaning of the written word.

The gaoler finished his meal, wiped his mouth on the back of his linsey-woolsey sleeve, and hauled himself laboriously to his feet. "Wait ye here," he grumbled, and shuffled out.

Within moments he returned with a tearful Robbin Chaney, who sobbed as she threw herself into Mimi's arms. "I knew it had to be you two who saved us," she cried. "I've never known such a horrid nightmare."

The gaoler smirked, then went off again.

Robbin was eager to learn how the rescue had been arranged. "What did you—"

"Later," Mimi said.

The gaoler returned, leading a dejected Dempster, whose ankles and wrists were chained. He brightened immeasurably when he saw his wife and their benefactors, and when his chains were removed, he started toward Robbin.

Richard clamped a restraining hand on his shoulder. "Patience," he said. "You sinners never learn, but we'll take you to dinner and try to teach you the error of your ways." He led the still-dazed younger man into the street, and Mimi followed with Robbin, whose weeping had turned to wild laughter.

"Hush," Mimi told her. "It may be against the law to laugh in this barbarous Roundhead town, too."

A few minutes later they were seated at a snug corner table in the dining room of the Sign of the Bear. "Bring our friends a sample of everything on the menu, if you please," Richard said to the proprietor, who hovered over them himself.

"You must have guessed," Dempster said, "that I was given only stale bread and water in gaol."

"I had something the gaoler called soup," Robbin said, "and the sanctimonious fraud promised me anything I wanted to eat if I— Needless to say, I refused."

"I'll kill him," Dempster stormed.

"You'll do no such thing," Richard declared firmly. "The longer you stay here, the more troubles you'll create. You're leaving Boston before sundown today." He told the Chaneys the whole story of their visit to Justice Platt, and at the end of his recital, he handed Dempster two five-sovereign pieces. "See if you can use these more judiciously."

"We can never repay either of you," Dempster

said. "I'm afraid we'll be indebted to both of you for years to come."

"You owe us nothing," Mimi said.

"But we do." Robbin was wide-eyed. "It would be wrong to accept so much money as a gift."

"Establish a solid place for yourselves, and we'll be satisfied," Richard replied. "You may repay the loan as you're able."

"Where should we go?"

Dempster shrugged helplessly as he looked at his wife.

"I've hardly become an expert on the New World in this short a time," Richard said. "But I kept my ears open wide this morning, and as I see it, you have two choices. Either you'll go south to a new colony called Rhode Island, and you'll find work there in a town called Providence Plantations, where they need masons and bricklayers. Or you can go on to another town called Newport, where most men catch fish for a living. There's also the start of a new shipbuilding industry there."

"I know nothing about bricks or masonry, fishing, or building ships."

"Then your only alternative is to start out toward the west. There are many villages and hamlets, most of their inhabitants people who couldn't tolerate the more unyielding attitudes of Boston's Roundheads." They were the only diners in the room, but Richard nevertheless took the precaution of speaking in a low tone. "You'll find someone who will give you supper and a bed tonight for a few pennies. Keep walking until you come to farm country that appeals to you, then stake a claim there. Just this morning a baker told me that's what he intends to do. He also told me his nephew has a working farm of one hundred and sixty acres somewhere to the west."

"What a huge estate," Robbin murmured.

"Not in the New World," Richard said with a grin. "Plus, reports claim that wheat, oats, rye, and barley grow here with greater success than in England."

"I'd need to let part of my property lie fallow while I cultivate thirty or forty acres," Dempster said thoughtfully. "But that's all right. I guess I've got to start thinking of farming on a larger scale."

Their first course consisted of shellfish largely unknown in England or Europe. Called clams, because of their tightly closed shells, these sea creatures had been steamed until the shells had opened from the heat, and as they were eaten, one by one, they were dipped first in broth, then in melted butter. Then came bear steak, which had been pounded to tenderize it. The spirits of all four rose as they ate.

"I was afraid of the food we'd find here," Mimi confessed, "but I've changed my mind."

Richard had to agree. "There's no need for anyone to starve here," he said.

After the meal, Dempster and Robbin bid good-bye to their benefactors, promising that they would meet again, and started off on foot toward the frontier. Both were cheerful, suppressing any doubts or fears they may have been feeling, and although they did not realize it, they were following in the steps of others who had come before them.

"They have courage," Richard said as they watched the young couple go off down the road.

"And confidence in themselves," Mimi added.

It was that spirit of self-assured optimism that Richard encountered again and again in the next two days as he spoke with people from every walk of life in Boston. The frontier beckoned, and anyone who could no longer tolerate the narrow-mindedness of those who were trying to create a society in their own image was free to go into the wilderness and make his own rules.

Writing a long report to the Earl of Newcastle, Richard concluded that although Boston was in the firm grip of the Puritans and could not be relied on for help in the restoration of young Charles II to the throne of his father, the same could not be said of the rest of Massachusetts Bay.

Ultimately, he wrote, *the frontier here, which creates a love of liberty in all men, will surely prevail. This colony cannot be judged by English standards, and in the short time I have been here, I have already seen the influence that the wilderness exerts on all but the most rigid of Puritans.*

He also reported all he knew about the man who had called himself Robertson, and after hesitating momentarily, he related the true account of the man's attack on him and its grisly climax. He enclosed the man's journal, adding his own speculation and Mimi's as to the reason it had been written in French.

When he accompanied Mimi to the brig, he closeted himself briefly with Captain Brennan, to whom he gave the packet containing his letter and Robertson's diary. "You know to whom this is addressed," he said. "I thought it safer to write no name on the outside of the package."

"Rest assured that it will be forwarded to the man to whom you wrote," the master of the *Anne* replied. "It will be in safe hands at all times and will not fall into the possession of the enemy."

It was strange to think of fellow Englishmen as enemies, but that was what they had become, Richard knew.

"Are you familiar with the system we use for the transmission of communications?" Captain Brennan wanted to know.

Richard shook his head. "I was told only that I would be informed at the appropriate time."

"Well, that time is at hand. Come with me." The captain led him from the cabin to the main deck, and nodded in the direction of the yardarm. "Do you see anything out of the ordinary up there?" he asked.

Richard looked up, but saw nothing.

"Ordinarily," Brennan said, "a ship doesn't fly her nation's colors in port. It isn't done, and the custom has been observed for many years. Whenever you see the Union Jack flying from a ship's yardarm when she is anchored or tied to a wharf, you'll know that her master shares our political sentiments. This signal was chosen because of its ambiguity: to those unaware of this system, it appears that the captain is perhaps sloppy or forgetful about hauling in his colors. It would be difficult for a Roundhead to prove that the captain is letting it be known that he is willing to take messages back to England with him."

"I won't forget," Richard said, and after shaking hands with the captain, went off to the cabin he had shared with Mimi on the long voyage to the New World. They had agreed they would part there, in private, rather than on the open deck, where their embrace would create troubles.

They kissed, then stood at arm's length. "I know we shall meet again," Mimi said.

"I'm sure of it," Richard replied. "I shall make it my first order of business to see Horace Laing when I come to Virginia, as I intend to do. I'll find you, no matter where you may be."

With one accord they kissed again, and Mimi clung to him. "I hate to admit this," she said, "but I shall miss you."

"It isn't too late to change your mind and stay with me," he told her.

"No, it's right that we go our separate ways," she replied, her voice firm.

"Just remember that my offer of marriage remains open," Richard said.

She nodded, smiled, and pushed him away.

Her insistence on leading her own life as she saw fit was similar to the feelings he had heard expressed by many Bostonians, Richard thought as he took his leave. Her independence was a sign that she would do well in the New World.

He stood on the wharf as the lines were released, and the seamen began hoisting the brig's sails. Then, as the vessel edged away from the pier, Mimi came on deck and waved.

Removing his hat and returning her wave, Richard told himself she was unique. He could not help contrasting her attitudes with those of Dorothea, who did only what she was told. Perhaps he was being too harsh in his judgment of Dorothea, but he knew himself sufficiently well to realize that he would miss Mimi far more.

He stayed on in Boston for only a few more days after the *Anne* sailed, and learning nothing additional of consequence, he started out for Rhode Island. His horse was frisky in spite of the saddlebags and sleeping blankets Richard had secured, and had to be curbed to be prevented from tiring himself too quickly. When they left Boston behind, the man and his mount entered a deep forest of maple, pine, ash, elm, and oak, and Richard breathed more freely. Boston had depressed him, but now he could forget the Puritans who made life so miserable for themselves and for everyone around them.

What astonished him was the difference between the colonies and England. Here, the wilderness intruded everywhere, and although he passed the log cabins and cleared fields that marked the presence of

117

farms, the forest soon closed in again, enveloping him. Familiar, rustling sounds that the untrained ear could not detect told him of the proximity of game, and he knew that even though a thin blanket of snow still covered areas of the ground, spring soon would come to this country of rolling hills and unexpected level areas.

In the afternoon, he came to a salt lick near a stream that meandered through the deep woods, and halting upwind of it, he waited; with any luck he might eat fresh venison before the day ended. At last his patience was rewarded when a doe appeared, and he brought down the creature with a single rifle shot, the sound echoing through the forest. Richard's rifle was one of a handful of similar hand-tooled weapons in England and in France that were perhaps unique. Certainly they fired accurately and lived up to their reputations and hence were infinitely more valuable than the ordinary musket available to everyone. That night he feasted on a venison steak at a fire he made in the open, and for the first time since coming to the New World, he was content.

He had taken the precaution of reloading his rifle as soon as he had fired it, a practice he had followed ever since he had first learned to handle firearms, and as he finished his meal, he reached for the weapon beside him, then leaped to his feet. Prince Henry sensed the approach of strangers, too, and whinnied softly.

Soon, two Indians appeared on foot, their faces smeared with dye, their buckskins worn. Their bows remained on their shoulders, and neither of the pair reached for an arrow; their whole manner convinced Richard that they were curious rather than hostile. He lowered his rifle.

The taller of the pair, a brave of about thirty, raised an arm in greeting, then in his own language said something incomprehensible to Richard.

Richard returned the gesture, and saw both of the

118

Indians staring at the remains of the doe's carcass, far more meat than he alone could possibly eat. "Help yourselves," he said, and when they did not understand, he told them in broad pantomime that they were free to use the meat as they saw fit.

They promptly built up his fire, carved chunks of meat, and placed them on a crude but effective spit. Then, as their meal cooked, they carefully separated the animal's hide from the flesh beneath it. They were using primitive but finely chiseled stone knives, and Richard marveled at their dexterity. This was his first direct experience with the copper-colored natives, and they interested him because these forests were their natural home.

Feeling more at ease with the white man, the Indians did their best to communicate with him while they devoured their meal. Ultimately, Richard was able to convey the message that he was traveling south, and the Indians, it developed, were going in the same direction. Returning his hospitality, they offered to guide him. Not until he indicated by his acceptance that he trusted them, did they smile.

Richard's horse fascinated the two braves, and both inspected the great beast at length, taking care not to approach Prince Henry too closely. The realization dawned on Richard that horses were alien to them, that there were no such animals in their tribe's possession.

That night, the two Indians slept in the dry clearing on one side of the fire while Richard, wrapped in a blanket, stretched out on the other, his rifle close at hand, as always. In spite of their apparent friendliness, he remained cautious, uncertain whether they would try to steal his horse or his equally precious rifle, which was much superior to the conventional muskets that were so unreliable. Therefore he slept lightly, but the

Indians did not betray him, and in the morning he felt more secure in their company.

The pair demonstrated their gratitude by cooking more venison for him, as well as for themselves. The shorter of the pair cut a line of tendon from the doe, made a hook with a long, spiked thorn, then astonished the young Englishman by using this primitive equipment to catch a fish in a stream that passed close to the campsite. Skewering the fish on a branch, the man roasted it over the coals, and when it was done, he offered it to Richard.

Already surfeited, Richard indicated that he appreciated the gesture, but preferred that the Indians eat it. This they did, splitting the fish with their stone knives and removing the bones swiftly and easily. Richard watched them, reflecting that anyone who wanted to live in the wilderness had a great deal to learn from these people.

He discovered that he himself had much to learn about Indians. When he mounted Prince Henry for the resumption of the journey, the two braves led him, both walking tirelessly for the entire morning, never pausing to rest, never showing the slightest sign of fatigue.

After traveling for another day through the forest, they halted at noon, and one of the Indians pointed through an opening in the trees. Peering ahead, Richard saw a stockade fence, with clusters of log cabins and more substantial buildings of brick on the far side and cleared fields on the near side. This, it appeared, was Providence Plantations, the core of the community that a clergyman named Roger Williams had founded a decade and a third earlier after his banishment from Boston, when he also had discovered his inability to tolerate the stern, unyielding ways of the Puritans.

One moment the Indians were there, and the next

they were gone, vanishing silently through the trees. Richard could hear them as they went their own way only because of his lifelong training, and he made up his mind to learn their language as soon as he could. No one, he told himself, could understand America without knowing the natives of this rugged country.

He rode slowly down the hill toward Providence Plantations, aware of the sentries who were watching his every move from the tower that dominated the palisade. From the heights, too, he could make out the small boats that rode at anchor in the half-circle of harbor that formed the inner rim of the town, and he assumed these were fishing craft. What struck him most forcibly was the diversity of Providence Plantations' architecture: dwellings and larger buildings were constructed in a bewildering variety of styles. There were simple log cabins, buildings made of stone, and several handsome houses of brick. The total population could not be greater than one thousand persons at the most, but it was plain that the citizens of the town had planted strong roots here and planned to stay.

The gates opened as Richard rode toward them, and a stocky man, clad in a buckskin shirt, linsey-woolsey breeches, and footgear of soft leather like that of the two Indians Richard had encountered, waved his musket in welcome.

"We figured you wasn't no Indian when we saw your horse and clothes," he called, "but we had to see the color of your skin to make certain. It don't pay to take risks these days. We permit entrance to Indians only when they are in the company of a white man."

Richard drew to a halt beside him. "Having troubles with the Indians?"

"Oh, a friendly little fuss with the Narraganset, you might say," the man replied. "Reverend Williams bought the land from them before he started Providence Plantations, but now we're a-bustin' at the seams, and the more farmland we claim for ourselves beyond the palisade, the more the Narraganset carry on. We're a-hopin' there won't be a shootin' dispute with them because we be a peace-lovin' people. But it don't hurt none to keep our powder dry."

"Where can I find lodging?"

The sentry took careful note of the cut and fabric of the stranger's clothes and the fit of his expensive boots. "For the likes o' you," he said, "you'll do best at Miz Gertie's, down to the waterfront. Just keep a-ridin' until you come to the water, and then turn left. You can't miss the place." He busied himself shutting the gates.

Richard followed the man's directions, wondering how he could identify Miss Gertie's, his instinct telling him to ask the sentry no more questions. People he passed en route to the waterfront kept themselves occupied with whatever they were doing and paid scant attention to the new arrival. A man mending a fishing net in his yard barely glanced at the rider, then returned to his task. A young woman dragging a cart filled with shiny new cooking utensils seemed unaware of his existence. She continued to trudge up the middle of the dirt road, forcing Richard to pull as far as he could to the side to make a path for her. Only two small boys throwing a ball to each other paused in their game long enough to wave.

After proceeding a short distance down the waterfront, Richard saw a hand-lettered sign, swinging from a post in front of a shingled, unpainted two-story building:

ROOMS TO LET
Only Genteel Folk Accepted
G. Allen, Prop.

Standing in the yard was a gray-haired woman wearing trousers under her skirt, energetically chopping down a tree with a long-handled ax. "The trouble with paper birch," she announced, "is that you need to keep the grove thinned out, or before you know it, you'll have a whole forest."

"You can't use the wood for much except kindling," Richard replied in the same easy, conversational tone. "But I understand the Indians use it for building canoes."

Apparently his demeanor pleased the woman, because she rewarded him with a smile. But her eyes remained sharp, and she absorbed every detail of his appearance.

"I was told to apply to you for temporary quarters," he said.

He took great care to speak politely, to smile, and to treat her with great respect. He knew the type, understood how she would react, and was taking no chances on having her regard him as glib.

"I get sixpence per day, payable in advance," Miss Gertie said. "Dinner is at noon sharp, supper is half-past five, and you get two candles every forty-eight hours you spend here—no more. Breakfast is whatever is left over from the night before."

Richard dismounted and handed her a silver half-crown. "This will take care of the basics for five days," he said. "I assume the stabling of my horse and feed for him will be extra, am I right?"

"You're wrong," Miss Gertie replied testily. "I run an honest hostelry. Besides, I don't know when I've seen a better-looking horse."

To Richard's surprise, Prince Henry, who disliked being touched by strangers and normally reacted by stomping and snorting, allowed himself to be petted and admired.

Soon the horse was at home in the stable behind the

main building, munching on some apples that Miss Gertie gave him, and Richard was shown to a room dominated by a huge, four-poster bed. "Are you quite certain you want to charge only sixpence per day?" he wanted to know.

"I'll thank you not to mock me, young man!"

He changed the subject hastily. "I wonder if a friend of mine has settled here in recent days. Her name is Mollie Williams, and she—"

"Not here," Miss Gertie replied. "She applied to me for a position as my cook, but I don't have enough guests here to hire anyone." She peered even more sharply at the new arrival. "You must be Master Dunstable."

He bowed.

"Mollie Williams told me about the voyage from England and how a certain lady gave her enough money for her to take time finding the place she wants. She couldn't find it here. Providence grows slowly. Everyone in Rhode Island is entitled to his own opinion, but folks hereabouts keep their thoughts to themselves, so Mollie's boy would have had problems in Providence. He speaks too freely for his own good. They went on to Connecticut, the next colony down the line."

Richard thanked her, wondering if he had correctly gleaned that the woman had Cavalier sympathies. "Mollie told you the cause of her predicament?"

Miss Gertie nodded. "You won't find sympathy here for Puritans," she said. "We accept anyone whose beliefs are sincere, provided he doesn't try to cram his views down the throats of others. Lapsed Puritans are welcome in Rhode Island, but those who try to make others feel the way they do are invited to leave the colony before they lose their good health. We don't hold with violence, you know, but those who preach that the only road to eternal salvation is their road

124

have been known to suffer accidents in Rhode Island. We value our freedom!"

Richard chuckled, then said, "There must be a strong Cavalier feeling in the colony."

She shook her head. "Mollie bragged how smart you are, but I see little sign of it, Master Dunstable. People in this colony don't do much of the bowing and scraping that kings expect of their subjects. All we want is to be left to ourselves." She walked to the nearest window and pointed. "What do you see out there, beyond the stockade?"

"The forest?" Richard asked.

"The forest, sir!" Miss Gertie said severely. "In a hundred years that forest will be gone, cleared by men who love their freedom. Rhode Island isn't Massachusetts Bay, where the population is expanding every year. To get along in Rhode Island you need to love liberty and be willing to die for it! That's why we say to the Roundheads and the Cavaliers—a pox on both your houses. We want no Old World quarrels here. We have enough to keep us occupied, taming the wilderness, maintaining a difficult friendship with the Narraganset, and trying to keep our young from being tainted with the bigotry and hatreds of outsiders. We don't give a hang whether England is ruled by a king or by Parliament. All we want is to be left alone to live as we see fit!"

In the days that followed, Richard discovered that Miss Gertie's thoughts were shared by virtually everyone he encountered. Religious freedom was guaranteed to the residents of the colony in a covenant made five years earlier with Parliament, and Rhode Islanders were so conscious of their liberties they carried a large chip on their collective shoulder, daring any and all outsiders to knock it off.

During the course of Richard's brief stay in the

colony, representatives came from Newport and War-wick, the other principal Rhode Island towns, for the purpose of joining Providence in discussing the tensions between the Puritans and the Niantic and Narraganset tribes. The entire colony was dedicated to Roger Williams's commitment to friendship with the Narraganset; therefore, the visiting Englishman had the opportunity to learn of the whole colony's views.

A dozen of the Rhode Island leaders gathered at Miss Gertie's on Saturday night for a dinner of boiled lobster, which started with a fish soup that everyone present called a chowder, and Richard was surprised when toasts were offered in home-brewed beer.

"To liberty!" Providence's delegate to the council declared, rising at his place and lifting his glass.

"To liberty," the others echoed, and drained their glasses.

"We don't tell the Puritans of Boston what prayers to recite, what hymns to sing, or what man-made rules to obey," the Warwick representative explained to the silent, observing Richard. "We expect the same courtesy from them in return, and when they refuse to reciprocate, which happens more often than not, we run them off our soil."

"Our ships sail as far as the West Indian Islands to trade," the Providence representative added. "We do business with New Haven, New Amsterdam, and the Indians. We go anyplace where we can earn a profit. But I'll be damned if our captains will put into Boston, no matter how much they might be able to earn there."

"It's been my observation that the Roundheads are a vindictive lot," Richard said. "Don't they try to even the score when you snub them?"

The representative from Newport looked at his red, work-roughened hands and chuckled. "Oh, they try," he said. "Frequently they claim the border needs re-

126

definition, that we're extending the boundaries of Rhode Island. But we have a map that was approved by King Charles and was ratified by the Long Parliament. So we show it to them every year, and they can't say much when they see the great seal of Parliament on the bottom of the map, right next to that of King Charles."

"I would think the royal governors would solve such problems," Richard said, and discovered that everyone at the table was staring at him.

"Some colonies may choose to take guidance from England," the Warwick representative said haughtily. "But Rhode Island doesn't entertain that particular attitude. We govern ourselves, and we swear no allegiance to either the Crown or to Parliament. We swear allegiance only to God, and we pray to Him to preserve our independence."

Richard was confused. "You do regard yourselves as an English colony?"

"Of course." The man from Newport was impatient. "You can tell for yourself that we aren't French or Spanish or Portuguese, sir!"

"Then you pay British taxes?" Richard asked.

Everyone in the room, including Miss Gertie, who presided at the table and ladled out the food, burst into loud, sustained laughter.

"You might say, Master Dunstable," the Providence representative said dryly, "that we pay when we must. With great reluctance."

The man from Newport grinned, revealing two rows of yellow teeth. "It's all a matter of pride," he said. "I do believe our Rhode Island sea captains are more adept at avoiding the payment of duties than those of any other British possession."

Richard began to grasp what these Rhode Islanders were trying to tell him. Independence—the right to do as they wished—was an obsession with them, so he said, "The Cavaliers are firm believers in the Church of England, while the Roundheads have developed the teachings of Calvin and Knox. But presumably they worship the same God. Would you permit a godless man to settle in your colony?"

They looked at each other in silence, and then the man from Warwick said quietly, "We wouldn't know he was godless, Master Dunstable, because we don't ask a man about his faith. That is something we regard as a private matter, to be determined by an individual's own conscience. We don't pry into matters that concern only a man and his Maker."

V

RICHARD spent a full week in Providence Plantations, and when he left the town he felt a grudging admiration for the people of Rhode Island, who practiced the liberties in which they believed so fervently. Certainly their concept of freedom was new and unique. England and most nations of Europe had an official state religion which the people were required to observe; alliances were based on the system of government and religion being intertwined. Even colonies were founded on that same principle.

But the pioneers of little Rhode Island, few in number and trying to eke out a living in the wilderness of North America, were living according to a revolutionary concept: a man's religion was his own private business, and it was his right—not his privilege—to believe and practice his faith as he alone saw fit. Freedom of conscience was a novel, daring idea, and the more that Richard pondered the matter, the more he approved.

Only in the free world of America, where men faced dangers every day of their lives with a determined calm, could such an idea come into being and grow. His report to the Earl of Newcastle would necessarily indicate that neither the Cavaliers nor the Parliamentarians could expect much active support in Rhode Island, and Richard guessed that officially he would have to disapprove of the new concept. But in actuality, he found he secretly admired the Rhode Islanders. If one of the powerful nations of the world, like Great Britain or France, ever adopted such an idea, that nation would be greatly strengthened. And if the concept spread to other colonies from Rhode Island, the appeal of the New World would become irresistible to those people of the Old World who were reduced to second-class citizenship because their way of worshiping God did not happen to be the same as that of their rulers.

Mounted on Prince Henry, he headed toward the southwest, occasionally catching a glimpse of the high seas and angry surf of the Atlantic from the crest of a hill. The Rhode Islanders had provided him with a crude map of the area between Providence Plantations and the small town called Pequot, urging him to go on to New Haven colony. One curious fact impressed itself on Richard's mind: there was no marker, no definition of any kind to tell him when he left Rhode Island and entered Connecticut. "The area is so sparsely settled," he was told, "that the problem of drawing a precise boundary won't become urgent for years to come."

In other words, Richard thought, someone who carved a home for himself and his family in these

129

boundless forests would not necessarily know whether he was a resident of Rhode Island or Connecticut. Even more significant, that lack of knowledge would have no bearing on the man's life. As nearly as the newcomer could determine, only in Boston did the geographical location of a man's dwelling have an effect on his way of life. Elsewhere he was free to do as he pleased, the colony in which he lived neither contributing to nor demanding service from him.

This was a life that Richard truly relished. He loved sleeping in the open, bringing down game, and catching fish for his meals, and what he did not already know about life in the wilderness, he was quick to teach himself. Through constant experiments he learned which roots and plants were edible, and once he found some forest produce he enjoyed, he invariably recognized it when he saw it again.

His clothes could not tolerate the strain of wilderness traveling, so he paid a tailor in Providence Plantations to cure the skins of several bucks that he shot, then to fashion trousers and shirts for him out of the stout leather that could withstand the punishment of rain and brambles. He was so much in his element that the problems of England seemed almost unreal to him, and frequently he had to remind himself not to dawdle on the trail. He still had a mission to perform.

One day, in the vicinity of the poorly defined Rhode Island–Connecticut border, Richard made out the sounds of human voices somewhere ahead. At almost the same instant, Prince Henry lifted his ears and became alert. Riding warily, Richard checked his rifle and pistol to make certain they were loaded, ready for use.

The trees thinned as he neared the crest of a rounded hill, and he drew to a halt in the shadows of a patch of evergreens, shading his eyes as he stared ahead. Five Indian braves were slowly circling some

130

object on the ground. Two jabbed at it with pointed sticks, while the others applied flaming brands they brought to life repeatedly in a nearby fire. Every time one of them jabbed at the object, he laughed and spoke aloud. Richard could not understand a word that was said, but he recognized the tone of voice as taunting.

All at once, he realized that the braves were torturing a fellow human being whom they had spread-eagled and tied to stakes. With his wrists and ankles held firmly in place, the writhing, silent victim could not evade the jabs nor the fire of his foes.

Richard first felt a sick revulsion for the scene he was witnessing, and that sensation gave way to an overwhelming feeling of outrage. No matter what the reason for the punishment, the odds against the victim were insurmountable, and his tormentors were prodding him for the sheer sport of it.

Weighing his own odds, Richard quickly made up his mind to intervene. "Steady, lad," he whispered to his mount, and raising his rifle to his shoulder, he squeezed the trigger. One of the torturers flung his arms high above his head, then collapsed onto the ground.

The other Indians heard the rifle shot, but could not figure out what had happened, perhaps because they were not anticipating the sound of a firearm's discharge, possibly because they had never known such expert marksmanship.

Reloading swiftly, Richard did not take his eyes from the Indians who were staring first at their fallen companion, then at each other. Again he raised his rifle, and he put his bullet between the eyes of a brave who caught a glimpse of the mounted man behind the fringe of trees and opened his mouth to shout a warning to his companions. He died before he could utter a sound.

"Go, Prince Henry!" Richard said, touching his

horse's flanks with his heels. The great beast needed no other signal and bounded forward, hooves thundering through the spring mud as he gathered speed, his rider again reloading the rifle.

The braves stared in awe and fright at the unexpected apparition, a white-skinned man riding on the back of a huge mount, bearing down on them with reckless speed. They scattered, running for their lives.

No shot is more difficult than one attempted at a moving target while the marksman himself is in motion, but Richard was equal to the challenge. He knew Prince Henry as well as he knew himself, and adjusted easily to the horse's jarring gallop. Raising his double-barreled pistol, he took aim and squeezed the trigger. A third brave sprawled on the ground.

The remaining pair were heading for the forest on the far side of the open space, and Richard knew they would disappear unless he acted with dispatch. He drew one of his throwing knives, waited until he had gained on the fleeing braves, then hurled it with all of his might. The blade plunged into the Indian's back, vanishing up to the hilt, and the brave went down, his lifeblood soaking his buckskin shirt as he died.

The last surviving member of the group turned to face the onrushing man and horse, his desperation giving him the courage to make a stand. He snatched his tomahawk from his belt, then steadied himself before hurling it.

Richard had another knife in his hand, but he had no chance to throw it. Prince Henry seemed to understand that this Indian was his master's enemy, and he bore down on the brave, his speed still increasing, a wild fire in his eyes, his teeth bared.

Too late the brave realized the stallion's intent, and turned away hastily after throwing his tomahawk, which sailed harmlessly over Richard's head. There was a thud as the horse ran over the man, but Prince

Henry did not slow his pace, and the warrior died under the great steed's relentlessly pounding hooves. The task complete, Prince Henry wheeled abruptly and halted.

Richard surveyed the carnage, aware that five men had been killed within moments and that he had the field of combat to himself. He dismounted hastily, retrieved the knife he had thrown, and hurried to the victim of the quintet. The Indian was alive and conscious, his pain-filled eyes reflecting his gratitude to the white man who had rescued him from torment.

Richard slashed the leather thongs that held the warrior fast. Clad only in a loincloth, the man had suffered some nasty burns and cuts, but had survived his ordeal in relatively good condition. To the white man's astonishment, the Indian addressed him in English. "The leaves of the red plant that grows near the evergreens will heal me and make me well again," he whispered.

Richard ran to the nearest pines, and to his surprise saw a number of small plants with clusters of dark reddish-brown leaves growing up through the last remnants of snow on the forest's floor. He cut them at their base with his knife, then returned to the Indian with them.

The warrior crushed the leaves between his fingers, then rubbed them into his wounds. The procedure must have been excruciatingly painful, but he did not flinch, his face remaining impassively expressionless. When he was done treating himself, however, a great sigh of relief shook through him. "Roaring Wolf owes his life to the white man with the thundersticks and the horse who knows no fear," he said. "Roaring Wolf will serve them well as long as the Great Spirit allows him to live in this world."

The Indian was short and stocky, and the wiriness of his arms and legs indicated that he was capable of

133

great stamina. His most compelling feature was his eyes, which were dark brown and unusually penetrating. They reflected an inner quality Richard was soon able to fathom as wisdom. The Pequot knew a great deal about nature and ways to survive in the wilderness.

Later, when Roaring Wolf came to know his benefactor better, he explained how he had acquired his name. It seems that years earlier when his tribe was at war and badly outmanned by neighbors, he dozed off while standing a long sentry duty. He awakened just in time to see a large band of enemy warriors approaching. Giving no heed to his own safety, he fired arrow after arrow at them, at the same time shouting at the top of his lungs. His colleagues later described his voice as being similar to that of a wolf that roared its displeasure when under attack by enemies. Roaring Wolf was obviously proud of his name, and also obviously had good cause for his pride.

Richard stared at him in fascination. "How do you happen to speak my language?" he demanded.

"It did not happen," the warrior replied. "I was the pupil of one who tried to teach me to love your God." Richard had not known that missionaries had been active in the area.

"I will collect more of the plants with red leaves," Roaring Wolf said, "and in two days my wounds will be healed. This is a secret known only by the Pequot. Then I will be strong again and will help you in all you wish to do." Reaching out suddenly, he plucked a throwing knife from the startled young Englishman's belt, hauled himself to his feet, and walked to the nearest of the dead braves. Richard had to avert his eyes when he saw Roaring Wolf neatly and expertly scalping the dead warrior.

Soon the brave returned, five scalps clutched in his hand. "You killed them in fair combat," he said.

"There are many in my tribe who would claim that one man cannot kill five Narraganset in battle, but I saw this miracle with my own eyes. You have earned the spoils." He offered his savior the scalps.

"I have no use for them," Richard said, feeling queasy.

Roaring Wolf shrugged, then tucked the scalps into the top of his loincloth. Returning the knife with a clumsy bow, he went off again, going from one fallen body to the next. Richard watched him as he took a buckskin shirt from one, trousers from another, and a pair of moccasins from a third. He acquired a knife, a bow and a quiver of arrows, and finally a tomahawk in the same practical, realistic way. He needed these essentials, and it did not seem to bother him that he was robbing the dead.

"Now we will go on your journey," Roaring Wolf announced. "You will lead and I will follow."

Richard wondered how anyone could travel so soon after being subjected to painful torture, but he was anxious to leave the scene and did not argue the point. He mounted Prince Henry, and as he set off again to the southwest, he deliberately walked his horse. The Indian made no complaint, and for more than two hours kept up the pace.

Afraid the brave might collapse at any moment, Richard finally halted and made camp beside a swift-running stream. Roaring Wolf gathered dead wood, made a fire, and after digging up some roots unknown to his benefactor, he first washed them in the little river, then placed them in the coals at the edge of the fire. Finally, using his new knife with dexterity and speed, he fashioned a spear, which he took to the stream. Lying on his stomach, he peered intently into the water, his body motionless. All at once, his arm flashed, and he grinned happily as he exhibited a large fish on the point of his spear.

As the meal was cooking, Roaring Wolf told his story. He was a warrior of the small Pequot tribe, he said, and was thirty-five summers old. His people had been severely punished by the Great Spirit, and Richard gleaned from his explanation that the tribe had been decimated by a plague of some sort. The Narraganset, the ancient enemies of the Pequot and far more numerous than their foes, had long contested the Pequot's control of superior hunting grounds and were now obtaining possession of them. Pequot braves were isolated, captured, and tortured to death, which had been the fate in store for Roaring Wolf prior to Richard's intervention; the women of the tribe were enslaved and the children were adopted by the Narraganset.

"Soon all the Pequot will be gone," Roaring Wolf said, looking moodily into the fire. "The hunting grounds of my people will become the hunting grounds of the Narraganset. But," he added, his homely face suddenly relaxing as he smiled, "they will not enjoy these lands for long. The fathers will not be able to pass these hunting grounds to their sons."

"Why not?" Richard's curiosity prompted him to interrupt.

The Indian pointed a forefinger at him. "Every moon, ships that look like great white birds bring more men and women with pale skins from far places to the land of my ancestors. Already your towns are larger than the towns of the Narraganset. Your people use thundersticks that kill their foes and bring game to the cooking fires. The Narraganset use the bows and arrows of their fathers, which are no match for the thundersticks." The finger jabbed in the direction of Prince Henry, who was foraging for some tender grass and shoots protruding through the rich spring soil.

136

"The men with pale skins bring beasts who carry them with great speed that the legs of the Narraganset cannot equal. So the greed of the Narraganset will gain them little. Soon, they will join their fathers in the land of spirits, and no man who lives in this land will remember them." He chuckled aloud, the notion giving him great satisfaction. Roaring Wolf interrupted his recital long enough to gather more plants with red leaves, which he rubbed into his wounds.

Richard was astonished to note that the burns and cuts were already far less inflamed and swollen than they had been. It was obvious that the primitive method of treating them was effective.

"It was the will of the Great Spirit that directed you to the place where the warriors of the Narraganset were taking the life of Roaring Wolf," the Indian declared.

Richard was too polite to suggest that sheer happenstance had brought him to the scene.

"So it is plain that the Great Spirit spared the life of Roaring Wolf for a purpose. I will devote the rest of my days to helping you overcome your enemies."

The young Englishman tried to dissuade him. "I became angry when I saw the odds against you and realized that you were being tormented. But you are not in my debt, and you owe me nothing."

The warrior shook his head stubbornly. "Great evil will come to me if I disobey the will of the Great Spirit. And I would shame my father and his father before him if I did not hold out the hand of friendship to him who saved me from death." Reaching into the fire, he picked up a small coal and, with no sign of feeling plain, crushed it in his hand. Then he dropped the ashes into the palm of Richard's hand. "I will go where you go," he said solemnly, "and I will do as you direct me to do."

For better or worse, Richard knew, he had acquired a companion for the duration of his New World travels.

Richard had long assumed that he was familiar with forests, and even though he could survive in the deep woods, he soon realized how much he could learn from Roaring Wolf. The Indian was not only infallible in noting signs of game, but was equally adept at detecting the recent presence of men in the forest. Richard gratefully listened to the warrior's advice, observing the way leaves that had been scattered and bent blades of grass revealed the proximity of other humans.

He learned, too, how many edible roots there were in the wilderness, and how to distinguish between plants and berries that gave nourishment and those that were poisonous to man. Plants that had medicinal properties were endless, and the young Englishman gave up trying to commit them all to memory, instead concentrating on the most useful and plentiful herbs.

He was also taught by example how to eat after the fashion of the Indians, wasting nothing. The staple of the Indians' diet was corn, supplemented by other vegetables and plants, he discovered, with meat, fowl, and fish taking a minor role in their nutrition. He found it more difficult to acquire the art of walking for hour after hour without tiring. He began to practice shooting with a bow and arrow, and his eye was so keen he quickly acquired the knack. His talent for throwing a knife made tomahawk-throwing an easy skill to acquire, but he had to admit he never would be able to hurl the clumsy weapon with the accuracy that Roaring Wolf took for granted.

The backgrounds of the two men were dissimilar in every way, but their love for the forest bound them together, and they soon established a solid rapport. Their communication transcended the use of words, and often a look or a hand signal was enough. The thought dawned on Richard that he had gained an ally who could prove of great value to him.

They traveled southward by easy stages until Roaring Wolf's wounds were healed, and after crossing the Pequot River, they came to the town of that same name. The inhabitants of the little port town were struggling to establish a foothold in the wilderness, and the lookout of the garrison seemed upset by the prospect of admitting Roaring Wolf to the town.

"You are welcome here, Master Dunstable," he said, "but we've made it a rule to keep out all Indians."

"Roaring Wolf is my friend," Richard replied, "and he goes where I go."

The guard was still nervous.

"Do you fear he'll steal from you?" Richard demanded. "I assure you, he already has all that he needs. Are you afraid he'll learn your strength and lead a band of warriors in an attack on your town? His tribe is scattered, and he is responsible to no one —other than to me." With great reluctance the lookout granted permission for Roaring Wolf to enter the town.

No rooms or taverns for visitors were available, but Richard and Roaring Wolf were offered a meal by one of the hospitable residents. Richard wanted to tell the leaders of the little community that they were making a grave error. Pequot had a total of only thirty-six home lots, and the residents were greatly outnumbered by the Indians of the area, according to Roaring Wolf. Common sense dictated the necessity of winning the friendship of the natives, instead of holding them at arm's length. But Richard had learned to keep his opinions to himself.

Pequot, founded by John Winthrop, Junior, he discovered, was surprisingly not a smaller version of Boston. Richard had come to a town directed by its inhabitants, among whom Winthrop held paramount authority. During the few hours he spent in the community, he learned that the citizens of Pequot might be Puritans, but they were not fanatical in their devotion to the cause. The wilderness, he decided, was far more of an active force here than it was in Boston, and consequently, the Puritanism of the inhabitants was tempered by a realistic appraisal of the harsh environment that surrounded the town.

Richard had a private word with a town leader, who was known by the title of constable. "Constable Palmer," he said, "forgive an outsider for interfering, but you'll do far better if you trade with the Indians of the neighborhood rather than deny them the right to enter your town."

"You think so?" the man asked uncertainly. "We debate the question often at town meetings."

"Well," Richard replied, "surely your people know they can catch more bees with sweet pollen than with vinegar."

Constable Palmer's guffaw belied his funereal appearance. "I never thought of it that way, sir, but you may be right! Folks here are inclined to be extremely cautious when their safety is at stake!"

Richard rejected the constable's plea, seconded by others, to remain overnight as his guest. No one offered Roaring Wolf quarters for the night, and Richard refused to accept shelter when his companion would be forced to sleep in the open, even though that was the arrangement the Indian would have preferred.

The journey to New Haven was resumed, with Roaring Wolf leading his friend along the shore of the Great Bay. They spent the night on the beach after feasting on clams, crabs, and oysters they gathered in the shallow salt water, and after beginning their inland march the next day, they came to a relatively narrow bend in the Pequot River, the largest stream by far that Richard had encountered on his travels. Roaring Wolf offered to build a raft that would carry them and Prince Henry to the west bank of the river.

The forest was more dense now, making it necessary for Richard to follow the Indian on foot. Prince Henry brought up the rear and, like a well-trained dog, followed his master of his own accord. They proceeded in this fashion until early afternoon, when Roaring Wolf halted suddenly, raising a hand in warning. Richard moved up beside him, while Prince Henry seemed to realize he could not make his way quietly through the underbrush, and halted, too.

Directly ahead, in a sun-dappled hollow, several young Indian girls were gathering berries, which they tossed into woven baskets. The girls chatted and laughed, and the scene was joyously pastoral, so Richard could not understand the expression of alarm on the warrior's face.

The Indian maidens were enjoying themselves thoroughly and were so carefree, so uninhibited in their movements that it seemed impossible for them to be in danger of any kind. In fact, as Richard watched them, he was struck by their similarity to young English girls at play. They had the same innocent quality, the same bubbling mirth, the same free spirit. But something definitely was amiss.

Roaring Wolf made a circular motion with one hand, indicating his intention of giving the girls a wide berth. He started around the hollow, and Richard accepted the decision, turning away from the scene ahead. As he did, something caught the corner of his eye, and he looked back to see a huge black bear standing upright behind one of the Indian girls who had inadvertently wandered too close to the edge of the clearing. She was unaware of her danger until her companions began to scream, and then she was rooted to the spot, terror robbing her of her ability to flee.

Regardless of Roaring Wolf's reason for withdrawing. Richard could not leave now. He raised his rifle to his shoulder, took aim over the head of the endangered young girl, then fired. His bullet caught the bear in the shoulder, sending him down on his side. The beast howled in anger, rolled over, then rose to his hind legs again and lumbered toward his attacker.

Richard was so astonished to see the animal coming toward him that he gaped at the bear for a moment. Then he drew his pistol from his belt and fired, but through carelessness or haste he missed his target, something that rarely happened. Furious with himself, he fired a second time.

His shot found its mark, but the five-hundred-pound bear did not stop. The wound that was inflicted on the bear landed close to the first, and the animal's roar of pain and rage echoed through the forest. Prince Henry answered the challenge, pawing the ground, and his neigh was loud and clear. Richard knew the bear would tear the stallion apart or break the horse's neck with a single swipe of his powerful forefoot. There was no time now to prevent his mount from joining in the combat. The screams and shrieks of the Indian girls mingled with the bear's menacing growls, adding to the confusion.

Richard stepped into the open, blocking Prince Henry's charge, and drew one of his throwing knives. For his own sake, as well as his horse's safety, he could not afford to miss. No encounters with wild animals in the royal game preserve had prepared him for the rush of the gigantic creature bearing down on him now, but he steadied himself, and knowing his life and Prince Henry's depended on his aim, he let fly.

The knife penetrated the bear's skull between the eyes. To Richard's horror, the monster continued to lumber toward him for a few more paces before collapsing in a heap. Making certain the bear was dead before he ventured any closer, Richard retrieved his knife. Only then did he hear Roaring Wolf say urgently, "The maidens are Mohegan. We must go!"

The warning came too late. A party of thirty warriors burst into the open, all of them armed with bows and arrows or tomahawks. The girls all spoke simultaneously, and the leader of the party, a stern-faced man of forty, raised a hand for silence, then pointed first at one maiden, then at another. After each related in turn the story of what had happened, the leader went to the bear, examined the dead beast carefully, and finally turned to Richard, an expression of wonder in his eyes. At last he spoke, saying something curt and stern.

"He wishes us to come with him," Roaring Wolf muttered. "Now I shall surely be killed."

Warriors surrounded the pair, taking care to avoid Prince Henry, and Richard realized that their plight was hopeless. He had no opportunity to reload either his rifle or his pistol, and even if he took the chance and tried, the odds for their escape were minuscule. Perhaps he could leap into the saddle and rely on Prince Henry's powerful, flashing hooves to clear a path for him, but if he escaped he would need to leave Roaring Wolf behind, so he abandoned the plan as quickly as it crossed his mind. He picked up his mount's reins and, surrounded by the warriors, allowed himself to be led off through the forest. For the better part of an hour, he trudged in silence, wondering if he could bear the pain and indignity of torture with the tight-lipped courage that Roaring Wolf had shown.

At last, they came to a cleared field where neat furrows had been hoed for planting. Beyond it stood a circular palisade similar to those that Richard had seen in Providence Plantations and Pequot. Inside the circle, there were oval dwellings covered with woven mats or with bark, the smoke of fires within them emanating from crude holes in their roofs. Scores of Indians appeared from nowhere, and women, old men, and half-naked children watched the procession in silence, with small boys and dogs joining the rear of the column. All were careful, Richard saw, to keep beyond the range of Prince Henry's hooves.

The two captives were conducted to an empty hut, and the horse was tethered outside. Air was admitted only through the door-flap of animal skin, and when it was lowered, the interior was as stuffy as it was dismally dark.

Roaring Wolf stoically seated himself cross-legged on the ground. "I tried to warn you," he said, no hint of bitterness in his voice. "How much better it would have been to let the bear send the maiden to her death!"

Richard's eyes smarted, and he blinked them in order to see his companion in the gloom. "I would do the same thing again," he said, "no matter what the consequences. What will happen to us now?"

His friend seemed indifferent to the fate that awaited them. "We will do what the Great Spirit wills," he said. "That which is done to us will be done at the will of the Mohegan, and I prefer not to think about it."

Suddenly weary, Richard seated himself on the hard ground and brooded. The ways of North American savages were inexplicable, he thought. Any other people would be pleased that a daughter of the tribe had been saved from a needless, cruel death, but it

144

appeared that he would be penalized for his interference, perhaps because his skin was white, possibly because his companion was a Pequot.

All at once the door-flap was opened, admitting air and light, and a young woman in doeskins stood in the entrance, holding a wooden bowl in both hands.

Richard recognized her as the maiden he had saved from the clutches of the bear. She looked older now that he had a chance to study her, and he guessed she was in her late teens or early twenties. Her features were regular and clean-cut, her cheekbones were high, and her full lips parted in a smile when she saw the man who had saved her life. Her huge, dark eyes expressed her gratitude to him as she entered the hut and, still holding the bowl, prostrated herself on the ground. Then, she said something in a singsong voice.

"Take the bowl and drink," Roaring Wolf whispered urgently. Following the instructions, Richard took the receptacle from the girl's hands, raised it to his lips, and drank. The brew was flavored with herbs, and the taste was so bitter, so alien that he shuddered.

Roaring Wolf snatched the bowl from his grasp and noisily drained the contents, then smacked his lips repeatedly in exaggerated approval. Then, he delivered what sounded like an endless address. The girl continued to gaze only at Richard as she listened to the diatribe. There was no way he could mistake the expression in her eyes. She wanted him.

When Roaring Wolf finished speaking, the girl took the bowl from him, rose to her feet and, after replying briefly and succinctly, withdrew. Perhaps she was being careless, but she left the flap open, and for whatever reason, Richard was grateful to her.

"What was all that?" he demanded.

The Pequot sucked in his breath. "It may be that we will not be made to suffer the death of a thousand torments. The girl you saved is Ilia-awi. She is the daughter of the sachem of the Mohegan. She made the drink for you herself." He sounded deeply impressed.

"No matter who made it, I'm glad you took it and drank it. I've never tasted anything worse."

"Your face told the way you felt. That is why I snatched the bowl from you and drank it myself, even though it was intended for you. It would not be wise to arouse the anger of the sachem's daughter. The Mohegan have many faults and are an ignorant, bad people, but they love their children."

"Are you telling me we may not be killed?"

"It is unlikely now." Roaring Wolf folded his arms across his chest and stared into space.

Nothing was more maddening, Richard thought, than Roaring Wolf's present unwillingness to communicate.

The next to arrive was a young warrior with fresh paint smeared on his face. He stood rigidly erect inside the entrance to the hut and raised his arm in greeting, the palm of his hand held perpendicular to the ground. Feeling a trifle foolish, Richard responded with a similar gesture.

The warrior spoke, apparently asking a question. Roaring Wolf replied at length, and the warrior withdrew. Wishing he could understand the language, Richard looked inquiringly at his friend.

"The Mohegan, as I told you, are an ignorant people. They have only seen a horse from a distance, so they think that Prince Henry is a god and that he has magical powers. They wished to know if he eats the food of humans, so I told the stupid warrior that he consents to eat apples."

Richard grinned and had a hard time controlling an urge to laugh when he saw through the entrance to the hut that the warrior had returned, slightly out of breath, carrying a basket filled with apples. He placed the basket on the ground, then pushed it with his foot toward where the horse was tied. Prince Henry sniffed, recognized the scent, and began to eat. The relieved warrior withdrew.

Richard was becoming convinced that no harm would befall him or Roaring Wolf. People who were solicitous of his horse's welfare would not injure or torture them.

A drum began to throb somewhere in the distance, then a second and a third were pounded rhythmically, too.

"Ah, it has started," Roaring Wolf said.

"What has?" Richard's nerves were ragged.

"You have a great surprise in store for you. The drums are summoning all Mohegan to the village." The Pequot chuckled, obviously enjoying the air of mystery he was helping to create.

Richard had already reloaded his rifle and pistol, which had not been taken from him, and he checked them automatically now.

An alarmed Roaring Wolf shook his head. "Do not shoot the Mohegan, I beg you!" he exclaimed. He had no chance to elaborate.

A group of a dozen warriors approached, all with fresh paint smeared on their solemn faces.

Their paint, which had beeen applied with a heavy hand, consisted of broad strokes of deep red, edged with thinner lines of white. They were attired in loincloths, moccasins, leggings that fastened behind, and fringed shirts that were closed with thonglike contraptions. They looked barbaric in the extreme, but Richard was becoming sufficiently acclimated to the New World to accept them in his stride. They drew to a halt outside the hut, and Richard recognized the leader as the man who had captured him. The warrior made a mercifully brief speech.

147

"He wants us to come with him," Roaring Wolf said. "I apologize for not answering your questions earlier, but I did not want to lift your hopes if I was wrong. But I am not wrong. The Mohegan are going to honor you."

Richard was relieved, but carried his rifle as he stepped into the open and was surrounded by the warriors. They led him through the strangely vacant town to the palisade gate, and there, in the open, Richard saw a vast crowd—hundreds, perhaps even a thousand men, women, and children gathered around a blazing, roaring fire.

Seated cross-legged at one side of the fire was a man of middle years whose elaborate headdress of feathers set him apart from all the rest. A half-dozen others, some elderly and some middle-aged, all with bonnets only slightly less elaborate, surrounded the man, who rose and extended his arm in greeting as the party approached.

Richard needed no one to tell him that he was meeting the sachem of the Mohegan and his principal aides, whatever they might be called. He returned the greeting.

The drums fell silent, and the sachem, speaking in a loud voice that carried through the twilight to the far edge of the crowd, made an address. Richard, understanding nothing that was said, heard the same words repeated again and again, and it was obvious to him that the chief of the Mohegan enjoyed public speaking. The young Englishman looked obliquely at Roaring Wolf, who stood beside him. The Pequot shook his head, and Richard understood; it would have been bad manners to interrupt the sachem.

The elders picked up the refrain, the drums began to beat again, and gradually the entire assemblage joined in, repeating the same words endlessly.

Roaring Wolf leaned closer to his friend. "The

148

sachem told his people of your virtues, and now the people of the Mohegan are singing your praises."

Richard stood self-consciously, a half-smile on his lips as he listened to the endless, singsong refrain. How Mimi would laugh if she could see him now! It was strange, he reflected then, that he should think of Mimi rather than of Dorothea.

At last the seeemingly interminable chanting came to an end, and the sachem lowered himself to the ground, inviting the guest of honor to follow his example. Richard seated himself in a cross-legged position, which he found uncomfortable.

Ilia-awi approached, carrying something she had taken from the fire, and prostrating herself on the ground, offered the contents of the platter to her father and to Richard.

"This is a very great honor," Roaring Wolf whispered. "You are being given the opportunity to eat the heart and the brains of the bear you killed." Feeling his stomach turn over convulsively, Richard didn't know how he could follow the sachem's example.

"You must eat," Roaring Wolf whispered insistently. "The Mohegan will be insulted if you refuse."

"I am not worthy to eat the heart and mind of my enemy, the great bear," Richard announced, and forced himself to take token amounts of the food on the platter. The Pequot translated his words.

The members of the council beamed. The white man not only had made a fittingly modest response in the true Indian tradition, but his refusal to eat left more of the delicacy for them. The contents of the platter, to Richard's relief, soon disappeared.

Now, dozens of the women were busy ladling out food for the entire crowd, and Richard noted that they worked methodically, in an orderly manner. They carried steaming victuals on wooden platters to

149

families, and these braves distributed the rations to their wives and children.

Ilia-awi continued to serve her father and the man who had saved her life, her frank gaze burning into Richard whenever she looked at him. The girl could not be accused of being shy.

Richard looked suspiciously at the contents of his serving and was encouraged by the aroma. Taking a deep breath, he lifted it to his mouth, and to his surprise he found the thick, souplike stew to be delicious. The basic contents were corn, which he recognized at once, having eaten it not only in Boston, but in Providence and with Roaring Wolf, and chunks of a meat with a flavor all its own. Not until later was Roaring Wolf able to tell him that the meat was moose, the Mohegan having been fortunate enough to have enjoyed good luck on a recent hunting expedition.

There was no need to identify the main course that followed the stew: the bear had been roasted after being cut into quarters, and there was enough to give everyone present a portion. The taste was strong, Richard discovered, but he entered into the spirit of the occasion, aided by a healthy appetite, and between bites he smacked his lips in the approved manner. Far more to his liking were little corn cakes and steaming squash, served in gourds and sweetened with honey. The Mohegan might be a primitive people, but their cooking was excellent.

After the meal, the sachem wiped his mouth on his sleeve, then rid himself of the grease on his hands by wiping them on his trousers. Richard did the same, glad he had purchased a suit of buckskin, thereby saving the English clothes that would be difficult to replace.

Everyone around him was grinning now, and the strains of strange music floated across the area. Two braves were playing flutelike instruments, hollow reeds with finger holes, and rattles and drums picked up the tempo. The entire assemblage began to stamp and sway to the music.

Ilia-awi approached Richard again, and this time there was no obsequiousness in her manner. She stood boldly before him, her face wreathed in a happy smile, and slowly extended both hands to him.

Richard needed a moment to collect his thoughts, but soon he realized the girl was asking him to dance with her. This was the first time he had seen an Indian dance, and there was no escape, so he grasped her hands in his, and the crowd roared in approval as she led him to an open area at one end of the fire.

Ilia-awi began to dance, her feet stamping in time to the beat of the music, and Richard emulated her, his hands on his hips. At first he was awkward, unsure of himself, but the dance was simple, and he was soon carried away by the spirit behind it. The girl flirted with the man, enticing him, and when he came after her, she retreated. Then, when she grew tired of this game, she made the advances, and he retreated.

Scores of other couples came into the open area and were soon dancing, too. Richard was astonished to discover he was enjoying himself. He forgot that the music was repetitive and simple, that the girl who was flirting with him so expertly was a wilderness dweller who could neither read nor write. The Mohegan, he was learning, knew what they were doing. The very repetitiousness of the dance aroused him, and he pursued Ilia-awi with a mock vengeance that soon became real, then retreated from her in haste when she became aggressive.

Both were laughing and breathless when the music stopped. He and this young Mohegan woman had not been able to exchange a single word, yet he felt that he knew her well. She grasped his hand and led him

151

back to her father. The sachem looked hard at the young couple who stood before him, his eyes bright. Then, folding his arms across his chest, he made a simple, direct speech to them. Ilia-awi averted her gaze and looked off into space.

Roaring Wolf materialized out of the crowd and translated for his friend. "The sachem gives his daughter to the great warrior who preserved her life. The great warrior will be given a hut of his own, and there he will sleep with Ilia-awi until the sun rises in the morning."

Richard's blood ran cold. At this time he could not afford the luxury of a liaison; he was devoting himself completely to the mission he had undertaken on behalf of the Stuarts and his country, and an affair with the Indian girl might well cause complications he could not predict. He had no way of knowing whether the offer was customary under the circumstances, or whether it would be followed by a demand that he marry the girl, which would be disastrous. Yet, in spite of all that his good sense told him, he knew he wanted Ilia-awi, who was making no secret of her willingness to give herself to him. He had to summon his willpower in order to shake his head.

Too late Richard realized he had committed a serious mistake. Roaring Wolf's expression of incredulous horror told him that he had erred, Ilia-awi was insulted, and the sachem was enraged. Well knowing that his future depended on the goodwill of the Mohegan, he blocked the girl's path when she would have flounced away.

"Hear me," he said. "Ilia-awi is the loveliest and most desirable of women."

Roaring Wolf translated hastily, and from the length of his statement, it was apparent that he was adding embellishing touches of his own.

"I did not know she was so attractive when I saved

her from the death embrace of the bear," Richard continued. "If I were to claim her body as a reward, I would denigrate the deed that I performed. I think too highly of her to sleep with her. I prefer to let my deed speak for itself. In this way it becomes a symbol of all that is good between us."

As Roaring Wolf translated, again adding his own words to the statement, Richard saw the sachem begin to thaw. His daughter was not being rejected, so his own honor remained intact.

Even more important, Ilia-awi accepted the explanation and was mollified by it. Her instinct had told her that this ruggedly handsome stranger, so unlike the warriors of the Mohegan, wanted her as much as she wanted him. But he was holding back because of his ideals, and there was nothing that could have flattered an Indian girl more.

Certain now that his approach was right, Richard bowed to Ilia-awi. "You will be present for all time in my thoughts and in my dreams," he said, knowing he was speaking the truth.

"The Great Spirit who guides and protects the Mohegan brought you to me in my hour of need," she replied, speaking softly. "He will not let us part, never to see each other again. I admire you all the more because you will not sleep with me now. That will await another time. The Great Spirit has not brought us together, only to separate us for all time. We will meet again in this world, of that I am very sure."

Richard continued to look at the girl as Roaring Wolf translated her words, and she gazed at him in return, her eyes steady, her bearing proud. Perhaps, he thought, primitive savages who were close to nature could foretell the future more readily and accurately than those who were too civilized for their own good. He knew, in ways that defied analysis, that she was speaking the truth. Their paths would cross again, and both would have cause to remember the death of the bear and its aftermath.

After spending three days on the trail that led to the southwest, Dempster Chaney estimated that he and Robbin had walked at least thirty miles. Had he been alone, he would have continued his journey, but he knew Robbin was tired, and the prospect of again trudging through forests and past occasional farms was too much for her.

He had not yet found the property that, he was convinced, he would recognize as his. The ten sovereigns that Richard Dunstable had given him were dwindling, and he realized that his dream of establishing a land claim and developing the property would need to be postponed. Robbin, who had led a sheltered life, deserved a roof over her head now, and it was wrong to wander on in search of an unattainable goal.

Dempster knew, too, that they had come far enough from Boston to escape both the Puritan influences and ways of life. The proprietor of the little country inn where they had spent the night was a bluff, hardy man, and the men of the neighborhood who had filled the taproom were hardworking farmers whose talk had indicated they were free from Puritan prejudices. Perhaps this was the area in which to settle and search for work.

So, as he paid the innkeeper for their lodging and food, Dempster asked casually, "Do you happen to know of anyone in these parts who could use the help of two able-bodied people, Master Greenleaf?"

The proprietor looked him up and down slowly, then inspected Robbin, too. "That depends upon what you can do," he replied.

"I was born on a farm in Devonshire and grew up there," Dempster replied, not adding that he had been trained as a gentleman and had planned to be a surgeon, not a laborer. "I daresay I know more about raising crops than most."

"And I'm not afraid to work, either," Robin added. "I can cook and sew, and I've spun cloth."

The innkeeper instinctively liked the forthright young couple and rubbed his chin reflectively. "Well, now, that does put a different light on the matter. I figured from your dress and manners that you were city folk—that you'd feel more at home in Boston than you would out here in the wilderness."

"May we never see Boston again!" Dempster exclaimed.

"Amen to that," Robbin said.

Greenleaf was lost in thought. "Everybody hereabouts knows that the Widow Browne sure needs help. Mrs. Hester Browne, who has a farm a couple of miles down the creek road. Her husband died two years ago, and she's had a hard struggle trying to farm her land herself."

"We'll go to see her," Dempster replied instantly.

"Hold on for a minute, young fellow," the innkeeper said. "Hester isn't the easiest person to get along with. She has the sharpest tongue in all of Massachusetts Bay, and she wants things done her way. You wouldn't find it easy living under her roof."

Robbin hesitated before she asked, "Is she of the Puritan faith, Master Greenleaf?"

"No more than anybody else in Taunton, young woman! All I said was that she's cantankerous, but she's in her right mind!"

"That's all right, then," Dempster said, and after thanking the innkeeper for his help and directions to the farm, they started out.

The village, which consisted of the inn, a general store, and a small cluster of houses, was soon left behind, and the couple started off on a narrow trail that led through deep woods. "This isn't very promising,"

Robbin said as she followed her husband. "The lady's farm must be terribly isolated."

Dempster shrugged. "We'll find out soon enough." He was becoming adept at avoiding fallen logs and other obstacles on the path.

Suddenly they emerged into the open, and directly ahead saw a large farm, the ground cleared of trees. The main house was two stories tall, of unpainted clapboard, and behind it stood a stable, a barn, a chicken coop, and a toolshed.

"There she is," Robbin said, indicating a gray-haired woman trying to handle a team of two large, gray workhorses who were pulling a plow through the ground. It was obvious to Dempster that she was fighting the horses rather than giving them their heads, and as a consequence, the plow sometimes was effective in turning over the earth and sometimes was not.

He cut across the open fields toward her, calling, "Mistress Browne?"

The woman halted her team, then wiped perspiration from her leathery, lined face. "Whoever you be, you're trespassing," she declared.

"I suggest you let your horses decide the path they'll take," he said. "They have an instinct for the line of least resistance, and you'll find it much easier to fill in the places they miss, later on. Like this." He moved toward the team, picked up the reins, plowed a straight furrow, then doubled back. As he had indicated, the horses were far more malleable.

Hester Browne watched him, her narrowed eyes bright. "You make it look easy, just like my Eddie did," she said grudgingly.

Dempster halted near her. "You have a large property here," he said. "Do you intend to plow up all of it?"

"All three hundred and twenty acres," Hester replied testily. "I've got to plant the entire property because I never know what crops will take and what crops won't."

"I see." He dropped to one knee, picked up a handful of plowed soil, and let it sift through his fingers. "Depending on the rainfall, which looks good judging by the trees, you'll do best here with wheat. And perhaps maize. I know very little about American corn, though. I presume you grow vegetables too, for your own use?"

"Naturally I do. Who be you, coming nosing around here, and how does it happen you know so much about my farm?"

"I only know what I see," Dempster replied gently, then introduced himself and his wife.

Hester Browne sniffed audibly.

"Green beans, cucumbers, and squash should do nicely here," Dempster said. "And depending on how much of your land you allow to lie fallow, you could raise sheep, too."

"My husband raised sheep, but I don't have the knack." The gray-haired woman stared at him. "You haven't answered my question!"

"Master Greenleaf, at the inn, said you could use some help. My wife and I are looking for work."

The young couple's clothes were travel-soiled but expensive, Mrs. Browne observed. "I can't afford the likes of you, though goodness knows I'm not too proud to admit that I can't earn the living that Eddie made here."

"We'll work for our room and board," Dempster said, "and we'll work out an arrangement to be paid a small share of the profits, too."

The widow laughed harshly. "There have been no profits since Eddie passed away."

"There will be." Dempster took his time looking out across the fields. The soil was rich, there were no

157

tree stumps, boulders, or other obstacles that he could see, and he knew of no reason why hard work shouldn't produce bumper crops.

"You show up out of the forest, as bold as you please, and you expect to be hired. Just like that. How do I know you're not a pair of rogues who will murder me in my sleep?"

"Do we look like rogues and murderers?" Robbin knew she should be civil, at the very least, but her indignation was too great.

"I'm none too friendly with folk of that ilk," Hester Browne replied, a hint of a smile appearing at the corners of her compressed mouth. "You and I will go to the house, where you'll tell me all about yourselves, young woman. Meantime your husband can finish what's been started here." Not waiting for a reply, she walked briskly toward the farmhouse. Robbin looked at her husband, shrugged, and followed. She had been given no choice.

Dempster removed his coat, folded it carefully and addressed the workhorses. "You two," he told them, "are going to earn your feed today!"

He plowed rapidly, the team responding to his confident handling, and in an hour he turned up much more soil than Mrs. Browne had managed in all her previous efforts. He had been aware of her peering out of the window at him from time to time, and he had given her enough of a sample. He unhitched the horses, giving them the opportunity to graze freely in the unplowed areas, and as he started toward the house, he saw the fence needed repair and that the barn door had been torn from its hinges. There was enough to be done to keep a man occupied here.

When he walked into the kitchen, where two partly consumed cups of tea rested on a table that needed to be scraped and sanded, he was startled to see Hester

Browne laughing heartily while Robbin stared at her indignantly.

"I told her the truth about us," Robbin explained, "and when I came to the part about Boston and what happened to us there, she started to laugh. She just won't stop."

"As the Puritans would say," Hester declared, stifling her laughter, "the Lord works in mysterious ways. You two deserved punishment for sleeping together before you were properly married. Oh, I understand the circumstances," she went on, giving Robbin no chance to interrupt, "but you could have been strong enough to resist temptation. You didn't, so you got what you deserved when the Boston constables threw you into prison for kissing in public!"

Dempster could see the point she was making, but nevertheless thought her sense of humor odd.

"I thought my Eddie and I were brave, coming out to the wilderness ten years ago and claiming this property," Hester said, "but at least we had our tools and our equipment and enough saved to buy whatever else we might need. You two came out this way armed only with your courage."

"It was necessity, not courage, that brought us out here, Mistress Browne," Robbin said firmly, dropping the cloth soaked in vinegar she had been using to clean a copper pan while they talked. "We had no choice."

"What will you do if I refuse to take you in?" Hester demanded.

"We'll search until we find someone who will," Dempster replied. "I can't believe that a man with my knowledge of how to operate a farm won't be able to find honest work."

"This isn't relevant," Robbin said as she peered into the parlor that adjoined the kitchen, "but you have a bench in there that badly needs a new cover."

159

"Don't I know it," Hester replied with a sigh. "But cloth is dear these days. Everything we can buy comes all the way from England."

"Do you have any flax?" Robbin wanted to know.

"The barn is half-filled with last year's crop. Everyone in the region had the same idea, and there was no market for all of it."

"In that case, I'll make you a new linen cover. I see you have a wheel." Robbin indicated a spinning wheel that stood in a kitchen corner.

"Aye, and no time to use it." Hester was silent for a moment, trying to make up her mind. "I suppose I have naught to lose by seeing how you'll do here. You're hired. For your room, board—and five percent of the profits."

"Make it ten percent," Dempster said quietly. "You said you've had none at all in the past couple of years, so you can see that ten percent of something is better than five percent of nothing."

"You have a bargain." Hester extended a bony hand. "But don't try to flummox or fool me, and don't—" She broke off as Dempster headed toward the door. "Where do you think you're going, young man?"

"There's plowing to be done," he said, "and with this spring weather, we need to be ready for planting." The door closed behind him.

She turned and saw Robbin energetically scrubbing the copper pan, so she muttered something about being behind in her mending as she headed for the stairs. It was true, she thought, that the Lord did His work in mysterious ways, and she felt ashamed of herself for being so flippant. She had been desperate, near the end of her rope when this young couple had appeared out of the blue, and if they lived up to their promise, she would never again doubt the Almighty's ability to work miracles.

160

VI

MOLLIE Williams was tired after the long journey to New Amsterdam from Providence Plantations, and after kicking off her shoes beneath the table at the Thorn and Thistle, she sat back gratefully, soaking in the atmosphere and enjoying the cold mug of ale that Angus MacNeill, the proprietor, had brought her.

"What I tell you is God's truth, Master MacNeill," she said. "The Puritans of Boston are as mad as those in England—nay, madder—and I fled from them as though Beelzebub hisself was hauling at me petticoats. Providence Plantations may become a fine town in time, and I've naught against it, but the birds made so much noise in the first hour of dawn, they had me wide awake. I'm a Londoner born and bred, I am, and I despaired of finding a civilized nook in this wild country until I saw New Amsterdam. Now then, I said to meself, here's a town for you, Mollie, me girl!"

Angus MacNeill grinned at her, revealing gaps where there used to be front teeth, then he absently smoothed his thinning, sandy hair. "Come to the windows with me, Mistress Williams. I feel as you do, and it's no accident that New Amsterdam is unique in all this land, even though we have a population far less than that of Boston."

Mollie searched frantically for her shoes, found them, and dutifully accompanied her host to the win-

161

dow. She was applying for a position here, so she was in no way able to refuse the invitation, much as she wanted to stay seated.

"Look yonder, to the right of the windmill, and what do you see?" he demanded.

"The fort, sir?"

"Yes, the little fort with the useless Dutch cannon that will blow up in the face of the man who has the nerve to fire them," he replied. "And over yonder, past Hudson's River?"

"It looks like chalk cliffs to me, Master MacNeill," she said dubiously.

"Ah, the Palisades, we call them. The beginning of a godforsaken wilderness that stretches all the way to the Pacific Ocean. Or so I'm told, though I don't intend to find out. And what do you see to the left of the fort? Long Island, another wilderness, save for the little town of Breukelen, where some who would farm want their own land so bad they're willing to risk their lives. And right here, surrounded by wilds, is New Amsterdam!" Beaming with pleasure, he led her back to the table.

Mollie followed, again disposing of her shoes, and took a swallow of her ale.

"New Amsterdam is like Holland, all right, but it's better," he said, beginning to laugh before he finished telling his little joke. "The Dutch, you see, are a minority here."

Mollie laughed dutifully.

"You think I jest." He began to enumerate on his thick, callused fingers. "The Dutch are reluctant to leave the prosperity in Holland to make the difficult ocean voyage. But we have Swedes from New Sweden who couldn't tolerate the wilds of the land. We have French Huguenots who were persecuted by Richelieu, then by Mazarin, damn his French soul. We have Jews who wanted a country where they could worship freely. We have West Indian planters who could not tolerate the hot climate, and we have a smattering of folk from Bohemia and Brandenburg, not to mention a boatload of settlers from the Kingdom of Naples."

Mollie was impressed, but tried not to show it. "That's most unusual, Master MacNeill."

"Aye, and it's what makes New Amsterdam the best and liveliest town in all of the New World. Do you know why, Mistress Williams? Because we have a philosophy here of live and let live. We accept a man for what he is, not for his religion or his nationality. We have British colonists who are fleeing the rigidity of the Puritans in England and in the New World, so that's why we laugh at the Puritans and thumb our noses at the Cavaliers!"

"Aren't the English who live in New Amsterdam loyal to the Stuarts?" Mollie was shocked.

"Why should we be? What did poor Charlie or his pa before him ever do for us? I built this inn with my own hands. I worked for years to save the money to be able to build it. I owe no debt to any man on earth, so I say to the Puritans and the Royalists, go on, chop off each other's heads. I'll have no pains in my neck as a result of their squabbling!"

Mollie nodded thoughtfully, and could see the man's point of view, which she wouldn't have understood before coming to America herself. The New World was physically removed from the Old World by thousands of miles, and the bitter disputes that had resulted in Britain's civil war were of little consequence to a people who now were trying to earn a living in a town controlled by the Dutch and surrounded by wilderness.

"I tell you all this for a reason, Mistress Williams," Angus MacNeill said soberly. "When I first planned this place, I thought I'd act as my own principal cook and barman. But I find I don't have the time. I've tried out three men for the job, one who couldn't cook and two who drank my best beer. You're a gift from Heaven, and I'd be a fool to let you get away. What wages do you want?"

Mollie shrugged. "I know nothing of what's paid here. At Whitehall I got all I wanted to eat, food to take home to me son, and three shillings per week."

"The Stuarts have a collection of marvelous gems, Mistress Williams, because they robbed the poor. You'll cook and tend the bar for me, and you'll get every other Sunday to yourself. I'll give you all your meals, wages of six shillings per week, and you'll keep the tips the patrons give you. You'll have your own snug quarters, too, with a fireplace of your own."

Mollie was overwhelmed. "You're most generous, Master MacNeill."

"Nay, I have need of you. Just remember what I told you about New Amsterdam. Don't encourage talk among the patrons about Cavaliers and Puritans. Keep in mind that New Netherland doesn't care what happens to England or the rest of the world, and you'll do fine."

"You can depend on it, sir. I'll weep for poor Charlie in me own snug quarters as I sit before me own hearth."

"When can you begin?"

"Now," she said. "Just tell me how many you expect to sup here tonight, and I'm off to the market."

"I've already bought all we'll need for tonight. You'll find the larders are filled. And Mistress Williams—the Thorn and Thistle isn't Whitehall, I hardly need tell you. We serve wholesome meals here, but I've been in the habit of buying what's cheapest at the market."

"I'll tell you a secret, Master MacNeill," Mollie replied. "The Stuart jewels didn't come only from the money they saved on the wages they paid me. Old

King Jamie went over the food bills hisself, and poor Charlie picked up the habit from him."

Angus MacNeill grinned at her. They had achieved a perfect understanding.

"There's just one more question to be settled," she said. "It concerns me son."

His cheerful smile faded rapidly. "That young Bart is a troublemaker."

"I beg to contradict you. He don't mean to cause a fuss. He has a hot temper and too big a mouth, but he's always surprised when there's trouble."

"Well," MacNeill said firmly, "I've heard him going on and on about King Charles, goading and poking and pushing until he can strike an argument. And I tell you plain, Mistress Williams, there's no room for the likes of that lad in my taproom. People come here to eat because they like the food and because the atmosphere is peaceful. The place would be in an uproar if I hired young Bart to wait on tables!"

Mollie hesitated. She didn't want to lose the post that had been offered to her, but she had to look out for her son's future, too. "What would you do if you was in me shoes, Master MacNeill?" she asked.

The proprietor of the Thorn and Thistle didn't want to lose the services of an experienced cook who could also attend to drink orders, so he relented. "There happens to be a place he might fit in. Does he know horses?"

"No more and no less than most," she said cautiously.

"Then he'll learn much about them. There's an opening in the stables for an ostler who will attend the guests' horses. I'll pay him two shillings per week, you can feed him his meals—which you'd do in any event—and he can sleep in the loft above the horses' stalls. That's the best I can offer him."

"On Bart's behalf, I accept with great pleasure," the relieved Mollie said quickly.

So the bargain was struck, and MacNeill took his new cook to the extensive kitchen, an outbuilding connected with the main portion of the Thorn and Thistle by a passageway. Mollie quickly asked questions as she familiarized herself with the hearth utensils, and contents of the larder, and MacNeill, equally brisk, replied succinctly.

"How much say will I have in working out a menu?" she wanted to know.

"Well, I urge you to check your plans for meals with me for a couple of weeks until you learn what our patrons like," he said. "Then you'll be on your own. With as many as a dozen guests spending the night, I'm too busy to bother. Your kitchen will be your own kingdom, Mistress Williams."

Nothing he could have said would have made Mollie happier. She threw some bones into a pot to make stock for soup, and as she busied herself, she began to hum under her breath.

"I haven't heard you sing for a long time, Ma." Bart had come in behind her.

Mollie turned to him with a frown. "Where have you been, lad?"

"If you must know," he replied defiantly, "a fine gentleman bought me two pints of ale, all for the pleasure of me company."

"What grand gentleman would seek the company of the likes of you?" she demanded.

Bart was short, but managed to look towering as he drew himself up haughtily. "His name is Laroche."

Had Richard Dunstable been present, he would have recognized the name as that of the principal Cavalier agent in the colonies, the man to whom he would report at the appropriate time. But Mollie remained blank. "And why did Master Laroche buy you two pints of ale, lad?"

"I was having a bit of a dispute with a pair of locals on the subject of King Charlie," he said proudly. "I lost me temper a mite when they said they couldn't care less what had befallen him. Master Laroche heard me light into them, and the ale followed, just like that. He says he wants to know you, too. He was impressed to no end when he heard you was on the staff at Charlie's palace."

"You'll keep your big mouth shut from now on," Mollie said. "I've arranged a job for you, courtesy of Master MacNeill—"

"He's sweet on you, Ma."

"Never you mind that, young man!" She told him in detail about the position she had obtained for him and the stipulations concerning Bart's behavior. "So you'll go to the stables right now. Report to the chief groom for work. And don't bother me again with your tales of grand gentlemen and pints of ale!"

Bart went off sulking, not bothering to thank her for intervening successfully on his behalf.

Mollie overcame her irritation with him by devoting herself totally to her work. She enjoyed cooking, and the new position was a challenge she intended to meet. It was true, as Bart had said, that Angus MacNeill was attracted to her. She was flattered and had to admit she was drawn to him, too. But he had hired her because of his need for the services she could perform at the Thorn and Thistle, not because of the potential of their personal relationship, so she would do her best to justify his faith in her.

The supper hour came, and as the dining room filled with guests the atmosphere in the kitchen became frenzied. Two waiters came in and out with orders, and Mollie was everywhere at once. She ladled soup, broiled steaks, put fresh fish on the fire, and

167

served portions of potatoes, vegetables, and salad greens with speed and expertise. The kitchen was her domain, and the waiters were brisk and businesslike in their dealings with her, recognizing her aura of command. Gradually the hubbub subsided, and as she sat down at last to eat her own supper, Angus Mac-Neill came into the kitchen, a broad smile lighting his square face.

"That was grand," he said, helping himself to a large portion of beef stew and sitting opposite her at the hardwood table. "I thought I was the only person alive who could keep the orders moving, but you're better at it than I am!"

Mollie thanked him with a smile and a nod. She well knew the praise was deserved, and having passed her first test with flying colors, she realized that she had made a secure place for herself.

"If you're too weary," Angus told her, "I'll take charge in the taproom tonight."

Mollie savored the taste of the fish she was eating before she replied. The flavor was delicate, unlike any fish she had ever prepared in London, and she wanted to commit the taste to memory. "I thank you most kindly for the offer, Master MacNeill," she said, "but —as you well know—the serving of drinks to them as wants relaxation before bedtime is child's play."

He remained solicitous. "Whenever you grow weary, then, close the taproom for the night."

She grinned and shook her head. "While there's an honest penny to be made, I'll earn it!"

He had been fortunate to find someone with her experience and capacity for hard work, he knew. "We'll go to the market together in the morning. I'll go with you until you come to know the butchers, fishmongers, and greengrocers." With Mollie relieving him of the chores that had tied him down, he would have the time to make the Thorn and Thistle the finest inn in New Amsterdam, and he would be in a position to construct the annex he had envisioned far sooner than anticipated.

When Mollie finished her meal, she went to the taproom, where she took up her place behind the long bar. Customers soon began to drift in, and she served them deftly, making small talk. Apparently the evening clientele included a number of locals, as well as travelers who had rented quarters at the Thorn and Thistle, and two of the former became involved in a loud argument while consuming their third mugs of strong ale.

Mollie promptly rapped a tumbler with a spoon, and everyone in the place looked at her. "I'll tolerate no blasphemy in my taproom," she announced, aware of the need to set a tone for the establishment if she hoped to maintain order. "And you'll take yourselves elsewhere if you're having a dispute."

One of the men who had been quarreling, a brawny fisherman, glowered at her. "Who are you to tell me how loud I can talk and what I'm to say?"

Mollie's expression became cold. "I happen to be mistress of this here room," she said. "I don't tolerate cursing, or those disturbing others who have paid for a pint and want to drink it in peace. If you can't abide by me rules, you will be asked to leave."

The fisherman hauled himself to his feet. "Who will run me out of here?" he demanded. "You?"

Mollie promptly picked up a bar knife and pointed it at the man, using it to underscore her authority. "I could call the constables and have you locked up for creating a nuisance, but that won't be needful. Mind your manners, and you'll be welcome here. Create a fuss, and I'll be obliged to run you off the property meself!" She emerged from behind the bar, the knife still pointed accusingly at the disturber of the peace.

To her surprise, the other half-dozen patrons applauded, none more vehemently than a dark, well-dressed man of indeterminate age who sat quietly at a corner table by himself. The fisherman flushed. This determined woman would cause him a great deal of trouble before he could subdue her, and he knew that if he tried, the law would be on her side.

"Sit you down!" she commanded.

The man sat.

Mollie went to him and picked up his mug. "You shall have some free ale, courtesy of the management, in return for behaving like a gentleman." She bustled back to the bar and refilled his mug.

The fisherman looked at her sheepishly as she placed it in front of him. "I—I didn't mean to cause a disturbance, ma'am," he said. "And I thank you for the ale."

Her smile indicated that she forgave him, while at the same time warning him not to forget his place again. She had not only won the encounter, but she knew the word of her victory would spread through the town, and that, consequently, she would have fewer problems in the future.

The dark, well-dressed man moved from his table to the bar and ordered a glass of sweet sack. "You handled that ruffian well," he said. "Forgive my curiosity, but would you have used that knife to drive him out?"

Mollie considered the question. "Aye," she replied laconically.

"You're an unusual woman, Mistress Williams," he observed.

Mollie peered at him sharply. His shrewd eyes were studying her, but she felt certain she had never set eyes on him until he had appeared in the taproom a quarter of an hour earlier. "You know me name," she said.

"I happen to know more than that," he replied. "I

170

know where you worked in London—and why you left to come to the New World."

She felt uncomfortable. "I'm an ordinary woman," she said. "Why should the likes of me be of interest to a grand gentleman?"

"Because," he said, speaking so softly she had to strain in order to hear him, "we share the same sentiments." He went through the motions of drinking a toast to the king-across-the-water, a gesture she hadn't seen since her voyage across the Atlantic. Mollie continued to stare at him as she awaited a fuller explanation.

"I had the good fortune to engage your son in conversation," he said. "He made no secret of his sentiments, and he told me of your great good fortune. We serve the cause in different ways, but you enjoyed the privilege of preparing the very meals that His Majesty ate. What satisfaction you must have felt!"

He actually made her work in the Whitehall kitchen sound far more important and rewarding than it had been. She had held the position because of the need to earn a living for her son and herself, and her loyalty to the Crown had nothing to do with her employment. In fact, she had disapproved of much that she had seen of King Charles and his way of life.

The man knew he was failing in his attempt to impress her. "My name is Laroche," he said.

As Mollie nodded, she knew she disliked Master Laroche. Something in his manner set her teeth on edge, but he was a patron of the Thorn and Thistle, and he had said and done nothing untoward, so it was her place to treat him with civility.

"I assume that you'd be willing to work for the restoration of the Stuarts to the throne. I know you'd be delighted to return to your former place of employment."

He was assuming far too much. "For the privilege

171

of serving Charlie," she said tartly, "I worked me fingers to the bone and was paid a pittance. You can have the privilege, Master Laroche. This is me first day here, but I tell you plain, I prefer an honest day's wages for an honest day's work."

"No one can fault you for that, Mistress Williams." He paid for his glass of sack, then made a point of leaving a half-crown on the bar.

"Don't forget your change, Master Laroche," she reminded him.

His smile was cheerless. "That's for you, Mistress Williams." Mollie well knew that she didn't deserve that large a tip, and even as she thanked him, she felt suspicious of him. In her experience, those who seemingly gave something for nothing had ulterior motives.

"What do you think of the French?" he asked suddenly.

The unexpected question bewildered her. "They've been the enemies of England as far back as anybody can remember. I suppose we should be thankful to them for giving young Charlie a roof over his head, and not go looking gift horses in the mouth. But I don't rightly trust the French, and I say no good will come out of this friendship they're showing the queen and her young son."

Her attitude did not surprise Laroche. The hatred of the English lower classes toward the nation that lay on the far side of the English Channel was deep-rooted. "I believe you're mistaken, but we'll let that pass," he said. "Mistress Williams, you're in a position to do the cause of the Stuarts much good."

"Am I now? A simple body like me?" She put her hands on her hips and challenged him, no longer hiding her suspicions. "How would I do that?"

"The Thorn and Thistle is the best inn in New Amsterdam," Laroche replied calmly. "Men of substance from England and from other colonies are guests here.

172

And as you surely know, liquor loosens men's tongues. You'll hear a good many conversations not intended for your ears in your new position here."

"If I hear anything that's none of me affair," Mollie replied indignantly, "you can count on it that it will pass through me mind like a sieve. I'm hired to tend bar here, not to gossip about things that are none of me concern!"

"You may pick up tidbits that could be valuable to the cause of young King Charles. It's your duty to repeat them to those who serve him!" His manner became stern.

"I—I didn't think of it that way." She felt less sure of herself.

"I'll be grateful for anything of importance that you can pass along to me—sufficiently grateful to reward you accordingly." He picked up the half-crown that he had left on the bar, then spun it on the polished surface.

Somehow, it didn't seem right to Mollie to be taking pay for the performance of what Laroche had termed a patriotic duty.

The coin clattered as it fell, and Laroche pushed it toward her. "We need to know our friends in the New World," he said. "And our enemies. It will take a great concentration of effort on the part of many good, devoted people to bring Charles the Second to the throne of his father and grandfather."

Her confusion growing, Mollie could only nod.

"You're not being disloyal to MacNeill by repeating anything of interest you may hear," he assured her. "And keeping your ears open, staying alert, will not interfere with the duties for which MacNeill is paying you. On the other hand, it isn't everyone who has your opportunity to serve the monarch—and to be handsomely paid in the bargain."

She knew Laroche was applying pressure, but she didn't know what to reply.

"I'll drop in from time to time, and we can have a little chat that will be mutually beneficial." He bowed, smiled faintly, and left the taproom quickly, not looking at any of the patrons.

Mollie was flattered by the thought that she had been enlisted, even involuntarily, as a spy for the Crown. All the same, she trusted her instincts, and she knew she neither liked nor trusted the smooth-talking Laroche.

New Haven was the most attractive and well-established town in the American colonies that Richard had as yet visited. The homes were substantial, the port area was busy, and although there was a Green similar to the Boston Common, the inhabitants of the affluent town preferred to keep their livestock at home and use the Green as a public park.

Less than an hour after Richard and Roaring Wolf arrived in New Haven, they were dining at a licensed tavern facing the Green. As they sat at their table, they were approached by a plump, smiling man of middle years. "I take it you're strangers here," he said, and the men exchanged introductions and background information. Richard soon learned that Adam Burrows owned a thriving fleet of merchant ships engaged in the encouraged intercolonial coastal trade, and that as the head of the colony's militia, he preferred to be addressed as Colonel.

"I migrated here from Lincolnshire a good many years ago," he said. "I wonder, do you by chance know Sir William Dunstable?"

"He was my father," Richard said.

"I knew him well, and we were good friends," Colonel Burrows replied. "I gather he's no longer alive?"

Richard nodded.

"In that event, you're Sir Richard! I insist that you and your friend stay at my home as my guests!"

Refusing to listen to Richard's polite protests, he supervised their move to his impressive waterfront house of red brick.

Roaring Wolf was relieved when he saw a large yard behind the house. "I will sleep there, in the open," he said. "The houses of white men are like boxes, and I feel shut up inside them."

Familiar with the ways of Indians, Colonel Burrows calmly agreed. Then he led Richard to his library for a chat, while Roaring Wolf took Prince Henry to the stable.

"You have a remarkable collection of books here, Colonel," Richard observed.

"I was fortunate, Sir Richard. When I first came to America, not too many people were settling in New Haven, so I took advantage of a half-empty ship to bring my entire library with me. What brings you to the New World?"

Richard became cautious. "If you knew my father, you must have been aware of the hereditary Crown post he held."

"Of course. As King's Forester. Ah, I see." Colonel Burrows folded his hands across his paunch. "I can guess the rest. The Parliamentarians abolished the position, as they have so many royal sinecures. And you're searching for a place to settle."

"Something like that." It was easiest not to admit too much.

"I hope you'll look long and hard at New Haven. Our sea trade doesn't equal that of either Boston or New Amsterdam, but we do a lively business nonetheless, exporting corn, beaver skins, and livestock. And our people are far friendlier."

"Then the Puritan influence isn't strong here?"

"It is a way of life for the older generation, Sir Rich-

175

ard. Our children, people your age, are devising their own codes of conduct and beliefs. We're all too busy, young and old alike, building our own trade and buying land from the Indians to let those generational differences disrupt peace and cooperation in our homes. Recently we had a request from Cromwell, asking us to pledge our allegiance to Parliament. So Tom Clayton, our leading merchant, and I signed the papers he sent us and shipped them right back to London. I doubt if Tom's son would have signed such a pledge. He's not so involved with the politics of England as is his father." He chuckled, then winked.

Richard was startled when an exceptionally attractive young woman opened the door and swept in. She was tall and blue-eyed, with long, blonde hair streaming down her back, and her gown of pale silk made no secret of her lithe figure. "I should have guessed you'd be cooped up here, talking business as uusal, Papa," she said. "Didn't you smell and feel spring in the air today? If I were you, I'd leap at the opportunity to spend the whole day on the waterfront docks. Anything to stay out-of-doors!"

"My daughter, Eliza," Colonel Burrows said proudly. "Sir Richard Dunstable."

As Richard bowed he could feel the girl's appraising glance, and he knew she was attracted to him, just as he was drawn to her.

Eliza Burrows would have attracted attention anywhere, in any country. Her hair, to be sure, was an unusual shade, and her eyes were an intense blue that was startling. Her figure, at least at first glance, appeared to be virtually flawless. She had a long neck, naturally square shoulders, a high firm bosom, a tiny waist, round but firm hips and long thighs. But these were merely the externals; what caused her to be striking was an intangible quality: she seemed to give

176

off an air, an electric current, an aura—something that called attention to her.

She had lived with her beauty sufficiently long that she did not rely on it and seemed to take it for granted. Rather, she depended on the vibrant inner warmth that exuded from her, that surrounded her and seemed almost to explode, so intense was it.

Richard had never encountered anyone quite like her. He was willing to acknowledge her beauty, but it was the extra dimension that utterly fascinated him from the moment he first set eyes upon her. He had no idea what this quality might be, or how it was affecting him; all he knew was that he found Eliza utterly captivating.

"Don't tell me you're content to sit behind closed windows on a glorious spring day, Sir Richard," she said. "That must be your horse I saw in the stable just now. A magnificent brute! If I were his master, nothing would prevent me from going out for a canter in the hills."

"As I was telling you, Sir Richard," the colonel said, "my daughter has her own ideas of how people should and shouldn't behave."

"I approve of Papa's regiment because they go on long marches to keep the frontier pacified," Eliza said with a laugh. "Otherwise, he leads too sedentary a life, and as you can see for yourself, he's toting some extra weight."

"I know the ways of this wench," Adam Burrows said, "having brought her up alone since early childhood, after my dear wife's death. I can tell you right now that she's planned on taking you for a ride down one of her favorite trails, and somewhere along the way she'll offer to change horses with you. She has it in her mind to ride your stallion, Sir Richard."

"Papa does have an uncanny ability to read my

mind on occasion," she admitted cheerfully. "Will you ride with me, sir?"

Richard had little choice, so he bowed his assent. Eliza went off to change, reappearing shortly in a riding dress, gloves, and boots. She led Richard to the stable, where she saddled a gelding, and then she walked to Prince Henry, patted him, and offered him some sugar.

The great stallion looked at her for a long moment, then took the sugar from her hand, and Richard had to admire his horse's instinct. Prince Henry seldom lost his dignity in the presence of strangers, but Eliza Burrows had made him an easy conquest.

The girl led the way inland on a trail through the forest, and Richard had to admit she was an expert horsewoman. She kept her seat well, and the gelding was under control at all times.

At last she turned. "There's an open meadow ahead, a perfect area for a race, if you're game."

Richard smiled and shook his head. "I'd hate to take unfair advantage of you," he said, "but your horse simply isn't a match for mine." He was too polite to add that Eliza wasn't in his class as a rider, either.

She grinned at him, a light dancing mischievously in her blue eyes. "You could equalize the odds by changing horses with me," she said, gathering her long hair into a ribbon, obviously preparing for an unencumbered ride.

Her father had been right, divining her intent from the outset. "It's all right with me," Richard replied, "but my mount usually has his own ideas, and I'm not so certain he'll allow you to ride him."

"We'll soon find out," she replied, and instantly dismounted.

He jumped to the ground too, and patted Prince Henry. "Boy," he said, "this young lady has it in her

178

mind to ride you. She means well, and she admires you, so don't mistreat her. What do you say?" The stallion pawed the ground and returned his master's gaze.

Eliza Burrows came up to the beast and murmured something that Richard could not hear. Then, without hesitation, she hoisted herself into the saddle. Prince Henry was as surprised as his master, and reacted instantly by bucking and kicking violently. The girl clung to her seat, even though the horse was plunging, then rearing back, running a few paces, and halting abruptly. Eliza had no intention of being thrown. The color was high in her face, her lips were compressed, and the light in her eyes showed that she was as determined as the stallion.

Richard was afraid she would be hurt if she were thrown, but he knew better than to interfere. The girl had forced herself on Prince Henry, and the battle was between them. If the stallion had persisted, he would have won the engagement, but he neighed loudly, then stood still. Obviously he had decided that the stubborn young woman was worthy of riding him.

Richard was surprised. "He likes you," he said.

She had won the first round against heavy odds, and it would have been natural for her to gloat. Instead she leaned forward, stroked the mount's neck, and murmured, "Good lad."

She had a real understanding of horses, Richard thought as he mounted the gelding.

"We'll start here," she said as they rode into the open. "In order to make it a fair race, I suggest we go to the line of elms over yonder—about two hundred and fifty yards—and then double-back to the starting line. Is that agreeable?"

"Very," Richard replied. "But I suggest you allow me to signal the start. My stallion won't cut loose for you unless I give him the word."

"Oh, no," Eliza said quickly. "That would remove

all the sport from the race. I'll count to three, slowly, and then each of us will be responsible for him—or herself—and his or her horse."

"Fair enough." He was sure Prince Henry would refuse to budge unless he gave the order, but the headstrong young woman would have to learn all that for herself.

"Ready?" she called. "One—two—three!"

As Richard spurred forward, shooting past her, he could see her whispering to Prince Henry. It was unfair to humiliate her, so he held the gelding in check. Suddenly his own mount roared past him. Prince Henry had reached an understanding with Eliza Burrows and was out to win the race.

A strange sensation of jealousy welled up within Richard. He alone had trained his horse, and no one else had ever ridden the great beast. Very well then, he would be forced to teach the wench and Prince Henry a lesson! The gelding responded to his touch and gradually regained the lost ground.

He drew even as they approached the line of huge elm trees, and Richard caught a glimpse of Eliza, her face flushed with exertion and pleasure, her blonde hair streaming behind her. It was apparent that she was relishing every moment of the experience.

Unfamiliar with the gelding's ways, Richard nevertheless managed to maneuver the steed into a sharp turn, and when Eliza had difficulty in turning Prince Henry, he gained about two lengths. For all practical purposes, that ended the race. He gave the gelding his head, and the animal ran freely, gaining yet another half-length. Richard could hear Prince Henry thundering behind him, and knew the mistake that Eliza was making. There would be ample time to tell her when they were done. He reached the finish line, then gently slowed the winning gelding to a walk.

Prince Henry was outraged at having been defeated,

and angrily tried again to throw his rider, bucking and plunging, halting for an instant, then rearing high into the air, his front hooves flailing wildly. Richard maneuvered the gelding close enough to seize the reins from the struggling girl. "Behave yourself this instant, sir!" he told Prince Henry. Responding to his master's command, the great beast became quiet and stood still.

"He's not accustomed to losing," Richard said, his tone apologetic.

"What did I do wrong?" Eliza asked quietly. "I could feel his power, but he didn't go all out for me."

"You should have given him his head, and he would have done the rest."

"I see. I'll know better next time—if there is a next time—and he won't be compelled to lose his temper with me. I'm sorry, lad," she told Prince Henry. "I should have realized that a horse of your intelligence would have known what needed to be done."

"Ride him back to your father's house, if you like," Richard told her. "He's feeling ashamed of himself, and he'll be convinced you've abandoned him if we change mounts now."

"Thank you, I shall continue to ride him with great pleasure. I'd give my soul to own a horse like this."

"He's not for sale."

"I should think not!" She sounded shocked. "Have you had him long?"

"I claimed him four years ago, the day he was born. His mother had been my favorite mare, and I knew the moment I saw him that there was no other horse like him."

"I knew it too, when I saw him in our stable. I'm sorry I tricked you, but I couldn't help it."

"Your father warned me what to expect. You ride well. I've never known a woman who has your understanding of horses."

181

"That's what comes of being reared by a father who had always wanted a son."

Richard's curiosity was aroused as they rode side by side through the deep woods on the trail back to New Haven. "Are you also familiar with firearms?"

Eliza laughed. "It's plain you're a stranger to the New World," she said. "For our own protection, parents teach their children to handle firearms as soon as they can lift a musket and handle the recoil. My father has made some good treaties with the Indians who live hereabouts, and they've learned to respect our militia regiment in recent years. But—until about two years ago, if that long—it wasn't safe in these woods. You never knew when you might be attacked. In fact, it was right about here, three years ago, that Ezekiel and I had the devil's own time fighting our way clear of an ambush."

What astonished him about her recital was her matter-of-fact tone. She seemed to take Indian ambushes for granted. "Who is Ezekiel?"

"Ezekiel Clayton. The son of my father's oldest friend and business associate. We grew up together. I'm sure the Claytons will be coming to supper tonight. Papa will want them to meet you."

Richard silently marveled at her lack of fear in the wilderness. The musket she carried as a matter of course was familiar to her, she had proved her ability to handle any horse, and the forest held no terrors for her. Yet she was feminine in every way, conscious of her beauty and willing to use it in order to achieve her ends, even the simple goal of riding Prince Henry.

"I enjoyed our outing very much," Richard told her as they dismounted, led the horses into the stable, and removed the saddles.

"I'm grateful to you for tolerating a spoiled brat's whims," she replied. "But this is a day I won't soon forget, I promise you that." Eliza's smile was angelic.

Later, changing for supper in his guest bedchamber in the Burrowses' spacious house, Richard had to warn himself to be careful. This girl was as lovely as Mimi Shepherd, and her self-reliance was an added magnet that made her even more attractive to him. He thought of Dorothea and wondered how she would fare in the New World. But such speculation was nonsensical, so he put her out of his mind.

When he came downstairs he found the Clayton family had already arrived. Thomas Clayton was a tall, spare man who had the self-assurance of someone who had fought for his place in the world and won it fairly. His wife, Mary, exuded charm and obviously had been a great beauty in her younger days. She, too, seemed sure of herself. Their son, Ezekiel, was a few years younger than Richard, with his father's dignity and his mother's bubbling nature.

Richard was totally unprepared for his introduction to the younger Clayton. "This," Colonel Burrows said, "is Eliza's betrothed."

So she was engaged to be married to the man! Surely she could have referred to him as her betrothed when she had mentioned being caught with him in an Indian ambush. Disappointed that her hand was promised, Richard was nevertheless relieved that he had not been overbold in displaying his own interest in her.

Ezekiel wore his clothes with an air and seemed very much in command of himself. He had good cause for his self-assurance; he was tall, his regular features gave him a handsome appearance, and he was athletic in build. Obviously he could give a good account of himself in hand-to-hand combat. Obviously, too, he spent a great deal of time out-of-doors because he was heavily tanned or windburned, which set off his dark hair and eyes to good advantage. Certainly he knew that he was attractive to the opposite sex.

Eliza chose that moment to make her appearance in an off-the-shoulder gown of ivory that would have been far more appropriate at a Whitehall assembly than in a New Haven house set on the fringe of the wilderness.

"Aha!" Ezekiel declared, bowing over her hand with mock gravity. "Sir Richard, I must warn you for your own good to beware of this charmer. It's apparent from the way she is dressed tonight that she intends to bedazzle you."

"She is succeeding," Richard admitted.

"Ezekiel," Eliza said severely, "I've heard your father tell you a hundred times that you talk too much. You should take to heart the advice he gives you."

"Well, everyone knows you're a flirtatious jade who collects admirers, the way that Sir Richard's warrior friend who is sleeping out in the yard collects scalps," Ezekiel replied.

She made a face, sticking her tongue out at him, before she escaped to the kitchen to check on the preparations for supper.

Richard was puzzled by the relationship. Eliza and Ezekiel obviously knew each other well and enjoyed their mutual teasing, but they did not behave like a betrothed couple. He had no chance to dwell on the matter, however, as Colonel Burrows handed him a glass of what appeared to be dry sack.

"Would you care to propose a toast, Tom?" the host asked.

"I drink to next year!" the elder Clayton said promptly, and raised his glass.

Richard took a small sip from his tumbler and almost choked on it: he had been served a fiery rum. Yet even Mary Clayton sipped with aplomb and seemed able to handle the potent drink. "May I ask the significance of your toast?" Richard asked as soon as he composed himself.

The others smiled, and Mary explained. "We live very near to the wilderness," she said, "and close to the forces of nature. Our towns, even a settled place like New Haven, are subject to Indian raids. We're at the mercy of the weather, and if it's bad, people starve because our lives depend on our crops. What we mean when we drink to next year is that we hope we'll all be alive, well, and prosperous in another year."

"That's true," Eliza said, coming into the quietly furnished parlor and accepting a small tumbler of rum from her father. "Richard asked me this afternoon whether I could handle firearms, and he seemed surprised when I told him I've used them all my life."

"In England, Sir Richard," Tom Clayton declared, "you take the law for granted, and the enforcement of it is almost automatic. That's why the people of the British Isles were so surprised by the beheading of King Charles."

"Here, we live with violence. We expect it in every aspect of our lives." Colonel Burrows motioned the guests to the dining room. Richard was surprised when Eliza took his arm, rather than her betrothed's, and led him to the table, where she seated him on her right.

"Every time I send one of my little tubs out to sea," Colonel Burrows continued, "I wonder if it will return safely. You need to know the fury of a West Indian hurricane to understand what I mean. It's enough for me to say that the officers and seamen on every ship in my fleet take their lives in their hands every time they go to sea."

A serving maid brought in a large tureen of soup, which Eliza ladled into bowls at the table. It was a chowder of whole clams, onions, and potatoes in a clear broth.

"They ruin this dish in Boston by cooking it in

cream," Mary said. "A good chowder should contain the natural clam juice, with nothing added."

Richard thought the chowder was delicious.

"This soup is a good example of what we're talking about," the elder Clayton said. "There must be twenty towns along the shore of New England now, and every one has a different recipe for this dish. What matters is that the clams are here for the taking. We've followed the example of the Indians, and we use what nature provides us."

"Well, I've eaten some unusual dishes since I've come to the New World," Richard said. "But I've discovered that my palate has adjusted rapidly to them."

The colonials nodded. "Bison meat is an acquired taste," Mary Clayton said, "but when you have a choice between bison or no meat at all, you quickly learn to like the taste."

"We live on bison, turkey, moose, venison, and fish," Eliza added. "Ezekiel and I have grown up here, and we scarcely know the taste of beef."

Ezekiel nodded, grinning at his parents and at Colonel Burrows. "On the rare occasions when beef is served, we try to show our appreciation of the luxury, but the truth of the matter is that we don't much care for the taste. Our cows are too valuable as milk producers to be slaughtered for their meat."

Richard drank in the information and began to understand the New World way of life for the first time. The main course was bison steak that had been marinated for two days in dry sack, oil, and herbs to make it less tough, and he had to admit he enjoyed the taste.

"Our principal concern," Colonel Burrows told him, "is our security. I estimate there are fifty thousand to one hundred thousand colonists on the seaboard, from New Somersetshire being claimed by Massachusetts Bay to the territory south of Virginia that has no name as yet. We cling to the Atlantic coast, where we've established a toehold, and we either trade with the Indians when we're fortunate or fight them when we must. I've heard many estimates of their numbers, but no one really knows how many are out there in the forests. All I know for certain is that we're obliged to live side by side with them in peace —or perish."

"How do you manage to maintain peaceful relations with them?" Richard wanted to know.

"They may be savages, but they understand justice," the colonel replied. "Here in New Haven we fine any man who tries to cheat or cozen them. The colony makes it a practice to pay for any land we acquire, and we give value received for furs and corn and other products we obtain from the Indians."

"Would that the Indians were our only worry," the elder Clayton said. "The Old World transfers its problems to the New. France and Spain understood the value of North America long before the British became aware of the potentials here, and both nations have thriving colonies to the north, the west, and the south of us. Naturally, they covet our growing civilization here. And frankly, it makes me nervous to see the hospitality that France is showing the Cavaliers. Cardinal Mazarin exacts what he deems to be appropriate reciprocity when he does a favor or extends a hand in friendship."

"The French, Dutch, and Spanish don't try to take your territory by force?" Richard asked.

Colonel Burrows shook his head. "No, we'd fight to the last man if they invaded us. But they use other, more subtle means. The French and Spanish offer bribes to our Indian neighbors to stir up trouble. They know the New Model Navy is preoccupied and going through changes at home, so they send privateers—unofficial ships over which they supposedly have no control—to prey on our shipping and destroy our lifelines to the islands of the West Indies and England itself. Every last one of my trading brigs is heavily armed, and my men know how to use their cannon."

Richard had been unaware of the colonists' struggle for the right to make their homes in the New World.

"Another great concern of ours is how to best utilize the services of the immigrants who are pouring into the colonies," the elder Clayton declared. "It was difficult for a number of years because we had a shortage of trained craftsmen and unskilled laborers. Inevitably, this forced wages up beyond accustomed levels in England. The court here in New Haven decreed specific wage and profit controls to prevent economic exploitation. We're getting more than our fair share of townsmen these days, but unfortunately they know nothing about carving homesteads for themselves out of the wilderness and then farming for a living. It's our responsibility to help them settle here, and perhaps to readjust our economic guidelines."

"Yes, the problems are increasing," Colonel Burrows agreed. "When a stonemason, shoemaker, bricklayer, carpenter, or tailor comes to the colonies, he's looking forward to the practice of the one trade he knows. It's a necessity to help him find his place in our society."

"That's why," Eliza said bluntly, "we don't give a hang for England's problems. We have enough of our own."

Ezekiel nodded emphatically. "Precisely so! The quarrels of the Puritans and the Cavaliers mean nothing to me. All I know is that we're required to pay duties to the mother country, regardless of whether a king sits on the throne or Parliament is the supreme authority in the land. We're worried about our own survival, and we'd like something in return for our money: troops to help us hold off the Indians—or arms, at the very least. We need protection of our merchant fleets."

"You can't expect automatic loyalty," Eliza said firmly. "England takes our furs, lumber, and other products, and charges us an export duty for the privilege. In addition, we pay an import tax on every skillet, every bolt of cloth we buy from England."

"Those of us who were born and bred in England have ties to her, naturally," Mary Clayton explained. "But the younger generation—your generation, Sir Richard—has grown up in the colonies. They take the rights of native-born Englishmen for granted, and they're far more outspoken than anyone would dare to be in the Old World in these trying times."

"I hadn't thought of it that way, but what you say is true, Aunt Mary," Eliza said. "I'm loyal to New Haven colony. I can also sympathize with the problems of Connecticut or Rhode Island or New Netherland because they're similar to our own, so I can understand them. I know that eventually all of us must stand together or fall separately. If I were a man I'd march to defend our neighbors because their fall would threaten our own survival. But I wouldn't lift a finger to put Charles the Second on the throne of England any more than I'd take up arms on behalf of the Puritans." The others obviously agreed with her, and the whole group looked at Richard, awaiting his reaction.

"I don't feel as you do because my background is different," he said. "I despise the Roundheads because they drove me from my country and confiscated my property, when the only crime I committed was that of being steadfast in my loyalty to the Crown." He looked at Eliza, then at Ezekiel. "But if I had grown to manhood here, I'm sure I'd resent having to pay a tax on every barrel of salt fish I sent back to England."

Eliza rewarded him with a dazzling smile. "You

189

don't yet know it," she said, "but you're already becoming a colonial. We're a new breed."

What she said was valid. A new breed was being formed in the wilderness of North America, where men breathed the clean, fresh air of personal freedom, and an individual was judged by his accomplishments, not by his family's standing.

VII

R ICHARD repeatedly extended his stay in New Haven. The gracious hospitality of Adam Burrows was one reason, and he felt that he was learning more about the colonies here each day than he had gleaned in all of the time he had so far spent in North America. He was forced to admit, too, that he was reluctant to part company with Eliza Burrows, even though she was betrothed.

To his consternation, Eliza flirted with him openly, frequently in the presence of Ezekiel Clayton, who seemed either not to know or care what she was doing. As an honorable man, Richard could not respond, but he knew he was strongly attracted to the girl. On several occasions, he made up his mind to go on to New Amsterdam, only to change his mind at the last minute.

Somehow, he reflected, he had to find the strength to resist the temptation to form a more intimate relationship with Eliza. His protracted stay in New Haven was helping him to understand the minds and hearts of

British colonials, and he could perform no greater service for the cause he represented than to portray conditions as he found them to the Earl of Newcastle and the other members of the Cavalier high command.

He suspected that Eliza was amusing herself at his expense, and one day, when her father was called to a conference of the New England Federation, he became sure of it. It would have been difficult enough for him to dine with her alone at noon, but she invited Ezekiel Clayton to join them, then seemed to go out of her way to create an awkward situation by devoting most of her attention to Richard.

Eliza lowered her voice and spoke huskily, with a personal immediacy whenever she addressed Richard, and she spoke to him almost exclusively. Her eyes widened whenever she smiled up at him, her lashes fluttered deliciously, and she seemed unable to illustrate her remarks without constantly touching his sleeve. She was aware of all the tricks of a professional flirt and obviously relished using them.

Ezekiel became aware of the young Englishman's discomfort, and said, "Behave yourself, Eliza!"

She sobered at once and stared down at her plate, but the corners of her mouth twitched suspiciously.

"The girl is a vixen, and I apologize for her, Richard," Ezekiel said. "Remember, Eliza, that Richard doesn't understand."

She nodded, then turned back to the guest. "Forgive me for teasing you. Ezekiel and I have been wondering if we might confide in you."

"Of course," Richard muttered, bewildered by the seemingly complex situation.

"You tell him, then," Eliza said to Ezekiel.

"As best I'm able. Our fathers have been close friends and business partners ever since they helped found New Haven. Eliza and I grew up together."

"You might say we had a sibling relationship," the

girl interjected. "I can't remember a time when Eze-kiel wasn't present in my life. We fought incessantly when we were younger."

"We did, indeed," Ezekiel confirmed, then laughed wryly. "Until I discovered that she wouldn't fight fairly. She'd kick, scratch, and bite, and if I became so exasperated that I hit her, she'd tattle to my parents and my backside would be tanned."

Eliza looked demurely innocent, but Richard knew that Ezekiel was telling him the truth.

"When we grew older," Ezekiel continued, "our fa-thers took it for granted that we'd be married. So did we, I guess."

"Ezekiel never formally proposed, and I never for-mally accepted," Eliza said. "We drifted into an en-gagement two years ago."

"And since that time we've been finding reasons—excuses, really—to postpone the wedding. I'd feel as if I were marrying my own sister."

"It's an impossible situation," Eliza declared. "We haven't wanted to hurt our fathers by telling them the truth, but they've been nagging at us lately to be married this spring, so we may be forced to tell them we want to go our separate ways."

"There you have it," Ezekiel said. "At the risk of embarrassing Eliza, I knew she was attracted to you from the day you came to New Haven. Now you know why she has behaved as she has toward you."

"I was trying to convey to my father—in a none-too-subtle fashion—that Ezekiel isn't the only man on earth for me. Quite the contrary. But you've been such a gentleman that you've refused to take the bait."

It annoyed Richard to discover that a baldly delib-erate attempt had been made to use him, but he couldn't help laughing. "If I had given in to my natu-ral inclinations, Colonel Burrows would have accused me of taking advantage of his hospitality and he'd have been justified to ask me to leave this house!"

"We wouldn't have allowed it to go that far," Eliza assured him.

"It strikes me," he said, "that you two have no choice. Go to Colonel Burrows and Master Clayton and tell them the truth."

Eliza and Ezekiel exchanged a long, despairing look. "He doesn't understand," the girl said. "Richard, we've tried to talk to them, but they won't listen. They've been looking forward to our marriage for so long that it's a fact to them. They're wonderful fathers, but they're headstrong men who believe only what they want to believe."

Ezekiel nodded in corroboration. "For once, Eliza isn't exaggerating," he said. "When I've tried to make my father see reason, he cuts me off by saying I simply don't know my own mind."

"There seems to be nothing we can do, short of refusing to go through with a ceremony," Eliza added.

"Surely there must be some way you can convince them," Richard said.

"Well," the girl replied, "I think Aunt Mary knows how we feel."

"We've gone to her, separately and together," Ezekiel went on. "She's influenced by my father, so she won't take us seriously, either."

"In time I could convince her," Eliza said. "But we don't have much time. Papa has even had a new house built for us, and now he and Uncle Tom have ordered furniture from England for it."

Richard found it inconceivable that the two fathers were so determined to go through with the wedding, but he sympathized with the young couple. "Would they listen to Mistress Clayton?"

"Oh, yes, provided she believed we really meant what we said," Eliza replied.

193

"And you think that you could persuade her you're serious?"

"She's more inclined to listen to me than to Ezekiel," the girl said. "If I could win her support, it would be a big help."

"Then what you need is time." Richard turned to the young man. "Are you familiar with the wilderness, Ezekiel?"

Ezekiel grinned at him. "I grew up in the forest. I'm more at home there than I am at my desk in Uncle Adam's shipyard, I can tell you."

"I'm making two major stops in my journey through the colonies," Richard said. "I'm going first to New Amsterdam, then on to Middle Plantation, in Virginia. You'd be welcome to come with me, if that would help. During your absence, it would be up to Eliza to convince your mother that neither of you wants to marry."

"Nothing would give me greater pleasure than to go with you," Ezekiel replied eagerly. "I'll need an excuse to travel, of course—"

"That's simple enough," Eliza said, interrupting him. "Tell Papa—and your own father too—that you believe you can arrange some business deals for them in New Netherland and Middle Plantation. They'll send you off with their blessings."

"That's precisely what I'll do," Ezekiel said. "It happens to be true that we have few trade agreements in either colony. I'm sure I can return with enough new business to make the trip worth my while."

Richard began to appreciate Eliza's cleverness.

"I'll go to my father right now, and I'll speak to Uncle Adam when he comes back from his conference. I appreciate this, Richard." Ezekiel was confident, and grasped Richard's hand.

"So do I," Eliza said. "You could have refused to help us."

"I haven't solved your problem," Richard said. "Only you can do that."

"I shall," she said. "I can be far more blunt with Aunt Mary than I can with Papa and Uncle Tom."

Ezekiel went to the front hall for his hat and musket. "Wish me well," he said. "With any luck you and I will soon be free of each other at last, Eliza."

They watched him from the parlor window as he rode off toward the harbor offices. Then Eliza looked up at Richard, her manner suddenly diffident. "You're kind to bear no grudge after what I did," she said. "I flirted with you outrageously."

"I enjoyed it," he replied candidly.

"I—I wasn't just trying to take advantage of you," the girl confessed. "It's true that you attract me—a great deal."

"Well, I didn't keep my reactions to you as much under control as I would have liked," he replied. "I didn't grasp the situation because I wouldn't have dreamed that any man would be reluctant to marry you."

She smiled slowly. "That's the nicest compliment I've ever been paid," she said.

"I mean it. It would be exceedingly easy to fall in love with you."

"That's because you don't really know me. I'm as headstrong as my father, and I always manage to have my own way. I know that I'm spoiled, and I freely admit I'm selfish."

Her frankness was disconcerting. "It may be your faults aren't truly as grave as they appear to you to be," he said.

"Don't humor me, sir. These past days haven't been as simple for me as you might think."

"That just goes to prove that you have a conscience," Richard said.

"I'd say that you know far too much about women," Eliza said.

"How can you tell?" he countered uncomfortably.

"You watched me as I flirted with you, and I could perceive you weighing my motives, speculating on whether I was trying to tempt you to bed me."

"Were you?"

"No, I'd have become frightened, and I'd have found some reason to hold you at arm's length."

"That's the way I had you figured," he said.

"But I knew from the way you were observing and measuring me that you've had experience, that you've had at least one serious affair."

His loyalty to Mimi kept him silent.

"It doesn't matter in the least," Eliza said lightly, seating herself on a small bench and spreading her full skirt. "I've always believed a husband should be more experienced in matters of love than his wife."

Richard was so startled he could only gape at her.

"Why don't you sit down?" she asked him sweetly.

He sank into a chair opposite her, still staring.

"I thought it only fair to give you warning, Richard. If Ezekiel and I break free of each other, I'm setting my cap for you. And not for the reasons you think. Your bride will become Lady Dunstable, but your title means nothing to me. In case you need reminding, I'm a new-breed American. With a little encouragement you could become one of the new breed yourself," she said with a smile. "Now, sir, since I've been honest with you, I think you owe it to me to be honest in return. What exactly are you doing in the colonies?"

"I explained all that the day we met. I'm traveling from one to another, becoming acquainted with all of them before I decide where to settle."

"You're concealing something from me, but no matter. It isn't any of my business, is it? For your own good, though, I think it only fair to tell you that you're a most unconvincing liar."

He raised an eyebrow.

"Something in your manner gives you away. I'm not certain I can pinpoint it, and I don't know if I'd tell you, even if I could. It helps a wife to know when her husband lies to her."

"You can't be seriously contemplating marriage to me," he protested.

"I've never been more serious in my life," Eliza replied, her blue eyes bright. "I've been waiting all my life for you. I know what I feel, and that satisfies me." She smoothed her skirt absently. "I hope you like New Haven and decide to settle here. I'll go elsewhere, if you wish, but my roots are here, and I don't like the thought of leaving Papa alone."

As far as she was concerned, their future together was settled. She was amazing. "I haven't yet seen New Netherland or Virginia," he said slowly, "but—so far, at least—New Haven is the only place I've visited where I feel at home."

Eliza was delighted. "Oh, I'm so glad!"

"Let me make a few basics clear to you, however," he went on grimly. "Please don't take it for granted that you and I will marry. I'm very much drawn to you, but I haven't fallen in love with you—"

"You will," she said, calmly interrupting him. "You held back your feelings because of the relationship you naturally assumed I had with Ezekiel. Now that you understand, it's just a question of time before you realize that you love me."

"My funds are limited, and I haven't yet decided how I intend to earn my living in the colonies. I'm not the sort who would live on his wife's income."

"It never crossed my mind that you would. A man who refuses to let a headstrong woman win a simple

197

horse race isn't the sort who would accept favors from anyone."

She knew him better than he had realized, and the knowledge made him all the more uncomfortable.

Eliza sensed his lack of ease, and rose to her feet. "You've been wanting to kiss me for days," she said. "You may."

Everything else was blotted from Richard's mind. Before he quite knew what he was doing, he was on his feet, sweeping her into an embrace. Eliza clasped his head in both of her hands and returned his kiss with a sincerity and passion that told him she had meant every word. Suddenly he stepped back, afraid his own desire would get the better of him. "This is premature," he said huskily. "You're still engaged to be married to Ezekiel."

She was shaken too, but recovered quickly. "I've now confirmed what I guessed—or divined—about you and me. Never fear, my dear, my betrothal to Ezekiel will be terminated, no matter how badly our fathers may be hurt. I have a reason now to be free, and free I shall be!"

Ezekiel Clayton won enthusiastic support from his father and Colonel Burrows for his plan to go to New Netherland and Virginia with Richard in an attempt to obtain new shipping contracts for the growing merchant firm. Plans for the journey were concluded quickly, and Ezekiel gathered his gear, intending to take his own gelding from the family stable.

No one was happier than Roaring Wolf that the journey would be resumed. The Pequot warrior had waited patiently, sleeping and eating in the Burrowses' yard, and he accepted the addition of another member of the party with resignation. "If the brave can shoot and follow a trail," he said, "he will be welcome."

Richard and Ezekiel said their good-byes at a supper given by the elder Claytons, arranging to meet at the Green at dawn the next day. Adam Burrows spoke for all three of the elders when he said, "We hope you'll return to New Haven and make your home here, Richard. There's a need in the colony for men of your caliber."

Richard thanked the colonel for his hospitality, said he would give serious thought to the prospect of settling in New Haven, and promised solemnly that he would return. His unfinished business with Eliza demanded it.

Richard did not dare look directly at Eliza, but glanced at her surreptitiously as he acknowledged her father's gracious remark. She was looking off into space, her expression dreamy.

He was awake long before dawn the next morning, and when he went down to the kitchen to prepare a predeparture cup of tea for himself, he was surprised to find Eliza already standing at the hearth over a kettle that was just starting to steam.

"You didn't think I'd let you go without saying a private farewell, did you?" she asked as she poured his tea into a cup.

"You make this more difficult for both of us," he replied.

"I daresay I do, but we'll be glad later. I've already told Aunt Mary that I'm coming to see her this morning, so I hope to have the issue settled before you even reach New Netherland."

"I hope you don't intend to bring me into the problem," he said. "I'd hate to have your father think that I abused his hospitality by making advances to his daughter behind his back."

Eliza could be forceful when she chose. "Trust me," she said abruptly.

"I do."

"And think of me—often."

"It will be difficult not to think of you." He hesitated, then took a major step. "I was betrothed before I left England," he said. "The engagement was ended by the girl's father because I was a Cavalier with a dubious future, and he already had a suitable Roundhead selected for her."

"She didn't elope with you?"

"She wasn't the type." Even now, he could not damn Dorothea. "The reason I'm telling you this is because she's been in my thoughts until you came into my life. Now I find it hard even to conjure up a mental picture of her."

"I'm glad," Eliza said simply. "And thank you for telling me. It will make this separation easier to bear."

He gulped his tea and glanced out of the window, where he saw the first streaks of dawn appear in the dark sky. "It's time for me to be on my way."

"I wish you Godspeed," she said. "May your endeavors, whatever they be, end successfully. And may you come back to me soon." She lifted her face to his.

Richard kissed her tenderly, then gazed at her for a long moment as he continued to hold her in his arms. "I'll have no trouble remembering the way you look," he said, and releasing her abruptly, walked out into the dawn.

Eliza stood silently at the window, watching him as he went to the stable for Prince Henry, then set out for his rendezvous with Ezekiel at the Green. His Indian friend trotted happily beside the stallion.

Drawing her dressing gown around her more tightly, Eliza sighed, then drank her own cup of tea. Somehow, she would have to make Aunt Mary understand. And she could not mention Richard. It was a miracle that they had sparked to each other, and she knew, in spite of their brief acquaintance, that a real romance would flourish if they had the time and the opportunity. It was up to her to create both.

Carefully rinsing out the teacups, she went upstairs to her own chamber, where she took her time dressing for the day. Her father was just starting his breakfast when she came down to the dining room.

"Bless my soul," he said. "It isn't often that I'm graced with your presence this early in the day."

"I have a busy day ahead," she said.

Colonel Burrows chuckled indulgently as he boned his broiled fish, which he ate with bread smeared with honey. "The house will seem empty without Richard Dunstable here," he said.

"Very empty," Eliza replied carefully.

"He'll be back," he said. "He doesn't give his word lightly, and he promised solemnly that he'll see New Haven again."

"I'm sure he will, Papa."

"I hope so. The town needs men of his caliber. He's still devoted to the Cavalier cause, which is natural, but time and three thousand miles of the Atlantic should soften and change his perspectives. We've seen it happen to others."

Eliza nodded, unable to carry on the conversation. Too tense to eat breakfast herself, she drank another cup of tea, and after her father went off to his waterfront office, she dawdled for an hour, killing time. Then she donned her lightweight cape of unbleached wool and walked the short distance to the Clayton house.

The dirt road was rutted, but it was so familiar to Eliza that there was no need for her to pick a path for herself. The stately elm trees that lined both sides of the road were budding, and she took that as a hopeful sign. Slowing her pace as she neared the house with the white portico, she quickly rehearsed what she intended to say, then raised the brass knocker on the door and released it.

Mary Clayton answered the summons herself. "Well," she said. "I was expecting you, but not this early. Come in, dear." She led the way to her sewing room. "You're just in time to help me measure the cloth for a new dress."

"Gladly, but first I want to talk to you, Aunt Mary." Eliza's throat was dry. "I don't quite know how to begin. It's a subject that Ezekiel and I have tried to discuss, but Papa and Uncle Tom are deaf to it, and I can only hope you'll understand and act as our ally."

The older woman looked at her calmly. "I understand far more than you think. You're going to tell me that your betrothal is a mistake, that you and Ezekiel don't love each other and never have."

Eliza swallowed hard and stared at her.

Mary smiled. "The reason your fathers haven't listened to either of you in the past is because they've wanted your marriage very badly. They saw the founding of a New World dynasty, and inasmuch as neither of you was interested in anyone else, they hoped against hope that proximity would take care of the problem. Well, it hasn't, obviously, and now the situation is changed—drastically."

Eliza's head swam.

"You and Richard Dunstable have found each other. Or think you have, which amounts to the same thing. Your father is no ogre, Eliza, and neither is my husband. They won't force either you or Ezekiel to go through with an unwanted marriage. They may be crotchety about it for a time, but I can promise you they'll understand and relent." Mary reached for a bolt of cloth. "This arrived from Leeds the other day. Rather attractive, isn't it? I thought of making it into a dress with a high neck and a straight skirt. What do you think?"

"Wait," Eliza said, and discovered she was short of breath. "How do you—know so much?"

"Dear Eliza, I'm almost fifty years old, but I'm not blind! The way you and Sir Richard avoided looking at each other last night was painful. And Ezekiel's idea of going off to New Netherland and Virginia to gain new business had to have been your idea, not his. I know my son, and his mind doesn't function that way."

Eliza laughed ruefully. "If you only knew the speech I'd practiced to convince you that Ezekiel and I aren't right for each other."

The older woman's smile faded, and she reached to pat the girl's face. "You'll never know how much I shall regret not having you for a daughter-in-law."

"I'm sorry, too." Eliza's eyes filled with tears. "You've been a mother to me, the only mother I've ever known."

Mary Clayton quickly recovered her composure. "It does no good to weep over what might have been," she said. "The breaking of your engagement won't end our relationship. My feelings for you aren't changed."

Eliza hugged her impulsively. "You won't mind if I still come to you for advice and help?"

"Mind? I'd be hurt if you didn't." The older woman became reflective. "It's always easier to see one's mistakes after they've been made. Adam, Tom, and I shouldn't have pushed you and Ezekiel together. If we had left you to your own devices, I daresay you'd have found each other."

"I don't think so. We feel as if we're related."

"So you are, even though you aren't blood kin. Now, tell me about you and Richard Dunstable. Are you sure in your own mind that you love him?"

"Very sure," Eliza said. "I didn't plan it, and it wasn't gradual. The moment I met him I knew he was the man I've been waiting for all of my life. And I was so unfair to him, Aunt Mary! I tried to force the issue by flirting with him, but the more I showed him my feelings, the more restrained he became. That made me admire him that much more!"

"Does he love you?" Mary asked quietly.

"I—I think so. He's too honorable to tell me in so many words until my engagement to Ezekiel is broken, and he's so self-contained that he doesn't show his feelings. But I can tell by the way he looks at me. I can't explain it, but I know what's in his mind and heart before he realizes it himself. I sense it, somehow."

Mary nodded gravely. "A rapport of that kind is unusual, and you're fortunate to have experienced it."

"What I find strange is that we've talked very little about things that matter. I know, for instance, that Richard has some reason other than finding a place to settle that's causing him to travel through our colonies, but he hasn't confided in me, and I've hesitated to ask him outright. I don't want him to think I'm prying into business that's none of my concern."

"I worry about you, not about Richard. He appears to be an upright, honest man, but you have no real understanding with him. Suppose he decides to make his home in New Netherland or Virginia. Suppose he doesn't come back here for you. I'm afraid you'd be badly hurt."

"Yes, I would," Eliza said, then smiled confidently. "But I can't imagine him just disappearing. If I'm sure of anything in this world, it's that I know he'll return to New Haven. Richard and I have too much unfinished business that needs to be settled!"

The journey to New Amsterdam was uneventful

for two days and nights. Ezekiel Clayton proved himself adept at wilderness travel, and even Roaring Wolf approved of his expertise. Certainly he was a welcome addition to the little party, his presence contributing to security in the forest. "The danger of Indian attacks is slight in this neighborhood," he said. "The real danger is encountering a band of robbers."

"There are highwaymen in the vicinity?" Richard was surprised.

"Not exactly, but they're outlaws, all the same. They roam in packs of up to a half-dozen men, and they make it a practice to halt and rob the unwary who travel between New Amsterdam and New England. We'll have to keep our eyes and ears open."

In spite of the precautions the trio took, however, robbers struck late one afternoon, when camp was being made on the bank of a small stream that flowed into the Great Bay. Richard and Ezekiel had dismounted and turned their horses loose to graze, and Roaring Wolf had gone down to the shore to gather shellfish for supper while his companions built a fire. Prince Henry gave the first warning, lifting his ears, pawing the ground, and neighing softly. Richard immediately reached for his rifle, which lay on the ground beside him. Ezekiel, equally alert, picked up his musket.

They didn't have long to wait. A party of five roughly clad men came into the open on foot, all of them armed with pistols and clubs. "Do what you're told and you won't be hurt," the leader called. "We're a-goin' to help ourselves to your horses. Just throw your purses on the ground, and we'll soon be on our way."

One of his confederates made the mistake of approaching Prince Henry, intending to take hold of his bridle. But the great stallion apparently sensed what was happening; snorting and baring his teeth, he reared, then brought his flailing front hooves down on the luckless bandit. The man tried to escape but was crushed, and Prince Henry ended his fury by stomping on his victim.

The incident, which took no more than a few seconds, distracted the attention of the other robbers long enough for Richard to raise his rifle and fire. He severely wounded the leader, whose scream of pain echoed down the deserted beach.

Ezekiel Clayton took careful aim with his musket and fired, too, his shot striking another of the thieves. Ordinarily a musket was not that accurate a weapon, but Ezekiel was close enough to make his shot good.

The remaining robbers started to retreat, and their rout was complete when an arrow sang out from the direction of the beach and caught one of them in the shoulder. The band had been unaware of Roaring Wolf's presence in the party, and they fled the scene, the wounded helping each other as they crashed through the forest. One of their number was dead, three others were injured, and only one escaped unscathed.

Richard calmly reloaded his rifle, then indicated the body of the dead robber. "We'll be wise to move our campsite, I believe," he said quietly, going to his stallion and calming him. Roaring Wolf insisted on cutting away the scalp of the dead robber before moving on.

Richard congratulated his companions on their quick responses and the accuracy of their respective muset and arrow fire, and after the camp had been moved, he ate with great relish his crabs, which had been baked in wet leaves. "I was hungrier tonight than I realized," he said.

Ezekiel looked at him curiously. "I've never seen anyone remain so cool in an emergency," he said.

Richard grinned as he tossed the remains of a baked

crab into the fire. "I believe in doing what needs to be done," he replied. "When a man gets excited he loses his ability to think clearly."

"You act as if you've spent your whole life in the wilderness," Ezekiel said admiringly.

Roaring Wolf, squatting on his haunches, laughed aloud. "Richard," he said, "is a mighty warrior."

The accolade was the highest praise that a man could receive, and Richard was pleased. "It's good to know I'm traveling with friends who don't panic, either," he said. Fishing another crab from the fire, he separated it from the wet leaves, then quietly returned to his meal.

No other violence marred the journey, and the following day at about noon, the trio reached New Amsterdam, a ferryman taking them across the East River to the wilderness of upper Manhattan. By midafternoon they reached the bustling town itself, and after inquiring of a passerby where to find lodging, they were directed to the Thorn and Thistle. While Ezekiel attended to their mounts, turning them over to a groom, Richard engaged a room from the amiably talkative Angus MacNeill.

"Our Indian friend isn't comfortable in white man's accommodations," Richard told him. "Can you suggest a place where he'll feel more at home?"

"Aye, sir, it's a common complaint of the redmen," Angus replied. "He'll be safer if he'll stay close by you. New Netherland and the Indians have had, to all our grief, a very difficult and bloody relationship. He'll be welcome to stay in the cellar, provided you'll pay for his space. Your friend will also be welcome in my kitchen—provided you'll pay for his meals."

"That I'll gladly do." Richard was pleased with the arrangements, because they satisfied Roaring Wolf. Ezekiel was eager to set up appointments for himself with various companies of merchants, so he set out for their offices on Hudson's River, a few blocks away. Richard decided to follow his usual custom of wandering around a city to begin his acquaintance with it.

He had to pass through the taproom in order to reach the street, and he was startled when he heard someone shout his name. He turned to see an overjoyed Mollie Williams emerging from behind the bar. She threw herself at him, kissing him soundly on both cheeks.

"What a wonderful surprise!" he exclaimed. "I traced you only as far as Providence Plantations."

"The life there wasn't for Bart and me," Mollie replied, still grinning broadly. "Ah, you look like a New World trapper in your buckskins. That's why I was so startled when I first saw you. I had to make sure it really was you."

Richard became conscious of Angus MacNeill standing a short distance away, scowling at him and at Mollie. "We crossed the Atlantic together," he explained.

"That we did, and it was the kindness of Master Dunstable that gave me the courage to travel from Boston all the way to New Amsterdam."

Richard was relieved by her care in avoiding any mention of his title.

"There are no customers here now, and none are likely to wander in at this hour," Mollie said, "so we can sit and tell each other the news. Do you know what's become of the Chaneys?"

Following her to a table in the empty taproom, Richard noted that Angus MacNeill's scowl deepened until, suddenly, he turned on his heel and stalked out.

"I believe I've made the proprietor jealous," Richard said with a chuckle.

Color flamed in Mollie's face. "He'll get over it soon enough when he realizes we're naught but old friends.

And if he stops to think about it, you're near young enough to be me son."

"I'd hate to be the cause of trouble between you and your employer, Mollie."

"The only trouble will be of his making," she said with a satisfied smile. "I need the work, but Master MacNeill needs me even more!" There was pride in her voice as she went on to tell him of her success at the Thorn and Thistle.

"I'm delighted for you. And how is Bart faring?"

The happiness faded from her face. "Still fighting the good fight for King Charlie. Master MacNeill made a place for him in the stable as an ostler, but he argues with one and all, even though most of the folk here wouldn't know the difference between a Cavalier and a Roundhead, and wouldn't care one way or t'other. I've warned the lad until I'm hoarse, but he won't listen. He's responsible for one strange happening, though." Lowering her voice, she told him about her encounter with the Royalist agent who had called himself Laroche. "I don't know what his game may be, so I've given him no information."

The Earl of Newcastle had told Richard he would report to a man named Laroche. "I believe he's what he says he is, Mollie."

Her eyes widened. "You'll vouch for him?"

"I haven't yet met him, so I wouldn't go that far. But I'm glad to learn he's in town, and I'm eager to make his acquaintance. Do you happen to know where he lives?"

Mollie shook her head. "Nay, but he drops in here near every night around ten o'clock for a glass of sack. In the time I've been here, I haven't known him to miss a night, so I'll arrange that you meet him this very evening, if you like."

"That won't be necessary," Richard said, not wanting to use her as a go-between. "Just point him out to me, and I'll attend to the rest."

"And you'll tell me whether I should accept some of the good money he's offered me?"

He could readily understand her wariness. Having worked hard for every penny she had ever earned, she was suspicious of Laroche's generosity. "After I've met him, Mollie, I'll give you my opinion of the fellow— for whatever it may be worth."

They continued to chat until Mollie had to return to the kitchen to prepare supper for the evening's guests. Her news that Laroche was in New Amsterdam, making a meeting possible that very night, altered Richard's plans. He returned to his room, where he wrote a long letter to Newcastle, telling him of the indifference to the Cavalier cause that he had found in Providence, Pequot, and New Haven.

Sealing the communication with a blob of wax, Richard set out for the waterfront on Hudson's River, hoping he could find a ship's captain with Cavalier sympathies who would carry the letter to Uncle William in France. New Amsterdam residents, he noted as he made his way down the cobbled streets filled with carts drawn by horses and mules, bustled far more than did the people of any other colony. Elsewhere, they strolled casually, but here everyone was in a hurry, darting between carts and needlessly endangering lives by boldly stepping in front of rapidly moving horsemen. If New Amsterdam citizens represented the new breed, they were a breed apart.

Slowing his own pace to a stroll when he reached the wharves, he could not believe his good fortune: a brig tied up at one of the first docks he saw was flying the Union Jack, a signal that her master was willing to act as a courier—unless, of course, the flying of the ensign in port was a careless accident.

He walked down the dock, saw the ship appeared deserted, and, cupping his hands, called, "Ahoy!"

A bearded man with thick, dark eyebrows emerged from a hatch. "What do you want?" he asked, his tone and manner surly.

"A word with the master of this vessel."

"I'm Captain Wardell." The man hooked his thumbs in his belt.

"A word in private, if you please, sir."

"Come aboard, then." The master's manner did not change.

Richard leaped onto the deck, and Captain Wardell led him below to a cluttered cabin.

Looking around, Richard found a dirty glass, and went through the ritual of extending it over water.

The seafaring man's attitude changed abruptly. He grinned as he went through the same gesture. "Why didn't you say so in the first place?" he demanded.

"It isn't the sort of information that one shouts across the wharf," Richard replied. "You sail soon for England?"

"Soon enough," Captain Wardell replied.

Trying to remain civil, Richard removed the bulky letter from the pocket of his buckskin shirt. "This won't add too much weight to your cargo."

The ship's master took the letter, saw it bore Newcastle's name, and frowned. "The earl is in France," he said.

"I know."

"I sail to Southampton."

"I was led to believe that communications could be forwarded to him through appropriate, safe channels."

"So they can, but the cost is dear. I'll have to charge you a gold sovereign."

The price was so high that Richard wondered if he

was being cheated. "A gold sovereign buys many things."

"In this instance, it buys safety," Captain Wardell replied bluntly. "The owners of fishing craft that smuggle letters across the English Channel lose their heads if they're caught by the Roundheads, you know."

Richard realized he had to pay the fee, and took a gold sovereign from his purse.

The master's eyes gleamed as he held the coin up to the light of a small oil lamp, then bit it to satisfy himself that it was genuine. "Your letter will be safe, and you can bet it will reach the Earl of Newcastle. I enjoy doing business with you, sir, and for your information, I'll return here in late July if you have more letters to send to good friends."

"I'll keep that in mind." Richard went ashore again as quickly as he could. Captain Wardell was motivated by greed, not a devotion to the Royalist cause, and Richard felt deep disgust for anyone who sought personal gain from a situation in which others risked their lives.

He strode briskly back to the Thorn and Thistle, unconsciously adapting himself to the pace of New Amsterdam, and the smell of clean sea air put him in a better mood. He found Ezekiel had already returned, much encouraged by his own venture.

"I was amazed to find how many merchants here know of Burrows and Clayton," he said. "It will be far easier than I thought to work out trade agreements with them. Trust Eliza to have thought of a clever way to expand the business. She's unique."

"That she is." Richard was reluctant to discuss her virtues with the man to whom she was still betrothed. "I suggest we go to supper, and I give you my word you'll be served a meal you won't soon forget. The cook here was on board ship with me crossing the Atlantic, and you'll search long and hard before you find her culinary equal."

The meal lived up to his expectations. The soup was thick with vegetables, the broiled cod was delicately flavored with herbs that neither of the hungry young men could identify, and the roast was so tender that Ezekiel found it difficult to believe he was eating shoulder of venison. The final course was a triumph, a pie of fresh spring berries cooked colonial-style, in a crust.

Angus MacNeill made it his business to be present in the dining room at the supper hour, and Richard hailed him. "I can't remember eating a meal I enjoyed so much," he said. "Give Mollie my compliments."

The innkeeper glared at him. "Tell her yourself!" he said curtly.

Richard knew how to rid the man of his unwarranted jealousy. "I shall do more than that. I'm traveling to Virginia to see the young lady who was Mollie's benefactress, and she'll be very happy—as I am—to learn that Mollie has found a position worthy of her talents."

Angus peered at him more closely, and then he became sheepish. "It may be I jumped to the wrong conclusions when I saw you and Mistress Williams a-hugging and a-kissing. You're not sweet on her?"

"Oh, I would be if I were older," Richard replied gallantly. "But she needs—and deserves—someone more mature."

Angus beamed at him. "I'll take your compliments to her myself," he announced, and headed toward the kitchen.

"Did he really regard you as a rival?" Ezekiel wanted to know after the proprietor was no longer within earshot.

"So it seems. People in love aren't quite sane, you know, at least according to my observations of them."

Ezekiel nodded. "Like the way Eliza flirted with

you, trying to force a confrontation with her father and mine."

"I'd like to make a pact with you," Richard said. "As far as I am concerned, you and Eliza are still engaged to be married."

"But you and she are——"

"That's irrelevant. The facts of the existing situation are at odds with the potentials of my own relationship with her. You and I work together effectively, as we proved yesterday when we were attacked by bandits. We're going to be on the trail together for a long time to come when we go to Virginia, and I suggest, for the sake of harmony, that we exclude Eliza from our discussions."

"Surely, if that's what you want." Ezekiel could not understand his companion's rigid code of honor.

Richard saw that the dining room was emptying. "Come along to the taproom, and I'll buy you a drink of ale." He made no mention of the meeting he hoped to have with Laroche, but thought it wise to remain inconspicuous.

The taproom was crowded, but the two young men were able to obtain one of the few empty tables. Most of the patrons were businessmen wearing brightly decorated suits and shirts with squared collars and deep cuffs. Mollie, busily taking orders and serving drinks, was the only woman in the room aside from a pair of obvious trollops who pouted when Richard and Ezekiel ignored them.

Mollie came to their table at once. "You set Master MacNeill on the straight road again!" she said. "I don't rightly know what you told him, but the storm has passed and the sun shines again, so that's good enough for me. I'm forever in your debt, Master Dunstable."

"I wish you all the happiness you want and deserve, Mollie," he replied.

"When I think of all you've done for me, I just wish I could find some way to repay you." She went off to the bar with their order.

Ezekiel was curious. "You say you crossed with her on the same ship, but she didn't call you Sir Richard."

"She was being discreet."

"I don't understand."

"I don't want to sound mysterious, Ezekiel, but there are aspects of my life it's best not to question."

He looked so somber that the younger man was abashed. "I didn't mean to pry—"

"No harm done."

Mollie approached with two tankards of ale, and as she placed one before Richard, she nodded in the direction of a table in the far corner.

He followed her gaze and saw a dark, inconspicuous man who could have been thirty or fifty, dressed in a suit of black. Only his multicolored waistcoat prevented him from resembling a Puritan.

Richard thanked Mollie, paying her for the ale, and tipping her generously. "I'm afraid I'll have to leave you to drink your ale alone," he said to the surprised Ezekiel as he stood, picked up his tankard, and made his way quickly across the room.

Dark eyes studied him intently as he approached. Richard took a seat opposite the solemn, dark man and quickly made the sign of drinking to the king-across-the-water. Then he waited until the man did the same. "I'm told you're Laroche," he said. "I'm Dunstable."

Laroche was surprised by the appearance of this rugged young man in buckskins. "Sir Richard?"

Richard nodded in confirmation.

"Judging by the way you look, I'd have sworn you were a hunter and trapper who has just come to town from the deep forests."

"That's where I've been, Master Laroche. Let's say I adapt to my surroundings."

"Well, you don't look as I pictured you." Laroche pursed his lips. "How did you know me?"

Not wanting to create trouble for Mollie, Richard merely shrugged.

A gleam of sardonic humor appeared in the man's dark eyes. "It's obvious, now that I think about it. You and Mistress Williams were shipmates."

Richard had to admit the man was sharp-witted. "I sent off a report today to our mutual friend in France."

"Ah, via Captain Wardell, no doubt." Laroche seemed to know everything. "And he charged you an outrageous fee for his services."

"That he did. A sovereign."

Laroche whistled under his breath, then shrugged. "We must build our house with the tools we have at hand," he said. "And speaking of money, do you have enough?"

"More than enough. I've lived frugally."

"Good." Laroche was relieved. "We're forced to live on the charity of the few who smuggled fortunes out of England, and funds for my operations aren't easy to obtain."

"Well, I shall impose no burden on you." Richard sipped his ale, reflecting that he could not warm to the gimlet-eyed man.

"I'm glad to hear it. Where have you been, and what was the nature of your report?"

"None too encouraging, I fear. Boston is a nest of Puritans. Providence Plantations, Pequot, and New Haven are too wrapped up in their own concerns to give a hang for our cause."

Laroche did not seem surprised. "You'll find most colonials react with indifference to anything that doesn't directly concern them. They fail to realize

216

how much the restoration of the Stuart line will benefit them. I have it on good authority that when young Charles gains the throne, he intends to encourage migration to the colonies."

"He'll win a loyal following far more quickly if he lowers the taxes the colonies are forced to pay on everything they import and export."

"Ah, you've been listening to local merchants."

"Their argument seems valid."

"It isn't our place to debate royal policy. We do what we're told."

Richard made no reply, but the thought occurred to him that the man chosen to lead the Royalists in North America was going out of his way to be unpleasant.

Laroche seemed to relent a trifle. "You'll find Virginia far different from the other colonies. The Puritans have established no foothold of any kind there, and the Cavalier sentiment is strong, or so I've been informed. I'll be anxious to learn your reactions." He delicately sipped his sack. "There will be no need for you to tarry here. I know New Amsterdam well, and the people here have no concern for either Cavaliers or Puritans. They are actively protesting the actions of their own Dutch authorities who place restrictions on their God-given right to earn as much money as they can in the shortest possible time. They refuse to give any assistance to the Royalist cause."

He spoke with an intense loathing that surprised Richard. "They can't be blamed for that. The English and Dutch have never been on easy terms, due to colonial land disputes and commercial competition."

Laroche's face remained expressionless. "After you've visited Virginia, come back here to me. By that time, I shall have other work for you to do."

His manner was so arbitrary that Richard wanted to remind him he was dealing with a volunteer who not only was paying his own way, but ultimately would be forced to earn a living. Instead he changed the subject. "Have you heard anything about the welfare of Mimi Shepherd?"

"All I can tell you is that she reached the colonies safely, which you already know. For whatever their reasons, the high command didn't see fit to recruit her for the—uh—special services you and I perform, so I have no cause to check on her well-being." Laroche looked as if the subject bored him.

Richard guessed that a spymaster, by definition, had to be cold-blooded and impersonal. Laroche was the first of that occupation he had ever encountered, and he was glad they would be going their separate ways in the foreseeable future.

All at once the man seemed to grow tense as he asked, "In your travels so far, what have you noted in regard to the relations of the various colonies with the French?"

"People here seem to think like people back in England, as nearly as I can judge." Richard shrugged. "In New Haven and Providence Plantations, they keep a wary eye on what's happening to the north, and they seem to believe the French can't be trusted. They think Mazarin covets the English colonies and wouldn't be above bribing the Indian nations of the area in an effort to stir up trouble."

"Do they offer any proof of the theory?"

"Not to me, but I feel precisely as they do. It's common knowledge that before his death, Richelieu lured German peasants into the French army and commissioned the construction of large carts for supplies. He spent money on the development of artillery, and whenever that happens, there's always trouble for us. Besides, they always demand a price, and there's bound to be some reason for the French to have offered a refuge to young King Charles."

"It's only natural that they would," Laroche replied. "After all, Queen Henrietta Maria was a princess of France."

"So she was, but the hospitality they've offered her and her children is a shade too convenient for my own taste. France has been our natural, principal enemy for more than five hundred years, and although she may hesitate to invade England despite the fact we've been weakened by the civil war, Mazarin well may believe he can occupy our colonies in North America and the West Indian Ocean without fear of starting a major war."

"That's an interesting conjecture," Laroche replied coldly, "but I can't give it much credence unless you substantiate it with facts. The economy of New France appears to be sound, young King Louis is earning large sums from the fur trade on the St. Lawrence River, and I'd be surprised if they took the risk of expanding. I could be mistaken, of course, so keep your eyes and ears open, and let me know if you find any hard evidence to indicate that they have designs on the English colonies." His tone and expression indicated that he refused to take the threat from Quebec seriously.

Richard merely nodded. He was surprised that the spymaster, who should have been alert to dangers from every source, should show so little concern for the possibility of a threat from Quebec.

VIII

A T Mollie Williams's request, Richard made it a
point to speak privately with her son before
leaving New Amsterdam. He found young Bart
in the stable of the Thorn and Thistle and deliberately
took him off to a waterfront tavern for a drink of ale.

"You look as if your work agrees with you, lad,"
Richard said with a smile.

"It ain't too bad. The work I do is easy, and I collect a heap of tips." Bart was cocky. "Ma got me the
job, you know. Just about the whole staff at the Thorn
and Thistle believes that Angus MacNeill is sweet on
her, but she won't even talk to me about him."

"From what I've observed, they're developing an
interest in each other. I think it's wonderful that your
mother has not only a position that suits her talents
but a chance to find personal happiness as well. She's
worked hard for many years, Bart—for herself and
for you—and she deserves all the good things in life."

"That she does, Sir Richard." The youth eyed him
a trifle suspiciously, now suspecting the true purpose
of this conversation.

"It would be a shame if her opportunities were
spoiled for her," Richard said pointedly.

Bart gulped his ale. "Ma asked you to have a talk
with me, didn't she?"

"You might say I volunteered to have a word or

two with you. Your mother tells me you've taken up with a gang of rough Cavaliers."

"I have the courage of me convictions, Sir Richard, and so do the boys who have become me friends."

"I'm not so sure that's wise, Bart. Director-General Stuyvesant has imposed heavy fines for violent disruption of the peace. The city has hired an interpreter to aid British merchants. This is a climate for enhancing the peace, not disturbing it. Such indiscretions won't be tolerated."

"They can't scare me none! I ain't afraid of them!" Bart spoke defiantly.

"You know where my own sympathies lie. But I don't make an issue of them."

"Well, I don't hold with keeping me views secret!"

"It's true, then, that you and your new friends go looking for Puritan sympathizers and then beat them?"

"They have a beating coming to them, Sir Richard. It was their kind who took off old King Charlie's head, it was. They killed me brother, John. And it was their kind that made life so miserable for Ma that she had to leave England and travel three thousand miles to start life all over again in the New World!"

"Where her son seems determined to create new messes for her." Richard was quietly emphatic. "Surely you know I hold no warmth for the Roundheads. I had to flee from my home to escape imprisonment, and property that belonged to my family for many generations was confiscated, all because I was loyal to the Crown. I have my own valid reasons to hate the Puritans, but I serve neither the cause of young King Charles nor my own case if I flaunt my sympathies. The Roundheads have won, at least for the present, so we've got to be patient until the clock pendulum swings back in our direction."

"I'm no coward, Sir Richard!"

"Do you think I am one?"

"You belong to the gentry. Your ways and me ways are different."

"Not as different as you may think. See here, Bart —most people in America wash their hands of the quarrels between the Cavaliers and the Puritans. I'm not asking you to change your views, merely to keep them to yourself. You and your friends are going to force the authorities to take notice of you. You're making it necessary for them to send you to prison for disturbing the peace—"

"We'll bash in a few heads good and proper before they can take us, I'll tell you that."

"Every head you bash will add time to the sentence you'll serve. Your mother will be disgraced and might well lose her new position, no matter how much Angus MacNeill needs her. And you may well ruin her chance for personal happiness, too. A public innkeeper like MacNeill must stay in the good graces of the authorities, you know."

"Just because he bows and scrapes to the authorities so he can make his money don't mean I've got to follow his example."

"For your mother's sake, Bart, I urge you to stay out of trouble."

"I ain't a little boy no more, Sir Richard. I've become a man, and I've got to act like one!"

Richard knew he was wasting his breath. Bart Williams had no understanding of the power struggle between the Cavaliers and the Puritans, and instead saw the complex problems only as they related to him. It was apparent that he would cause troubles for his hardworking mother as well as for himself in his misguided efforts to prove his manhood.

Dempster Chaney labored in the fields of Hester Browne's farm from dawn until dusk seven days a week, as if motivated by an unrelenting, supernatural force. Robbin felt compelled to prove herself too, scouring the house until it shone, preparing meals, and spinning cloth. Neither uttered a complaint about their long hours, and their employer, dubious of the young couple at first, gradually softened.

"You two make me feel tired just watching you!" she told them at supper one evening. "My Eddie and I worked hard all our lives, but I feel downright lazy when I compare my efforts to what you do!"

Dempster paused in his eating of the roast turkey. "When there's chores to be done, ma'am," he said, "there's only one way to do them, so we pitch in."

"That you do." Suddenly, the gaunt woman's smile vanished, and she gasped and clutched her right side, grimacing in pain.

"Is something wrong, Mrs. Browne?" Robbin asked solicitously.

"I—I don't rightly know. Maybe I got me a touch of indigestion, but it's an odd place for it." She touched the lower portion of her abdomen.

"Perhaps we should call in a physician," Robbin suggested.

Hester Browne forced a smile. "That's easier said than done, child. Old Doc Carey lived on the other side of the pond, but he passed away the year I lost my Eddie. Now, I don't rightly think there's a physician between here and Boston." She gasped again, the color draining from her face. It was obvious that her distress was genuine.

Dempster cleared his throat. "Ma'am," he said diffidently, "I was a student at the Royal College of Surgeons in Edinburgh until the Roundheads ruined my chances of becoming a doctor. If you don't object, maybe I might examine you."

"I reckon you'd best do it," the tight-lipped woman

replied. "I get these pains that shoot through me like a knife was being stuck into my innards."

The meal was forgotten. Encouraging the older woman to lean heavily on her, Robbin assisted Hester to the parlor, and there she stretched out on the sofa. Dempster bent over the patient, gently probing the area she indicated. Every time he released the pressure of his palpating hand, she winced.

At last he straightened. "It appears," he said, "that you have an infection of some sort in your appendix. Fortunately it's a simple enough ailment to diagnose. Less fortunate is the fact that the appendix must be removed."

"In the medicine chest near the hearth," Hester said, "I keep some phials of herb medicines for emergencies. You know where to find them, Robbin."

"Indeed I do." Robbin started to leave the room.

Dempster called her back. "Don't bother," he said. "All the herbs in the world won't rid Mrs. Browne of the infection. I'm sorry, ma'am, but that is the truth."

"What needs to be done?" Hester bit her lower lip.

"The appendix must be cut out," he replied firmly. "It's an operation for a surgeon." He shook his head, then added grimly, "But there is no surgeon between the farm and Boston. Even if we rigged up a cart to carry you to town, the jouncing on the road would worsen your condition, and the appendix might rupture. In that event—you'd die. The infection would spread to all of your internal organs, and there would be no way to save you."

"You're sure, Dempster?" Robbin demanded anxiously.

"Very sure. This is one of the first things we learned at Edinburgh."

"Can you perform the surgery on me, young man?" Hester demanded, pausing between phrases as pains shot through her.

224

"I've removed two appendixes in my time, both under the direction of a senior staff surgeon. I've never tried doing it alone, and I can only hope I remember all that needs to be done."

"If this . . . infected organ isn't removed, you say —I'll not live?"

"Your chances won't be good, ma'am."

There was a long silence, and they could hear the ticking of the clock that stood on the parlor mantel.

"Then I have no choice, and neither do you, young man. Operate, and do your best!"

Dempster made no move for a time, then he suddenly squared his shoulders. "Do you happen to have any laudanum in your medicine chest?"

"I—I think so." Hester gasped and shuddered. "Doc Carey gave us a supply when Eddie needed it, and it hasn't been touched since he passed on."

"Show me," Dempster said to Robbin, who led him to the kitchen and opened a cupboard that stood above the stove.

He scanned the contents quickly, then removed a phial containing an opaque liquid. Removing the stopper, he sniffed the contents, touched a bit to his tongue, then nodded. "We're in luck so far. Robbin, thread a slender needle with the thinnest silk thread you can find. Get me some clean cloths, and a bottle of brandy."

"You're sure that you know what you're doing, Dempster?"

"I'd best be very sure. Hurry." He cleaned off the kitchen table, scrubbed it with a brush and then, while it dried, hurried back to the parlor. "Don't try to walk. Just clasp your hands around my neck."

Hester Browne obeyed silently, and he carried her to the kitchen, placing her on the table. Robbin returned with the various items he had demanded. Dempster busied himself sharpening two kitchen

225

knives on a whetstone. One was a small utility knife that could be used as a scalpel; the other was a long, heavy carving knife that Robbin had used to cut the turkey they had been eating, and its appearance suddenly became sinister, threatening.

Hester Browne, suffering spasm after spasm of intense pain and nausea, averted her gaze.

Dempster could not tolerate the worry he saw in his wife's eyes. "Now go to the woodpile," he told her, "and bring back a small slab about an inch deep. Hardwood, preferably. And while you're at it, you'd best fetch several more oil lamps. I'll want as much light as we can produce. I'll need some clothespins too, the kind you use to hold wash on the line."

His requests seemed odd to Robbin, but he seemed to know what he was doing, so she asked no questions as she hurried off to do his bidding.

Dempster measured a dose of laudanum in a glass, added water, and handed it to Hester, raising her head with one hand. "Drink this right down," he told her. "It has a very bitter taste, so don't stop drinking until you've drained the last drop."

"What is it?" she asked faintly.

"An opiate," he replied. "What I'm about to do won't be easy for either of us, but the laudanum will dull the pain for you." He refrained from telling her that, even with the aid of the medication, the surgery would be excruciatingly painful. She dutifully accepted the drink, almost gagging twice, but somehow getting it down.

Robbin returned with the various items that her husband had requested. He pulled over a small table, and laid them out after rinsing them in brandy. The strong odor of the potent liquor filled the room and added to Robbin's sense of growing queasiness.

Dempster rearranged the lights to his satisfaction, then rolled up his sleeves and washed his hands with soft, yellow soap. "Stand up there, behind Mrs. Browne's head," he told his wife. "Can you hear me, Mrs. Browne?"

The laudanum had taken effect quickly, and the gray-haired woman nodded groggily.

"Put this chunk of wood in your mouth, and when I start, bite down hard on it. It will help you to withstand the pain. I promise you I'll work as fast as I can."

She understood him, the expression in her eyes indicating that she trusted him implicitly, even though her life was at stake.

Robbin closed her eyes and swayed on her feet.

"We'll have none of that," Dempster told her firmly. "I'll need your help, so you can't afford to faint. Take a cloth and use it to wipe perspiration from her brow. If need be," he added in a lower tone, "you'll have to hold her arms at her sides and prevent her from thrashing around on the table. That's paramount. I prefer not to tie her down, so you'll need to stay alert."

Robbin got a firm grip on her emotions. Never had she seen her husband so earnest, so determined.

"All right," he said. "Give her the block of wood. Mrs. Browne, the incision will be the worst of it."

Robbin placed the block of wood in the patient's mouth, and as she did, she saw her husband standing with his eyes closed, his lips moving. She realized he was praying, so she prayed too, not knowing what to expect and calling on Divine Providence to guide him.

Dempster bent lower over the patient's abdomen, probed with two fingers, then picked up the utility knife. Robbin held her breath. Moving swiftly, he made an incision about four inches long. Hester Browne shuddered, emitting a sound that was part scream, part moan.

227

In order to reduce the patient's bleeding, Dempster used the clothespins to clamp the exposed flesh. They were far less effective than the surgical clamps he had known in Edinburgh.

To Robbin's horror, he seemed to be digging deeper, so she concentrated her attention on Hester Browne, who was sweating heavily, her wide-open eyes reflecting her agony.

There was no sound in the room but the crackle of logs in the kitchen fire as Dempster worked, trying to recall all he had been taught so long before. His instructors had told him that he had a natural feel for surgery, and he was relying on that sixth sense to see him and his patient through the crisis. He labored quickly, his fingers surprisingly nimble as well as strong, and he paused only once to wipe away beads of his own perspiration that were stinging his eyes and threatening to blind him.

"Aha," he said at last, "I've got it."

Robbin could not look at the small, bloated object that he deposited in a bowl. Hester Browne was moaning continuously now as her teeth sank into the hardwood gag in her mouth. The worst was over, Dempster knew. He tied off blood vessels and removed the clothespins one by one, pausing occasionally to wipe away blood with a cloth soaked in brandy. At last he picked up the needle and thread, closed the lips of the incision, and sewed it. Then, pouring more brandy on a clean cloth, he wiped the patient's skin. "We're done, Mrs. Browne," he said wearily, and removed the wood from her mouth.

She understood the gesture to indicate that the operation was ended. "It—still—hurts," she managed to say.

Quickly washing his hands again, he mixed a smaller dose of laudanum and gave it to her. "This should put you to sleep," he said. "When you wake up tomorrow, you should be feeling much better." He turned to Robbin. "We'll wait until she's asleep before we move her to her bed. It will be far less painful for her that way."

His wife indicated that she concurred.

"Tell me—before the opiate takes effect," Hester Browne whispered. "Did you rid me . . . of the diseased part?"

"I did, Mrs. Browne. You'll be fit and fine again in a matter of days."

In spite of her pain, she managed to smile at him. "I'm not Mrs. Browne," she said. "Not to you. Call me . . . Aunt Hester." She drifted off to sleep, the smile still on her face.

Dempster helped Robbin carry her to her bedchamber, where Robbin dressed her in a nightgown, and then they returned to the kitchen to clean up the room. They worked in silence for a time, with Robbin scrubbing energetically. "I've never been so frightened in all my life," she said. "How did you manage to remain so calm?"

Dempster grinned at her. "If I'd allowed myself to be scared," he replied, "I couldn't have done what was necessary."

"You missed your calling, my dear. You seemed to know exactly what you were doing every minute. Somehow we've got to save the money for you to go back and finish surgeons' school. You have a talent that shouldn't be wasted."

He felt shaken inside, but when he extended his hands he discovered they were steady. "I won't be welcome at Edinburgh as long as the Roundheads are in power," he said. "And by the time they're out, it will be too late. No, Robbin, I seem destined to live as a farmer, like my father and grandfather before me. I don't wear my religion on my sleeve, the way the Puritans do, but I still put my faith in the Almighty, and I'm content to live as He directs." Smiling at her, he went to a cupboard and took out two glasses, into which he poured a small quantity of brandy. "I prescribe a little of this for internal use," he said. "We used quite a bit of it."

"Why did you wipe all the instruments you used with brandy?" she asked, taking a glass from him.

Dempster shrugged. "No one knows why," he said, "but they discovered at Edinburgh that patients suffer fewer fevers and infections after surgery when brandy is used liberally during an operation. I just did what I've been taught."

She raised her glass to him. "You've accomplished one thing tonight, Dr. Chaney. Our days of being on trial here are over. I believe you've guaranteed us a home here for as long as we want to stay."

"God bless Hester Browne," he said, and drained the contents of his glass.

Robbin drank too, but reflected that she would not be content to let her husband spend the rest of his life as a farmer. In some way she could not yet foresee, she would make certain he returned to school to earn his degree as a surgeon. His performance tonight proved where his real talents lay, and she was determined that he would have a chance to develop them to the full.

The holding of Horace Laing, outside Middle Plantation, was an extensive estate devoted to the growing of tobacco, for which there was an ever-increasing demand in England. Obviously the plantation was a profitable enterprise. The main house was constructed of red stone, with the upper stories shingled in wood, and virtually all of the handsome furnishings had been imported from England. A large staff, which included a cook, a butler, and several housemaids, attended to the needs of the host and his guests.

Certainly Mimi Shepherd felt completely at home here. Laing had been absent from the plantation when she had first arrived, but he had left orders to make her welcome, and this the staff had done, expertly attending to her needs. She could close her eyes and imagine herself back in her own London town house.

Now Horace Laing had come home, and they were dining together by candlelight for the first time. A burly man in his early forties, with the healthy tan of one who spent most of his days out-of-doors, he was endowed with a rugged charm. Only his accent was a trifle strange: he spoke so precisely, so deliberately that he sounded as if he were speaking English with the care of one to whom the language was alien.

Expensively attired in a suit of nubby raw silk, he was at ease in his surroundings. The tablecloth and napkins were of thick, creamy damask, the dinner service was made of fine bone china, and the flatware was gleaming silver. Even the goblets and glasses were fashioned of sparkling crystal, worth a fortune in England and far more in the distant land to which they had been transported.

Certainly, Horace Laing was not impervious to feminine beauty. Mimi had elected to wear a strapless gown for her first dinner alone with him, and she knew by the expression in his eyes that he appreciated her appearance.

"I owe you an apology, Lady Dawn," he said. "Had I known when you were arriving, I'd have altered my business arrangements accordingly. I didn't expect you to spend weeks here unattended."

"Oh, I assure you I was very well attended, Master Laing," she replied. "Your staff is superb, and I wouldn't have guessed that any help could be that well trained in the New World. I went out for a long

231

canter every day, and I've even explored the wilderness beyond your property. What's more, your library is marvelous, and I've availed myself freely of your books."

"You relieve my concern," Horace Laing replied gallantly. "I hope you exercised caution in your explorations of the wilderness. The forests here aren't as innocent as they seem. I've tried hard to bring civilization as I know it to the New World, but beyond my cultivated fields lies another realm. As recently as five years ago, it was explosively dangerous and cruel. Thankfully, the treaty approved three years ago seems to have completely subdued the tribes, but one cannot be too careful."

"I saw no one when I went for rides," she assured him. "Your chief groom told me to keep watch for Indians who might be hostile, but I didn't see any. Thank you for your concern."

A serving maid came into the dining room and filled their wineglasses. Horace Laing went through the ritual of drinking a toast to the king-across-the-water. Mimi instantly did the same.

"I understand that the Roundheads were eager to prevent your departure from England," he said.

"Apparently so. They boast that they don't wage war against women, but I appear to have been a special case."

"Because of your father's rank, I assume."

"Partly that," she replied candidly. "But also, I'm sure, because there were rumors about King Charles and me."

"I see." He was too much of a gentleman to inquire whether there was any substance to the story.

"But it worked out well for me, thanks to Sir Richard Dunstable."

"I've had good reports about Sir Richard. He appears to be competent."

"If it weren't for Richard," Mimi said with a smile, "I wouldn't be here today."

"Then I owe him my gratitude as well. Do you think our cause is doomed in England, Lady Dawn?"

"For the present I can see little hope for us. Parliament has been ruthless in crushing the opposition, and Cromwell has proved clever in playing on the sentiments of the people."

"Then our only hope rests with the French, I take it," Laing declared.

"The French? Hardly." She made no attempt to hide her scorn.

"Young Charles is the guest of Mazarin, and Queen Henrietta Maria, after all, is the aunt of the Boy-King Louis the Fourteenth. It strikes me that we'd be wise to accept all the help that Paris offers," Laing said earnestly.

"You can be sure there are conditions tied to French help. I may be prejudiced, of course, because I'm not welcome in France myself these days. Queen Henrietta Maria is none too fond of me. But I don't base my opposition to the French on personal grounds. In all the years my father was a member of the Privy Council, he argued successfully against forming any close alliance with France. He always said they'll throw one arm around your shoulder and pick your pocket with their free hand."

"With all due respect to Sturbridge, who was a distinguished diplomat, if he were alive today I'm sure he'd sing a different tune."

"You didn't know my father," Mimi replied firmly. "His mistrust of France was basic."

"Well, as I see our situation, the Cavalier party is disorganized and has no funds. If we're to put young Charles on the throne, we'll certainly need the assistance of the French navy, and it may be we'll require help from their army, too."

"I don't know how long it has been since you spent any appreciable amount of time in England, Master Laing," Mimi said heatedly, "but you misjudge the temperament and the patriotism of the English public. Let one French warship sail into English waters, let one battalion of French troops land on our soil, and the people will become united behind Cromwell and Parliament. Not only will the Roundheads win the complete support of the vast mass of people who have taken no part in the quarrel between the Cavaliers and the Puritans, but most of the Royalists will rally behind Cromwell's banner, too."

"Do I gather correctly that you would be one of the first to change sides?"

Mimi shrugged prettily. "I'm relieved that it's a decision I don't need to make. Let's just say I'd be sorely tempted."

Horace Laing nodded thoughtfully, then changed the subject. "I hope you'll join me in a glass of port, Lady Dawn. I usually reserve port for the men, totally ignoring the fact that a lady might appreciate the bouquet and taste of a rare old port, too."

"Kind sir, I'd be delighted to join you," she said, convinced that he was charming.

By use of a bellpull, he summoned a serving maid who had anticipated his desires, appearing with a decanter of port wine and two glasses. She placed them on the table before him, then stood back while he served the beverage.

Calling Mimi's attention to the floral centerpiece on the table, Laing reached surreptitiously into a waistcoat pocket and removed a packet containing a gray powder, which he slipped into his guest's glass before he filled it with port. Mimi was busily inspecting the floral arrangement and noted nothing untoward.

The serving maid could not help but realize what her master was doing, but she stared off into space, her face wooden, and when he nodded to her, she placed the silver glass in front of the guest, then silently withdrew. Whatever Laing's motive, she was familiar with his routine.

He solemnly went through the ritual of offering a silent toast to the king-across-the-water. Inasmuch as they had started the meal in the same way, Mimi thought that here was a man truly devoted to the Cavalier cause, so she followed his example before sampling the sweet wine.

"There are two schools of thought about port," he said. "Some prefer it served in a clear glass so they can enjoy holding it to the light and seeing the color of the wine. I prefer a silver cup because I'm convinced it enhances the taste. I import it from a vineyard in the north of Portugal. It takes a bit of doing to bring it across the Atlantic because its importation has not officially been approved, but I import it in bulk, so I don't mind paying a premium to a shipper for my pipes of wine."

Mimi listened to him politely, but found herself becoming so drowsy she could scarcely hold up her head. In an attempt to rouse herself, she took another large swallow of her port. She knew her smile was fixed and hoped her eyes didn't look as glassy as she feared they were. She could never forgive herself for falling asleep at her first dinner with a host who was doing everything in his power to please her.

Laing continued to talk at length about his method of bringing the wine to the New World from Portugal. He saw his guest struggling but slowly losing the battle to remain awake, and his voice droned on steadily.

Not until Mimi slumped in her chair, her breathing deep and even, did he fall silent and reach for the bellpull.

The serving maid did not appear to notice that the Lady Dawn was fast asleep.

"Tell Simms I'm ready for him," Laing directed.

The woman disappeared, and a heavyset man in butler's livery came into the room, glanced at Mimi, and grinned. "I wondered how long this one would last after you came home," he said. "You wasted no time."

"There's none to waste, is there?" Laing demanded. "You may remove her to the cellar, Simms."

The man scooped Mimi up into his arms. "What's the treatment to be this time?"

"Lady Dawn is more self-reliant and headstrong than the others. I believe she'll require a special treatment in order to break her spirit quickly. Tell Anna to strip her."

The butler nodded, his eyes gleaming.

"No, Simms," Horace Laing said sharply. "I forbid you to go near her. Your techniques may be effective with some, but Lady Dawn is of very high rank, and she'd be so outraged by your—uh—devotion to her that she would become all that much more difficult to break down. Tell Anna I said she's to receive no visitors and is to be given the silent treatment."

"As you wish," Simms said sulkily, and made his way out of the room, easily managing the dead weight of the unconscious woman in his arms.

Alone at the table now, Laing refilled his glass with port, twirled it, and drank. A hint of a smile appeared at the corners of his mouth, but his eyes remained dark and hard.

Mimi's first conscious thought was that she was thirsty, that never before had she craved water so badly. She sat up, startled to discover that she was reclining on a small cot instead of the four-poster bed in her guest suite. Then she realized she was completely nude. But her thirst came first, and she poured water from a carafe that stood on a crude bedside table into a glass, and not until she drained the contents did she look around.

Scarcely able to believe what she saw, she realized she was in a cell, a chamber no more than twelve feet long and eight feet wide, illuminated by a small oil lamp with the wick burning low. The walls appeared to be of solid stone and were sweating; that fact, combined with the absence of a window, convinced her that her place of detention was underground. Between her and freedom stood a heavy door of solid oak, and she knew even before she raised the latch that it was locked.

Conquering the panic that threatened to overwhelm her, Mimi sat shivering on the cot, and as she tried to reconstruct what had happened, she wrapped herself in the single, thin blanket that had covered her. Gradually she began to recall the previous night's events: she had been dining with Horace Laing, and as she had been drinking her port wine, he had told her in boring detail about his trials in importing it.

Of course! The port! Now that she recalled it, the wine had tasted curiously metallic. She had attributed that to the silver goblet. But why should Laing have gone to the trouble of drugging her and making her a prisoner? The strange dilemma in which she found herself made no sense. The removal of her clothes had made her vulnerable, but she was not prepared to tolerate this outrage. Wrapping the blanket around her as best she could, she picked up the slop jar, the only weapon in the cell, then rattled the latch hard.

After a time Mimi heard footsteps on the stone floor outside her cell, and when a key was inserted into the lock, she raised the slop jar over her head, intending to hurl it at an attacker.

Instead a broad-faced woman in nondescript attire came into the cell, barely glancing at the prisoner. In one hand she carried a tray, which she deposited on the little table.

There was food on the tray, but Mimi was too angry to care. "I demand to know why I've been made captive!" she cried. "And how dare you take my clothes! I hold Horace Laing responsible, and I demand to see him at once!"

The woman calmly ignored the prisoner's outburst, and picked up the carafe and empty water glass.

Mimi thought of hurling the slop jar at the woman, but the rumble of male voices in the corridor outside the cell accented her helpless state. One man—or a dozen—could assault her, and there was nothing she could do to protect herself.

Slowly she lowered the jar. "Please," she begged, "why am I being treated this way?"

The woman did not reply. Instead she withdrew with the carafe and the water glass, and a key grated harshly in the lock.

Mimi was so furious that she trembled violently, and no longer able to stand, she sat abruptly on the edge of the cot. Her common sense told her to control her temper; there had to be a reason she had been imprisoned, a reason for the woman's silence. As she grew calmer she became aware of the aroma of food and realized she was ravenously hungry.

Whisking a cloth from the tray, she realized that at least her captors had no intention of starving her. On a platter were thick slices of ham, cheese, and smoked whitefish. Beside the plate was a loaf of bread, still warm from the oven, a crock of fresh butter, and a wooden tankard filled with a mild ale.

Forcing herself to eat slowly, Mimi analyzed her situation. It was difficult to believe that a man who lived as ostentatiously as Horace Laing would have gone to all this bother in order to rob her. Surely her money wasn't worth the effort, although her jewels—

which had been in the family for generations—were worth a king's ransom. If he had coveted them, how much simpler it would have been to kill her and dispose of her body in the nearby wilderness. No, she was being kept alive for a reason.

It was difficult to judge the passage of time, and after Mimi ate her fill she crawled back onto the cot. Perhaps an hour or two later, the woman gaoler returned to remove the tray and fill the lamp with oil.

Mimi deliberately remained silent. The woman appeared surprised by her prisoner's change in demeanor, but made no comment as she removed the serving tray and the dishes.

Perhaps, Mimi reflected, she was employing the wrong tactics. Nothing ventured, nothing gained. It was a long, tedious wait until the next meal was brought to the cell, but this time she unleashed her frustration in a rage, demanding an explanation for the way she was being treated. The woman paid no heed to her, and might well have been deaf and mute.

Only the serving of meals marked the passage of time. Mimi slept and daydreamed, then deliberately called to mind the puzzles that had been the rage at the court of Charles I a few years earlier. Puzzles had always bored her, but solving them now helped to maintain her sanity.

She was held captive for about three days and nights before there was a sudden change in her routine. One day, the female in charge brought Mimi a complete set of her own clothes, a hand mirror, and her cosmetics case. Washing as best she could in the tub of cold water that the woman had also dragged into the cell, she dressed quickly. The gown that had been selected for her was unsuitable for a prison cell, and Mimi couldn't help grinning at her reflection in the mirror. She looked incongruously frivolous in a dress with wide, frilly cuffs of organdy and a matching collar that framed a deep neckline. The mere fact that she was dressed restored a measure of her confidence, and after she used her cosmetics and brushed her hair, she felt better able to cope with whatever might lie ahead. She suspected that her incarceration was entering a new phase.

The woman reappeared to remove the tub of water, and when she deposited a bottle of wine and two glasses, Mimi knew she was due to receive a visitor. She registered no surprise when Horace Laing appeared and bowed formally. "You'll forgive me if I occupy the only seat," she said coldly.

"I don't mind standing," he replied, leaning against the wall.

"Apparently the wine has been served to celebrate our reunion," she continued, filling the two glasses, "but if you don't mind, you'll drink first. The last time we drank together I suffered rather extraordinary consequences."

Obviously admiring her spirit, he raised his glass to her. Mimi went through the ritual of drinking to the king-across-the-water. The gesture surprised Laing, but he recovered and did the same.

"Now, sir, the time has come for an explanation of the horrendous treatment to which I have been subjected!" she said.

Laing looked uncomfortable. In similar circumstances, the earlier prisoners had been cowed and sullen, enabling him to take the lead and direct the conversation into channels he wanted to explore. But this bold aristocrat had a will and a mind of her own, so he was forced to talk on her terms. "I am not what I seem," he told her.

Mimi's high-pitched laugh echoed from the stone walls of the cell. "You, sir, have a most profound grasp of the obvious. Tell me you're in the personal employ of Oliver Cromwell, and I swear to you I shall not be surprised."

"I am not employed by Puritans, and I am no Cavalier, either. I have the honor of serving His Christian Majesty, Louis the Fourteenth, and I report directly to Cardinal Mazarin himself."

Mimi stared at him without blinking. "I'll be damned," she said softly.

"Whether you are, or whether you accept the salvation that is offered to you, remains to be seen." Little by little, Laing was gaining control of the situation. "My real identity is irrelevant to your situation. It is enough that you know me as Horace Laing."

"You wouldn't be flattered, sir, if you knew what I'm thinking of you!" she retorted. "What astonishes me is that you've gone to so much trouble to maintain a false front."

"The stakes are enormous, and Mazarin plays only to win. Think of Europe, my dear Lady Dawn. With England safely under French control, France can spread her influence and bring Spain, the German states, and the Low Countries under her wing. It is not too farfetched to say that even the Archduke in Austria will be forced to conclude a treaty of peace and friendship with France, as will Russia and the Ottomans. As for North America, all of it will be absorbed into New France."

"A wonderful dream, sir, and I envy you the sweep, the scope of it. The American colonies will be French. France will stand astride all of Europe, and every head will bow to your boy-monarch. But reality has a way of upsetting dreams. You can accomplish Mazarin's goal only by first subduing the English. But they're as indigestible today as they were at Agincourt long before your day and mine!" Mimi faced him proudly.

"It is not Mazarin's intention to fight the English,"

Laing replied somberly. "He well knows and respects their valor in battle. Wars are expensive, and he can accomplish his ends far more cheaply, with no loss of life. England has met her match in Mazarin!"

"I'm sure he'd be pleased to know how much you admire him, but I fail to recognize his many accomplishments, aside from causing me great distress and embarrassment."

Laing refused to be distracted by her sarcasm. "Hear me, Lady Dawn," he said. "At the moment Cromwell reigns triumphant over a divided, bitter England. Only a king can reunite the country—the legitimate monarch, Charles the Second. Do you agree?"

"So far, sir, we have little cause for argument." She looked across the cell at him, challenging him.

"Young Charles suffers from the familiar Stuart weakness, a liking for beautiful, exciting women. His cravings are already being cultivated and indulged. Mark my words, when he returns to the throne of his father, he will be accompanied by at least one mistress in the pay of France, and others will follow her. He will be a marionette manipulated by a puppeteer in Paris."

Mimi was aghast. "Damnable, but clever," she admitted.

"First, however, he must be restored to the throne. Mazarin needs able assistants to accomplish that goal, and you have long held the place of honor at the top of his list of potential recruits. Your qualifications are unique, after all. You are capable of gathering information available to virtually no one else, so your value to Cardinal Mazarin, therefore, is extraordinary."

She hadn't been aware that Cardinal Mazarin even knew of her existence, and she stared at him incredulously. It was obvious to her that he was sincere.

"In certain fields of endeavor, particularly as an agent who will influence the thinking of a nation, one woman can be as effective as one hundred men. Your credentials are impeccable. As the sole surviving member of one of England's greatest families, you have access to the entire nobility. Your beauty and charm speak for themselves. Even I have been impressed by them."

He was so much in earnest that her blood ran cold. The French seemed prepared to go to any lengths to obtain her services.

"You appear to be intelligent, and it is our understanding that you speak French fluently, which is also helpful to us. The one quality you lack is ruthlessness, a determination to allow nothing to stand between you and the goals we have set, but you can be taught that quality."

"By you, no doubt."

"I have been selected to act as your instructor," he replied gravely. "There are many nobles in England who care nothing for the causes of the Puritans and the Cavaliers. They are your first targets, and their defection to France must receive the first priority."

"I loathe the Roundheads with all my being," Mimi said, "but I prefer to see England ruled by Oliver Cromwell than to see her become a pawn of France!"

"Your patriotism is misguided. Mazarin decided long ago that you were necessary to the fulfillment of his aims, and he always gets what he wants. You have been under observation for a long time, Lady Dawn. We don't know what became of the agent, a man known to the English as Robertson, who was keeping watch over you. He sailed with you from England, but he was not on board the ship when you anchored in Boston."

Realizing that Laing was scrutinizing her carefully in order to assess her reaction, Mimi concealed her shock. So the man Richard had killed on board the brig had been in the employ of France rather than the Puritans, as she and Richard had assumed. Now she knew why he had written his journal in French. "He was washed overboard during a storm, the captain told us. That's all I know about the matter."

He couldn't determine whether she was telling the truth. "Poor Jean-Pierre," he said. "He was a devoted servant of France. But no matter. If you are willing, your instructions will begin at once. I neglected to mention that you will have no financial concerns if you cast your lot with us. I know your funds are limited because I have taken the liberty of counting the gold in your purse. But I have been authorized to assure you that no limits will be placed on the sums you will be privileged to draw from the royal treasury of France. There will be no need for you to change your style of living, Lady Dawn."

"Suppose I decline to accept Cardinal Mazarin's generosity. What then?" she demanded.

"I urge you to think twice before rejecting such an opportunity," Laing said.

"You haven't answered my question."

"Think of your situation," he told her. "Surely you don't enjoy your confinement in this miserable cell. Surely you must recognize the helplessness of your predicament. I have seen to it that you've been served edible food, and as a special favor I allowed some clothes to be returned to you today."

"I find your generosity overwhelming."

"Not at all," he said seriously. "You have a mind of your own, and I far prefer to have your voluntary cooperation than to force you to work with us. A reluctant agent is not the best agent. You'll continue to be served the same meals that I myself eat, and I shall have your clothing boxes brought to you, even though they'll make this cell far more cramped. I'm prepared to be patient, Lady Dawn. Think about all I've said to you today, and I'm sure you'll see the wisdom of working loyally with us."

Mimi bit back an angry reply.

Laing strolled to the door. "Take your time. You have little else to occupy yourself, so choose wisely. Although I don't like to threaten, the privileges of enjoying your wardrobe and eating fine food can be withdrawn." He bowed and left the cell.

Mimi faced the door defiantly until the key grated in the lock, then she crumpled onto the cot. It was one thing to maintain a brave pose in front of her captor, but now that she was alone, despair overwhelmed her.

She knew now that she had become a pawn in an international conspiracy being devised for the highest of stakes, the domination of Europe and the bloodless conquest of the British colonies in North America. Pitted against her was the wily first minister of France, who had all of the resources of a powerful nation to back him up. Charles I, her protector and friend, was dead, and his forces had been scattered and rendered impotent.

She had spoken the truth when she had said that she preferred to see Oliver Cromwell rule England than to watch a proud nation become an instrument of France. She could see no way out of the trap. Laing would continue to hold her prisoner until she agreed to become an agent of France, and he would apply pressures that would become intolerable.

Worst of all, she stood alone. In fact, no one in a position to help her even knew of her predicament. The Earl of Newcastle was in France, presumably near young Charles II, who was himself being corrupted by the French. And on this side of the Atlantic only Richard Dunstable knew where she had gone, and he had no reason to suspect that she had fallen victim to foul play.

In spite of the odds against her, she had no intention of giving in. Fighting back tears, she clenched her fists and glared at the closed door. "Never!" she vowed aloud. "Never!"

IX

THE American wilderness was a land of bounty to those who knew how to benefit from it. Game was plentiful, with deer and rabbits everywhere, and spring added northward-bound ducks and geese to the larder. Fish abounded in clear, swift-running streams, and Roaring Wolf taught Richard a new trick in forest living. The Pequot packed fish in green leaves and then suspended it over a low fire in a hammocklike contraption fashioned of vines. The result was beautifully steamed food. At times during the cooking, Roaring Wolf added small amounts of water to the leaves to retain moisture. There were enough wild berries for a man to eat his fill, and Richard learned to distinguish edible plants and roots at a glance. Never had he enjoyed food more.

He was fortunate, too, in his choice of companions. Roaring Wolf was in his natural environment and made all aspects of wilderness living seem easy. Ezekiel Clayton was familiar with the endless forests, too, and seemed never to tire. The trio moved southward through New Sweden and Maryland at a relatively leisurely pace, making steady progress in their journey to Virginia.

The wilderness was considerably different from the woods of Lincolnshire that Richard had known and loved. There were no poachers here, no civilized intruders greedy for forbidden game. The sweet, resinous scent of pines was everywhere, and often, when there was a break in the stands of towering oak, maple, and ash, the effect created by the sunlight slanting down into the open space was like that of sun streaming through a cathedral window.

As Richard became more familiar with the North American wilderness, his awe at the very size of the forests gradually led to an understanding of the fierce love the colonists felt for their new homeland. The quarrels of the Old World seemed petty here, and the man who cooperated with the natural forces lacked nothing. The forest provided him with food and drink, clothing, and a healthy body. Above all else, it gave him a sense of peace that was unique in Richard's experience.

"I can see the attraction of the wilderness for men like your father and Adam Burrows," he said to Ezekiel one night as they sat at their campfire, feasting on broiled venison and trout. "I wondered how men of their caliber could be content living so far from English civilization. Now I wonder how anyone in his right mind could be content anywhere else than here."

"We have a saying we've borrowed from the Indians," Ezekiel replied. "The sap that runs in the trees finds its way into a man's bloodstream."

"This is true," Roaring Wolf said. "White men who come to the forest know nothing of its ways. They learn from warriors, and soon they act more like Indians than Indians themselves." The uninhibited laughter of all three was a reflection of the comradeship that bound them together.

"I came to the New World not knowing what to expect here," Richard said. "Now that I know, I'll never willingly live in England again. I feel more at home here than I do in the house where I was born and reared—which is just as well, seeing that it's been taken from me." He laughed again, without bitterness.

They rolled themselves up in their blankets to sleep, and at dawn they awakened, washed in a creek, and ate cold venison and fish for breakfast before resuming their journey. As always, Richard was excited by the challenges that a new day on the trail would offer.

As they started to break camp, however, Roaring Wolf suddenly raised a hand in warning, then bent low, with one ear close to the ground. Richard did the same and heard the approaching thumping of many footsteps. He looked at Roaring Wolf for guidance.

"Large party of braves comes this way," the Pequot said. "Too many warriors for us to hide. Better to stay here and let them see us."

Richard promptly checked his rifle and pistol, and the other two made ready their own weapons.

Soon they could clearly hear the sound of a rapidly approaching party, and from the crest of the hill near their campsite, they saw a band of braves making their way rapidly toward the east, all armed with bows, arrows, and tomahawks, all with red and purple paint smeared on both their faces and bare torsos.

Roaring Wolf courageously stepped into the open, and while the others covered him with their firearms from their hiding places, he raised his hand, palm outward in a gesture of friendship.

The column halted, and a weary, middle-aged brave, whose bonnet identified him as the leader of the group, came forward. They spoke for some time in low tones. Richard, whose deficiencies in the languages of the Indians made it impossible for him to understand exactly what was being said, tried to deduce the meaning from the Indians' gestures, posture, and expressions. Ezekiel strained to hear, but could pick up only an occasional word or phrase.

Suddenly, Roaring Wolf turned and beckoned to his companions. They came into the open too, and Richard took care to cradle his rifle under one arm while he raised the other in the traditional greeting of Indian friendship.

"This," Roaring Wolf explained, "is Sha-wa-na, sachem of the Conestoga. He leads one hundred warriors, and he is troubled. The Conestoga are being chased by a band of their ancient enemies, the Iroquois, who have three warriors for each of the Conestoga. The Iroquois know that most warriors of the Conestoga have gone far into the wilderness to hunt. It is that time of year. The Iroquois will attack the main town of the Conestoga, burn it to the ground, and make slaves of the women and children. Only Sha-wa-na and his braves stand between the Iroquois and their bloody goal."

Richard looked at the exhausted, worried sachem, and impulsively reached a decision. "You say there are three Iroquois warriors for each of the Conestoga?"

Roaring Wolf nodded.

"Perhaps we can make the odds more equal with the aid of our firesticks," Richard said.

Ezekiel Clayton grinned broadly. "I'm going to enjoy this," he said. "The Iroquois are noted for their viciousness toward their captives. They deserve being taught a lesson they won't forget."

Roaring Wolf translated the offer for the sachem, who promptly reached out and grasped Richard's forearm as he spoke solemnly.

"The Conestoga," Roaring Wolf translated, "will never forget the friendship their white brother offers them in their hour of need. Tell us what needs to be done."

A battle plan had already formed in Richard's mind, and he spoke quickly, decisively. "Divide the warriors into three groups, with one double the size of the others. Let the smaller parties conceal themselves on the flanks in the forest—there, and there. The large group will hide in the forest here, on the side of this hill. None will open fire on the enemies until I give the word."

As Roaring Wolf translated, the Conestoga warriors, bewildered and eager for leadership, obeyed with alacrity.

"Roaring Wolf," Richard said, "the success or failure of that which we will attempt depends on you. For many days you have seen Ezekiel and me using our firesticks. You have examined them often. Do you think you can reload them swiftly? Do you think you can teach a Conestoga brave to do the same?"

The Pequot nodded solemnly. "I will do this for you. I will ask Sha-wa-na to help. My fingers are not as nimble as your fingers, but the Great Spirit will help us."

"Good. Now listen carefully. You too, Ezekiel. I want the Iroquois to think they're facing a large company of white men who carry firearms. Shoot your musket, and Roaring Wolf will reload it while you discharge your pistol. Sha-wa-na will do the same with my weapons. My idea is to establish and maintain a steady stream of fire at the Iroquois. I want to convince them that they face a whole company of marksmen, so you'll both have to reload quickly, Roaring Wolf. And Ezekiel, you and I will be obliged to make every shot count."

Sha-wa-na nodded in approval when Roaring Wolf, who was examining the firearms critically, explained to him what Richard had in mind. "The Iroquois," the sachem declared, "have no fear of other nations. But

250

no Indian can stand up to the magic of the white man's firesticks."

Roaring Wolf and Sha-wa-na were given a supply of powder and lead, and while they practiced the reloading operation, Richard and Ezekiel led their horses to the far side of the hillcrest and tethered them there. The coming battle would be better waged on foot.

A random thought flickered through Richard's mind and caused him to smile at himself. He, who should be concerning himself with the conflict between the Cavaliers and the Roundheads, felt so at home in the American wilderness that he was committing himself to a fight between two tribes of whose very existence he had been unaware only a short time earlier. He had promised his support to the outnumbered Conestoga, however, so he was determined that they win a victory.

As he and Ezekiel returned to their place of concealment behind a thick stand of oaks and brambles, Roaring Wolf raised a hand in warning. The Iroquois were approaching.

Richard had to admire the stealth of the native braves. One moment, the wooded section directly ahead appeared deserted; the next, it was swarming with Iroquois warriors, their faces and bodies streaked with bright green paint. Obviously this was the enemy's vanguard or scouting party, and the braves advanced cautiously.

To open fire now would be to give away his entire plan of action before the main bodies were joined. So he turned to Sha-wa-na and drew a finger across his throat. The sachem understood at once and reacted accordingly, silently signaling to his own men.

Richard would never forget the astonishing spectacle that followed. One by one, the twelve to fifteen Iroquois scouts seemed to be swallowed up by the earth itself. The waiting Conestoga struck with swift brutality, making no sound, and their knives disposed of the entire advance party. Not until later did Richard become conscious of the discipline the Conestoga were exercising; aware of the need for continuing secrecy, they refrained from their customary removal of the scalps of the dead.

Now the main body of the Iroquois came into sight, the brawny, copper-skinned braves making no attempt to conceal themselves because they had no reason to suspect that they were walking into a trap.

"Now, Ezekiel," Richard muttered. "Fire at will—and keep firing."

The rifle and musket spoke almost at the same instant, the former killing one Iroquois warrior in the front rank, the latter wounding another. Dropping his rifle to the ground beside the tense, waiting Sha-wa-na, Richard took aim with his pistol and fired twice. When he saw yet another Iroquois drop to the ground, he decided not to keep count of the casualties. Dropping his still-smoking pistol, he reached for his rifle again, and had to wait only a moment for it to be reloaded.

Thanks to the skill of the sweating Roaring Wolf and Sha-wa-na, who paid no attention to the enemy and concentrated solely on the vital task they had been given, the rifle, musket, and pistols were reloaded steadily, enabling Richard and Ezekiel to keep up an uninterrupted fire. Troops familiar with firearms would have understood the nature of the hoax and been quick to pinpoint the enemy fire, but the Iroquois had never before encountered sustained gunfire in battle and had no idea they faced only two men.

The war chief of the Iroquois came forward, resplendent in a feathered bonnet, and Richard felt a grim satisfaction as he put a bullet between the man's eyes. The Iroquois, leaderless and confused, gave in to a sudden panic and began to withdraw from the field.

"Now!" Richard yelled. "Let the Conestoga attack!"

Roaring Wolf barely had time to translate before the Conestoga, whooping loudly, let fly at their foes with a hail of arrows, then fell in behind the retreating Iroquois.

It was too dangerous now to continue the gunfire for fear of striking down a friend rather than a foe. "Continue your fire," Richard told Ezekiel, "but aim over their heads."

Ezekiel was quick to grasp the principle at stake, and obeyed the order.

Sha-wa-na followed in the wake of his warriors, who were relishing the unusual experience of driving the Iroquois off through the forest and, consequently, were fighting even more ferociously than they otherwise would have done. The sounds of combat became fainter in the distance.

No quarter was given and none was expected. The Conestoga, showing no mercy to their foes, scalped the living who had been wounded, as well as the braves who had been killed.

Sha-wa-na returned to the command post. "My brothers," he said, "there is a rich harvest of scalps that awaits you."

Roaring Wolf looked at Richard, silently entreating for permission to share in the spoils that his efforts had helped to create. Richard waved him forward. "Go ahead," he said. "You're welcome to any scalps I might claim."

"Mine, too," Ezekiel called after him, and calmly began to clean his musket and pistol.

Sha-wa-na and Roaring Wolf soon returned, with bloody, dripping scalps hanging from their belts. It was plain that both were gratified with the results of the battle.

The Conestoga warriors drifted back, their war chiefs reporting to Sha-wa-na, who finally allowed his wooden features to relax in a smile. "More than ten times ten Iroquois warriors lost their lives this day," he announced proudly. "The sons of the Conestoga and their sons after them will sing songs in praise of this great day in the history of our nation." He raised his voice and summoned his warriors, who clustered around Richard and Ezekiel.

"Let all who fought in this battle mark the faces of the Pequot and the white brothers whose firesticks broke the power of the Iroquois," he said in a loud voice. "Let their likenesses be engraved in your hearts, my children, as you would chisel them in stone or wood. They are our brothers for all time and will always be welcome wherever the Conestoga live and hunt. We are a proud people who do not wish to be in debt to anyone. So our medicine men will offer prayers to the Great Spirit that the day will come when we will be able to repay the debt we owe to the white brothers and the Pequot whose help made it possible for us to defeat the mighty Iroquois in battle!"

Hester Browne sat in an armchair, a blanket keeping her warm, a mug of steaming tea on the table beside her. She seemed lost in thought as she stared out at the fields where Dempster Chaney's industry had spread a mantle of green crops. She seemed preoccupied, so Robbin did not disturb her, and instead was content to remain nearby in case she was needed.

"Ah, he's through with work at last," Hester muttered to herself.

Dempster came cheerfully into the house. "The bean crop looks even better than I thought," he announced. "We'll have at least one hundred bushels more than I expected to send off to the Boston markets."

Robbin knew how important the size of the produce yield had become to him. "Wonderful!" she said.

Hester did not react, and it was plain she hadn't heard him.

Dempster looked at her in concern. "You're not suffering a setback after all the fine progress you've been making, Aunt Hester?"

She jerked her mind back to the present. "Indeed I'm not. I'm stronger every day, and by the end of the week, I hope to make those new scarecrows you want for the west forty." She smiled, then sobered. "I want a word with you, young man. With you too, Robbin."

"Let me wash up, and I'll be right back," Dempster said as he went off to the kitchen.

Hester nodded vaguely, then once again peered out at the gathering dusk that enveloped the Massachusetts Bay farm. Her behavior was strange, and Robbin felt a stab of apprehension, even though she told herself there was no cause for concern.

Dempster returned to the parlor, rubbing his hands together. "I see you're cooking venison stew with dumplings and brown gravy tonight," he said with a grin. "How did you know I had my mouth set on that very dish?"

"Because," Robbin replied with a laugh, "you've mentioned it day and night for almost a week."

"Sit down, both of you," Hester commanded.

Her tone was so abrupt that they sat, and Robbin's laugh died away.

"Young man," the proprietress of the farm said gravely, "I owe my life to you. You showed skill as well as courage when you took the diseased part from my body, and those are qualities I admire. If it wasn't for you, and for all that Robbin did for me too, I wouldn't be sitting here now, as chipper as you please."

255

Dempster was embarrassed by her praise. "I did what was needed, that's all," he said.

"Nonsense and fiddlesticks! Now, I'm not a wealthy woman, not by any means, but I can't see letting a natural talent like yours go to waste. I've decided to pay your way at the surgeon school in Edinburgh so you can complete your training."

Dempster was stunned. "I'm more grateful than I'll ever be able to tell you for the offer, Aunt Hester," he said. "But how will you get along here without me?"

"I'll be able-bodied again as soon as my strength returns. Robbin is healthy and strong. Between us we'll manage."

Dempster leaned forward in his chair and put his hand over hers. "Your generosity overwhelms me, Aunt Hester, but I wouldn't dream of accepting. Not only do I refuse to beggar you, but surgeon school belongs to my past, not my present or my future. I doubt that the Roundheads would even permit me to register."

"We'll see about that," she snapped. "There are some Puritan clergymen in Boston who call themselves friends, so we'll see how much influence they can muster on your behalf."

"This may be difficult for you to understand," the young man replied, "but even if my entrance at Edinburgh were guaranteed, I wouldn't accept. Once, I had a dream of becoming a surgeon, but the Roundheads shattered the dream. They did me a favor because I've rediscovered the soil, which is my true love."

"You aren't just saying it because you're reluctant to accept my money?" the woman demanded suspiciously.

"I'll prove it to you." He turned to his wife. "I did what we discussed last night."

"I'm glad for you," Robbin replied softly. "I knew it was right when you mentioned it."

Hester Browne was perplexed. "I dislike mysteries, and I can't abide talk I don't rightly understand."

"Aunt Hester, I've found myself," Dempster told her. "I've planted my own roots in the soil of New England, and they're spreading. This is my homeland now. I've put England behind me for all time, and that includes surgeon school. The militia has been campaigning for recruits, so I went into the village to-day and signed up."

"Did you now?" Hester was startled. "Fancy that!"

"I proved to the recruiting sergeant that I can handle firearms and a sword," he continued, "and my education being what it is, the sergeant seemed to think I'll be awarded a commission, at the very least as an ensign. He said the decision would be made by the Massachusetts Bay high command, but I'll be notified in due time. By early summer, at the latest."

Robbin jumped from her chair and kissed him. "I'm proud of you," she said.

"Well, the way I see it, what with the Indians of the neighborhood getting restless, I'd be less than a man if I didn't live up to my obligations to you two."

"What obligations do you have to me?" Hester demanded, sounding angry.

"I live under your roof and I eat your food," he replied. "It seems to me the least I can do in return is to protect you from Indian attacks!"

Hester blew her nose loudly in a handkerchief she took from her sleeve, and then, still flustered, she sipped her tea. "If there's anything I can't abide it's cold tea!"

Robbin immediately rose again. "The pot is on the stove," she said. "I'll bring you a fresh cup."

"You'll do no such thing, young woman! Land o' Goshen! You'd think I was an invalid the way you pop up like a jack-in-the-box! You'll stay seated until I tell you that you're excused!"

Robbin sank slowly back into her chair, thinking that the older woman's convalescence was making her crotchety.

"I knew, deep down," Hester said, "that you wouldn't accept my offer to send you to Edinburgh, young man. You're too proud for your own good, and you forget that we're taught pride cometh before a fall. Well, I have another scheme in mind, and this time I intend to have my way. Is that understood?"

"Yes, ma'am," Dempster replied meekly, knowing how to mollify her.

She settled back in her chair. "With my Eddie gone, I'm alone in the world," she said. "The Almighty didn't see fit for me to bring children into being, and I have no other relatives. Then the Lord sent me you two, out of the blue."

Robbin started to speak.

"Don't interrupt, young woman!" Hester glowered at her. Never had Robbin seen her in such a foul mood.

"Mind you, what I tell you now is what will be. There will be no arguments, no discussions. Tomorrow morning, first thing, you'll ride over to Solicitor Burnham's and ask him to call on me, Robbin. Tell him I'll appreciate the courtesy, seeing as how I've been ailing and haven't the strength to call on him. I want him to prepare two documents for me. One is a new Last Will and Testament, in which I leave all my earthly goods to you two. The other is a property agreement that makes us equal partners. From now on we'll share equally the profits of this farm." She glared at them. "Do I make myself clear?"

"Very clear, Aunt Hester," Robbin said, and tears came to her eyes.

"We'll have none of that. You should know by now

that I can't tolerate sniveling!" Robbin couldn't help laughing through her tears.

Hester turned to Dempster, her manner still ferocious. "I haven't heard you say a word, young man!"

"For one thing, you've given me no chance to get a word in edgewise, Aunt Hester. And for another, I'm so surprised that I've run out of breath."

"A body has a right to deal with what's hers any way she sees fit, so I'll stand for none of your arguments to the contrary, Dempster Chaney. Not only did you save my life by performing surgery on me, as cool as you please, but you work your fingers to the bone around here. Not even my Eddie, may the Lord have mercy on his soul, worked as hard as you do. That's why we'll share, and share alike from now on!"

"Aunt Hester," he replied huskily, "you're an old fraud. You remind me of a poodle I had when I was a boy. He was old and toothless, but he raised such a storm, barking and growling whenever a stranger came to the door, that people thought he was a mastiff or a sheep dog, at the very least."

Hester Browne opened her mouth to protest further, thought better of it, and merely muttered, "Hmph!"

"You've made it clear that we have no choice, that you've made a final decision in matters that concern all three of us. Very well, I won't embarrass you by telling you how grateful we are. That will spare us another scolding." Dempster grinned as he stood and went to her. "But you forget that love and affection flow two ways at the same time. You've adopted us. Fair enough. Robbin and I are now adopting you, too." He went to her and hugged her gently.

Robbin followed him, kissing the woman's leathery cheeks. "If we don't stop all this chatter and eat supper soon," she said, "my dumplings will be as hard as the rocks I've been digging out of my kitchen garden."

259

That night Aunt Hester's appetite improved sharply and she devoured every scrap of food on her plate.

Mary Clayton elected to wait until a Sunday noon, after church services, to break Eliza Burrows's news to her husband and the young woman's father. She invited Adam and Eliza to dinner, telling the daughter in advance to arrive at least a half-hour late.

Colonel Burrows lost no time apologizing for his daughter's tardiness. Accepting a hot buttered rum from Tom Clayton, he said, "Eliza doesn't understand the value of promptness, no matter how much I lecture her. She was still primping when I stopped at home for her just now. Seeing she didn't even have the decency to come to church with me, you'd think she could have been ready on time."

"Eliza is late," Mary replied immediately, "because I requested it. You two gentlemen are the victims of a female conspiracy." Adam and Tom looked at each other, then at the smiling Mary.

"Have a swallow—a large swallow—of your drinks and brace yourselves."

"What in thunderation has gotten into you?" her husband demanded irritably.

"One step at a time, if you please." She deliberately seated herself on a cushioned stool and faced the two men who stood together at the hearth, facing her suspiciously.

"Why should you have asked Eliza to be late?" Colonel Burrows wanted to know.

"I wanted an opportunity to talk freely and frankly with both of you," Mary replied, her smile fading. "You've nurtured a dream for many years, and it's painful when a dream bubble bursts. You forced Eliza and Ezekiel to become betrothed. Between the two of you, you gave them no choice. As a dutiful wife and a loyal friend I tried to accept your plans, even though I

260

knew in my heart they would never materialize. Having grown up together, they regard their relationship as that of a brother and sister. There's no spark of romance that flows between them."

"There will be plenty of time for romance after they're married," Tom Clayton growled.

"Agreed," Adam Burrows said emphatically. "They're young, and they don't know what they want."

"They know they don't want each other, as they've tried to tell you many times," Mary said forcefully. "Ezekiel may not know what he wants, but he's relieved—beyond measure—that Eliza has lost her heart to someone else."

Colonel Burrows looked as if he had been slapped across the face. "How could that be?" he asked in bewilderment.

"All I find surprising is that it didn't happen a long time ago—to both of them. I swear, Adam, some men are blind. There was a lovely romance budding, right under your nose, and you refused to recognize it."

"Who is the man?"

"Sir Richard Dunstable. I gather he's very much interested in Eliza too, but refrained from expressing his feelings because she was betrothed to Ezekiel."

The colonel drained his drink. Tom Clayton refilled both glasses.

"It could be worse, I suppose," Adam said at last. "Young Dunstable could be useful to us in the business."

"Yes, it would be easy to find a spot for him," Tom agreed.

Mary lost her temper. "Business! Is that your only reaction? Two young people tried hard to please—and submit to the will of—their fathers at the cost of their personal happiness until the strain became too great. I'm proud of Eliza, and I'm proud of my son! And to the devil with what all this does to your precious business plans!"

Eliza had the misfortune to arrive at that moment. She glanced uncertainly at her father, then looked at Mary.

"They know now," Mary told her.

"I'm sorry, Papa," the young woman said. "I tried to tell you, but you wouldn't listen to me. Uncle Tom, I hope you understand, as Aunt Mary does, that my feelings are no reflection on Ezekiel. He's a wonderful person, my best friend, and I wish him all the happiness I want for myself."

The elder Clayton made a gallant attempt to smile. "I've thought of you as a member of the family for so long that it won't be easy to get out of the habit."

"Don't try," Eliza said, and impulsively hugged him.

Adam was still in a whirl. "Why Dunstable?" he demanded.

"I suppose I could tell you a hundred reasons, Papa," Eliza said earnestly. "But it should be enough that I didn't fall in love with him on purpose. It just happened."

"He's established no roots in the New World," her father replied. "That isn't necessarily a handicap, of course. And he is a baronet, so you'd become Lady Dunstable if and when you marry him."

"As if that mattered," Eliza said scornfully. "I know it means nothing to Richard. He prefers not to use his title."

"Life in the colonies is already influencing him," Mary said. "That's all to the good."

Adam walked slowly to a chair and sank into it. "I'll need time to digest all this," he said, shaking his head.

Eliza went to him. "I didn't flout your will deliberately, Papa, and the last thing I wanted was to hurt you. But there are some things that can't be controlled. I know you meant well and were thinking of my welfare."

He looked up at her, his eyes revealing his inner turmoil. "I've got to admire your spirit, Eliza," he said. "I brought you up to be independent, so I suppose I should have expected something like this." He hauled himself to his feet, then embraced his daughter. "Does Ezekiel know how you feel?"

"Of course!"

"And Dunstable?"

"I didn't keep my feelings secret," she replied defiantly.

"Does he reciprocate?"

"I—I have reason to believe he does."

"Well," Adam said, "he hasn't seen fit to ask me for your hand. So, until he does, you can only surmise he feels as you do. Don't count on a marriage to him, Eliza. You can't know him all that well after so brief an acquaintance, so you have no way to judge the permanence of his feelings for you."

The young woman shook her head vigorously, causing her long, blonde hair to dance. "I know he loves me as much as I love him."

"Your father is right, dear," Mary said, "and he doesn't want you to be hurt. Richard may have commitments or relationships you know nothing about, and until you're formally engaged to him, he has every right to change his mind."

The incident began innocently enough. A delegation of three Puritan commissioners arrived in New Amsterdam from Boston at the request of Director-General Stuyvesant to discuss the New Englanders' charges that the Dutch endeavored to stir up an Indian revolt against them. The meetings were not scheduled to start until the following day, so the trio went to the Thorn and Thistle for supper. There Bart Williams saw them and could not resist the temptation to amuse himself at their expense.

His own workday at an end, Bart hastily summoned several like-minded youths, and they waited for the trio. When the commissioners emerged from the inn after supper, they were subjected to a barrage of eggs, fruit, and rotten fish. Several small children joined in the fun, chanting, "Dirty Roundheads," while a number of sympathetic citizens came to the aid of the besieged Puritans.

A full-scale riot ensued, and only the arrival of the local constabulary on the scene prevented serious injuries and property damage. A dozen men were arrested, Bart among them, and all were charged with inciting a riot. All twelve were held pending trial the following day.

Director General Stuyvesant had committed himself to reform and had forbade sabbath-breaking, brawling, and drunkenness in the disorderly town of New Amsterdam. The senseless, unjustified attack infuriated him. He sent to Magistrate Pieter van Dijk, the justice who would hear the case, a personal note in which he declared that the honor of New Netherland was at stake.

The courthouse, located only a stone's throw from the scene of the crime, was crowded to capacity the next morning, and among those in attendance was Mollie Williams, who was badly upset. Angus Mac-Neill, who had accompanied Mollie, tried to soothe her.

"The defender appointed by the court for Bart and the other lads is competent," he said. "You can be certain he'll do his best."

Everyone stood when Magistrate van Dijk came into the courtroom and took his place on the bench. The shackles worn by the defendants were removed in an antechamber, and the entire group looked sheepish as they filed into the chamber under the watchful gaze of constables armed with six-foot staffs of heavy wood. Mollie noted at once that the new shirt she had only recently made for Bart was torn.

The facts of the case were soon established. The visitors from Boston told their story, saying they had been subjected to an unprovoked attack after dining at the Thorn and Thistle. A parade of witnesses described the development of the riot, and an officer of the constabulary told the court how order had been restored.

Bart was identified as the leader of the band of attackers, and when he was called to the witness stand, Magistrate van Dijk himself questioned him.

"Are you acquainted with the plaintiffs?"

"I never saw them in me life until last night, Your Honor."

"Then why did you attack them?"

"Because they're Roundheads." Bart smirked.

"And you consider that a cause for assault?"

"I sure do, Your Honor. We live as we please here, and we don't need these hypocrites telling us to pray. Let them keep their long noses out of our affairs!"

Bart was excused, and the official statement in Bart's defense pointed out that no one had been seriously harmed and no property damaged.

Magistrate van Dijk was not impressed by the argument. "I do not happen to hold the beliefs of those who call themselves Puritans," he said, "but that does not give me the right to ridicule those who do, to subject them to abuse, or to try to harm them. It has been suggested that Boston tries to impose its principles on all who go to that city, but that is Boston's business, and Boston is not New Amsterdam. This city is unique in all the colonies. Living in our midst are people of many nationalities and faiths. All of us are citizens of New

Netherland. It is our duty to live together in harmony. Tolerance of the views of others, tolerance of what sets them apart from us is what causes us to be different from the savages who inhabit the neighboring wilderness. If we are tolerant, we shall flourish; if we are not, then we are doomed."

The defendants were called to the bench for sentencing. The court took their youth into account and was prepared to be lenient, but order had to be preserved in the streets of a town that took pride in its new desire for civility. Bart, as the ringleader, was fined thirty guilders, and each of his confederates was fined fifteen guilders. Those who could not pay would work off their fines in gaol at a rate of one guilder per day. Bart, who spent his wages as rapidly as he earned the money, faced twenty-one days of imprisonment.

Mollie blinked back the tears that threatened to erupt. "Master MacNeill," she said, "I've never in my life been in debt to anyone, but I'll be forever obliged to you if you'll advance me the amount of Bart's fine."

"That I will not, Mistress Williams," Angus replied firmly. "I know how your heart must ache for your one and only child, but you'll do him no favor if you buy his freedom for him."

Mollie was too proud to beg; she stood rigidly erect, the color drained from her face.

"You heard what Magistrate van Dijk said about tolerance," Angus went on. "I happen to agree with him, and so do you. What your son thinks—if there's any thought at all that enters his mind—is hard to tell. But give him twenty-one days on bread and water to digest the magistrate's words, and he'll think twice afore he attacks strangers who have committed no crime worse than that of appearing in our streets dressed in black."

Mollie knew in her heart that he was right, but

could not admit it. "Think of the disgrace a prison term will cast on Bart."

"Think of how fortunate he is that none of the Puritans was killed or maimed. Then he'd swing on a gibbet, Mistress Williams."

She drew in a sharp breath and, unable to speak, could only nod.

"This could be the making of the lad," Angus said. "I swear I won't hold this against him, and he'll have his post as an ostler at the Thorn and Thistle waiting for him when he's released."

"You're good to him, and I won't forget your kindness. Do you think they'll allow me a word with Bart afore they haul him off to gaol?"

"We'll soon find out." Angus piloted her to the front of the courtroom and identified her to the sergeant of the constabulary. A moment later, Mollie stood facing her son in an anteroom.

Bart grinned at her. "I knowed you'd come for me, Ma," he said. "But there's no need for you to bear the expense. I'll pay you back at a rate of a shilling per week."

"I've not paid your fine, boy," she told him.

He looked at her in astonished dismay. "They'll give me naught to eat and drink for three weeks but bread and water. And I'll work from dusk until nightfall breaking stones to be used in making new roads."

"Then, me lad," she replied, tight-lipped, "mayhap you'll learn to appreciate that eggs, apples, pears, and peaches are grown for folk to eat and aren't intended to be thrown." Her head high, she marched back to the courtroom where Angus awaited her. "I'm in your debt, Master MacNeill, for showing me the error of me ways. The boy was as brazen as you please, expecting me to pay the fine! A diet of bread and water will be the best of medicine for him."

Angus was relieved that she took no offense at his

267

refusal, but a principle had been at stake, so it had been impossible for him to compromise.

They walked in silence back to the Thorn and Thistle, and finally Angus said, "You might like the day to yourself, Mistress Williams."

"And who would cook dinner and supper for them as will come crowding into the taproom?"

"I'll stand in for you myself."

"You'll do no such thing, Master MacNeill, I thank you for being so thoughtful. With naught to do but brood, I'd soon feel sorry for meself, when me only real sorrow is for the day I brought that useless boy into this world."

"Well," Angus said with a smile, "it will do no harm if I lend you a hand."

Mollie returned the smile. "It isn't easy for me to say this to one who pays me wages, but you're a darling man, Master MacNeill."

Angus turned scarlet. Mollie was equally embarrassed, and they compensated for their feelings by working furiously when they returned to the kitchen. Pots and pans clattered, Mollie threw ingredients into a bowl and stirred vigorously, while Angus kneaded a shell of dough in which to wrap a venison roast. Both were on the verge of declaring their feelings, yet both were too shy, so they took refuge in the bustle.

The kitchen door swung open, and Bart swaggered in, his walk as brazen as his expression. "A good day to you both," he said. "Ma, I hope you'll be a-cooking plenty of victuals for dinner. The bread they gave me in gaol was stale. And Master MacNeill, there's no need to hire a replacement for me. I'm on me way to the stables this very minute." He began to strut toward the back door.

Mollie and Angus stared at the youth as if he were an apparition, and then the woman found her voice. "Wait!" she commanded.

Bart halted and turned, his grin insolent.

"The last we knew, you were on your way to prison for three weeks. But here you be, as bold as you please. What happened?"

"It seems there are folk in New Amsterdam who feel the same way I do about Roundheads. The very sight of the hypocritical psalm singers makes them sick."

"What happened?" she demanded, her knuckles whitening on the ladle she held in a tight grasp.

"A fine gentleman showed up and paid me fine so I was set free, that's what!"

Mollie glared at her son suspiciously. "And just who was this fine gentleman, pray tell?"

"Master Laroche, that's who! Friends do favors for each other, he told me, and he paid out me penalty in gold as quick and easy as if it was threepenny bit!"

Trim, healthy, and in high spirits after their journey through the wilderness, Richard, Ezekiel, and Roaring Wolf arrived at Horace Laing's estate outside Norfolk. As they started up the long driveway, lined on both sides by graceful linden trees, Ezekiel stared hard at the portico supported by four ornately carved Corinthian columns, then paused.

"Maybe Roaring Wolf and I had best find ourselves lodging elsewhere," he muttered.

The Pequot felt as he did, and nodded. "Too fancy here," he said.

"Rubbish," Richard replied briskly. "I wouldn't insult Master Laing's hospitality by having you go somewhere else. Just look at the house, and you know he has plenty of room for all three of us. Besides, from what I have heard of him, he'll be delighted to have us here! Come along!"

Not waiting for a reply, he rode up to the front door, dismounted, and knocked. Simms, the stone-

269

faced butler, led the trio into the house and alerted his master of their arrival.

Horace Laing greeted his guests in the library, an impressive room lined with bookshelves that stretched from floor to ceiling. "Sir Richard, you've been expected for some time, ever since you first landed in Boston. Master Clayton, I know of your father by repute, although I've never had the pleasure of doing business with him. And Roaring Wolf, an honorable warrior is always welcome here."

"I will sleep in the yard," Roaring Wolf replied, "and I will get food from your kitchen. The beds of white men are too soft, the tables where they eat are too clumsy."

"Of course," Laing replied urbanely. "I sometimes have Powhatan guests, and they feel just as you do. Sir Richard, I can offer you and Master Clayton adjoining chambers, and I hope you're prepared to stay with me long enough to have made your journey worth your effort. Your horses have been attended?"

"Indeed they have, and I've taken the liberty of warning your chief groom to provide my stallion with a stall of his own."

"You may be certain that we'd treat a stallion in no other way," the still-smiling Laing replied. "Hot water will be brought to your rooms at once, gentlemen. Roaring Wolf, I trust the pond behind the stables will be sufficient for your needs. We'll gather here for a cup of cheer before dinner at noon, gentlemen." He bowed them out, and Simms waited to conduct them to their rooms.

Horace Laing's genial smile vanished as he closed the door of his library behind the guests. He threw himself into a leather armchair behind his desk, then picked up a quill pen, and chewed thoughtfully on the end. Here was an unexpected obstacle to his neatly made plans.

It was true that Sir Richard's visit had been anticipated, and Laing had been looking forward to the arrival of the promising new recruit. Dunstable, like Lady Dawn, was a special prize. The young man was in robust health, an expert shot, a fair enough swordsman, and as the King's Forester who had lost his hereditary position when the Puritans had taken full control of England, he was certain to arouse sympathy in Cavalier circles. Mazarin himself had marked Dunstable's file for Laing's personal attention.

Horace Laing had expected to handle the recruiting of Dunstable in his usual manner, just as he was now doing with Lady Dawn, and as he had done with all who had gone before her. A few drops of the apothecary's special powder in a glass of port, a stay of long or short duration in one of the cells below, and another agent would join the ranks of the English who were working for France. After all, Dunstable had no ties to anyone in the New World, and his disappearance would not create even a ripple of excitement or interest.

The presence of Ezekiel Clayton caused many complications. He was of no use to France and, consequently, would have to be eliminated. But that would prove awkward. His father was a prominent New England merchant and was associated in business with a wide network of influential officials. If he vanished into thin air, an inquiry might be launched, and Laing wanted no colonial militia probing into dark corners. He himself might slip, and there was always the possibility that the members of his staff, no matter how much he trusted them, might blunder. If the militia of the English colonies learned of his plans to bring all of their territory under the French flag, the task would become far more involved, and the chance of success would be lessened drastically. Yes, he would need to find a way to neutralize young Clayton.

As for the Indian, Laing dismissed him from mind. He felt only contempt for savages, whom he regarded as stupid brutes, and a knife neatly inserted between the ribs of the warrior called Roaring Wolf would dispose of him.

Unfortunately, he would need time now to work out a foolproof scheme. Very well, he would make the best of the situation while he played to the hilt his role of jovial host.

When Richard and Ezekiel reappeared in the library at noon, he prepared stiff drinks of brandy for his guests, thinking the strong liquor would affect them quickly and forestall questioning on subjects he would prefer to avoid.

But Richard politely took a single sip of his drink, then left it untouched. "Tell me how Lady Dawn is faring," he said. "I've been eager to hear about her."

Laing was prepared for the inquiry. "A charming young lady, isn't she? I enjoyed her stay with me, although her lack of interest in political affairs was somewhat surprising."

"She is like so many of us," Richard replied. "She took it for granted that people would remain loyal to the Crown, and she didn't dream that Parliament would try to usurp King Charles's royal prerogatives. Where is she these days?"

"She became interested in the new colony being formed to our south, Carolana," Laing replied glibly. "A number of new settlements are being formed down there by Cavaliers, and she went off to join them."

"Really?" Richard couldn't picture Mimi making her home in a frontier community totally lacking in the comforts of civilization she not only enjoyed, but took for granted.

Laing didn't want him to become too curious about the woman's whereabouts. Realizing by Richard's attitude that he had erred in some way, he tried to compensate. "I had a number of guests while Lady Dawn was visiting here," he said. "Among them was a nobleman whom she had known at Whitehall, and I believe he influenced her decision to join the party that was planning to establish a new settlement."

Richard shook his head. The story didn't quite ring true, but he had no reason to doubt Horace Laing's word.

"I expect to receive word on their progress at any time now, Sir Richard. Perhaps I'll be fortunate enough to get a letter while you're still here." The best way to allay Dunstable's unformed suspicions would be to nip them in the bud. Later in the day, Laing would forge a note from a leader of the Carolana settlers. He would present it to Dunstable in the morning, making certain it contained a reference to Lady Dawn, stressing that she was well and content with her life on the frontier.

Laing realized he was walking a tightrope, that his hitherto foolproof operation was in jeopardy. He would be obliged to proceed with great care.

X

ROARING Wolf needed few comforts to make himself at home anywhere. The overhanging roof of a little smokehouse in the yard behind Horace Laing's mansion provided him with shelter in case of rain, the kitchen staff had been notified that he was to be provided with food, and his blanket was the only bed he required.

The main house was the largest private dwelling he had ever seen, and the coming and going of a large staff fascinated him. Sitting motionless in the sun, his back propped against the smokehouse wall, a pipe clamped in his teeth, Roaring Wolf amused himself by observing and identifying the hired help. The cook who had given him his noon meal was already familiar to him, and he wondered why both the groom in charge of the stable and the handyman carried knives and pistols in their belts. It seemed odd to him, too, that the butler, whose name was Simms, exerted so much authority over the others. They appeared to fear him, and when he gave an order they jumped to obey.

The ways of whites were strange. First Simms came stealthily to the backyard and, taking a key from a ring, unlocked a heavy door. When he opened it, Roaring Wolf caught a glimpse of stairs that descended into a cellar. The groom and the handyman stationed themselves outside the door.

Then a grim-faced serving maid in a starched uniform that looked uncomfortable came from the kitchen outbuilding carrying a tray of food. She marched past the groom and the handyman, disappearing down the cellar stairs.

Roaring Wolf had nothing better to occupy him, so he was content to remain propped against the wall of the smokehouse. After a wait of about a half-hour, as white men counted time, the maidservant reappeared, and the food on the tray was gone. Then Simms carefully closed and locked the door again, and the groom and handyman went off about their business.

Removing the pipe from his mouth and absently tapping the bowl against the palm of his hand to empty it, the Pequot pondered what he had just witnessed. He came to the conclusion that the cellar had an entrance of its own, separate from the main portion of the house, and that a meal had been served to someone who either lived or was hiding there. But why had the door been locked? And why did the groom and the handyman stand guard when it was open?

Unable to answer the questions, Roaring Wolf became restless. Curious about whites and the way they lived, he made up his mind to investigate further, but he knew better than to attempt to force the locked door. He was enjoying the game he had devised for himself, so he waited with the utmost patience until all members of the staff had taken themselves elsewhere.

Then, needing an excuse to approach the building, he drew his tomahawk from his belt and hurled it at a small silver birch that stood at one side of the cellar. The blade imbedded itself in the trunk, and he strolled to retrieve it, never once looking in the direction of the cellar.

Ah! At ground level was a window that had not been washed in many months; the pane of glass was filthy, rendering it opaque. That window was perfect for his purposes, so Roaring Wolf made his way slowly back to the smokehouse wall, propped himself against it, and fell asleep.

He awakened shortly before sundown, stood and stretched, then went off to the kitchen.

"It's you again," the cook muttered, carving a thick slice of ham, then placing it on a board with a slab of corn bread and thrusting the food at the Indian, her eyes angry and resentful.

Roaring Wolf's face remained expressionless as he accepted the food. Taking it to his resting place, he consumed it slowly. When he was finished he licked his fingers, wiped his mouth on the sleeve of his buckskin shirt, and went off to the pond for a drink of water.

By now night had fallen, and the Pequot no longer moved lethargically. The yard was dark, but he took no chances, creeping toward the house. He approached the window and, drawing his knife from his belt, pried it open silently. His guess had been right: it had not been locked from the inside; the dirt caked on it indicated that the butler and the rest of the staff had forgotten its existence. Opening the window gently so he wouldn't dislodge the dirt, Roaring Wolf lowered himself to the ground, slithered through the opening, then silently closed the window again, using his knife blade to ease it shut. Now he found himself in a stone-lined corridor with a stone floor. The odor was musty, indicating a lack of fresh air. Momentarily closing his eyes in order to acclimate himself to the dark, the Pequot saw an open door on one side of the short corridor, and hurried to it. Beyond it stood a cell, furnished only with a cot, and he knew for certain now that this place was a prison of some sort. There was a rusty key in the lock that he removed with some difficulty, guaranteeing that he could not be locked inside the cell should his presence be discovered.

On the opposite side of the corridor stood another door similar to the one that stood ajar. It was closed, and a crack of light made by a burning candle or an oil lamp showed on the floor. Roaring Wolf concluded that the cell was occupied.

All at once the Pequot heard the outer door being unlocked, so he drew back farther into the cell. Then he heard two sets of approaching footsteps. Peering out from his place of concealment, he saw Simms, toting an oil lamp, followed by the serving maid, who carried a tray of cooked food.

By the light of the lamp Roaring Wolf saw a key protruding from the lock of the door opposite him, and he guessed that it could not be removed. The metal used by whites grew rusty in damp weather, and it was uncomfortably damp in this cellar. The door was opened, and the serving maid entered silently.

Roaring Wolf was astonished to see a young woman

in a dress of shimmering silk in the cell. Her skin was fair, and he took note of her shoulder-length red hair and her eyes, which were a startling shade of green. Obviously she was a captive, even though she was dressed for a party of some sort.

As the fascinated Pequot, his presence still undetected, continued to watch, the red-haired young woman sat on the cot in her cell and ate her meal, totally ignoring the serving maid. Neither spoke a word. Then the maid withdrew, Simms closed and locked the door, and the maidservant walked ahead of him into the open. The experience was so extraordinary, so eerie that Roaring Wolf almost imagined he had been dreaming. But the hair and eyes of the prisoner had been so vivid that he knew what he had seen had not been a fantasy.

The retreating footsteps halted, the outer door was relocked, and the Pequot heard no sound but his own breathing. He was tempted to unlock the cell door opposite him, but the ways of whites were so contrary to his own that he didn't want to inadvertently offend his host or Richard. He would report what he had seen to Richard, who would interpret the incident for him. First, however, he had to exercise still more patience and wait until he was certain the way was clear.

He listened outside the closed door of the cell, but could hear nothing, although the light continued to show under the door. He waited for a long time, then departed as he had entered the cellar, first assuring himself that Simms, the groom, and the handyman were no longer loitering outside.

Now he faced the problem of how to convey what he had learned to Richard. Laing and his guests were still at supper, so Roaring Wolf walked purposefully to the side door of the house, slipped inside, and then rapidly climbed the inside stairs. There were so many rooms in the house that he became confused, but he looked in them one at a time, until finally he recognized Richard's rifle and saddlebag in a corner of a chamber on the third floor.

Relaxing and grinning, he seated himself cross-legged on the floor, folded his arms, and waited patiently in the dark for his friend to appear. After a long time he heard voices on the stairs, listened intently, and nodded when he recognized Richard's and Ezekiel's voices deep in conversation. Rising to his feet, he moved out into the corridor.

Richard, who was saying something to his companion, broke off abruptly when he saw the silent Indian awaiting him. Roaring Wolf raised a hand in warning. The baffled pair followed him into the bedchamber, and Richard closed the door behind them. Knowing the Pequot was not given to melodrama, he looked at him and waited.

Roaring Wolf quickly described what he had seen in the cellar, explaining how he had made his way there and relating what had aroused his curiosity.

"Describe the prisoner again," Richard said, his mind whirling.

"Young. Very pretty. With very red hair. And eyes the color of young oak leaves in the spring."

Richard drew in his breath as he turned to Ezekiel. "This makes no sense, but Horace Laing appears to be holding Lady Dawn Shepherd captive!"

Ezekiel didn't know what to reply.

"You're sure, Roaring Wolf?" Richard demanded incredulously.

"Very sure," the Pequot replied.

"I'm damned well going to get to the bottom of this!" Richard started toward the door.

Ezekiel remained level-headed. "Wait!" he said, grabbing hold of Richard's arm. "Whatever is responsible for all this, it's a serious business. I heard Laing lie to you today about Lady Dawn going off to Carolana. He has a considerable household staff—not to mention the field hands who may or may not be loyal to him. In any event, we're outnumbered, and we could find ourselves in a nasty situation."

"You're right, of course," Richard said, halting abruptly. "Why Mimi is a prisoner isn't relevant at the moment. We've got to rescue her first, and then we can ask questions."

"Precisely so," Ezekiel Clayton replied. "If you go to Laing with what we've just learned, we lose the element of surprise."

Richard thought rapidly. "Roaring Wolf, can you lead us to the lady?"

The Pequot's broad grin was sufficient reply.

"Are there enough horses in the stables for all of us?"

"Plenty of horses," Roaring Wolf assured him.

"And there are no guards stationed outside the cellar now?"

"Guards come only at mealtime."

"It seems to me there's no time like the present," Richard said. "I see nothing to be gained by waiting until tomorrow night. I propose to rescue Mimi right now, get our horses and whatever additional mounts we may need from the stable—and then make a break for freedom." Richard picked up his rifle, checked it and then his pistol. "All right. We'll sneak out and let Roaring Wolf show us the way. Bring your saddlebag, Ezekiel, because we won't be coming back up here." He hesitated for a moment. "It's a dark night, but I suggest we use no candles or lamps. We'd be asking for problems if we show any lights."

"We don't need lights," Roaring Wolf said.

Ezekiel agreed. "We got along fine in the wilderness without oil lamps."

"So be it, then." Richard loosened his knives in his belt. "Once we set Mimi free, I suggest we head

279

straight for Middle Plantation and swear out a warrant for Laing's arrest."

"Let's rescue the prisoner first," Ezekiel said as he went off for his own saddlebag and weapons.

They met in the corridor and, with Roaring Wolf in the lead, crept down the stairs.

What they did not know—and could not have known—was that Horace Laing was still in his library, writing the letter he intended to produce the following day to prove that Lady Dawn was thriving in Carolana. He heard the soft footsteps on the stairs, then stole after the trio after first alerting Simms and sending him to rouse the other men on the household staff.

The Pequot led his companions into the side yard, then made his way directly to the cellar window. Richard left his saddlebag on the ground outside, then followed Roaring Wolf deep into the dark cellar, with Ezekiel Clayton close behind. Roaring Wolf pointed toward the closed prison door with the light showing beneath it.

At that moment they heard a key turning in the lock and the door creaking open. Several dark shapes loomed at the top of the stairs.

Roaring Wolf braced himself, and Richard drew his pistol. "Fetch Mimi," he told Ezekiel softly. "We'll hold them off here."

"Who goes there?" Horace Laing called. "Come out with your hands over your heads now!"

Richard replied by firing his pistol twice, first at the taper that Simms held, then at the armed man himself. The landing suddenly became dark, and the butler stumbled and screamed, pitching headlong down the stairs.

Ezekiel Clayton hurried down the dark corridor, guided by the light he saw beneath the door. He tried turning the key in the rusted lock, but in his haste he wedged it more securely. "Stand away from the door!" he commanded, and blew off the lock with his pistol, then raised the latch.

Mimi Shepherd stood facing him in the light of her oil lamp, wide-eyed and bewildered, but even in this moment of crisis showing no fright.

Never had he seen anyone so lovely. "I'm Ezekiel Clayton. I've come with Richard to get you out of here," he said.

Mimi unhesitatingly opened a clothing box and removed her jewel case. "I'm ready," she said.

Ezekiel hastily reloaded his pistol. "Don't take the lamp. It makes too good a target. Stay close behind me."

Asking no questions, she followed his orders, and they crept down the corridor, halting when they saw the activity directly ahead.

As Richard reloaded in the dark, Roaring Wolf detected a movement near the open cellar door. He hurled his tomahawk at the shadow, and a man's howl echoed through the stone vault, indicating that the Pequot's aim had been accurate.

Yet another figure appeared at the top of the steps, and Richard saw the burly groom, armed with a musket. His pistol spoke twice more, and the man slumped to the ground.

"Dunstable," Horace Laing seethed, "you've interfered in matters of state that are none of your concern!"

Richard turned to see the outraged Laing bearing down on him, a sword in one hand. There was no chance to reload his pistol, and knowing his rifle was useless at such close range, he retreated hastily before the onrushing Laing, stumbling over the body of Simms. On the stone floor beside the butler was the sword he had dropped. Richard bent down, snatched it, and straightened just in time to deflect a wicked thrust from Laing's blade.

"No!" Mimi shuddered, and Ezekiel, a pistol in one hand, encircled the woman's shoulders with his free arm, shielding her.

Roaring Wolf fitted an arrow into his bow, but the duelists were dancing back and forth so quickly and erratically in the uncertain half-light that the Pequot was afraid to release it.

The corridor was narrow, the damp stone flooring underfoot was slippery, and the light was bad. Horace Laing was an expert swordsman, and in his rampant fury he was determined to kill the man who had spoiled his carefully conceived plans.

Richard knew when their swords clashed that he had more than met his match. His touch with a blade was less skilled than that of his foe, his reflexes slower. He parried a vicious thrust just in time to save himself, and was pressed backward step by step to the inner end of the corridor. Then, suddenly, Horace Laing was gone, appearing to have vanished into thin air.

But Roaring Wolf, whose night vision was superior to that of his companions, was not fooled. He saw Laing leap up onto a stone block, preparing to demolish his enemy from the greater height. The Pequot unhesitatingly unloosed his arrow, the twang of his bow echoing faintly down the length of the underground chamber. The arrow penetrated Laing's chest, and he toppled to the stone floor.

"All enemies are dead now," Roaring Wolf de-. clared.

"We don't know how many others may be around," Richard said. "Are you all right, Mimi?"

"I—I think so, Richie," the shaken woman gasped.

"All right. Let's get out of here." Suddenly belying his own words, Richard snatched one of his throwing knives from his belt and hurled it with full force at the prone body of Horace Laing. A pistol that had been pointed at Mimi slipped from Laing's grasp as he died.

The full impact of her captivity was suddenly felt by Mimi, and she found it difficult to breathe. She buried her face in Ezekiel's shoulder, leaning on him for support.

Richard retrieved his knife. "I saw him just in time," he said. "We have no way of knowing how many male retainers may be at large here. Certainly the serving maids have heard the sounds of pistol shots. Roaring Wolf, take the lead. Ezekiel, you shield Mimi and follow close behind me."

They hurried to the stable where Prince Henry greeted his master by whinnying. Losing no time, they saddled the stallion and Ezekiel's gelding, found a mare for Mimi to ride, and another gelding for Roaring Wolf. Within a short time they were on the road that would take them to Middle Plantation.

"My money is gone," Mimi said, on the verge of tears, "and I've had to leave all my clothes behind. All I've managed to salvage are my jewels."

"You're safe now, and that's all that matters," Ezekiel said, trying to comfort her as he rode close beside her.

"What I want to know is why Laing was holding you prisoner, Mimi," Richard said.

She told her story, her voice breaking as she related her helplessness and frustration. Ezekiel's expression indicated that he found her story unbelievable, but Richard accepted every word literally. He clearly recalled how Robertson had conferred at length and in private with the French *enseigne* when the brig bringing him and Mimi to the New World had been halted on the high seas, and that Robertson's journal had been written in French. Obviously a great conspiracy that threatened the future of England and her colonies had been exposed.

"I might have guessed it would be you who would find me, Richie," Mimi said tremulously.

He stared hard at her and petted her hand. "You've held up well during your ordeal," he told her. "I don't know anyone else who would have your courage."

They looked hard at each other and what they did not say was far more significant than the words they spoke. Somehow, for reasons neither of them understood, their mutual attraction had vanished; they were no longer interested in each other as man and woman, although as colleagues bound together in a great adventure with enormous stakes, their ties were still indissoluble.

"Your captivity wasn't in vain," he said. "You've done a great service for England, and you've accomplished even more for her colonies here. All of us are in Roaring Wolf's debt for being so observant."

The Pequot, clinging in terror to his saddle, was in no mood to accept praise.

"We've left at least four dead men behind us at Laing's estate, and your story will be hard to prove, Mimi," Richard said. He carefully refrained from saying that by making the conspiracy public the French would be alerted to their own activities. He had surmised enough about espionage to know that the advantage lay with the nation that knew what to expect from its foes. "I've changed my mind about going to the local authorities in Middle Plantation. Laing was a personage of consequence in the community here, and we might spend days being questioned about tonight's events. I suggest we leave the area as rapidly as possible." Richard added to himself: *And give me the chance to report these developments to colonial leaders I know I can trust.*

284

"I won't need much persuasion," Mimi said, "but where I'll go, I can't imagine."

"Let me worry about that," Ezekiel told her. "I'm sure my family will give you a warm welcome."

"We'll go straight to the waterfront and see if we can find a ship that will take us north," Richard said, reflecting that travel through the wilderness would take too long.

Smudges of the early, false dawn streaked the sky as he rode at the head of the little party as they approached the Kecoughtan harbor, where, in spite of the early hour, there was a great deal of activity. Fishermen were heading out into Chesapeake Bay for their day's work, their torches glowing brightly at a half-dozen docks, and Richard felt encouraged when he saw a merchant ship's crew on deck, obviously making ready to put out to sea.

Dismounting hastily, he left his companions waiting for him while he went to confer with the master of the ship. "May I ask your destination, sir?"

"New Amsterdam." The captain looked askance at this man who smelled of burned gunpowder.

"Can you take four passengers—and four horses?" Richard knew he had to make the offer interesting. "You'll be paid a sovereign in gold for your trouble."

A gold sovereign would substantially increase the master's personal profit on his three-day voyage, and he brightened. "I have stalls on board for the animals, so they'll be no problem," he said. "But I have no quarters available for you. I can feed you in the cabin, that'll offer no problem, either. But you'll have to sleep on deck."

Richard unhesitatingly reached into his purse for a gold sovereign.

A short time later, with the horses snugly penned in the hold, he and his companions gathered on the aft deck where they tried to stay out of the busy crew's way. "You'll be roughing it on deck for three days, Mimi, but the sea air should bring some color to your face. How long did you spend in that confounded cell?"

"It felt like forever, but actually it was about two weeks." The girl rubbed her arms and smiled. "The most welcome sound in the world was the shot that Ezekiel fired when he blasted the lock."

"I'll never forget the way you looked," Ezekiel replied with a grin. "As cool as you please, accepting my introduction as if we had just met at a lawn party."

She joined in his enjoyment. Richard noted absently that they had struck a good rapport, and he was glad. It was odd, he thought, but he could look at Mimi without thinking that they had ever been intimate. His relationship with Eliza had supplanted Mimi in his thoughts; come to think of it, he no longer yearned for Dorothea, either.

Waiting until the ship sailed and the excitement died away, Richard sat down with Mimi and told her to recount every word of the talk she'd had with Horace Laing in her cell. It was important, he said, that she remember every detail.

The woman realized he was in dead earnest and did her best to methodically comply with the request. Ezekiel listened to her narrative with great sympathy, but could not understand why Richard remained stone-faced, memorizing every detail.

The voyage was uneventful, marred only by the seasickness of Roaring Wolf, who was badly frightened to find himself sailing on one of the great white birds that he had viewed previously only from a safe distance. The wilderness held no terrors for him, but the rolling blue-green ocean, with its mountainous waves that caused the frail vessel to pitch and toss, made him miserable.

Richard spent the better part of the voyage analyzing the information that he had gleaned from Mimi. As nearly as he could judge, the French conspiracy obviously was not confined to Laing and the members of his household. The man who called himself Laroche had to be in the pay of Cardinal Mazarin of France, too, as did one or more high-placed Cavaliers who had either followed young Charles II into exile or were living inconspicuously in England. Richard thought of his dear friend the Earl of Newcastle and wondered how he would react to this knowledge.

Preoccupied with the problem and its many implications, Richard was only vaguely conscious of the growing intimacy of Mimi and Ezekiel. They spent literally all of their time together, conversing at great length, and at night when they slept on deck, Ezekiel took care to place himself adjacent to Mimi, ready to protect her with the loaded pistol he kept close at hand.

On the last morning of the voyage, Richard revealed something of his plans to his companions. "We'll go straight to the Thorn and Thistle Inn," he said, "because I have some unfinished business with a gentleman there. Ezekiel, you'll scour the waterfront and arrange a sailing for us tomorrow on a ship that will take us to New Haven without delay. It's urgent that I see Colonel Burrows."

"Will there be time for me to attend to some errands of my own?" Mimi wanted to know. "I'm traveling in the only clothes I have to my name, and I'm sick of them. It's important that I look presentable when I meet Ezekiel's parents, you know."

Richard nodded, but the significance of her statement escaped him.

"I've decided to sell a ruby ring that has no particular sentimental value. That will give me enough money to buy some clothes and cosmetics in New Amsterdam."

"Very well," Richard said. "But Roaring Wolf and Ezekiel will go with you everywhere."

The others looked at him blankly.

"Horace Laing may be dead," he said somberly, "but you have other, far more important enemies, ruthless people who will stop at nothing to gain their ends—one of which is the recruitment of Lady Dawn Shepherd to the cause of France. Ezekiel, I charge you and Roaring Wolf with protecting Mimi. Don't allow her out of your sight for a single minute on shore. Where she goes, you two will go. And when you search the waterfront for a ship to take us to New Haven, Mimi will accompany you."

"It's that serious?" Mimi asked gravely.

"It's more serious than you know," Richard assured her. "Just do what I ask. and you'll be all right."

They landed at noon, their horses were led from the hold, and the party went straight to the Thorn and Thistle. There, Richard engaged two rooms, one for himself, the Pequot, and Ezekiel, the other for Mimi. Then, while they went off on their errands, he turned with a smile to Angus MacNeill, who had been loitering in the vicinity, obviously seeking a word with him.

"How is our Mollie?"

"She has news for you, both good and bad, and it'll be best if she tells you herself. Will you come to the kitchen with me?"

Richard accompanied him to the kitchen, where Mollie, wrapped in an apron, was testing a cake with a long straw. She put down the straw, wiped her hands on her apron, and hurriedly approached, her face wreathed in smiles. "Me prayers have been answered, Master Dunstable," she said. "You're the very man I've been aching to see." She turned to Angus. "What have you told him?"

"Nothing. All I said is that you have news both good and bad."

"The good first, then," she said, and smiled shyly at the balding innkeeper. "Master MacNeill has done me the honor of proposing marriage, and I've accepted him," she said.

Richard kissed her on the cheek and grasped MacNeill's hand. "My best wishes to both of you! You'll have a wonderful life together, and the Thorn and Thistle will become the best inn on the entire seaboard."

"That it will," Angus MacNeill assured him.

"But there's bad news to temper the good." Mollie lowered her voice so the assistant cook and waiters could not hear her. "Me Bart has disappeared."

Richard was startled.

"Mistress Williams ain't saying it right, sir," MacNeill declared. "The lad didn't vanish into the blue, like you might say. One day he was gone, but he left a note for his ma, he did. He said he was going off to Quebec to make his fortune."

"Why Quebec?" Richard tried to conceal his surprise, but guessed that young Bart had been recruited in the service of France.

"He took us by surprise, he did," Mollie replied with a deep sigh. "Me and Master MacNeill, we didn't know he had as much as a nodding acquaintance with anyone up there. Seeing as how you wasn't around to give us advice, we consulted Master Laroche, and he told us not to worry, that Bart is sure to do fine there."

Laroche again! Richard's eyes narrowed as he said, "I'm intending to have a little chat with Laroche this very evening. I assume he still comes here for a late-evening drink."

289

"He's as regular as the tide," Angus assured him.

"I'll find out what I can for you," Richard said. "I'm interested in his reasons for thinking Quebec offers opportunities to the lad."

Mollie and Angus insisted that he dine as their guest, then piled his plate high with food, which embarrassed him. He took his time, dawdling over the meal, and it was late afternoon when Mimi and her escorts returned, all three laden with packages containing clothes she had purchased.

The woman was in high spirits, the first time since her ordeal that she seemed like herself. "Now I can feel presentable when I meet Ezekiel's parents!" she said enthusiastically.

Richard wondered why the meeting was so important to her, but Ezekiel's news obliterated everything else from his mind.

"We're in luck, Richard! One of Uncle Adam's coastal brigs is in port and will have her cargo loaded in time to sail on the morning tide tomorrow. We're welcome on board, and although we'll be a mite cramped for space, we'll reach New Haven in far less time than we'd need on an overland march through the forest."

Only Roaring Wolf was gloomy over the prospect of another sea voyage.

Mimi deposited her packages, then went off to the kitchen for a joyful reunion with Mollie.

"You didn't tell me what a remarkable person Mimi is," Ezekiel said to Richard.

A light slowly dawned. "Are you smitten?"

"From the moment I saw her, and she feels the same way! What I find astonishing is that she puts on no airs, and she doesn't give a hang about her rank."

"As you say, she's remarkable," Richard replied, feeling infinite relief. With Ezekiel in love with the daughter of the late Earl of Sturbridge, whom his parents were certain to welcome warmly, he would have no obstacle in his wooing of Eliza Burrows. But he could not allow himself to dwell at length on the mercurial Eliza. The future of the colonies was at stake and required his complete concentration.

That evening the party dined at leisure, and Richard gave specific instructions to Mimi and Ezekiel. "Ask no questions, but do as I say," he told them. "Wait about five minutes, no more, and then follow me into the taproom. You'll find me at a table with a dark-haired man who looks as if his supper disagreed with him. Take a table at the far end of the room and make sure you sit where he can see you. Most important, pay no attention to me or to him."

"There is obviously some reason for all this," Mimi said.

He nodded. "You were Horace Laing's prisoner for two weeks, and that's reason enough. When you want to be rid of vermin, you smoke them out." Richard refused to say anything more. Stifling their curiosity, they agreed to do his bidding.

Angus MacNeill came to the table, and as he had been asked, he told Richard that Laroche had arrived and was seated at his usual corner table.

Richard rose abruptly, then made his way into the taproom by a roundabout route, so Laroche would not see him as he approached. He halted by the man's table, then said quietly, "Good evening, Master Laroche. May I join you?"

The agent's training stood him in good stead, but he nevertheless gaped at Richard for a moment, his face registering astonishment before a mask again covered his face. "By all means," he said.

The shock he displayed so plainly, if briefly, convinced Richard that the same fate Mimi had suffered had been in store for him, too. He believed that Laroche was working for France, and soon he would be able to put that theory to the test.

"You stayed only a short time in Virginia, I take it," Laroche said.

"Circumstances made it unnecessary for me to prolong my visit there." Richard did not elaborate.

"You saw Horace Laing?"

"A charming man. He takes his duties as a host seriously." That, Richard reflected, was an understatement. From the corner of his eye, he watched Mimi and Ezekiel make their way to a table directly in Laroche's line of vision. "By the way, I encountered an old friend at Laing's plantation. You aren't acquainted with Lady Dawn Shepherd, I believe you said."

The man nodded.

"There she is, in the blue gown—the woman with red hair. Once you've seen her, you aren't likely to forget her. Don't you agree?"

Laroche's jaw dropped as he stared at Mimi. Recovering his aplomb quickly, he managed to murmur, "She's very lovely." Obviously something had gone amiss with Laing's recruiting operation, but he could ask no questions of the sharp-eyed young baronet who was studying him so intently.

The last doubts vanished from Richard's mind. Laroche had been a party to Laing's recruiting scheme, which meant that the supposed chief of New World operations for the Cavaliers was actually in the employ of France. Richard found it difficult to hold his anger in check, while Laroche seemed to be calculating his next move.

"I'm pleased you've returned at this particular time," Laroche said briskly. "Our friends in England want a personal report, and so do our principals in France. If you're willing, I'd like you to sail in about ten days, when a safe ship will go off to England."

"I'm not sure I can afford the luxury of making another journey this soon," Richard temporized.

"Your fare and other expenses will be paid," Laroche replied quickly. "The voyage will cost you nothing but your time."

"In that case, I might be able to arrange it." Richard wondered if he would be entering another trap.

"Are you acquainted with Lord Blankenship?"

"Slightly." Richard had gone to London every year to receive his pay as King's Forester from Blankenship, who had served as assistant secretary of dispensing of funds at the court of Charles I.

"Good. You'll find him awaiting you in England at the Royal Arms Inn, at Dover. Return here nine days from today, and your passage will be waiting for you. Master MacNeill will be given a packet for you."

"A round-trip passage, I trust?" Richard asked quietly.

"Naturally," Laroche replied quickly, almost too quickly. "You've become familiar with the colonies during your stay in the New World, so you're more valuable to the king's party here than you were previously."

Richard knew it could prove dangerous to make an immediate decision. "If I can't settle my own affairs in time to make the voyage, I'll be in touch with you."

"I hope you'll see fit to go. You're better able to give a comprehensive report than anyone else."

Richard nodded, rose to his feet, then said casually, "Mollie Williams tells me you approved of her son's going off to Quebec to seek his fortune there."

"Indeed I did," the man replied smoothly. "The future of the English colonies depends on Anglo-French trade, and any man who knows Quebec will be valuable to the exporters."

"I see." What Richard saw was that Laroche would be difficult to back into a corner. The man was as clever as he was lethal.

The little coastal ship ran her owner's pennant to the yardarm as she entered the New Haven harbor, and the unusual gesture brought both Tom Clayton and Colonel Adam Burrows to the dock. The partners tried in vain to conceal their surprise as Ezekiel came ashore escorting a red-haired beauty, both of them beaming. "Lady Dawn Shepherd," he said, "allow me to present my father and his partner, Colonel Burrows."

Mimi's smile was devastating. "I'd have known you anywhere, Master Clayton," she said. "Ezekiel looks so very much like you."

Richard, watching from the deck, where he was supervising the debarkation of the horses, knew from the elder Clayton's broad smile that Mimi had made another conquest.

Following the couple ashore, with Roaring Wolf at his heels, Richard immediately sought Colonel Burrows. "I need to confer with you in private at once, sir."

Adam Burrows nodded as he led the way to his sparsely furnished office. He assumed that Richard intended to ask him for permission to court Eliza, and he had to admit to himself that the young Englishman was wasting no time.

"Colonel," Richard said as soon as they were seated, "when I came to the New World I accepted an assignment from the Earl of Newcastle as a Cavalier agent, and in that capacity I fear I have discovered a conspiracy that threatens the very foundations of the Enlish colonies."

Adam's smile faded.

Richard launched into a detailed recital, beginning

294

with the vessel that had brought him to the New World having been halted on the high seas, followed by the attack launched on him by the man who had called himself Robertson. He described Laroche, then gave a crisp account of Mimi's harrowing experience under Horace Laing's roof. The colonel hitched forward in his chair as he listened to the story of the woman's rescue.

"Finally," Richard said, "I saw Laroche again in New Amsterdam the night before last." He gave a full account of their talk.

The commander of the New Haven artillery company leaned back in his chair as he assimilated the information. "Obviously you believe that this Laroche is secretly in the employ of the French, and obviously you have ample evidence for that belief."

"I couldn't prove it in a law court, but I'm convinced of it, sir!"

"Well, it sounds likely. We've had indications of late that the French in Quebec are stirring up the Indian tribes on our entire frontier. They're being bribed with blankets, whiskey, iron cooking utensils, and trinkets, that much we know. But not firearms. The French are too clever to arm allies as unreliable as tribes that will favor anyone who gives them gifts. Putting all of the facts together convinces me that our frontier settlements are going to be inundated with Indian raids this summer."

"What will you do about it, Colonel?"

"Pass the word to our sister colonies, of course," Adam replied firmly. "I was reluctant to alarm them, especially when men are needed to bring in the crops. But there's no longer any choice. Massachusetts Bay, Rhode Island, and Connecticut will be wise to follow the example I intend to set. I'm calling the council of war regiment to duty. It's too bad your stay in Virginia was cut short, but I'll notify the authorities there too, so they can be prepared for a summer of hard fighting."

"I see." Richard was silent for a moment. "Now, sir, I'd like your advice in a personal matter. I don't know if Laroche suspects I know too much and is setting a trap for me by suggesting that I go to England and possibly to France."

The colonel pressed his fingertips together. "It seems to me you have no choice. In England and in France, too, there are men posing as representatives of the Cavalier party who are actually in the pay of France. Give them free reign and Mazarin will achieve his ends. England would become a helpless French possession, and the *fleur-de-lis* banner soon would fly over the capitals of every English colony in North America. You're in a unique position to prevent those catastrophes. You can uncover the identity of the traitors. I can't force you to expose yourself to danger. No one can. But I urge you to take the risks."

"You confirm my own decision," Richard replied quietly. "I'd made up my own mind to go."

All at once, Adam grinned at him. "There are ways to reduce the risks to a minimum, but we'll speak of that later. If I don't take you home with me now, Eliza will be furious with both of us. You've never faced her when she loses her temper, or you'd know the rage I'd prefer to avoid."

All at once Richard's self-confidence vanished. "Do I gather correctly that Eliza has spoken to you about me, sir?"

"At length," the colonel replied drily.

"I hope you don't mind, Colonel."

"I'm a realist, or try to be. And what with Ezekiel so obviously in love, it does simplify matters."

"Then I have your permission to pay court to Eliza?"

Adam Burrows grinned broadly. "Neither of us has

an alternative," he said. "Eliza has set her cap for you, and what she wants she usually succeeds in getting!"

Prince Henry was so lively after being cooped up on board ship again that he had to be restrained on the short ride to the Burrows house.

Eliza looked indignant as she came to the door. "The very idea!" she exclaimed. "The least you could have done, Papa, was to let me know that Richard was expected. My hair is a mess, I've been wearing this old gardening dress all day, and I don't even have on a smidgen of lip rouge."

"Richard, maybe you can handle her better than I," the colonel said, and hastily went off into the house.

Roaring Wolf was eager to escape from the irate young woman, and took the horses off to the stable.

"You look fine to me," Richard said mildly. "Exactly as I've pictured you in my mind."

"Is that a compliment or an insult?"

"I intended my observation as a compliment."

"In that case," she replied, her mood changing swiftly, "I forgive you." She threw herself into his arms.

They embraced and kissed sincerely, and both were shaken by the depth of their emotions now that their separation had come to an end. "Your father has granted permission for me to court you," he said, "and your worries over Ezekiel are at an end." He told her what he deemed appropriate for her to know about Mimi, making no mention of his own affair with her.

"Then there are no obstacles in our path," Eliza said.

"No obstacles, but there are complications," he replied. "My stay here is limited."

297

"But you've just come back!" she cried. "What must I do to persuade you to stay?"

"There's nothing you or anyone else can do," Richard told her.

"You may find this hard to believe, Eliza," Colonel Burrows said as he came into the parlor, "but there are matters in this world more important than what you do or don't want."

"Do you know about his new travel plans, Papa?"

The colonel nodded, but had no intention of taking her into his confidence. Eliza turned to Richard for an explanation, but he took his clue from her father and offered no elaboration, either.

She looked at one, then at the other. "I suppose," she said, her tone scathing, "that your secret is connected with the precious security of New Haven."

"Something of the sort," her father admitted.

"Well, I'll tell you one thing, and don't forget it, either of you! I've worried myself sick over Richard for the last time. You're not going anywhere without me again, Richard Dunstable!" She swept out of the room, partly to indicate a conclusion to the discussion, but also to make herself more presentable.

Later, attired in a silk gown of deep red, with her hair piled high on her head, she enjoyed a far better mood, and was delighted when a servant brought a supper invitation from Mary Clayton. "Good," she said. "I'm anxious to meet the woman who has captivated Ezekiel."

"His taste is impeccable," Richard said. "I'm sure you and she will become fast friends."

Eliza was on her best behavior when she accompanied Richard and her father to the Clayton house. She was quick to appreciate Mimi's patrician beauty and seemed pleased by Ezekiel's choice.

The elder Claytons made it plain they were delighted with Mimi, and Ezekiel had an announcement

298

to make before supper. "I've been waiting for Mimi all of my life," he said, "and now that I've found her, I intend to lose no time. The banns will be posted tomorrow, and after three days we'll be married."

Richard gallantly offered a toast to the bride and groom. The newlyweds, it developed, would take up residence in the new house that had been built for Eliza and Ezekiel.

"That is, if Eliza doesn't object," Mimi interjected quickly. "Ezekiel has told me all about his relationship with you, and I'm well aware that you have a vested interest in the house, which I haven't even seen as yet."

"You're welcome to it, Mimi," Eliza said. "I hope you'll be as happy there as I would have been miserable. Anyway," she added, glancing at Richard, "my own plans aren't really settled yet. It appears that I'm going to be doing some traveling before I settle down." Richard laughed, as did Colonel Burrows, and Eliza took care not to mention that she wasn't joking.

Before the party went in to supper, Mimi contrived to have a moment alone with Richard. "Thank you for your discretion," she told him.

"You can rely on me."

"I know," she said, and squeezed his hand before turning back to her betrothed and smiling radiantly at him.

Never before, Richard reflected as he sat at the supper table, had he been so aware of the power of seeming adversity to change people in a positive way. Mimi, the complete aristocrat, had begun such a transformation from the moment she fled England, and it was apparent that she would be content to spend her days in a middle-class New Haven home as the wife of a young merchant. She seemed so sure of her destiny, and so did Ezekiel, neither of them questioning whether she could be happy in a life so unlike that for which her whole previous experience had prepared her.

Mimi seemed to read Richard's mind. "In all the days and nights I was cooped up in that cell of Horace Laing's," she said slowly, looking around the supper table, "I had nothing to read, nothing to do except review my life. I realized that most of my values were artificial, most of my precepts false. I did what was expected of me at court, and I really think the Puritans did me a favor to strip me of my inheritance. I knew then that all I wanted was a relationship in which I could place my trust. And in came Ezekiel, spoiling for a fight, his pistol still smoking after he shot out the lock!"

"I've always believed the poets exaggerated when they wrote about love at first sight," Ezekiel added, looking affectionately at his betrothed, "but the moment I first saw Mimi I realized how wrong I had always been."

"I'll take some of the credit," Eliza said. "I told you for years that you'd know the real from the superficial."

They lingered for a long time at the supper table, and when Colonel Burrows adjourned to the study with his host for a private discussion, he suggested that Richard escort Eliza home. "I want to tell Tom about our talk earlier in the day, Richard," he said.

Richard held Eliza's cape of light silk for her, and after saying good-night to everyone present, they started back to the Burrows house, walking hand in hand down the street lined with lindens. "You didn't tell me you and Mimi had slept together," she said calmly.

He stared at her. "Whatever prompted you to say that?"

"Really," she said with a light laugh. "I knew it the instant you greeted each other. It was obvious."

300

"Only to you," Richard replied. "You'll do Ezekiel a disservice if you mention it to anyone else."

"Believe it or not, I know when to keep my mouth shut. When are you going to confide in me—or must I continue to ferret out your secrets?"

"We'll see what your father has to say."

"Then I'll never know. And now that I'm free, when do you intend to propose to me? We were reunited ten hours ago, and I had no idea you could be so backward."

"The question has been very much on my mind," he admitted. "But it would be unfair to propose now. I have a delicate, dangerous, and complex mission still to perform, and I won't become my own master until it's done."

"You're as bad as Papa with your military secrets. Very well, sir, I don't require a proposal, though I'd have enjoyed one. I shall simply take it for granted that we're going to be married. When shall it be?"

"Wait until I return. We'll discuss it then."

"Oh, how I envy Ezekiel and Mimi. Just think, in three days they'll be husband and wife. Aren't you jealous of them?"

He shook his head, unable to explain to her that he would be risking his life on his journey to the Old World, and consequently could not tie her down to an advance commitment.

"You force me to behave rashly, sir. I want you to remember that." Eliza looked up at him, her blue eyes shining in the pale moonlight.

"You're a hussy," Richard told her. "You know how much I want you."

Eliza's quiet smile told him the issue was far from settled.

The church that faced the New Haven Green was crowded with guests attending the wedding of Lady

Dawn Shepherd and Ezekiel Clayton. The citizens of the town took advantage of this rare opportunity to wear their finery. Most men would be reporting for duty with their battalions and separate companies later in the day, but Colonel Burrows had demonstrated his compassion by signing an order that permitted Ezekiel to report for duty one week late. Eliza Burrows attended the bride, at the latter's request, and this simple act stifled the gossip of the many who had assumed that Eliza harbored ill will for the woman who married Ezekiel. Richard Dunstable stood up with the bridegroom and looked so distinguished that the mothers of eligible daughters stared at him. But they changed their minds when they saw the proprietary look in Eliza's determined eyes when she and Richard followed the bride and groom down the aisle at the end of the ceremony. Roaring Wolf observed the ceremony and festivities with his continued interest in the ways of the white man.

A lavish reception was held in the garden behind the Clayton home, and roasted meats, fritters, vegetables, and a variety of fresh shellfish were served. There was a potent rum punch, and a milder version for those so inclined. Innumerable toasts were offered to the health and longevity of the bride and groom.

The only reminder of Mimi's past were her earrings of diamonds and sapphires, which she wore with a matching necklace. Regal in a gown of ivory satin and lace, she looked every inch the daughter of an earl.

"I wish you a life of great joy," Richard told her as he kissed her lightly after the ceremony. "Ezekiel, my congratulations. You're the most fortunate man in the world."

"I'm forever grateful to you for suggesting I travel through the colonies with you—and for ordering me to fetch Mimi when we were attacked in Laing's cellar," Ezekiel replied. "You changed my life."

302

Eliza delighted in presenting Richard to more people than he could remember. Her hand firmly grasping his arm, she made the rounds of the garden beside him, and he was pleased that she introduced him as Master Dunstable rather than Sir Richard. She knew he preferred not to use his title, and that was good enough for her.

At last, after everyone had eaten and Richard, in his capacity as the groom's attendant, had offered a formal toast to Mimi and Ezekiel, the bridal couple departed for their own new home. Now the atmosphere became more relaxed, and as Eliza chatted vivaciously with her friends, Richard couldn't help thinking that the lives of the young colonials depended on what he could learn about the French conspiracy. It did not matter whether they were men or women, young or old, Cavaliers or Puritans. They were an integral part of the new breed of which Eliza was so proud: they were committed to new lives in a new land, and their future rested in his hands.

Colonel Burrows threaded his way through the crowd, approached his daughter, and asked, "Do you suppose I could borrow Richard for a time?"

The girl's grasp on Richard's arm tightened. "Not today, Papa! I forbid it!"

"You may forbid all you please, but it's necessary all the same. I'm leaving at dawn tomorrow to muster the council of war up and down the length of New Haven Colony, and it's urgent that I speak to Richard in private. Now."

The disgruntled Eliza reluctantly released her hold on Richard's arm, and he followed the colonel into the house. They went to Tom Clayton's study, and Adam closed the door behind them.

"I took my partner into my confidence," he said, "and we believe we've worked out a scheme that will offer you maximum protection while taking as few

303

risks as possible. First, I suggest you write tomorrow to Laroche and give your letter to Tom, who'll send it straight to New Amsterdam by intercolonial rig. Tell Laroche you'll arrive at the Royal Arms in Dover in approximately a month, and that you're providing your own transportation. Supply him with no details. The less he knows, the safer you'll be."

"How will I provide my own transport, Colonel?"

"Through Tom and me," Adam replied with a smile. "We have a one-thousand-ton frigate in the West Indian trade, the *Bonnie Anne,* that's big enough for an Atlantic crossing. We've taken Captain Hooper, the most reliable of our ship's masters, into our confidence. He'll carry a cargo of furs and lumber so the voyage will be legitimate, and what with the ironware he'll bring back, we'll make a handsome profit. What's important is that he'll sail you to Dover and wait for you. If you're sent to France, he'll take you there and will wait again to bring you back here."

"I see. That's clever of you. And convenient for me."

"It is the least we can do for you—and for ourselves. Not even Mazarin will dare to abduct you and either do away with you or force you in some way to serve France—not when you have your own means of transportation. Mazarin may be smart, but a pair of old colonials can prove themselves smarter. What Mazarin might have forgotten is that most of us have had military training in England where men had a military obligation to fulfill for the homeland. This is our home now, and we are ready to pass on our military experience and knowledge to benefit our children and our children's children. The younger men— like you, like Ezekiel—are building a life of seemingly limitless opportunities and rewards. Our experience, teamed with your youth, strength, and emotional ties to the New World, is a combination no one can conquer. God be with you, young man. The future of the new breed depends upon your courage and success."

XI

RICHARD wrote a carefully worded letter to Laroche in New Amsterdam, and Tom Clayton saw to it that the communication was dispatched without delay. Clayton introduced the young Englishman to Captain Hooper, a bluff, hearty giant, who wrung his hand.

"Be ready to sail in two days' time, Master Dunstable," he said. "And don't worry your head none. I'll see you safely to England, to France if need be, and back home again. I've been told your situation, and you'll come to no harm traveling with me."

Richard could not keep his departure a secret from Eliza Burrows and braced himself for a confrontation with her. "I'm leaving in two days' time," he told her as they sat together at noon dinner in the Burrows house.

"You're leaving sooner than Papa led me to expect. May I know where you're going?" Her calm was astonishing.

"To England, possibly to France. I won't tarry long in either country."

"Is England safe for a Cavalier these days?"

"Not for this Cavalier. That's one of the risks I'm obliged to take."

She nodded thoughtfully. "Papa is providing a ship for you, I suppose."

"How did you guess?"

"I know Papa. The only ship in his fleet big enough for an Atlantic crossing is the *Bonnie Anne*."

He saw no need to conceal that fact from her. "You're right again."

She smiled serenely. "You'll like Captain Hooper. I've known him since I was a little girl. I was frightened to death of him for years, but then I realized that his gruff ways are just a front. Well, we'll need to get you ready for the voyage. If there's anything you want me to get for you, just put it on a list and give it to me."

Richard studied her for a moment. "Thank you, Eliza," he said. "You're taking this news like a lady, and you're asking me no embarrassing questions that I'd be reluctant to answer."

"You don't know me as well as you may think. I can be practical when it's necessary. You'll leave Roaring Wolf here?"

"Yes, and Prince Henry, too. I hope you'll exercise him occasionally."

"Every day," she said solemnly. "And when you return, we'll make our marriage plans."

"I—I can't afford the luxury of looking that far ahead," he said. "I'm not avoiding the question, and my reluctance has nothing to do with you. I'm on the trail of something that's vital to the future of the colonies, and if certain people—unscrupulous, ruthless people—learn that I have uncovered their schemes, my life won't be worth a ha'penny."

"I honestly wasn't trying to trick you into proposing to me now. You told me of your own volition about Dorothea, and I found out about Mimi on my own. I

306

know there is no one else in your life now, and I also know from the way you look at me how much you love me. That's quite good enough for me. We'll wait until the appropriate time to talk about marriage."

He covered her hand with his. "To think that I dreaded telling you I'm sailing in two days!"

Her smile was soft. "You have enough on your mind, and I just wish I could help you in some way."

"Your attitude is a great help."

"I meant doing something active. Ah, well. You'll sail on the late-afternoon tide, I presume?"

"Yes, that's when Captain Hooper wants me on board."

"In that case I'll be very busy collecting good foods for you to eat on the voyage. Trust me."

"I do," Richard said.

He had just enough time to organize his belongings for his departure: he had a new suit made, appropriate for presentation if he should be called to the court of young King Charles II. He brought new powder for his guns and spent as much time as possible with Eliza, who was happy to accompany him on his errands.

On the day of his departure he found a large cloth-covered hamper awaiting him in the front vestibule, and he knew that Eliza was keeping her promise to provide him with delicacies. He went to the stable to bid farewell to Prince Henry, and the stallion seemed to sense the pending separation. Finally, he piled his belongings into a wheelbarrow, which Roaring Wolf insisted on pushing, and they made their way to the harbor together. There his gear and the hamper of food were transferred to the ship, which lay at anchor in the harbor, and he was surprised and pleased when the newlyweds appeared to see him off.

"I have a fair idea of what may be in store for you," Mimi told him. "Be careful. Horace Laing was fanatical

307

in his beliefs, and others of the same stripe must be equally devoted to the cause of France."

"I wish I were going with you," Ezekiel said. "We make a good team."

"So we do," Richard replied, "but you have other responsibilities now."

"Where is Eliza?" Mimi wanted to know. "I thought she'd be here to say good-bye."

Richard concealed his disappointment. "So did I, but her nose must be out of joint because I'm making this voyage."

Ezekiel sympathized with him. "Handling Eliza is like trying to stuff quicksilver into a bottle. You never know from one moment to the next what she's going to think or do."

The gig from the *Bonnie Anne* was waiting, and the boatswain signaled to Richard that the time had come for them to leave.

Mimi reached up and kissed him. "May you be alert to treachery," she said. "Our colony's future depends on you."

Ezekiel grasped his friend's hand. "Good luck and good hunting," he said.

Richard went up to Roaring Wolf, who was standing quietly by the emptied wheelbarrow. He extended his hand to the Pequot, who grasped his wrist.

"This may be my most difficult farewell, my friend. We have grown close and have enjoyed a most unusual friendship. You call me your leader, but you are my teacher. I am grateful to you for your loyalty, bravery, and company. I hope you will be here in New Haven when I return, but I do not want to insist that you stay." Richard scanned the Indian's inscrutable face, hoping to read an indication of the Pequot's plans.

"I will be here when you return. You are my white brother. The Great Spirit has intended your path and

308

mine to run side by side. I will honor the wishes of the Great Spirit always," the warrior assured him.

Richard and Roaring Wolf stood silently for several moments, savoring the closeness and feelings of mutual respect they were unable to express. Then Richard turned and moved toward the *Bonnie Anne,* glancing briefly over his shoulder with hopes of seeing Eliza. His effort was unrewarded.

As soon as the passenger came on board, Captain Hooper weighed anchor, and the ship threaded a path for herself through the crowded harbor, her jibs filling.

Richard stood at the starboard rail and watched the New World recede. When he had sailed from England, he had felt sad and uncertain of what was in store for him. But now he knew America, and he was surprised by his reactions. The communities that clung to the edge of the forest had become his home, and he was determined to return to this land of promise. He had found his true self in the wilderness, and he realized that he identified with the sturdy, independent, and self-reliant people who were creating a new way of life for themselves in a place where a person was judged solely by accomplishments, character, and ability to cope with adversity.

He had joined the new breed, and for their sake he would do his best to get to the bottom of the international conspiracy that threatened the colonies. Only the failure of Eliza Burrows to say good-bye to him marred his mood, and though he tried to accept her behavior, he did not succeed.

Feeling frustrated and annoyed, he abruptly turned away from the rail and went below, where a pleasant surprise awaited him. His quarters were spacious, he had a real bed rather than a bunk, and there were several chairs, a table, and a rug on the deck, all making his cabin seem like a living room. Thanks to Adam Burrows, he would travel in real comfort.

That night at supper, Richard discovered that the ship's cook was competent and the two mates were intelligent young men, so the voyage promised to be pleasant. "The Atlantic is calmer now than at any other time of year," Captain Hooper told him, "and we should have tailwinds all the way across. I expect to reach Dover in four to five weeks."

After supper Richard went for a stroll on deck, but the lights of New Haven, twinkling and fading in the distance, reminded him of Eliza, so he returned to his cabin before his mood became too melancholy. Opening the hamper, he discovered that Eliza had packed several books for him, so he read for a time before retiring.

The next day he found they were out of sight of land, and he settled in for the long voyage. American seamen, he soon found, were unlike their British counterparts in that they needed neither goading nor strict discipline. Every man knew the performance level expected and understood the reasons his tasks were important. The men worked well together, and there was no need for the boatswain to patrol the decks with a length of knotted rope to prod the sloppy, the lazy, or the recalcitrant.

The winds remained favorable, as the master had predicted, and the sea was calm, so the ship cut rapidly and smoothly through the green-blue water. The days were so much alike that Richard made a small chart for himself to mark the passage of time. On the fourth day of the voyage, Captain Hooper invited him to his great cabin for dinner at noon, and proved to be well informed about the New World.

"The colonies are just beginning to live up to their potential," he said. "New England is more self-sufficient than Virginia for sustaining a chosen way of life, but that will change as our population grows and we continue to develop our colonial unity. We have waterpower and all the wood we need, and there's sure to be coal under the ground, so it's just a matter of time before we develop our strength. Then we'll be truly independent, able to stand on our own feet."

He was interrupted by a tap at the door, and one of the mates stood on the threshold, scowling unhappily. "I hate to spoil your dinner, Captain," he said, "but we've just found a stowaway on board."

Eliza Burrows came forward, the mischievous expression in her eyes belying her demure manner. "I apologize for any inconvenience that my presence may cause," she said.

Captain Hooper was on his feet, and so was Richard, both of them staring at her apparent nonchalance.

"I told you that I didn't intend to be separated from you again, Richard," she said. "You didn't believe me."

He nodded and swallowed hard, still unable to accept the fact that she was actually on board the ship.

Captain Hooper groaned and ran a hand through his thinning hair. "I've worked for your father for twenty years, but this will cost me my job," he said. "We're too far out in the Atlantic to turn back now!"

"That's why I waited until today to come out of hiding," Eliza replied blithely. "I know the *Bonnie Anne* as well as I know my own house, so it was easy to hide myself and my clothing boxes in the hold, although I must admit I'm tired of the cold meat and bread I've been eating. Aren't you going to invite me to join you for dinner?"

Captain Hooper could only sputter helplessly.

Eliza took pity on him. "I left a note for my father," she said. "I took full responsibility for what I've done, and I made it very clear to him that neither you nor Richard had any idea of what I was going to do. Papa is a fair and just man, and he won't blame either of you."

"But why have you done this?" Richard found his voice.

"I've already told you. I refused to be separated from you again. Besides, I can help you. We have much to discuss."

Captain Hooper turned to the mate and said in a constricted voice, "Be good enough to ask the cook to prepare a plate of food for Mistress Burrows."

"Please, Captain, hold the food for the time being. If you will excuse us, Miss Burrows and I seem to have several matters to discuss," Richard said as he took Eliza's elbow and guided her swiftly and none too gently to his cabin.

Eliza was surprised at Richard's brusqueness as he shoved her into his cabin and closed the door behind them, then turned to glare at her.

"Your audacity knows no bounds. You have placed Captain Hooper's professional standing in jeopardy. You have made my own mission even more dangerous, if that is possible!"

Eliza stared at Richard, and her high spirits vanished. She had misjudged his reaction.

"You may," he continued, "find it possible to gain easy forgiveness from your father, but you will not from me. If it had been convenient for you to accompany me on this voyage, you most assuredly would have been invited. But no, I said it was impossible, and here you are nonetheless."

"Richard, I—"

"You must have everything your own way, is that it, Eliza? Is that how it's always been for you? Is that how it always must be? Well, I am sorry. And your future husband, whoever he may be, also has my deepest sympathies."

Richard had exhausted his fury, and sank into a chair.

Eliza felt as if she had been knocked off a horse and couldn't regain her breath. Her heart was pounding wildly and she felt a depth of regret and remorse previously unexperienced in her young life. *Could he mean this?* she thought. *Could he really be through with me?*

"Please, Richard. I only did this out of love for you. I cannot bear to be away from you, not knowing where you are, but knowing that you are in danger. I can help. That's why I came, so I can help. Your enemies will be my enemies."

He lifted his gaze and found her face. She sank to her knees in front of him, afraid to touch him, but unable not to. She placed her hands on his knees, and looked up at him imploringly.

"Eliza, this is no pleasure cruise. When we reach England, I will arrange passage for your voyage directly back to your father. He seems to be able to deal with your obstinacy more calmly than I. I am sorry, Eliza, but I will move my belongings out of this cabin so you may have your privacy and your reputation. I will move elsewhere as soon as Captain Hooper can find the space."

"Richard, please listen to me. Now your enemies will have two people to deal with. It's bound to be twice as safe for you that way. I was not raised to be like your women in England. I have been taught to deal with danger, to protect myself, and to think quickly. I am capable of assisting you. I will go where you tell me, I will stand by you just as I would if we were attacked by Indians in New Haven—or in a frontier fort. That's how I was brought up."

Richard, having vented his spleen, was beginning

to calm down, and her words were making some sense. If the French tried to convert him to their cause, they would have to convert Eliza, as well. Order began to be created out of chaos. Although she was impulsive, she was also intelligent. If he could curb her behavior, it could work.

"You would be placing yourself in danger. Your father would never forgive me for this," Richard said.

Eliza began to take heart. He was speaking to her again, and his color was returning to normal. "I left my father a note, I told you, assuming all responsibility for my actions. I knew it could be dangerous, Richard; I could draw that from the little you were willing to discuss with me. I will stand beside you. How better could I prove my love?"

He melted; placing his hand on the back of her head, he stroked her long, blond hair. She leaned her head against his knee and tried to regain her equilibrium. Clearly, he was considering what she had said. She waited silently for his verdict.

"Eliza, you deserve a sound spanking. Your behavior is reprehensible. However, I feel your intentions were honorable. Because of that, I will reciprocate in kind. I will ask the captain to perform a marriage ceremony immediately, so I can make an honest woman of you."

Her hair danced as she shook her head vigorously. "I am grateful to you for your offer, but I must decline. I owe it to my father to be married only in his presence."

"Be realistic," Richard said hoarsely. "How can you and I sleep apart in the same bed?"

"We'll let nature take its course. You are an honorable man, and I am quite sure you'll marry me when we return to New Haven. A wedding ceremony is only a technicality. Papa would never forgive me if I married in his absence."

She was too much for him. "Let's return to Captain Hooper. I am sure he is anxious to know how you are faring."

Back in the captain's quarters, they briefly explained the arrangements.

"For my own protection," Captain Hooper said, "you'll sign a statement to the effect that you insist on moving in with Master Dunstable, but you refuse to marry him."

"Word it as you please, and I'll gladly sign it." She smoothed her skirt. Obviously she had changed her clothes before revealing to the crew that she was a stowaway. "I'll be obliged to you if you'll have my clothing boxes moved to the cabin from the forward hold, Captain."

Captain Hooper shrugged helplessly. He knew how headstrong she could be.

They were interrupted by the steward, who appeared with Eliza's meal. Announcing that she was ravenously hungry, Eliza began to eat. The steward was instructed to remove Mistress Burrows's wardrobe chests to Master Dunstable's cabin.

Captain Hooper sensed that a great deal had transpired between the two passengers, and he was greatly relieved when they excused themselves after the meal to return to their now-shared cabin.

Richard closed the door and bolted it shut. He sat down on the chair and watched Eliza as she unpacked her belongings. He reflected with interest that he had condemned Dorothea for her inability to control her own life. Now, he was confounded by Eliza's behavior at the opposite end of the spectrum.

When her organizing was completed, she turned to face him.

"I've gone to a great deal of trouble to arrange this

rendezvous," she said. "Do you find me so much less attractive than Dorothea, so much less desirable than Mimi?"

He was goaded, as she had known he would be, and when he came to her, taking her in his arms, her lips parted for his kiss. Their differences immediately became irrelevant, and whether they were married or unmarried had no bearing on their present situation. They had curbed their desires long enough, and now, suddenly, all restraints were removed.

Eliza's lovemaking was as frank, as natural as her approach to Richard had been. She wanted him urgently, and she cast aside her inhibitions, responding to his caresses with an all-devouring passion that further inflamed him. She gave herself to him totally, holding back nothing, and he was overwhelmed by the need to conquer her.

As their desire expanded, they became unaware of their surroundings, and seemed to float freely from dizzying heights. They acted and reacted instinctively, giving and taking, demanding and yielding. They became one, and Eliza's scream of ecstasy mingled with Richard's moan of sheer gratification.

"Richard, you know how much I love you," she murmured, her eyes shining.

He did not reply in words, but instead made love to her again, then for a third time. Her insatiable desire matched his, and each existed only for the other. Richard no longer wondered whether his love for this fascinating vixen was genuine; it was proof enough that she had the power to arouse him repeatedly.

The afternoon passed, and at last he rose to light the oil lamp that was held in place by a bracket beside the bed.

Eliza giggled. "I wonder what I could have been thinking when I packed some books in the food hamper," she said. "Who'd want to read when we could be making love?"

Richard grinned at her. "I wonder why you go out of your way to make shocking remarks," he said.

She shrugged. "I don't know why," she replied. "I say whatever comes into my head, and sometimes I'm surprised myself at what comes out."

"That," he told her, "is a tendency you'll learn to curb, my love. You've elected to play a dangerous game, and a single slip could prove fatal for both of us."

"Never fear," she said, her smile fading. "I'm Adam Burrows's daughter, and now I've become your woman. I'll be equal to any test."

They made love all the way across the Atlantic, with the master and crew of the *Bonnie Anne* discreetly ignoring their impropriety. No one on board had forgotten that Eliza was the daughter of the ship's owner, no matter how unorthodox her conduct.

The mood changed abruptly one night at supper when Captain Hooper told the couple, "We'll put into the English Channel later this evening, and we should reach Dover by noon tomorrow."

Later, in the privacy of their cabin, Richard's mood was grim as he cleaned his rifle and pistol. "Take your lead from me," he told Eliza. "Say as little as possible, keep your eyes and ears open, and if danger threatens, do as I tell you without argument or discussion."

"I'm prepared for any emergency myself," she replied, and showed him a little poniard, razor-sharp, that fitted into the palm of her hand.

"That's a lethal weapon, not a toy," he said. "Have you ever used it?"

"No, but I'm prepared to do whatever is needed," she said seriously.

317

In the morning they packed their belongings before breakfast, and after eating they stood together on the deck, looking at the coast of England. Captain Hooper joined them.

"I'll need about twelve hours to dispose of my cargo, no more," he said. "Then I'll be available whenever I'm needed. If there's time I'll pick up a cargo of kitchen utensils and pots, but only if you don't need me to sail away quickly. Just remember I'm at your disposal. Your requirements receive my first attention."

"We won't forget," Richard told him.

Shortly before noon they saw the white chalk cliffs of Dover ahead, the heights above it dominated by an ancient castle, frequently rebuilt, that dated back to the time of the Roman conquerors. Sail was reduced as the *Bonnie Anne* eased her way into the small, cramped harbor, and after her anchor was dropped, the Puritans' harbor officials came on board. Somber men attired in unrelieved black, they studied the ship's manifests, then gave Captain Hooper the approval that made it possible for him to engage in trade.

"Take ashore with you only what you'll need for a day or two," Richard told Eliza. "And make certain your clothes are inconspicuous, even drab. You're in the land of the Roundheads now."

"I've packed a dress with long sleeves and a high neckline, and I'll hide my hair under a linen cap similar to what women in Boston wear."

He nodded in approval, hesitated, and decided to leave his rifle on board the ship. His sword and pistol, together with the throwing knives concealed beneath his dark coat, should be sufficient protection. In the New World it was taken for granted that a man would carry his rifle or musket wherever he went, but this was England, and different behavior was in order.

"We'll stay at an inn called the Royal Arms," Richard told Captain Hooper before they disembarked. "We'll register there as Master and Mistress Burrows, and you can expect to hear from me within the next twenty-four hours."

"If there's no word from you, I'll come in search of you," the ship's master promised.

They went ashore in the master's gig. Richard had expected to experience a rush of emotion, but he felt nothing when he stepped onto the solid ground. England was no longer his home and had become alien soil.

He hired a carriage and driver, then placed their one small clothing box in the rack on top of the coach himself.

"Be ye strangers to Dover?" the driver asked.

"Aye, that we are," Richard replied, broadening his accent. "We're from Lincolnshire."

"Be ye troubled there by snooping Roundheads?"

"We have no complaints," Richard replied diplomatically. "In the North we've found that those who tend to their own affairs are left in peace."

"Would it were that way here," the coachman muttered. "What with laws against this and laws prohibiting that, we may as well all be dead."

Uncertain whether the man was speaking in earnest or was in the hire of the Puritans, Richard nodded vaguely, but made no reply. England was obviously still permeated by fear and uncertainty.

On the drive to their inn, Eliza stared out of the carriage window, drinking in the sights of the mother country. Every road was cobbled, which impressed her, and many of the buildings of stone and brick were very old. And she was fascinated by the people who filled the narrow streets. Without exception they were attired in black, gray, or brown; they stared straight ahead as they walked sedately, and the children looked like miniature versions of the adults.

The proprietor of the Royal Arms not only resembled a clergyman, but had a minister's grave manner, and as soon as he departed after seeing "Master and Mistress Burrows" to their room, Eliza asked, "Now that we're here, what do we do next?"

"Well," he said, "it was useless to ask for Lord Blankenship, who, if he is here, is sure to be using an assumed name. The Roundheads would be keeping a close watch on the assistant secretary of funds of King Charlie's court. Let's go to the dining room and see if he is there."

Eliza busied herself at a mirror, tucking her blonde hair under a close-fitting cap. "How do I look?"

"Far too pretty for a Puritan," he replied, and kissed her. "If we should meet Blankenship, watch and judge him closely. The fact that Laroche set up the meeting with him makes me suspect him of being a French agent."

Eliza nodded, then preceded him down the stairs to the inn's dining room, her manner appropriately grave. They found a table near an open window that overlooked the harbor and were conscious of being studied by other diners. Eliza, Richard noted with satisfaction, played her role perfectly, sitting with downcast eyes, her hands folded in her lap.

He glanced casually around the room, then stiffened. Seated several tables away was a Roundhead with a bony, angular face, dressed in solid black; a chill shot up Richard's spine when he recognized Lord Blankenship posing as a Puritan.

Their eyes met for an instant, and Richard knew he had been recognized in return.

"He's here," Richard said quietly. "Three tables away, directly behind you. The next move is his."

Eliza nodded casually, and studied the bill of fare.

Both ordered steak-and-kidney pie, which had long been one of Richard's favorite dishes, but he was surprised to discover it had lost its savor. He preferred the game of the New World.

Blankenship finished his meal, paid for it, and stood. As he walked past Richard's table, a small pellet of folded paper dropped from his hand, landing near Eliza.

Continuing to eat with one hand, she scooped up the pellet in the other and dropped it into her purse, her motions so swift, natural, and fluid that even someone watching would have been unsure of what he had seen.

Blankenship was gone, and Richard did not turn in his chair. He and Eliza finished their own food, then returned to their room, where she removed the pellet and stared at what was written there: "Olde Tavern, six," she read.

"I gather he wants us to meet him at six o'clock this evening at a place called the Olde Tavern. I do believe we'll go for a stroll and see if we can find the Olde Tavern."

"Wouldn't it be simpler to inquire of the proprietor?"

He shook his head. "Never. That would be revealing too much."

They went out for a walk and soon discovered the location of the Olde Tavern, a modest establishment that occupied the first floor of a Tudor-style house. It was located only a few minutes' walk from the Royal Arms, and Richard strolled past it without halting. "Now," he murmured, "just in case we're being watched, we'll go into a shop nearby and buy something."

"That will be easy," she said, and led him to a shop directly across the road from the tavern, where she purchased a collar and a set of cuffs in stiff, white lawn. "Tonight," she told Richard, "I shall look like every other Puritan woman in this dismal town."

It was true that the collar and cuffs caused her to resemble the women of Dover. She was a chameleon, and her scrubbed face, modest gown, and demure manner made Richard, by association, less conspicuous. He had to admit that her presence was a bigger help to him than he had anticipated.

Precisely at six o'clock that evening, they walked into the Olde Tavern, where Lord Blankenship awaited them at a table set for three. "God be with you, niece," he said loudly, kissing Eliza on the cheek. "And with you, nephew," he added as he bowed and shook Richard's hand.

The lively expression in Eliza's eyes indicated her appreciation of the charade.

"We can speak freely here until the place fills up," Lord Blankenship said softly. "The proprietor is one of us, even though the Roundheads come here in large numbers." He stared at Richard accusingly. "I expected you to come alone."

"Permit me to present you to my wife, sir," Richard replied.

The courtier raised an eyebrow. "Laroche mentioned no wife."

"I wasn't married when I last saw Laroche. My wife's loyalties are identical to my own."

Blankenship studied the woman. "Well, she's handsome, and she certainly looks like a Puritan. You could be useful to the cause, ma'am."

"You're kind to say so, sir," she replied smartly.

"We'll waste no time on the amenities," Lord Blankenship said after they had been served with glasses of ale. "I await your report, sir."

Richard told him in detail about conditions in the colonies, stressing the indifference to the quarrel between Cavaliers and Puritans everywhere but in Bos-

322

ton. As he talked he had the feeling that Blankenship already had a thorough understanding of the position taken by the colonies, and he wondered if he had been sent across the Atlantic on a fool's errand.

When he finished his recital, Blankenship downed his glass of ale, coughed slightly, and turned to Eliza. "As a colonial, I daresay you're grateful to France for the support she gives to the young king."

"I am not, sir," she responded at once. "The French never give anything without demanding full payment in return."

"You may change your mind," Blankenship said with a genial smile, and ordered their meal from a waiter who approached the table.

The oxtail soup was fragrant, and as Richard ate it slowly he awaited a fuller explanation of the courtier's cryptic remark.

"You have a singular honor in store. As soon as passage to Cherbourg can be arranged for you, you'll be received by the young king so you can report to him in person."

So they would be going to France! "We already have a ship at our disposal. Tell me when we're expected, and we'll be there," Richard said.

Blankenship artfully concealed his surprise. "That's convenient, I must say. You'll be met by someone you know and have reason to trust. He'll await you at the stone quay inside the Cherbourg breakwater the day after tomorrow."

"We'll be there," Richard promised, thinking that in France it might be easier to distinguish a traitor who appeared in the guise of a patriotic Cavalier.

"I trust you'll have suitable attire for your presentation," Blankenship said to Eliza. "His Majesty doesn't appreciate a Roundhead appearance." He looked up, his face darkening when he saw a party in somber attire approach a nearby table. "Uh oh. Be careful to speak softly. Here is the Warden of the Port, damn the luck."

The Warden of Dover was the most powerful official in the town, and Richard glanced up casually at a pudgy, waxen-faced, self-important man clad in black. He was escorting a woman, and they were followed by three other men. The woman also wore the black of a Puritan, but she was young and exceptionally pretty. Richard's heart skipped a beat, then pounded furiously when he saw her. It was Dorothea!

Eliza looked at him curiously, aware that the color had drained from his face.

"Dorothea!" he muttered.

Eliza turned slowly, and saw the shock in the other girl's eyes when she spotted Richard. She sat facing him, unable to tear her gaze from him as she replied absently to a remark made by her husband.

Richard was aware of his danger—and Eliza's. He was on the proscribed list, and if Dorothea revealed his identity, he would be imprisoned, then held indefinitely without a trial. Eliza could expect the same fate.

But his alarm faded when it dawned on him that Dorothea had no intention of betraying him. The expression in her limpid eyes was tender, and she continued to stare at him as if he had risen from the dead.

Eliza also knew there was no danger. As the proprietor came forward obsequiously to greet the honored guest, she studied the dark-haired girl and knew her love for Richard was still a living force.

Richard became conscious of the concern in Dorothea's eyes, too, and he felt as if he were suffocating. Here, almost within reach, was the girl he had idealized and worshiped from afar. Beside him sat his mistress, whom he felt honor-bound to marry. Never had he felt so disoriented.

Blankenship was still speaking, but neither of the others at the table heard a word he said.

Dorothea's focus widened to include those at Richard's table, especially Eliza, who returned her gaze. Richard realized that, in ways too subtle for him to grasp, the girl from his past and the girl who represented his present and his future, were communicating. Eliza raised a hand, placed it on Richard's sleeve for no more than an instant in a proprietary gesture, then withdrew it. Dorothea understood, bowing her head for a moment in recognition of the gesture. Then she put her past behind her, turned to her husband, and spoke to him with animation. Richard turned away from Dorothea, looked at Eliza, and grinned at her.

She stared deeply into his eyes and knew that all was well between them. He had buried a ghost that had haunted him, and his clear smile indicated his present feelings.

"Is this good beef?" Eliza asked lightly. "I've eaten it so seldom that I can't judge it."

"It's very good," Richard assured her. She refrained from hugging him and creating a spectacle.

"You'll see the future in a new light after your visit with our friend," Blankenship continued.

"The future," Eliza replied, "couldn't be more promising than it is at this moment."

"Amen to that," Richard said.

Blankenship looked at his dinner companions, unable to understand their coded comments. He concluded that the proximity of the Warden of the Port was responsible, and he decided to bring the evening to a conclusion. His purpose in holding the meeting had been to arrange for Richard's reception at the court-in-exile, and it would serve no useful purpose to prolong the session.

"I suggest we leave separately," he murmured, then stood. "Good-bye, niece. May God be with you. Until we meet again, nephew, may the Lord watch over

325

you." He watched them as they made their way out of the tavern, both of them avoiding looking in the direction of the table occupied by the Warden of the Port and his party. Trained to observe human conduct, he thought it odd that the pretty young brunette at the Warden's table studiously averted her eyes when the departing couple brushed past her.

Richard made no mention of the encounter with Dorothea. "It struck me that Blankenship was anxious for us to gain a good impression of France. But that isn't proof that he's in the pay of France."

"Perhaps we'll learn more when we visit the court."

That night their lovemaking was more impassioned and more tender than it had ever been. The accidental meeting with Dorothea had sealed their own relationship.

The *Bonnie Anne* threaded her way through the harbor of Cherbourg, the low-lying hills of France in the background, and Richard knew this was truly foreign soil. The dock area was patrolled by soldiers in the gold-and-white uniforms of France, heavily booted, all carrying cumbersome sabers; riding herd over the merchant ships in the harbor were two frigates of the French navy, their powerful cannon more than compensating for the clutter on their decks that no British officer would tolerate.

Captain Hooper came and stood beside Richard. "I don't like this situation," he said. "You'll be at the mercy of the French every minute you're ashore here."

Richard shrugged. "I've calculated the risks, and I have no real choice. All that worries me is Eliza's safety. I've tried to persuade her to stay on board until I return, but she refuses."

"She's been headstrong all her life, accustomed to having her own way," the captain replied. "I don't envy you. Colonel Burrows will be wild if something happens to her."

"I can look after myself," someone behind them said.

Richard turned and was astonished by Eliza's appearance. She was wearing a gown of shimmering pale silk that hugged her torso tightly, then was elegantly decorated with cascades of ruffles from her hips to the hem. The most dramatic feature of her gown was its neckline, which plunged daringly and was adorned by insets of lace. The crew gaped at her. Eliza thoroughly enjoyed the sensation she was creating, and lightly fingered a long, dangling earring. "I've been saving this dress for a special occasion, and I thought I'd give the young king cause to remember me," she said with a smile.

"You're tempting fate," Richard told her, hurriedly enveloping her in a lightweight cloak of matching silk. "I'm not sure this is wise."

"There are times," she replied archly, "when a woman's natural assets are more potent weapons than a man's firearms. This is such a time."

He knew it would be impossible to persuade her to change into more modest attire.

The *Bonnie Anne* inched toward a berth inside the stone breakwater, then tied up at a dock. A squad of French soldiers appeared, taking up positions at the foot of the dock, but no harbor officials came to the ship for the customary examination, so it was plain that the vessel was being accorded special treatment.

"I'll wait for you right here until hell freezes," Captain Hooper confirmed.

"I hope we won't be obliged to stay in France that long," Richard replied, gripping the master's hand, then escorting Eliza ashore.

As he started down the dock, a familiar, gray-haired figure, resplendent in a plumed helmet and beribboned waistcoat, appeared at the foot of the dock. "Uncle William!" he cried.

The lines in the Earl of Newcastle's wrinkled face deepened when he smiled. "Welcome to France, Richie," he called.

Richard presented Eliza as his wife, and she surprised him by dropping in a deep curtsey, which was so graceful that it seemed like second nature to her.

Newcastle studied her openly, nodding in approval. "You've outdone yourself, boy," he said. "Now I know that His Majesty will give you a hearty welcome."

He conducted them to a luxurious carriage that bore the Stuart crest, and Richard noted at once that a troop of French soldiers, fifty strong, surrounded the vehicle. Obviously they would not only travel in style, but were under the protection of the government of France.

Newcastle chatted easily as the team of matched bays drew the carriage at a rapid clip down a road of crushed gravel lined with manicured trees. The queen was well, he said, and at present was paying a visit to the court of the Boy King, Louis XIV. "She is given every privilege of her rank here, and her grief over her husband's martyrdom has been assuaged." Charles II, now twenty years old, was grateful to his hosts and was saved from overwhelming French influences by receiving a steady stream of visitors from England. "We may fool ourselves, of course," Newcastle mused, "but we think the tide is turning in His Majesty's favor. We feel, and so does Cardinal Mazarin, that it won't be too long before King Charles is restored to the throne."

"You see Mazarin yourself?" Richard asked.

"Regularly," Newcastle replied proudly. "He takes a keen interest in our affairs."

A little too keen an interest, Richard told himself.

The earl continued to gossip about the court-in-exile. James, Prince of Wales, the younger brother of Charles II, was moody and unpredictable, inclined to spend his time reading English history rather than availing himself of the pleasures that were his for the taking. "You wouldn't know that he and Charles were brothers," he said.

Richard had the feeling that the Stuart court was a world of its own, far removed from reality, and what surprised him was Newcastle's deep involvement in it. That was to be expected, however, since the earl's own fate was so closely tied to the fortunes of the young monarch.

After an hour's drive they approached a château that stood high on a hill, its medieval towers and buttresses dominating the productive farms in the valley below, as it had done for centuries.

"When you make your report to King Charles," Newcastle said, "don't ramble. Be concise. His Majesty is easily bored by details."

French sentries armed with sabers and muskets stood guard duty outside the château, and the security precautions were thorough, the carriage halting repeatedly while an officer checked the identities of those inside. "We take no risks here," Newcastle explained. "We take no chance that Roundhead fanatics will try to assassinate or kidnap him."

It was a simple matter for the French to keep Charles II isolated, Richard reflected, allowing him to see only those of whom Mazarin approved. The realization made him uneasy, and he wondered how the young monarch managed to keep in touch with day-to-day affairs in England.

When they reached the château, a servant in Stuart livery—who, it rapidly developed, spoke not one word of English—conducted Richard and Eliza to a suite where they could refresh themselves before being presented to the king. Richard paced the chamber restlessly, paying no attention to the spectacular view of the valley below, while Eliza sat before a mirror arranging her hair. "I have the strange feeling here that we're cut off from the whole world by the French troops," he said.

The Earl of Newcastle conducted them to the great hall of the château, where, even though the sun stood high overhead, scores of French tapers were burning, casting their reflections on the huge, priceless tapestries that covered the stone walls.

Groupings of ladies and gentlemen, all elegantly attired, sat at small tables, amusing themselves at cards or with dice, occasionally pausing to take silver wine cups from one of the many servants in attendance. Richard's presence created no stir whatever, but the gentlemen looked up from their games to inspect Eliza, while the ladies scrutinized every detail of her appearance, their eyes measuring their own looks against the standard created by the newcomer.

Lolling on a bench set on a dais at the far end of the great hall was an athletic-looking young man with long, brown hair, informally attired in a shirt of white silk, open at the throat, and snug-fitting black breeches. Reclining on a mound of pillows beside him was an almond-eyed girl of about the same age, who fed him tidbits from a tray of sweets and occasionally lifted a cup to his lips.

Richard instantly recognized Charles II. He had the long Stuart chin and thin, almost Roman nose of his father and grandfather, his forehead was high, and, although he was totally preoccupied with the young woman whom he was fondling, his brown eyes were sharp and penetrating. But what was Charles doing here? He had moved from France to the island of Jersey months ago.

The Earl of Newcastle cleared his throat in order to

gain his monarch's attention. "Your Majesty," he said, "I have the honor to present your loyal subjects, Sir Richard and Lady Dunstable."

Richard bowed low, and Eliza, smiling because she had been called Lady Dunstable for the first time, sank to the floor in a deep curtsey.

King Charles took another sip of wine, then forcibly removed his attention from his companion. His eyes were slightly glazed as they slid past Richard, but he came to life as he gazed at Eliza. "Have something to drink," he said in French, much to their astonishment.

Richard accepted a cup from a servant, and went through the ritual of drinking to the king-across-the-water. His gesture amused King Charles, who chuckled as he reached for the pliant playmate beside him on the divan.

Somehow Richard managed to give his report on conditions in the colonies, his voice sounding hollow in his own ears. He was prepared to swear that the man who would become the master of the New World when he regained the throne did not hear a word. Charles studied Eliza with obvious relish, then busied himself fondling the breasts of his unidentified companion, who wriggled in pleasure at his touch.

Richard spoke briefly, poignantly, knowing he was wasting his time.

"We appreciate your loyalty to our person and our cause," Charles said automatically when Richard finished his recital. "Rest assured you will be duly rewarded when we return to England." He smiled, then added in French, "Stay to dinner, why don't you?" Not waiting for a reply, he embraced the girl beside him.

Newcastle signaled to Richard, and they backed out of the hall as King Charles devoted himself to serious lovemaking. Richard could not conceal his revulsion, drawing a deep breath of fresh air in the corridor.

"Who is the wench?" Eliza asked contemptuously.

The earl shrugged. "Her identity doesn't matter. His Majesty's appetite is insatiable, and he's kept well supplied. He comes back to France from Jersey periodically just for relaxation of this type. I should have warned you what to expect."

"It seems to me," Richard said, "that I've traveled three thousand miles in vain."

Newcastle shook his head. "Not at all," he replied gently. "The purpose of your journey soon will become evident to you."

Richard knew only that he was glad to put the château behind him, and he could tell that Eliza felt as he did. He was serving a monarch whose corruption by the French made him unworthy of the risks taken and the sacrifices made in his name.

Not until the carriage started toward the south after moving down the hill did it occur to Richard that Cherbourg was not their destination. "Where are you taking us, Uncle William?" he asked.

Newcastle's smile was enigmatic. "Trust me."

They rode in silence for a time, and Richard dared to think the unthinkable: was it possible that the Earl of Newcastle, the inheritor of one of the greatest and most distinguished English titles, could have sold out his country's interests? Was it conceivable that he was in the pay of France?

Newcastle's voice intruded on his thoughts. "I'm sorry your dinner has been delayed," he said, "but you'll find the wait well worth the increase in your appetites." He seemed pleased with himself.

After a drive of another hour or two, still surrounded by the cavalry escort, the carriage rumbled into the sleepy market town of Saint-Lô, its ancient walls and towers, which dated back to Roman times, reminding Eliza and Richard of the wooden palisades that protected the communities of the New World from the dangers of the wilderness.

A few farmers driving carts that had been emptied of their produce at the open-air market stared at the carriage and troops, but otherwise the dusty street was deserted. In the center of Saint-Lô, in between the town hall and an imposing church, lay several one-story buildings, the weather-beaten sign on the front gate identifying them as a monastery. Richard was surprised when the gate was opened by smartly uniformed sentries, and the carriage drew to a halt before what appeared to be the main building. Several brown-robed monks glanced up from their work in a vegetable garden, then returned to their labors.

Newcastle led the young couple down a silent corridor, and there was no sound but that of their heels clicking on the tile floor. At last the earl paused before a closed door and tapped tentatively.

"Come in, William," a deep voice boomed from within. "I've been expecting you."

Richard and Eliza found themselves in the presence of a gray-haired priest who was seated behind a desk piled high with papers in an otherwise bare room. A smile lighted his gentle face as he stood and extended both hands. "Ah, Sir Richard, we meet at last," he said. "And this is Lady Dunstable. I commend your eye for beauty, Sir Richard."

The priest's manner and appearance suggested sophistication and worldliness, and Richard was not shocked when he was presented to Jules Cardinal Mazarin, Regent and Principal Minister of the Realm. Here was the man who had never been consecrated as priest but had risen to the rank of cardinal through nepotism, general lack of public interest, and shrewd diplomacy.

"You haven't dined as yet?" Mazarin asked.

333

"Good! I bring my chef with me whenever I'm called away from Paris, so I can offer you a passable meal." Gathering his habit closely around him, he led them down the corridor to the refectory, a bare room with whitewashed walls, and seated himself on a bench at a scrubbed table.

The meal was one of the most memorable that Richard had ever eaten, although he was too dazed to fully enjoy the rich soup and the dishes of fish, fowl, and meat that followed in profusion, served by silent monks.

Very much at his ease, Mazarin conversed fluently on many subjects, surprising Eliza and Richard with his wealth of knowledge of the English New World colonies. He seemed familiar with the business affairs of Burrows and Clayton, he knew the New England Federation militia had been called to duty only five weeks earlier, and he made a passing reference to the recent marriage of Lady Dawn Shepherd. It was obvious that he kept himself well informed.

At the conclusion of the meal he had their wine glasses refilled, then glanced meaningfully at Newcastle.

"His Eminence has kept you under observation for a long time, Richie," he said, "and concluded that a personal meeting was in order. We apologize for wasting your time with Blankenship in Dover, and for the charade to which you were subjected today, but both were necessary for you to grasp the situation in which we find ourselves."

So it was true, Richard thought, his heart sinking. Newcastle was a traitor who was betraying England for French influence and gold.

Cardinal Mazarin laced his slender fingers together. "Politics imitates nature," he said in his gentle, cultured voice, "and like nature, she abhors a vacuum. For generations France and England have been Europe's greatest powers, each balancing the other. Now Cromwell has destroyed that equilibrium. Consequently Spain has been stirring, the Holy Roman Emperor in Vienna dreams of extending his realm, and even the Czar of Russia thinks of increasing his power. That is not to be. France and England are the two most civilized nations in the West, and if they are not to share the rule, then one or the other must dominate. Thanks to the blunders of Cromwell, it is the good fortune of Louis the Fourteenth to become the master of Europe and of the New World."

"It was not accidental that you met Charles the Second," Newcastle interjected. "An amiable enough young man, but I watched your faces, and I know you have judged him for yourselves."

Richard felt ill, and a glance at Eliza told him she too was stunned.

"The common people of any nation are ill-informed in matters of politics," Mazarin said, "and must be led. You have qualities of leadership that have called you to my attention, Sir Richard. And you have chosen a mate worthy of you. Together you will be instrumental in bringing the English colonies of the New World into the fold of France."

Eliza expected Richard to protest and refuse, but to her astonishment he said nothing. A few moments of reflection explained his prudent silence: no force had been used, but they were the prisoners of France, isolated in a little market town far from the ship that awaited them at Cherbourg. Mazarin, with a troop of his own guards at his disposal, could eliminate them from the face of the earth with a wave of his patrician hand. He had placed them completely in his power.

"The man you know as Laroche is exceptionally able and understands both our goals and our methods," Mazarin continued. "You will operate under his jurisdiction. Naturally, France will be grateful for your efforts."

"And France is generous," Newcastle said with a faint smile.

"Your rewards will be ample," Mazarin declared. "I am not niggardly in my dealings with those who show loyalty to our ideals, just as I am severe in my treatment of those who betray us." Nothing in his expression or tone indicated that he was threatening the couple. "We must strike while England is disorganized and confused. Earthly power and glory are the just spoils of the bold and the swift." He paused, then asked quietly, "May we count on your help, Sir Richard?"

Richard knew that only one reply was possible if he and Eliza hoped to leave Saint-Lô alive. "You may, Your Eminence."

"I applaud your good judgment," Mazarin said. "And you, Lady Dunstable?"

Unable to trust her voice, Eliza could only nod. She and Richard had been maneuvered into becoming French puppets.

"Splendid," Mazarin said, rising quickly to his feet. "Much work of importance remains to be done, and I shall anticipate glowing reports of your progress from Laroche."

The cardinal was a man who prided himself on his subtlety, and never would he do anything so crass as to issue threats blatantly and openly. Having made his position clear, he reached into the girdle that encircled his waist, and there, adjacent to his ivory rosary beads, was a short, exceptionally sharp double-bladed knife that he plucked out and held carelessly. He flipped it over in the palm of his hand, then grasped it and absently sliced a sheet of parchment with it. The knife was so sharp that it instantly cut through the sheepskin without making a sound. Smiling benignly, Mazarin tested the blade with his thumb as if thinking of something else, but his meaning was very clear. Either Richard and Eliza did precisely what they were told, or they had only a short time to live. His threat was all the more brutal because it was indirect. Still smiling and nodding, he left the refectory.

"Both of you have displayed wisdom beyond your years," Newcastle said when the door closed behind the principal minister. He drew two bags of gold from his belt and placed them in front of the young couple. "The wealth of France is as unlimited as her gratitude to those who serve her."

Richard wanted to hurl the gold into his face, but instead he took the bag and slipped it into his own belt. This was not a time for heroics. Eliza hesitated, then followed Richard's example.

"There is no choice, really, in selecting the path I now follow," Newcastle said. "Oliver Cromwell is despicable. Young Charles is unfit to rule. So France offers the only hope of salvation."

It was so easy to rationalize, to believe what one wanted to believe, Richard thought bitterly. Perhaps there was no choice in the Old World, but America offered an alternative, the freedom to live according to the principles of liberty espoused by the new breed.

"You have been privileged to meet and break bread with a great man," Newcastle said, then smiled as he stood. "You'll be back at your ship in time to sail for the New World on the evening tide."

Ashamed of the commitment he had been forced to make, and despairing for the loss of an old family friend, Richard's greatest regret was that he had pulled Eliza with him into ruin and disgrace.

XII

THE summer weather was benign and the sun shone brightly on the green-blue Atlantic, so the westward voyage should have been carefree. But Richard and Eliza were miserable.

"I should have known better than to try to outsmart the shrewdest man in France," he said in self-disgust. "For all the good it does, I know the identities of the traitors to England, and I recognize the dangers to the colonies. But my own hands are tied: either I cooperate with France, or I'll be knifed in my sleep."

"Don't feel too badly," Eliza said bravely. "We were amateurs playing professionals' games."

"The worst of it is that you've become involved," he said. "I should have seen the pitfalls when they tried to recruit Mimi, but instead I delivered you into their hands."

"You can't blame yourself for my involvement," she replied. "I went into this with my eyes open and I gave them the opportunity to use me, too."

"There is a way out for you," he said. "When we reach New Haven, you can refuse to have anything more to do with me. Just drop me permanently. Then I'll report to Laroche that you were too flighty to be reliable, and you should be safe."

Eliza's blue eyes blazed as she stared at him. "Are you trying to get rid of me?"

"For your own welfare and protection, yes," Richard told her.

"What a convenient excuse!"

"You're wrong," he said earnestly. "But I prefer to give you up to seeing you suffer the degradation of being forced to act as an agent for France. If I loved you less, it would be simple enough to drift with the tide."

"Did I hear you correctly?" she demanded. "Did you say that you love me?"

"Of course! Why should that surprise you?"

She looked at him and slowly shook her head. "In all the weeks we've been living together, this is the first time you've said you love me."

"I thought you knew." Richard was defensive.

"I guessed it," Eliza said. "I even assumed it. But I still like to be told."

His smile was a trifle sheepish.

"That settles the matter," she said decisively. "I've been frightened by the depth of our commitment to France and our inability to wriggle out of a menacing situation. If you didn't care for me, I might have been willing to accept your suggestion that we part, even though I know Papa would be terribly upset. But it happens that I love you too, and nothing in this world is going to separate us. That includes Cardinal Mazarin!"

He realized she had tied his hands, making it impossible for him to protect her. "Then we'll simply have to do our best to outwit Mazarin and his people, impossible though that may seem."

"Together we can do anything!" Eliza said confidently, and embraced him.

It was true, he knew, that he had come to love this woman with her fiercely independent mind and will. Somehow he would have to shield her from the ruthless foes who were determined to make England a mere puppet of France and to gain possession of the New World colonies for themselves.

Captain Hooper was not looking forward to his ship's return to her home port. "Colonel Burrows will nail my hide to a wall," he said on the last night of the voyage as he entertained the young couple at supper in his cabin.

"Leave Papa to me," Eliza said. "I'll take care of calming him."

The following day, as the ship eased into her berth at the New Haven port, the ship's master nodded in the direction of the dock. Adam Burrows was pacing there, a frown on his face, his eyes angry.

Eliza insisted on going ashore alone. "You can't blame Richard or Captain Hooper for what's happened, Papa," she said as she embraced and kissed him. "I accept full responsibility."

"Are you married?" Adam demanded.

She shook her head and smiled. "Not yet, but I soon will be. Richard offered to marry me the instant he discovered I stowed away, and I refused only because it wouldn't have been right to hold the ceremony unless you were there."

She had succeeded in disarming him, as she had known she would, and his anger melted away into relief and joy at having his daughter home again. Her behavior no longer shocked him. He had been her father too long for that.

A short time later, at dinner in the Burrowses' house, Richard gave the colonel a full report on their meeting with Lord Blankenship, their reception at the court-in-exile of King Charles II, and their climactic session with Cardinal Mazarin. "I've offered to part with Eliza so she won't become involved with the French, but she refuses."

"It's too late for that," she said. "Besides, our love

340

is more important than the dangers to which we may be subjected."

Colonel Burrows's reaction surprised them. "You've wanted a life of adventure for a long time, Eliza," he said, "and now you've taken a bigger bite than you may be able to digest. But the situation may not be as bad as it seems."

They looked at each other, then at him.

"Every able-bodied man in the colonies has been mobilized for what promises to be the fight of our lives," Adam Burrows explained. "The French have been smarter than I gave them credit for being. We've had reports that the two biggest Indian nations of the border country, the Algonkian and the Micmac, are moving hundreds of warriors down the Pequot River. They intend to split Connecticut and New Netherland from Massachusetts Bay and Rhode Island, and gobble us piecemeal. Indians don't think in such terms, so the maneuver is French-inspired, but our scouts—and Roaring Wolf is worth his weight in gold to us—report that there are no French troops on the march against us, only a handful of mercenaries. We're badly outnumbered, but the threat of a common enemy has served one purpose: it has united the British and Dutch colonials in a military action of common defense. Therefore, I have every confidence that we'll give a good account of ourselves. What has worried me is that even if we beat back the attackers, France won't give up. It will be convenient, to say the least, to have a daughter and son-in-law who can keep the colonies informed on what new schemes the French may be devising."

Richard felt better than he had at any time since he and Eliza had been dragooned into service by Mazarin. "You're suggesting we become triple agents, sir. I'm supposedly working for the Cavaliers, although I

341

have no heart for their cause after seeing the young king."

Eliza nodded in emphatic agreement.

"We've been forced to work for the French," he went on. "Now you're suggesting that we go along with them so we can report their plans to you."

"That's the general idea," Adam Burrows replied. "It won't be too easy, I daresay, and you'll be in danger every minute. But we've been given an opportunity to learn the long-range thinking and planning of the French, so I'm compelled to urge you to take the risks."

"I'll do it gladly," Richard said. "But I still hesitate to let Eliza become too involved."

"You can't stop me," she said with spirit. "And neither can Papa. I have an investment here too: I am concerned for both of your welfares and for the security of my home. You can't expect me to withdraw my active support."

Her father nodded and sighed. "All right, Eliza, Richard—we'll have to move one step at a time," he said. "I came to New Haven to move every available ship to the mouth of the Pequot River. It's coincidental that I happened to be here when you landed. The first order of business is your marriage, and then I've need to rejoin the combined colonial militia."

"I hope you'll let me come with you, Colonel," Richard said. "I'm a fair shot, and I can not do nothing while others fight for the freedom of the colonies. This trip to England and France has taught me what to put first, and the colonies have become my home."

"You'd leave your bride behind?" Eliza demanded.

"You'll stay right here," Richard told her firmly.

The rector of the New Haven church agreed to waive the customary three-day waiting period following the posting of banns because of the wartime situation. Adam hastily rounded up the senior Claytons as witnesses, and the wedding was conducted in much haste. But the rush in no way detracted from the solemnity of the occasion.

This was no ordinary marriage, and Richard was conscious of the bride's need to be sheltered and protected from influential, unscrupulous foes in this international conspiracy that would stop at nothing to achieve power and wealth. Eliza, in spite of her eagerness to do her share, was far more vulnerable than she realized.

At the end of the ceremony the newlyweds kissed, then accepted the good wishes of the Claytons and of Mimi, who was delighted by the marriage. "I'm so glad that circumstances have worked out for you as they have," she said. "I don't know of any two people—except Ezekiel and me—who are so well suited."

The bridal couple's honeymoon consisted of sharing a glass of wine at the Burrowses' house. "If you're coming with me," the colonel told his new son-in-law, "you'll have to leave right now."

Richard nodded, then took his bride in his arms. "Stay out of mischief while I'm gone," he told her.

"I shall," she promised, "provided you'll come back to me so I can enjoy being Mistress Dunstable." She clung to him for only a moment, then made their parting easier for him by smiling impudently.

Richard knew nothing of the military situation that faced the colonies, but understood why he had been so prompt in volunteering his services. He was going off to fight to preserve a way of life that was unique, and someday, when he and Eliza had a family, he wanted their children to enjoy the benefits of a new kind of civilization, a world in which all were born equal and had equal opportunity to make of their lives what they wanted.

Prince Henry whinnied and pawed the ground in pleasure at the sight of his master, and as Richard started off with Colonel Burrows along the coast trail, he had to hold the stallion in check.

As they rode, Adam Burrows briefed his son-in-law. "Our scouts tell us that the Algonkian and Micmac are traveling downriver by canoe, and if their estimates are accurate, we'll face at least one thousand warriors. The bulk of our defending force will be my own regiment, about three hundred and fifty strong. New Netherland has sent us one hundred British volunteers living in the Dutch colony, Rhode Island and Connecticut have contributed fifty, and Plymouth and Massachusetts Bay, which have recognized the dangers to all of us, have sent two hundred."

"Then we're outnumbered by several hundred."

"Unfortunately we are. I hope to block the mouth of the river with cannon on board a half-dozen ships that will force the enemy to land. But we're handicapped by a lack of Indian allies of our own—warriors who will understand what the enemy will do next."

"I can see where they'd be useful," Richard said. "You have no alliances with any neighboring tribes?"

"The French have proved far more shrewd in their dealings with the natives. We've paid them for land we've taken, but we haven't actively cultivated their friendship. The French have made them welcome in Quebec and ply them with gifts, and their policy pays off. Now, when we need the advice of war chiefs, there's no time to develop a relationship."

Richard's mind worked rapidly. "Do I assume we're riding straight through to your camp area?"

"It's only forty-five miles," the colonel replied. "It shouldn't unduly tax our horses."

"Do you speak any of the Indian languages? I've learned a little from Roaring Wolf, but I'm far from fluent."

"I've picked up enough to make myself under-

344

stood," his father-in-law said. "What do you have in mind?"

"The Mohegan are indebted to me," Richard replied. "I'm wondering if the time hasn't come to cash in that debt. We'll be riding only a few miles from one of their main towns. It might be worth our while to pay them a visit."

"Well," Adam Burrows said, "at the rate the Algonkian were leading the enemy, they won't reach our defense lines for at least another forty-eight hours. I suppose we have nothing to lose by trying."

So, late in the day, they made a detour inland, and as they had anticipated, two Mohegan sentries appeared out of the bush. Richard promptly raised a hand in friendly greeting, and the colonel addressed the braves in their own tongue. "We wish to meet with your sachem on a matter important to him and to us," he said. The request was unusual, and the warriors hesitated.

"You do not remember me?" Richard asked quickly. "The Mohegan are noted for their memories, but they have already forgotten the man who saved the life of Ilia-awi."

Adam translated his words dutifully, and the attitude of the braves changed at once. They peered hard at Richard, then professed to remember him, and one of them raced ahead to a sentry outpost. Soon Richard and the colonel, following at a more stately pace with the other sentry, heard the beat of drums echoing through the wilderness, announcing their arrival.

Adam glanced at his new son-in-law, then decided to trust him completely. Ordinarily he would have hesitated to ride to the village of one of the most warlike of the New England tribes, but Richard showed no fear, so the visit must be worth the risks.

As they drew near the town, they discovered that the entire community was turning out to greet them, with warriors old and young, staid women, and hordes of children pouring out of the palisade gates and inundating the fields of corn and squash.

At last Richard saw the familiar figure of the sachem, surrounded by his war chiefs, medicine men, and the tribe's elders, with Ilia-awi, wearing a dress and leggings of beaded doeskin, half-concealed behind them.

Richard dismounted promptly, surprising himself by delivering a long speech, translated by the colonel, in which he stressed his friendship with the tribe.

The sachem replied in kind, making it clear that he whose skill with a firestick was unequaled anywhere was welcome.

Not to be outdone, Richard introduced his father-in-law as the most illustrious of white war chiefs.

His exaggeration embarrassed Colonel Burrows, who nevertheless translated the younger man's remarks literally, and was rewarded when the Indians raised their arms in salute to him.

The Mohegan considered the occasion adequate excuse for a feast, and scores of volunteers dug a large pit, filled it with firewood and, after lighting it, went off to their storehouse for several sides of buffalo. The whole town seemed eager to participate in the preparation of the feast.

Richard, meanwhile, removed his hat, then bowed low to Ilia-awi. The girl obviously was pleased by his attentiveness to her, and several of the older women nudged each other slyly. But Richard had no intention of taking unfair advantage of Ilia-awi's still-obvious interest in him.

Richard bided his time, having learned the ways of Indians. He could see Colonel Burrows becoming restless, aware that the hour of attack by the Algonkian and Micmac was drawing closer, but he refused to become agitated. Just as one survived in the wilderness by patiently flowing with the forces of nature, so one dealt with the natives of the wilderness.

At last the food was prepared, and Ilia-awi herself served her father and the two guests. She was appropriately reserved in her manner toward Adam Burrows, but cast aside restraint and eyed Richard boldly. He knew he would cause far more harm than good if she gained the wrong impression, so he only nodded to her politely as she handed him each dish, doing nothing that would cause her to believe he was personally interested in her.

At last the meal came to an end, and the sachem rose to his feet. Relishing his role as a public speaker and proud of his ability to play on the emotions of his people, he spoke at great length, extolling the virtues of the white war chief and particularly those of the unselfish friend of his people.

The night was advancing, and Colonel Burrows was finding it difficult to curb his impatience.

Then Richard stood and offered a reply, which his father-in-law duly translated for him. His opening words were so unexpected that he captured the attention of the Mohegan people. "My brothers," he said, "we sit side by side in peace for the last time. Soon these forests and hunting grounds, which we share in peace, will be soaked with blood.

"Even as I speak to you, the land is about to be invaded. The mighty Algonkian and the ferocious Micmac have sent forces of invaders to drive the English and Dutch settlers from the soil. Rest assured that the colonists will resist! Oh, yes! Their firesticks are ready, and they will stand bravely to the challenge, even though the invaders number as many as the trees in the forest."

The unexpected sobriety of his alarming speech had fully shocked his hosts. The sachem's face revealed nothing, but his knuckles turned white as he gripped

347

the bowl of the long pipe he held in his hand. Others, including the tribe's medicine men and war chiefs who sat directly behind him, were less able to hide their feelings, and stared in fascinated horror at Richard.

Making up his speech as he went along, Richard decided to simplify. These Indians had no understanding of European politics, were untouched by the rivalries of the English and French, and would not understand that the warriors who were about to invade their homeland had responded to French goading. It was enough that the Algonkian and Micmac were bent on conquest far from their own homeland. Everyone knew, he declared, that the invaders were ruthless men who showed no mercy to their foes. Warriors who dared to oppose them would be killed and scalped. Women and children would be dragged off to the north to become the slaves of the rapacious Micmac, the servants of the dreaded Algonkian.

He and the white war chief should be at their posts at this very moment, Richard continued, rallying and preparing their men for combat. But they had stopped off in the land of the Mohegan in order to warn their friends and neighbors of the impending danger.

As he spoke, the traditional cold indifference of the warriors gradually gave way to indignation, then to outright anger. A young warrior broke the spell by uttering a fierce war cry that echoed through the nearby forest. "Death to the Algonkian!" he shouted, brandishing a tomahawk. "Death to the Micmac!"

All at once dozens of braves were on their feet, uttering similar cries, and in the bedlam it was impossible for Richard to finish his address.

"I reckon you've accomplished your purpose," the colonel told him. "I've never seen anyone communicate with Indians any better!"

The sachem conferred briefly with his elders, medicine men, and war chiefs, then raised a hand for silence. "My brothers," he said as the crowd gradually became quiet, "the Mohegan, who hunt where their fathers and the fathers of their fathers hunted, thank you for the warning you have brought to us. How soon do you march against the invaders?"

"Now," Colonel Burrows replied promptly, not bothering to consult Richard first. "At once!"

The sachem nodded, then turned back to the throng. "How many warriors will march beside our white brothers to defeat the strangers who invade our sacred soil?"

The fighting men of the tribe responded with one voice, their suspicion of the English and Dutch settlers in abeyance in light of this greater, more immediate peril.

A war party was organized with dispatch. A total of one hundred twenty-five warriors daubed their faces and torsos with fresh paint, filled rawhide bags with strips of sun-dried venison and a few handfuls of parched corn, and shouldered quivers of arrows, then pronounced themselves ready to depart. Their leader, a hawk-faced war chief named Ro-an, gripped the forearms of the two visitors to demonstrate his fealty to them. Soon the party was on the trail, led by Colonel Burrows and Richard, who rode while the warriors trotted tirelessly behind them.

"You've brought us reinforcements of the best kind when they were desperately needed," Adam Burrows said.

"If we had more time, I think I could persuade the Conestoga to march north to join the defenders."

"I knew you were resourceful," his father-in-law said, "but I'll never understand how you've made allies of at least two tribes in no time at all!"

They traveled the better part of the night, and it was still dark when they stood their mounts at the crest of a hill and looked down at the broad mouth of the Pequot River. No campfires were burning, and the only signs of a defense force were the small ships riding at anchor, their unlimbered cannon shimmering in the pale moonlight.

Colonel Burrows cupped his hands over his mouth, then gave a credible imitation of an owl.

There was an answering owl cry from the thick foliage ahead, and then a sentry in buckskins appeared, his musket ready for use. "Ah, it's you, Colonel," he said. "Some of the men was getting jittery because you hadn't showed up yet."

"I was delayed," Adam Burrows replied. "Show our good allies to a place where they can conceal themselves."

The sentry stared in astonishment as the half-naked warriors of the Mohegan filed forward silently. Shaking his head in wonder, the sentinel quickly led them down the hill.

The colonel conducted Richard to his own command post, a small clearing with a view up the river. There they turned their tired horses loose to graze, and an orderly brought them a cold breakfast of corn bread and fish, which they washed down with a bitter ale.

Adam Burrows took no time to rest. "Pass the word that I'm back," he told an aide. "We'll hold a meeting of the high command here in an hour's time. Meanwhile I want a report from the scouts." Using the knife that he carried in his belt, he removed the bones from his fish and began to eat.

Admiring his calm at a time when extreme danger threatened, Richard could better understand and appreciate Eliza. She, like her father, couldn't help responding to a challenge.

The first to arrive was Roaring Wolf, who was so overjoyed when he saw Richard that he emitted a low cry of pleasure, then embraced his friend. "I was afraid you would miss the battle!" he said.

"Never fear," Richard assured him, "I have a nose for a good fight."

Ezekiel Clayton appeared, clad in buckskins that camouflaged him so completely that he wasn't visible until he stepped from the screen of trees into the clearing. "Well, well," he said. "You've come back from Europe just in time!"

"Richie hasn't been idle since he landed yesterday," the colonel said with a chuckle. "He and Eliza were married less than two hours after they came ashore, and on our way here from New Haven we stopped off long enough to pick up a hundred twenty-five Mohegan warriors."

Ezekiel pumped Richard's hand. "I'm so glad you and Eliza married," he said simply.

"I had little choice," Richard replied. "She decided to become my wife, and that was that."

Ezekiel joined in his laugh, then asked, "Are the Mohegan reliable?"

Roaring Wolf frowned. "Mohegan are cowards," he declared flatly.

Richard had no intention of becoming engaged in a dispute with the Pequot. "We'll find out soon enough," he said.

The colonel had exercised patience, but now he asked sharply, "What reports do you have on the enemy's progress?"

"A scout came in less than an hour ago." Ezekiel glanced at Roaring Wolf for confirmation.

"He is a Pequot, so he can be trusted," he said. "The Algonkian and Micmac are in no great hurry. They stop to hunt and fish whenever they need fresh food. If they keep up their present pace, they will reach the mouth of the great river before the sun sets tonight."

"Good. We'll give them a suitable reception. Did the Pequot scout count their numbers?"

351

"There are many," Roaring Wolf replied with a shrug. "With them are ten or twelve white men who speak in the tongue of New Haven."

Colonel Burrows was incredulous. "They speak English rather than French?"

Again Roaring Wolf shrugged. "The Pequot is an honest man, and was close enough to the white men to touch them. He swears they spoke English, and I believe him."

Adam Burrows was baffled, but wasted no time on conundrums that he couldn't solve. "We'll find out the meaning of this mystery soon enough," he said.

The leader of the New Netherland contingent arrived with the captain in command of the Rhode Island troops, and they were soon followed by the captain of the Connecticut militia and the colonels commanding the Massachusetts Bay and Plymouth colony regiments, accompanied by two aides. One of them, a lieutenant, was compactly built and tanned, his manner reflecting the self-confidence of a man who knew what he wanted in life and was well on his way to achieving that goal.

Richard stared at him, then stared again. "Dempster! Dempster Chaney!"

Equally startled, Dempster grasped the hand of the benefactor who had made it possible for him to establish himself in the New World.

As they chatted, bringing each other up to date on the developments in their lives, Richard reflected on the remarkable changes in his protégé. When they had first met, Dempster had been timid and confused, hoping for success in America but unsure of how to achieve his ends. Now he was a man whose brains and brawn had given him a solid base, and his devotion to the cause of liberty marked him as a member of what Eliza called the new breed.

"Robbin had mixed emotions when I volunteered to

352

join this expedition," he said. "She'll be lonesome, but saw the need for me to come. If we can teach the Algonkian and the Micmac that they'll pay a high price for aggression, the Mohawk and the other powerful tribes that live to the west of us will leave us in peace. There are some who argue that New Netherland has no business interfering in the British colonials' quarrels, but they're shortsighted. There are too few of us on these shores, so we stand or fall together."

Colonel Burrows sent Roaring Wolf for Ro-an, the Mohegan war chief, for whom he would translate, and when they arrived together he called the meeting to order. "Gentlemen," he said, "our situation is much improved in the past forty-eight hours. First, I was able to assemble the fleet of brigs, barques, and frigates that you see blockading the mouth of the river. Every last one of those ships is armed with two or three cannons, and although their marksmanship might not qualify them as experts by British or French standards, their guns can make one whale of a racket when they're fired. I'm confident they'll persuade the enemy to come ashore on the west bank of the river, where we'll be waiting for them. If the ships do that much for us, they'll be accomplishing their purpose.

"Our other need was equally urgent," the colonel went on. "My son-in-law, Master Dunstable, stepped into the breach and persuaded the Mohegan to send a strong war party to aid us in the fight. I ask Ro-an, their war chief, to station himself beside me during the coming battle to predict how the enemy will react."

Roaring Wolf translated rapidly, and Ro-an smiled, obviously pleased that he would play a key role.

"Tell the braves of the Mohegan," Colonel Burrows continued, speaking to the war chief in his own tongue, "that they must be patient. I intend to hold them in reserve, then send them into battle only when the time is ripe. We face a cruel and determined foe, but the Mohegan will gather a rich harvest of scalps if they follow orders."

"The braves of the Mohegan," Ro-an replied solemnly, "have not only the courage and strength of the bear, but also the cunning of the wolf. They will do as they are told, and will win glory as well as scalps."

"I intend to deploy the units in depth on the near bank of the river," the colonel told his associates. "We'll keep ourselves well concealed in the forest so the enemy won't be able to learn our strength. It is important that all militia units hold their fire until the last possible moment and then make every shot count."

"Apparently, sir, you're relying on our ability to cause the enemy to panic," the Massachusetts Bay commander said.

"Exactly so." Colonel Burrows's expression was grim. "As I understand Indian tactics, their aim, always, is to overwhelm their enemies. But neither the Algonkian nor the Micmac has ever faced massed musket fire, which can be a terrifying experience for them, provided your troops hold steady when they're rushed. There you have my basic battle plan, gentlemen. Feel free to discuss it and suggest modifications."

Dempster Chaney cleared his throat. "It strikes me you're relying on the element of surprise, at least to some extent, Colonel. But the cannon fire you'll utilize in order to drive the war canoes ashore should tell the Algonkian and Micmac that a land force will be waiting for them in the forest."

"So it will, Lieutenant," Adam Burrows replied. "But they've undoubtedly been told that we have few settlements in New Haven and Connecticut, and they'll expect to meet a far inferior force. Our numbers are not equal to theirs, but I'm relying on their losing the desire to fight when they realize they're not going to

354

roll us back and send us fleeing from the field. What do you think, Ro-an?"

The Mohegan war chief listened to Roaring Wolf's translation and was lost in thought for a time, his arms folded across his chest. "The war chief of the colonists," he said at last, "also has the cunning of the wolf. The enemy will fear for their lives when you do not run, and then they will wish only to withdraw from the field with honor."

"That brings up an interesting point," the New Netherland commander said when the war chief's comment was translated. "By working together we've been able to accumulate a force to effectively challenge the enemy. But next time we may not be so fortunate. The Indian nations of this continent can send thousands of warriors into battle against us, while the best we can do is muster hundreds. Every sachem and every war chief in America, regardless of his tribe, will hear of this battle and will judge us accordingly. I say that we show the enemy no mercy, that we kill as many as we can. Other tribes will recognize the power of our firearms, and we'll be left in peace."

Richard was strongly inclined to agree with him. There was no place for the chivalry of the Old World in the wilderness of North America.

But the colonel from Plymouth was shocked by the suggestion. "Surely you won't lower our standards to those of the barbarians we're going to meet in battle!" he declared.

"That's exactly what I propose," the New Netherland officer replied. "The Mohawk, the Seneca, and the other tribes of the Iroquois Confederation, the most powerful Indian force anywhere, make their homes in territory claimed by my colony. If we turn soft, no farm, no village, and no town in New Netherland will be safe. Savages understand only the language of brute force."

"You're right, Major," Colonel Burrows said. "The survival of our civilization on the shores of the New World is at stake today, so we're obliged to be as ruthless as our foes. This is not time to consider the moral niceties of the situation. I want every militiaman under your command to realize that once he opens fire, he's to keep firing as long as one enemy warrior is still alive. We expect no quarter—and we'll give none!"

Shortly after noon the grim-faced militiamen deployed, taking up the positions in the forest that they would occupy when the fighting started. A peaceful beach, curved like a half-moon, stood on the near shore, with sand dunes behind it and the forest moving down to the scrub vegetation behind the dunes, and here Colonel Burrows massed his greatest strength.

"The way I see it," he said, "the strip of beach promises the braves a safe landing, so they're almost certain to come ashore here. We'll prepare a welcome for them accordingly."

He gave the honor of first emplacement in the line of battle to his own troops from New Haven, and then Connecticut, explaining his reasoning to Richard. "They'll be defending their own soil," he said, "so they'll fight harder than anyone else."

The Massachusetts Bay and Plymouth regiments were assigned a position directly behind that of the men from Connecticut, with the New Netherland volunteers, the Rhode Islanders, and the restless Mohegan being held in reserve, deep in the forest to the rear. Ezekiel Clayton demanded the right to station his company of veteran Indian fighters in the vanguard, directly behind the crests of the dunes, and Colonel Burrows could not deny him the privilege. His men, being the most experienced, would be least likely to panic or confuse orders in the heat of combat.

Then, when the colonel was satisfied, he withdrew to his command post at the crest of the hill from which he could see the whole field spread out below, and calmly ate parched corn and sun-dried venison. Richard followed his example, and although the food was dry, he discovered he enjoyed the taste. Perhaps, after going without sleep all night, he was hungrier than he had realized.

"Now that everything else is settled," he said quietly, "perhaps you can devote a moment or two to deciding what part I'm to play in the battle."

Colonel Burrows blinked in surprise. "I've assumed you'd stay right here with me," he replied.

Richard shook his head. "I'm a civilian with no training in strategy or tactics," he said. "I'd be of little use to you here other than as a messenger."

His father-in-law hesitated and frowned.

"I know what you have in mind," Richard said. "You don't want to run the risk of seeing me killed or badly wounded in the fight. It wouldn't be easy for you to face Eliza. But I have a responsibility to myself to do my fair share. Remember, sir, that I have a quarrel with the French, who are responsible for this invasion. They've tricked my wife and me into working for them as spies, so I have a private score to settle with them."

The colonel sighed. "I might have known you'd feel this way," he said. "What do you have in mind?"

"I want to join Ezekiel's company," Richard said.

"But they're in the most exposed, dangerous position of any troops in the entire force!"

"I assure you, sir, that I'm not being heroic. I just want to be stationed where I can do the greatest amount of good. I've fought Indians only once, when we helped the Conestoga in a battle with a superior force of Iroquois. I don't pretend to be an expert in the Indian style of warfare, just as I don't pretend to

357

have a military mind. But—if I do say so—you don't have a marksman in your whole command who is my equal. Turn me loose to do what I do best, and I promise you I won't disgrace you—or Eliza."

It would be wrong to shelter him, Adam knew, and the request could not be denied. "Go ahead," he said with a sigh as he extended his hand. "I can't stop you. And I'm forced to admit I admire my daughter's choice!"

Richard grinned at him, then started down the slope toward the Pequot River, his rifle cradled in one arm. It was odd, he thought as he threaded his way past troops who were sprawled on the ground of the forest, that he felt nothing. He had volunteered for an exposed position in a battle for his wife's homeland— his adopted homeland now—yet he felt neither fear nor an anticipatory tingle of excitement. Perhaps the sunlight gleaming on the broad ribbon of water below him was lulling him into a false sense of security. Crouching low as he left the shelter of trees, he made his way to the crest of a high dune where Ezekiel Clayton was at ease. "I figured you could use some help," Richard said.

Ezekiel chuckled. "I made a private bet with myself that you'd show up here, Richard," he said. "I couldn't imagine you missing all the fun." His smile faded slowly. "I'm damned glad you're here. We'll need all the help we can get."

Richard carefully surveyed the scene. The dunes were about one hundred yards from the inner rim of the beach, and he estimated that if the enemy charged, he would be able to fire and reload his rifle at least twice, perhaps three times before being forced to use his pistol, so the odds were favorable.

Certainly the veterans who made up Ezekiel's command were unflustered by the imminence of a fight for their lives. Some ate parched corn and sun-dried venison, a few dozed, and several sat quietly, lost in thought as they contemplated the almost pastoral scene.

There was a stir in the forest underbrush, and scores of hard-eyed men watched Roaring Wolf emerge from cover and stroll forward nonchalantly, his quiver filled with arrows, his bow slung over one shoulder.

"Too many moons have passed since we have faced an enemy together," he told Richard as he dropped to his haunches, plucked a blade of grass, and chewed on it.

"Does the colonel know you've joined us?" Ezekiel wanted to know.

The Pequot shrugged. "Roaring Wolf does not serve the colonel."

Richard and Ezekiel exchanged a quick glance, and both appreciated Roaring Wolf's presence with their unit. Ro-an would interpret the enemy movements for Colonel Burrows, but they would also have an Indian who would know and understand any sudden shifts in the tactics of the Algonkian and Micmac.

The afternoon wore slowly, endlessly on. Occasionally the hum of a mosquito, the call of a gull, or the buzz of a yellow jacket sounded loudly in the silence, with a slight breeze ruffling the waters of the Pequot River as it flowed toward the Great Bay. The ships of the little flotilla anchored at the mouth of the river rocked gently, and the gunners on the decks sat beside their cannons and dozed.

Then, in late afternoon, the lookout on the tallest of the ships silently signaled the quarterdeck. A moment later a red signal flag fluttered as it was hoisted to the yardarm.

The enemy had been sighted, and the defenders came to life. The gunners on the ships struggled to their feet, and there was a rustling sound in the forest as the militia braced for action. Richard calmly

359

checked his rifle and pistol, even though he knew they were loaded. The veterans yawned, then stretched out on their stomachs behind the crest of the high dune.

At last, after a wait that seemed interminable, the lead canoe of the enemy flotilla came into sight as it swept around a bend, the paddlers bending to their tasks in unison.

All at once the river was filled with war canoes, some carrying Algonkian warriors with purple paint on their faces and bodies, others filled with Micmac, who wore blue paint. One of the frail craft in particular caught Richard's attention. Although it was being rowed by Algonkian, its occupants were white men, clad in buckskins. Apparently these were the white leaders of the expedition who had been identified by a scout as English-speaking.

The river was at least a half-mile wide at its mouth, and seemed to be alive with the formidable force sent by the French to harass and conquer the English and Dutch colonies.

As the warriors became aware of the presence of the merchant ships at anchor, they faltered, then slowed dramatically. The white men conferred, an order was shouted, and the lead canoe gathered speed again, apparently intending to break through the cordon.

The roar of a cannon sent seagulls by the hundreds rising high into the air, their wings flapping frantically. One by one the other guns joined in the ragged salvo. The aim of the cannoneers was erratic, to say the least. Most shots fell short, with iron balls falling into the water at least fifty feet from the lead canoe, while several others sent their shots sailing high over the heads of the invaders.

Any New Model Navy officer who had witnessed the scene would have regarded the marksmanship of the gunners as deplorable, but, as Colonel Burrows had predicted, the steady cannon fire had the desired effect. The warriors knew they were the targets of these huge weapons that belched fire and smoke, and realizing there was no way they could retaliate, they turned their frail craft toward the beach that lay on the western shore.

The gunners obeyed the orders they had been given and kept up a steady fire, their aim not improving in spite of their efforts to sink the canoes.

The occupants of the canoes, much to their credit, retained their composure, and the craft hesitated offshore until several could approach the beach simultaneously. Then they were propelled toward the beach at top speed, the warriors leaping out into waist-high water and fitting arrows into their bows as they waded ashore in unison.

The well-disciplined men concealed behind the dune watched the enemy land and group together on the beach, none of them revealing his presence by firing prematurely. But Ezekiel Clayton twisted around, his gaze fastened on a clearing at the crest of the highest hill behind him. He was waiting for a direct order to repel the invaders.

The warriors were forming in ranks on the beach, with the buckskin-clad white men urging them to open their ranks and spread out.

All at once the enemy was in motion, and while canoe after canoe discharged its passengers, a force of at least two hundred sturdy Algonkian headed at a trot toward the sand dunes.

A red flag attached to a stick swept toward the ground at Colonel Burrows's command post. Ezekiel Clayton felt infinite relief, knowing he could not have restrained his men much longer. "Fire at will!" he called.

A number of his wilderness fighters were proud of

their speed as well as their skill, but none could match the marksmanship of Richard Dunstable. His rifle spoke sharply at least a full second before any other gun was discharged, and an Algonkian whose feathered headgear marked him as a war chief pitched forward, then lay face down in the sand. Other Algonkian were dropping, too, as the marksmen took a deadly toll.

But the warriors soon demonstrated their courage, proving it was not accidental they were universally feared. The survivors of the first salvo held their places, other braves came forward to fill the gaps in the line, and then the entire body was on the move again, sending a hail of arrows sailing over the crest of the dune at their unseen enemies.

Reloading coolly but hastily, Richard got off a second shot, then a third. By now the warriors in the lead were close enough for him to see their faces clearly, and they were not panicking, even though their enemies were armed with firesticks that were taking a heavy toll.

Richard expected to be engaged in hand-to-hand combat at any moment, but suddenly the line halted, and then the wave receded, with the warriors still sending arrows over the top of the dune.

An arrow grazed Roaring Wolf's arm, then embedded itself in the hard-packed sand of the dune only inches from his face. He plucked it out, then studied the craftsmanship of its maker. "Algonkian are good fighters," he said in grudging admiration. "They fight like Pequot."

"They're hard to discourage," Ezekiel admitted. "If they hadn't retreated when they did, they'd have been right on top of us."

"It looks like we have a day's work ahead, that's sure," Richard said, aware that he had come to life when the battle had started. He watched the enemy regroup on the shore, exhorted by the white men in buckskins. Something vaguely familiar about one caught his attention, and he peered intently at the man, then was almost overcome by astonishment. He was staring at Bart Williams!

Now he understood the enormity of the crimes being perpetrated by the French. Young men who were courageous but whose intelligence was limited were being recruited from the English colonies by the French to act as the invasion's leaders. In that way, should any one of them be captured, he would be regarded as a traitor to the English colonies. France would not become involved. The scheme was both audacious and clever.

"What's wrong?" Ezekiel asked him. "You look as if you've just seen a ghost."

"I believe I have," Richard muttered, and thought of Mollie Williams, who had sacrificed so much in order to bring her son to America, where he could have an opportunity to make something of himself.

"When they charge again," Ezekiel said, "pick off their white leaders. Pass the word."

Even as Richard repeated the order to the men beyond him, he knew he didn't have the heart to kill Mollie's son. The directive that Ezekiel had just given was sound, to be sure, for without the guidance of the whites who commanded them, the Algonkian and Micmac well might falter. But knowing Bart's background made a difference. The lad was a confused Cavalier, not a traitor, and the real villains were men like Cardinal Mazarin, the Earl of Newcastle, and Laroche, who took advantage of the Bart Williamses of the world for their own purposes. Hating France with all his being, Richard braced for the next assault.

The purple-smeared Algonkian advanced again over a broader front, and this time they held their fire.

Roaring Wolf recognized the tactics at once. "Algonkian will wait until they see us before they shoot arrows," he said.

The maneuver made no difference to Ezekiel. "This time," he said, "we'll wait until we can count their teeth before we open fire."

Three white men were accompanying the advancing braves, and Richard felt a wave of nausea sweep over him when he recognized Bart Williams as one of them. He wanted to shout a warning to the stupid lad, but instead he peered down the length of his rifle. His heart hammered, and cold sweat beaded on his forehead, which he wiped angrily with his sleeve.

The onrushing Algonkian were no more than a stone's throw away when Ezekiel called again, "Fire at will!"

Richard took aim at Bart, then suddenly changed his target, instead bringing down the warrior beside him.

Ezekiel Clayton didn't know Bart, was unfamiliar with his story, and felt no sympathy for him. Taking careful aim, he squeezed the trigger of his musket.

Bart Williams halted, a look of utter astonishment on his face as he pitched forward on the side of the dune, his blood turning the yellow sand a bright shade of crimson.

"Now all enemies come," Roaring Wolf said.

Again he proved accurate. The Micmac formed a blue wave behind the wall of purple as the invaders hurled their entire force at the one point.

The woods came to life behind Ezekiel Clayton's New Haven and Connecticut companies as the Massachusetts Bay and Plymouth volunteers charged to the aid of their comrades who held such an exposed position.

Richard reloaded and fired, reloaded and fired, his every movement faultless. Had he stopped to think of the overwhelming odds against him, he would have been numbed by fear, but the mere act of shooting down one warrior after another was sufficient to keep him rooted to the spot.

Recklessly ignoring their own casualties, the braves continued to advance. Ezekiel knew his exposed position on the dune soon would be overwhelmed. "Retreat!" he called above the din of battle. "Draw back to the main line in the forest!"

Richard brought down a warrior, then reloaded and fired again at another who was in the act of throwing a tomahawk at him. The sharp blade missed him by a hair's breadth, then buried itself in the sand behind him.

The senseless death of Bart Williams so infuriated him that he gave no thought to his own safety. These savages had been sent by France to crush and humiliate the English and Dutch colonies, and he had no intention of retreating. "I'm taking my stand right where I am," he declared, making himself heard above the blood-curdling whoops of the advancing Indians.

Roaring Wolf heard him and quietly stood beside him. So did three other members of Ezekiel's band, all of them firing and reloading as rapidly as they could.

Ezekiel Clayton and the bulk of his company reached the safety of the concealed front ranks in the forest before they realized that five of their band had refused to budge, becoming an island in a sea of surging Algonkian and Micmac. Before Ezekiel could react, however, a company of Massachusetts Bay militiamen raced forward into the open, led by Dempster Chaney, who knew only that the man responsible for his happiness was in grave danger.

Richard had no chance to reload his rifle now. He fired both barrels of his pistol point-blank at two warriors, then began to hurl his throwing knives at the foes who surrounded him, his companions using their muskets as clubs to ward off the enemy.

Ezekiel Clayton could not allow strangers from Massachusetts Bay to rescue members of his own unit. "Forward again, lads!" he called.

Colonel Burrows was in despair as he watched the unorthodox scene unfolding below him. Ezekiel had been right to order his band to retreat, and the Algonkian and Micmac would have been decimated had they followed into the heart of the defenders' formation. But his stubborn son-in-law had refused to move; a handful of others had followed his example, and the situation was rapidly degenerating into chaos.

His alarm increased as he watched Lieutenant Chaney's men engage in hand-to-hand combat with the foe, followed quickly by Ezekiel Clayton's veterans. He knew he was losing control of the situation, his superior arms nullified by the inability to fire into the midst of the swirling, charging masses of men engaged in hand-to-hand combat. He had to act quickly to restore some semblance of order—or at least contribute to the mass pandemonium.

Turning to the eager Ro-an, who stood beside him, he said, "Go! Lead your warriors into battle!"

The war chief needed no urging, and within moments the Mohegan, anxious to prove their valor, hurled themselves into the fray.

Richard knew that his personal situation had eased a trifle. Braves painted purple and braves painted blue were falling through no effort of his own. Roaring Wolf stood behind him, wielding a tomahawk with deadly efficiency, and as Richard bent to pick up his rifle, he found himself face to face with Dempster Chaney.

"At last! I finally have a chance to help you," Dempster shouted above the din.

The bulk of the New Haven, Plymouth, Connecticut, and Massachusetts Bay militiae watched the struggle helplessly, unable to intervene, until several young men conceived the same idea at the same moment. Breaking ranks, they raced into the open to join the free-for-all. Scores of their comrades followed them, and Colonel Burrows laughed aloud. The techniques of Indian-fighting he would describe to his colleagues in his report on the fray would make mighty strange reading.

Now it was the turn of the Rhode Islanders and the British volunteers from New Netherland to surge forward, and the fight spread quickly over the dunes and onto the beach. Refusing to be deprived of their share of glory, these militiamen eagerly brought down every foe they could find.

Richard felt no concern for his own safety. Every time he clubbed down a warrior wearing purple or blue paint, he was ridding himself of frustration. Every enemy was a representative of France, which had not only maneuvered him and Eliza into bondage, but had caused the needless death of Mollie Williams's son. He had no idea that bodies were piled around him, that the Indians who saw him in action would write songs about his ferocity and prowess. He knew only that he was obtaining vengeance, and the taste in his mouth was sweet, even though there was a hard core of bitterness within him that would not dissolve.

The surviving Algonkian and Micmac were bewildered by the turn of events. Never before had they engaged in combat with a foe so eager to meet its enemies face to face, and as the realization dawned on the braves from the north that they were losing the battle, they rapidly lost their appetite for combat. Their war chiefs had lost none of their skill, and somehow they managed to form the remnants of their battered force into cohesive units that gradually retreated toward the water.

But the wild white man—whose refusal to retreat

367

had been responsible for the turn of battle—would not allow the enemy to escape without further punishment. Richard had the opportunity to reload his rifle at last, and calling, "After them, lads!" he fired, reloaded, and started down the dune in pursuit.

Hundreds followed him, firing into the ranks of the desperate savages who were trying to reach their canoes. The Mohegan ran amok, scalping indiscriminately, and Colonel Burrows knew he would never be able to write a report that would describe the scene accurately. When the canoes of the invaders were launched, and weary Algonkian and Micmac bent low over their paddles straining every muscle in their efforts to leave the site of their defeat, they left behind more than half of their total force.

Colonel Burrows had ordered that no quarter be shown the enemy, and none was given. The Mohegan reaped a rich harvest of scalps, a reward sufficient to cause them to sign a treaty of alliance with the men of New Haven and Connecticut. And it was no accident that the Micmac and Algonkian never again waged war so far from their homes. The white men whom they had faced in battle were not only armed with magical firesticks, but they fought with a deadly ferocity that put even the dreaded Seneca and Huron to shame.

Feeling faintly cheated now that the battle had ended so abruptly, Richard returned to the spot where he had taken his stand and methodically began to collect his throwing knives. He was still engaged in the grim task when Ezekiel Clayton found him.

"I wonder if Eliza knows she has married a madman," he said as he pumped his friend's hand. "I've heard of people going berserk in battle, but watching you in action is the first time I've ever seen such madness."

Richard thought he was exaggerating. "All I knew,"

368

he said, "was that I'd been insulted enough by the French, and I was damned if I was going to retreat." He hailed Roaring Wolf and they clasped forearms. "Well done, my friend!"

The Pequot looked at him proudly. "I knew from the day you saved my life that you are the greatest of warriors. The sons of our sons will sing your praises!" He hurried off to collect still more scalps.

Richard went in search of the Massachusetts Bay regiment, and finally located Dempster Chaney. "I'm much obliged to you for your help," he told the young farmer. "It didn't occur to me at the time that I was taking such risks."

"What set you off?" Dempster wanted to know. "You looked and acted demented."

Richard told him about the death of Bart Williams.

"So that's the game that France plays. Poor Mollie."

"I'll have to write her a letter, and it's a task I dread," Richard said. "I'll have to be truthful with her, but I'll omit mentioning that I saw a Mohegan scalp him."

"Yes, there's no reason to cause her needless pain. You're going to settle in New Haven, Richard?"

"I imagine I will, although I've had no chance to think about the future. I have a wife now, and I have no intention of living on the charity of my father-in-law."

"We'll meet again, I'm sure of it," Dempster said. "I don't know when or where it will happen, but our paths are sure to cross."

"Until they do, give my love to Robbin, and tell her that Mimi thinks of her often, too."

As they parted company, Dempster wondered how it had happened that Richard had married someone other than Mimi, who was now married herself. But he was too polite to ask, which was just as well, because Richard could not have offered him a logical explanation. It was enough that he had lost his heart elsewhere, as had Mimi.

At Colonel Burrows's direction, the dead were buried. The casualties suffered by the defenders were surprisingly light; most injuries were incurred during the hand-to-hand melee, so their wounds were superficial.

Hunting parties were sent into the wilderness, and they returned with enough game for a feast. Campfires were lighted, and that night the victorious celebrated. Colonel Burrows set an example for intercolonial cooperation by inviting all of the officers to dine with him and making a point of asking Ro-an and the subordinate Mohegan war chiefs to be present, too. So the militia leaders of New Haven, Connecticut, New Netherland, Massachusetts Bay, Plymouth, and Rhode Island dined together, and as they talked they were surprised to find they held similar aspirations and goals. More alike than they had realized, they learned that all were devoted to the principle of independence and were determined to lead their own lives without interference from their European governments. They were united, too, by their fervent desire to prevent France from gaining control of their rapidly expanding towns and farms.

A smiling Colonel Burrows refused to reveal where he obtained the wine he served that night. Richard assumed he had stored quantities of it on board the merchant ships that had played such a decisive role at the onset of the battle. But he knew his father-in-law was enjoying the bewilderment of his pleased guests, so he made no mention of his guess.

"I offer a toast to every man who fought today," Colonel Burrows said, raising his cup at the end of the meal. "The Algonkian and the Micmac—and, above all, their French masters—did us a great favor. No one colony could have repelled them alone. But we have learned from our victory that by standing together, shoulder to shoulder, we are invincible. We and our brave allies, the Mohegan, have struck a blow for liberty that will long be remembered."

"To liberty!" the colonel from Massachusetts Bay cried, and the officers rose spontaneously to their feet, then drained their cups in silence.

"It is appropriate on an occasion such as this," Colonel Burrows declared, "to mention those who distinguished themselves in battle. But the list is too long, so I shall save those mentions for the reports I shall send to the governors of the individual colonies. I cannot resist, however, calling your attention to one fact for which I am grateful. It is fortunate that my son-in-law is a civilian and holds no commission in the militia of New Haven or of any other colony. His civilian status saves me from the need to solve an impossible dilemma, whether to order him tried by a court-martial for refusing to obey orders, or whether to promote him for gallantry in action beyond the call of duty."

A roar of laughter erupted, and some of the officers cheered.

Richard had the grace to flush, and felt he had to respond. "I publicly apologize to Captain Clayton for my refusal to obey his order to retreat," he said, "but my hatred for the French and my contempt for their methods interfered with my better judgment. As I intend to apply for a militia commission in the immediate future, I promise my conduct will be more orthodox hereafter."

Again he was cheered, and Dempster Chaney embarrassed him by proposing a toast to "the man who wouldn't retreat."

The celebration ended on that convivial note, and the officers went off to their own camp areas. Early the following morning the army disbanded, with the various units heading for their homes. The troops from New Haven marched with the New Netherland militia and were accompanied by the Mohegan, who were proud of the role they had played.

At Colonel Burrows's request, Richard rode with him at the head of the column, and as they made their way down the trail that cut through the wilderness near the shoreline, the older man asked, "What are your plans for the future?"

"I'm not sure," Richard replied. "I'll want to discuss the matter with Eliza, although she knows no more than I about how much time we'll be obliged to spend on missions for the French. I just wish I could tell them to go to the devil."

"The connection you've established with them is too valuable for that," the colonel told him. "You can be certain that the failure of the Algonkian and Micmac to crush us will cause Cardinal Mazarin to redouble his efforts to gain control of the English colonies. I can appreciate the satisfaction you'd enjoy by thumbing your nose at them, and I know you want to protect Eliza, but you can't afford to neglect an opportunity to learn from the inside what France may be plotting against us."

"I don't have the temperament for espionage work, but I'll do my duty," Richard said.

"The very fact that you and Eliza are unlikely double agents increases your value to us. That's why I prefer not to give you a commission in the militia at present. You'd place yourself in even greater jeopardy if the French learned that you were reporting their activities to me."

"I suppose you're right, sir," Richard conceded grudgingly. "I reckon I'll need time to adjust to the role that I'm going to play. Meantime I'm thinking of establishing a land claim on some wilderness property and developing it."

"Have you had any experience in farming?"

"Not really, but—"

"Neither has Eliza, and in my opinion neither of you is suited to farm life. Tom Clayton and I will be delighted if you'll accept a post in our business."

"I must decline, sir, with thanks."

It was not difficult for Adam Burrows to read his mind. "You're rejecting my offer," he said, "because you think I'd be creating a place for my daughter's husband."

Richard nodded.

"I wonder what you'd say," the colonel declared, his voice quiet, "if you knew that Tom and I discussed ways of tempting you to join us long before I had any idea that you and Eliza were interested in each other."

Richard was startled, and could only stare at him.

"I'll grant you know nothing about ships and nothing about trade," Adam said, "but you could learn. Look at the problems from our point of view. Tom and I are growing older, and there's no one but young Ezekiel to succeed us. Meanwhile the colonies are growing so rapidly that the volume of our business has more than doubled in the past two years. And if the present pace of immigration is maintained, which is likely as people in England and Scotland become disillusioned by the power struggle between the Puritans and Cavaliers, it will multiply again in the years ahead. We need someone who knows men and enjoys their respect. You'll become famous as the hero of yesterday's battle. So all I can tell you is that even if you weren't my son-in-law, I'd ask you to name your own price."

Richard studied him closely. "You mean what you say, sir? You aren't just making work for me because I'm Eliza's husband?"

"I'd be doing her a disservice and insulting you, as well," Adam said firmly.

373

Richard's objections crumbled. "In that case, sir, you have a new hired hand. As to wages, pay me what you think I'm worth."

They clasped hands, and the issue was settled.

The column spent two days on the wilderness trail, the Mohegan warriors taking their leave and heading inland at noon of the second day after exchanging vows of friendship with the colonel.

The merchant ships had already brought the news of the victory to New Haven, and the town prepared a celebration worthy of heroes for the conquerors of the Algonkian and Micmac. Huge bonfires lighted the Green, where tables were spread with food contributed by the grateful citizens, and a fife-and-drum corps welcomed the militiamen. Virtually the entire population of the town and surrounding countryside was on hand to cheer the troops, who straightened their ranks and marched proudly in time to the beating drums.

Colonel Burrows doffed his hat repeatedly as people raised their voices to acclaim him and his men. Richard felt an unfamiliar thrill of excitement as he searched the crowds that lined the cobbled street, looking for the face of the woman he loved. He had to admit that Eliza had been absent from his mind for days, but now the realization flooded him that she was actually his wife.

At last he saw her, standing arm in arm with Mimi Clayton at the edge of the Green, the light of the huge fires playing on their hair. Others were cheering lustily, but Eliza stood silently, one hand at her throat, her glowing eyes fixed on the hero who was her husband.

Colonel Burrows halted the column, and it seemed like an eternity before he gave the order to break ranks. Richard leaped to the ground and embraced Eliza, only vaguely aware that Ezekiel had brushed past him and lifted Mimi off her feet. Eliza showed no reluctance to return her husband's embrace, and their kiss was so prolonged that the crowd cheered.

Eliza caught her breath when he released her. "I'm told, sir, that you did your best to be killed in action!"

"Something like that," Richard said, realizing that the story of the anger he had felt when he had seen Bart Williams leading the enemy savages would have to await a more appropriate time.

"I don't know whether to be proud of you or whether to scold you," she said. "But I'm so relieved to find you well that I'll do neither."

Ezekiel Clayton turned to them, his arm encircling Mimi's slender waist. "A reception like this," he said with a grin, "makes fighting a battle worth the while."

Only when well-wishers engulfed Richard, with the men anxious to shake his hand and the women congratulating him, did he realize how renowned he had become. He and Eliza were separated repeatedly by the crowd, and he was offered more food than he could eat, more ale and mead and rum than he could drink.

He shared Colonel Burrows's concern for the reception being accorded the New Netherland militiamen, and was relieved when he discovered they were being inundated by the hospitable people of New Haven, too. The rivalry between colonies was forgotten, and all who had fought and won the battle were being honored equally.

Eliza came to Richard's rescue when he was surrounded by an admiring throng of young women. "Pardon me, ladies," she said sweetly, her hold on his arm firm, "but I've come to claim my husband."

"It strikes me I've done my duty now," he told her as she led him away. "How much longer are we obliged to attend this reception?"

"That decision is entirely yours, sir," she replied demurely.

"In that case," Richard said, sweeping her off her feet and carrying her to the waiting Prince Henry, "we're leaving now." Her happy sigh as she curled her arms around his neck indicated that she did not object.

The Burrowses' house was deserted when they arrived there, and together they removed Prince Henry's saddle, then fed and watered the stallion.

"It seems as if we've been married forever," Richard said as they started toward the house.

"No, not quite that long. I've waited patiently for my honeymoon, Master Dunstable."

"Your wait has ended, Mistress Dunstable," he replied huskily.

Their lovemaking followed their usual pattern, at first swift and savage, then prolonged and tender. Not until they were satiated did they talk.

"Your father has persuaded me to work for him," Richard said. "He swears he would have offered me the post even if we weren't married."

"He means it, and with good cause," Eliza replied. You'll receive offers from every man of business in the colony after your exploits in battle. But I'm glad you'll work for Papa. I'll enjoy knowing that our children will inherit a thriving business one day." She paused, then told him news of her own. "I wasn't inactive while you were off at war. I've found us a house of our own. It's just right for our needs, and we can have it for five hundred sovereigns. I'll use my dowry to pay for it."

"You'll do no such thing. I can scrape together five hundred sovereigns, although we'll be short of cash for a time."

Eliza started to protest, then thought better of it. Her husband's homecoming was too important to be spoiled by a marital disagreement.

The next morning they went together to see the

house, and Richard was well pleased with the property. The rambling structure was solidly built of gray fieldstone, and was situated on extensive land only a short distance from Colonel Burrows's house. It was modest, as were the furnishings that came with it, compared to the estate that Richard had been forced to abandon in Lincolnshire, but he truly was sinking his roots here. He and his wife had acquired a vested interest in the New World.

That same day, while Eliza supervised the move of their personal belongings, even riding Prince Henry to his new stable behind the main dwelling, Richard went to work. He had long meetings with Colonel Burrows and the elder Clayton, then he studied the all-important ledgers, and finally Ezekiel took him on a tour of the company's docks and warehouses.

"My head is spinning, Ezekiel," he said at last. "But the principles of the operation are simple enough. We buy as cheaply as possible, we sell for as much as the market will bear, and we hold merchandise in storage for as short a time as possible."

That evening, the first in his new home, Eliza met him at the front door with a kiss. His wages were sufficiently generous for her to hire a cook and a serving maid, but she prepared their first supper herself. Although the menu was simple, he found the meal delicious.

They quickly established routines, and a few evenings later they invited Eliza's father and the Claytons to supper.

Mimi Clayton offered a toast that fit the occasion. Lifting her glass, she said, "May all of us flourish in the New World!"

Soon after they were seated at the table, there was a pounding at the front door, and Richard excused himself to answer the summons.

A stranger stood on the threshold, the dust of the

377

road thick on his boots and cloak. "Be this the home of Sir Richard Dunstable?" he demanded.

Richard nodded, his heart sinking. Only the French called him Sir Richard. "I am he."

The man thrust a square of parchment into his hands, then returned to his waiting mount and clattered off into the night.

The communication was addressed to "Sir Richard and Lady Dunstable," and Richard broke the seal with reluctance. The message itself was succinct: *"Meet me at your earliest convenience on a matter of urgent importance. L."*

The hope that he and Eliza could lead normal, peaceful lives vanished abruptly. They were being summoned to duty by their French masters.

Putting the communication into an inner pocket, Richard returned to the supper table, where he tried to carry off the pretense that nothing out of the normal had occurred. Eliza knew from his expression that he was disturbed, but she asked no questions. Her guess was confirmed when the Claytons prepared to leave after the meal, and Richard asked his father-in-law, in an undertone, to stay.

They saw the Claytons off, and then Richard handed Eliza the square of parchment. "The life we hoped to lead here is too good to be true," he said. "Reality has caught up with us."

Eliza read the brief message in silence, then gave the parchment to her father.

"The 'L' stands for Laroche, no doubt," Colonel Burrows said.

"So I assume, Colonel."

"I must hand it to the French. They're wasting no time after the defeat of the Algonkian and Micmac. Very well, you'll sail to New Amsterdam on one of our coastal brigs that leaves in the morning. This journey will give you the chance to become acquainted with our customers in New Netherland."

"I'll go, but I'm sailing alone," Richard replied. "I refuse to allow Eliza to become embroiled."

Eliza squared her shoulders. "This order was addressed to me as well as to you. I couldn't do battle against the forces sent by France to subdue us, but I can fight them in my own way. And I shall."

"I'll find a valid excuse to leave you here," Richard said.

Her blonde hair danced as she slowly shook her head. "We're engaged in a war of wits with the French, and the whole New World is the prize that will be taken by the winner. I insist upon my right to insure that the just are victorious."

Her father smiled in approval. "I knew you'd feel that way," he said.

Richard shrugged bleakly. He had done his best to prevent Eliza's involvement, but had failed, and now she would be obliged to share whatever risks he faced. "So be it," he said.

THE AMERICAN PATRIOT SERIES
Volume II
THE GREAT DECEPTION

The year is 1650. Peter Stuyvesant and the Dutch colonists in the New World are now threatened by the English settlers, who perceive America as a permanent home in which to live, worship, and grow toward a more secure future.

War is imminent as the English colonials expand toward Dutch settlements, and as Stuyvesant provides the Indians with firearms and the inspiration to use them.

Richard and Eliza Dunstable, forced to act as espionage agents for France, are now involved with the wily Peter Stuyvesant. They travel to many parts of the New World, gathering information for the Dutch, French, and British colonials with whom their sincere loyalties rest.

As they practice the deeply felt belief that they represent a "new breed"—free thinking, free acting, responsible only to their vast and promising new land—Richard and Eliza face danger, intrigue, and the possibility their marriage will not survive the challenges they have undertaken in service of their great new land . . .

THE GREAT DECEPTION
Coming soon from Ballantine Books